HARBINGER

THE SULLIVAN GRAY SERIES

H.P. BAYNE

Cover art by H.P. Bayne with art licensed through depositphotos.com

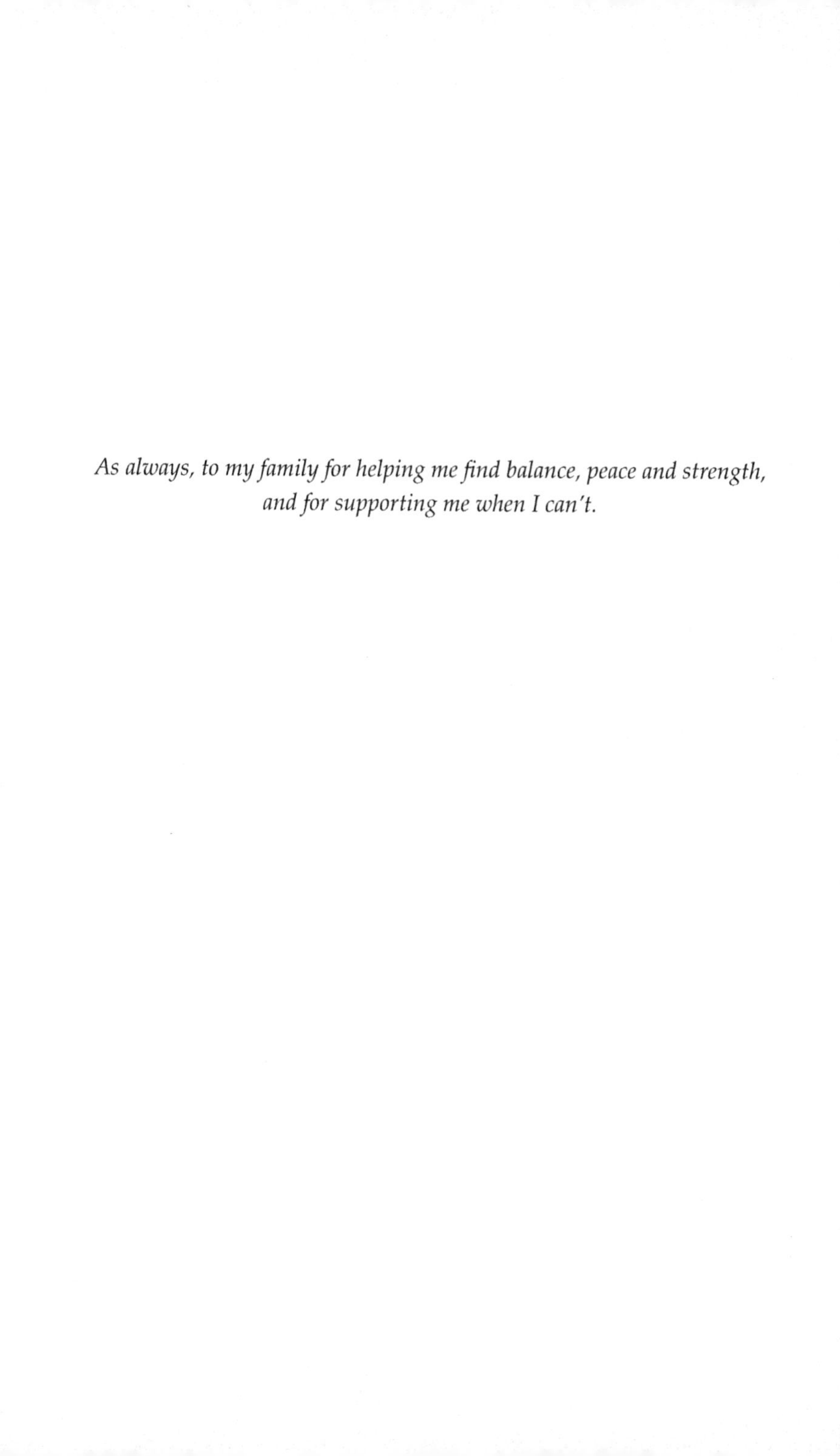

As always, to my family for helping me find balance, peace and strength,
and for supporting me when I can't.

1

THE WIND RATTLED the thinly paned windows of the small apartment. The creak of glass turned the unnerving howl into a viable threat.

Sullivan "Sully" Gray had been asking his uncle Lowell Braddock to replace the windows for the past year, but the man—despite the exorbitant size of his net wealth—always found a convenient way to forget. While he had poured enough money into his pub downstairs, the same didn't hold true for the three suites above the Black Fox.

It might have helped were the other two rented out, but Lowell couldn't be bothered with the inconvenience of acting as landlord. Sully wasn't viewed by his uncle as a tenant so much as a live-in employee, not family so much as the foster kid he was.

Not normal so much as an attention-seeking liar or a certifiable freak.

Sully urged away the dark thoughts as he rolled onto his side, facing away from the orange glow of the streetlights. He closed his eyes to the places in the room the light didn't touch. He'd shut the bar down half an hour ago, but he'd never been as good at doing the same with his brain. Too much went on around him all day.

And far too much at night.

This night would prove no different.

He jumped to the sound of smashing glass, his eyes snapping open and straining against shadow, ears tuned to the anticipated sounds of another break-in. They happened at the Fox sometimes, local addicts looking for ways to get at the liquor or anything that might be left in the till.

Tonight's noise was unaccompanied by the usual thudding of feet or clattering of bottles. What that meant, he didn't know.

He reached for his phone beside him and slid from under the covers, battling the chill in the room. After pulling on the jeans and long-sleeved T-shirt he'd left rumpled on the floor, he stepped into a pair of untied runners. He grumbled out a curse when his toe rammed into the dresser.

Unsure where the sound had come from, he decided to check the pub and the adjoining staff-only areas first. He considered phoning the police—his older brother, Dez, was on duty, and would get here in about ten seconds if Sully called in—but decided against it. If the only intruder—given the protests the windows continued to make—was the wind, he didn't want to come across as panicked. Not until he knew for sure he had something to panic over.

And there was the other always-unsettling possibility—the one now making itself known in the form of a wide-eyed older man standing in the bedroom doorway.

He appeared solid. They always did.

But Sully had learned to tell the difference long ago between the living and the dead.

This was a new ghost, so he brought with him a large degree of unknown—and an equally large degree of uncommon terror. Sully had been seeing the dead for as long as he could recall and, over time, bone-shaking fear had dwindled to a far-more-manageable anxiety. They still startled him, but rarely was he afraid.

This time, a creeping dread rapidly boiled over into outright panic, threatening to send him from the room, the apartment and even the building at a dead run.

Unlike many of the ghosts Sully encountered, this one presented no immediate sign of fatal injury, although the way his body appeared to be seizing likely provided some clue. His eyes were unnaturally wide, his mouth gaping in a silent scream that had Sully working hard to keep his own at bay.

Like the others Sully had seen, the ghost hovering in the doorway had a luminescence in the dark. The man, somewhere in his sixties, had thin, grey hair and an unkempt layer of stubble over both cheeks and chin. He swam within baggy, pale yellow drawstring pyjama pants and a matching top. His hands, balled into tight fists at his side, spoke more to tension than aggression.

His sudden presence provided another possibility: the glass-breaker was not the kind of person the police would be able to slap a pair of cuffs on.

Even so, there remained a solid chance the noise was, in fact, a living, breathing intruder, one Sully would need to report. To make sure, he needed to slip past the ghost blocking his path.

Sully closed his eyes and took a measured breath as he tried to rationalize that the terror wasn't his own. In dealing with the ghosts of murder victims—the only ones he ever saw—he'd learned the hard way their emotions could affect him. He'd taught himself how to block out feeling, but this one wasn't so easy.

It took longer than he'd cared to admit to reach a place where his mind wasn't reeling in fear, and his heart not threatening to explode inside his ribcage. It could have been a few seconds or a full minute, but Sully at last felt his nerves settle into something he could almost call comfortable. He opened his eyes.

The ghost stood directly in front of him.

Sully fell back, his shock finding voice in a short, sharp yelp. The man was way too close. But as Sully stared at him with what felt like it must be a mirroring expression, the spirit disappeared.

The terror dissipated like smoke after an extinguished blaze, until Sully felt the return of a semblance of normal. The whole episode had likely lasted thirty seconds. It felt like thirty minutes.

Remembering the noise downstairs, he grabbed the baseball bat he kept by the door and crept from his suite. The ambient glow of the streetlights filtered through the landing window, and Sully sought the shelter of the shadow in the corner, listening.

Silence. He was relieved the ghost wasn't following him. Remaining alert to the possibility of a living, breathing intruder was difficult enough without a dead, terror-inducing man at his shoulder. Sully steeled his nerves, and lifted the bat so the business end was close to his right ear, ready to swing.

He started down the steps.

It was darker where he emerged into a back room that accessed the rear exit, the offices and employees-only area. To the right was the door to the bar. That door—stronger, with a better lock than its predecessor—was supposed to be locked after hours, but it had been damaged during a fight a few nights ago. Lowell hadn't yet managed to get the locksmith to look at it, nor had he ever bothered installing an alarm.

After giving his eyes a moment to adjust, Sully headed there first.

The door was shut, but that didn't make the next step easy from a psychological perspective, Sully having to summon courage before grasping the handle and pulling.

The last time he'd done this, an intruder had rushed him from the other side, hitting him with the steel door in the process and leaving a nasty goose egg on the edge of his forehead. This time, he was ready, standing just to the side of the door as he anticipated a possible repeat.

None came. Nor was there any sound from inside the bar to indicate an intruder of the human persuasion.

Not that it meant anything. While any trespasser Sully had encountered to date had been easily startled, it was possible someone had heard him coming and was hiding.

He slipped through the door and flicked on the lights.

Searching the room and the customer bathrooms at the back, he found nothing. No human burglar, no ghostly visitor. Nor, he observed, were there any broken windows or bottles.

Leaving the bar lights on, Sully flicked on the one in the employees' area. Nothing. The last place he could think of was the manager's office down the hall.

Hugging the wall, Sully made his way there. The door was shut; from behind it came the sound of someone rifling through papers and supplies.

Betty Schuster, the Fox's manager, would come in after hours on occasion, but never at two-thirty in the morning. When she did turn up during non-business hours, she always put on the lights and left her office door open.

This wasn't Betty.

Sully guessed the door would be locked, so he went back down the hall, intending to conceal himself in the side alley to keep watch while he talked to police.

With the bat tucked under his arm, he dialled 9-1-1 and eased the back door open, slipping outside. There, he reported the break and enter.

"I'm heading down the side alley," Sully told the operator, a woman he'd talked to several times in the past.

"Don't get too close," she warned. "It's not safe. Just sit tight where you are. Police are on their way."

Sully was fine with the idea of not getting too close, but he wanted to be near enough he could provide a description, given the guy would probably bail once he heard sirens. He didn't tell the operator he was taking a few more steps in, knowing he'd be setting himself up for a balls-busting.

In the distance, and getting closer, was the sound of a siren; Sully didn't need to be psychic to know Dez was pedal to the metal as he made good on the big brother role he'd perfected since Sully had been placed with the Braddocks at age seven. Three years older, and significantly taller and more broadly muscled than his foster brother, Dez came by the role of protector naturally, and he'd never outgrown it in the fifteen years they'd known each other.

It wasn't until the sirens—he could make out at least two—were close enough to make it clear they were coming this way that the intruder decided enough was enough. A solidly-built man dressed in jeans, a dark hoodie, gloves and a balaclava crawled out the broken window and started down the alley.

Toward Sully.

"He's coming this way," Sully told the operator, before slipping his phone into the pocket of his jeans. Despite the material, he could hear the operator trying futilely to continue the conversation.

With the intruder now running in his direction, Sully figured he had his hands full.

The man had been looking over his shoulder toward the street, probably expecting the police to come from that direction. He pulled up short at the sound of Sully's shouted, "Hey!"

In the glow from the lights of the small parking area, the two men locked eyes.

The moment passed quickly, wide-eyed surprise giving way to a determined glare that had the man rushing at his would-be opponent. Sully readied the bat and swung, a move that would have laid out most of the intruders he'd encountered. He was fast, always had been. But this guy was faster, spinning away from the swing so it only caught his side a glancing blow. As he moved, the man grasped the bat, and it was only the fact Sully kept himself in shape that prevented the weapon from being yanked away from him.

As the sirens approached, the man released the bat, throwing Sully off-balance and leaving him open to a leg sweep. He hit the pavement hard, retention of the bat proving pointless as the man drove a booted foot into his side and gut.

A combination of the assault and the impact on pavement drove the air out of Sully's lungs, had him struggling for breath until it came back in a round of hacking coughs. Around that, he could make out the sound of the man sprinting off.

Still coughing, he managed to roll to his hands and knees. A car braked hard, followed by the slam of a door. Then more rushed footfalls, these ones coming toward him with a shout of his name.

"Sully! Sully, you okay?"

He nodded between racking coughs, which didn't prove good enough for Dez.

"Are you hurt?"

A head shake, no, this time.

"Which way did he go?"

Sully managed to extend an arm and point to the right. Dez picked him up and half-dragged him to the passenger side of the car. Having been deposited inside, Sully sat, getting his wind back while Dez drove the area in search of the guy.

In the end, despite a half-hour hunt that came to include five separate police cars, they found nothing.

They returned to the Black Fox where forensic identification members had been called in to look for clues.

"There have been a few business break-ins around Riverview lately," Dez explained as Sully sat on the back stairs, filling out a written statement. "Could be it's our suspect. You're lucky. He stabbed the last guy who caught him at it. What the hell were you thinking, going out there?"

Sully gave up on the statement for the moment. He'd known the scolding would be coming, and Dez would expect his full attention.

"You're right. It was stupid."

"Damn right it was stupid. You had no idea if the guy was armed. We're seizing guns left, right and centre off the streets these days. You could have gotten yourself shot."

"I know. Okay?"

"So, why do it?"

"I thought maybe I could get close enough to get a description."

"If you're close enough to get a description, you're close enough to get shot. Not worth it. Let Ident do their job."

But after an hour of dusting and swabbing the scene, Ident came up with nothing.

Sully had notified Betty, and she'd come in, swearing up a storm, in the midst of the fingerprinting. She had stalked to her office in search of Sergeant Joe Peterman, and the resulting conversation had been terse enough to send snippets of it down the hall.

The Ident officers seemed happy to be leaving.

"Looks like a professional job," one of them told Sully and Dez. "We can't find any sign he removed his gloves, and he brought a long rubber car mat with him for the window ledge so he wouldn't cut himself crawling in. We checked the mat, but no obvious hairs, fibres or substances showed up. Could be he just bought it. We'll take in a few items we seized for further analysis, but it's not looking promising for evidence."

Dez returned his attention to Sully as the Ident officer and his partner left with the seized and bagged evidence. "Did you or Betty call Lowell?"

"Not yet. Guess I should."

"Let Betty," Dez said. "She's the manager."

"I'm the assistant manager. And I'm the one who was here. No sense his crapping on her for this."

"No sense his crapping on you either. Tell you what, I'll call him. Betty's likely to be held up with Joe for a while."

While Dez made the call, Sully headed down the hall to where Betty and Sergeant Peterman—the officer who had taken over the night's investigation—were digging through the office, looking for anything that might have been taken.

Betty excused herself and joined Sully, leaving Joe to take advantage of the break to go outside for a smoke.

"Anything?" Sully asked.

Betty's headshake was a tight one. "Not that I can see. Listen, would you mind pouring me a rye and water from the bar? I don't normally drink this late but, given the circumstances, fuck it."

She turned back into the room as he left to fill her request. He'd taken a couple steps when he heard the sound of tape being ripped off something and the sound of her muttering, "Thank Christ."

Sully ducked back inside. Betty faced a section of cheap wood panelling which lined the office. "Everything okay?"

She spun, eyes wide and mouth open as she stuffed her hands into the pockets of her jacket. "Jesus, Sully. Don't scare a gal like that."

"Sorry. It sounded like you found something."

"Oh." Betty ducked her head, but looked back up at him. She pulled her hand from a pocket and uncurled her fingers, revealing a pale blue thumb drive. "Just some family photos and history I've been compiling. I thought maybe it was gone."

"Why would anyone want your family photos and history?"

"They wouldn't," she said. "Just that it's on a thumb drive, and sometimes thieves take those thinking they contain important classified information. Always do on TV, anyway."

Sully smirked. "Who would think you've got important classified information? You moonlighting as a spy or something?"

"Don't be stupid."

Sully had gotten to know Betty fairly well over the past four years, and he could read people. He sensed this person—this friend—was lying to him. He risked not going for the ordered drink, suspecting she'd only made the request to get him out of the room, anyway.

In a low voice, he asked, "What do you think the guy was after?"

"How the hell should I know? Peterman there kept asking the same thing. I don't keep anything important here. Just employee and business records, tax records, my personal tax returns. I've got an extra copy of my will here. There's no cash, sure as hell no drugs or expensive goods. The computer's so old it's going to crap out any day now. I can't imagine what someone would want coming here and breaking in."

Sully couldn't say he knew either, but he suspected it might have something to do with the thumb drive Betty had returned to her pocket—whether or not she was prepared to admit it.

She must have seen his eyes drifting that way. "Sully, please don't tell anyone about the thumb drive. It's just my personal stuff and it means a lot to me. I don't want to risk it getting seized as evidence and accidentally erased. That's all. There's nothing important on it, all right?"

Sully watched her eyes and, while she blinked a little more than normal, she didn't look away. She was doing her utmost to convince him and, short of ratting her out or wrestling it away from her—moves that would make working here unbearable going forward—there wasn't a whole lot he could do about it.

Nor did he know he should do anything. He didn't have any clue what was on that drive, and rational thought suggested she could be telling the truth.

Except, deep down, he knew she wasn't.

2

Lowell Braddock started his pharmaceutical company from the ground up. It had been at the forefront of a number of successful medical breakthroughs thanks to skilled chemists and a willingness to take a few well-placed risks with his money.

LOBRA employed a hefty portion of the city's scientifically minded, and it had achieved a reputation for being one of the best places to work in Kimotan Rapids if you had the skillset to earn your way in.

Lowell surrounded himself with the best of everything, be it people, places or things. He drove the most expensive cars, had both a penthouse in the city and a sprawling estate to the west, and was photographed at charity events and highbrow social gatherings with KR's elite. He gave frequently and had a hand in a number of local businesses, having been credited more than once with keeping some of them afloat through the economic crunch that had hit within the past few years.

As free with money and credit as he was in handing out a well-deserved compliment, he was the sort of guy most people wanted to be close to. To the world at large, Lowell Braddock was a good man.

Sully knew better.

He'd long since accepted he might well be the only person in the world who saw the other side of the man, the darkness he worked so hard to keep hidden. Despite Lowell's best attempts to conceal the black side of his soul, it continued to lurk just below his shiny exterior, hunched there like a poisonous toad, beady eyes ever watching and waiting. It was nothing like the surface Lowell presented to the world; well-dressed, handsome, tall and elegant, Lowell could charm the socks off the oft-curmudgeonly Christian Ladies' Club one minute with a well-turned speech, and impress smart-ass teens the next with his love for extreme sports and hot cars.

Perhaps most frustrating to Sully was that Lowell's inherent charm didn't fail him in the family department. Lowell and his brother Flynn—Sully's foster father—were like night and day in some respects, but Flynn loved his younger brother nonetheless. And Mara—Sully's foster mother—was close with Lowell's wife, Kindra, so that holidays were rarely complete unless all of them were together. Dez looked up to his father, he also adored his uncle, had grown up anticipating the best birthday and Christmas gifts thanks to Lowell's generosity. While Lowell was a blind spot for Dez, the younger Braddock was observant enough to recognize the tension between his brother and uncle. Dez had never pursued it, whether out of concern for trespassing too far into Sully's personal feelings or simply because he didn't want to face any more pain within his little family unit. Either way, Dez had Sully's back around Lowell—always had—but he did it without rocking any boats.

Sully held his own course and kept his misgivings to himself. Flynn, Mara and Dez Braddock had taken him in as a kid, but he'd learned by then nothing was ever set in stone. At the end of the day, Lowell was still blood and Sully was not. He had no doubt the Braddocks loved him like true family, but there were ways in which he wasn't prepared to test the strength of that bond. Lowell was the granddaddy of all tests.

Lowell and Sully had an understanding they'd held to since

those early days. They spoke to each other civilly, treated each other fairly and kept any unfavourable views to themselves. Most days, it worked. On the days it didn't, they simply ignored the resulting questions and moved on.

There was no ignoring Lowell now, as he swept into the Black Fox, wearing a facade of concern. He took in the scene and breezed out to find the lead investigator.

"He insisted," Dez explained to Sully. "Third break-in here in as many months. He's anxious about it."

The suggestion being Sully should be anxious too. And he was, just not for the same reasons Lowell was likely to be.

Sully didn't say anything else to Dez on the matter; there wasn't much to add. Dez went off to talk to his uncle, leaving Sully in the bar nursing a beer. It was only a matter of time before Lowell came over to politely demand an explanation, and it took seconds rather than minutes before the bar's owner was sliding onto the chair across from Sully.

"The sergeant's still busy with Betty in the office," Lowell said. "What happened, this time?"

Sully provided the obligatory narrative, detailing the night's events from the initial noise to the confrontation in the alley. He left out the bit about the ghost; Lowell didn't go in for that sort of thing, thought Sully was somewhere just this side of crazy. Lowell had tried to do him one favour over the years, though: seeing to it Sully had a running supply of sleeping pills. There had been many nights over the years those pills had come in handy.

"Were you hurt?" Lowell asked.

Sully felt the smile plucking at the corners of his mouth. As Sully was obliged to provide an explanation, so Lowell had to go through the motions of concern. This was how the two of them worked.

"Fine, thanks."

"Did you happen to get a look at him?"

"Nothing that's much help. He was masked. But he was a

pretty big, solid guy, and he knew how to handle himself. Not like the last couple of boozers who smashed in here."

"And it seems like he focused on Betty's office rather than the bar," Dez added. "That's a new one."

"It certainly is," Lowell said. "Any idea what this guy was after?"

Sully shrugged, making efforts to appear like he was studying the label on his bottle. It was usually easier not to look at Lowell, just answer his questions and get on with things. "No idea. Betty said she doesn't know either."

"Do you believe her?"

That had Sully glancing up, and he found Lowell watching him closely, studying him as if wanting to read and to dissect his thoughts.

"Why wouldn't I? Are you suggesting she's lying?"

Lowell offered his own shrug and sat back with crossed arms. "You tell me."

"There's nothing to tell. Maybe the guy thought we kept the float back there or something. I really don't know."

"Just seems strange," Lowell said. "Most people break in here for one reason. They're after booze and smokes, maybe whatever might be left in the cash drawer. That means the bar's the target, not the offices."

Dez usually ended up cutting into Sully and Lowell's conversations, and he blessedly picked that moment. "Most people around here know you own the place, Uncle Lo. Maybe they weren't thinking of it as Betty's office, but yours."

"I don't spend a lot of time around here. Why would anyone think that?"

"I don't know. But there are quite a few people in this neighbourhood who don't think things through very well before committing a crime."

"Except, by Sullivan's description, this intruder doesn't seem our usual smash-and-grab type. I'd say it sounds almost professional. Which leads me back to my question about what he would have been after."

"Maybe you're better off waiting and asking Betty," Dez suggested. "Sully doesn't know."

"He works closely with her. I just thought he might have a theory, that's all."

But Dez's words had the desired effect, Lowell giving up on the mild interrogation and heading off to check back in with Betty and Sgt. Peterman.

Sully waited until Lowell was out of sight and earshot before turning back to Dez. "Thanks."

"He's not meaning to come down on you," Dez said. "He's got questions. So do you and I. He's right that it's not your typical bar break-in."

"I know that. Look, maybe Betty's got some idea as to motive, but I don't."

"I know, Sull. I wasn't suggesting otherwise. I'd just like to get this sorted out sooner rather than later. Whoever broke in is still out there and, like we've all said now, it's got the feel of a professional job. I don't like the idea of you being here on your own until we've picked this guy up."

"I don't think I'm in any danger. He could have taken me out but he didn't. I didn't get the impression he was out to seriously hurt me."

"Even so," Dez said. "If he got what he came for, then it's all good. But if he didn't, chances are he'll be back once the heat dies down some. And if he's desperate enough to get his hands on whatever he came here for, there's no predicting how far he might go to get it—or who he'll go through."

THE SEARCH of Betty's office turned up no sign of anything missing or any additional items the intruder might have left behind. Sgt. Peterman summoned Sully to go over a few questions he had about his statement.

By the time Sully had provided what extra information he could, Lowell had sent Betty on her way, and Dez had been dispatched on another call. Once the police took their leave, Lowell and Sully remained behind to clean up.

They boarded up the window and swept up the shattered glass. Having ensured the place was as secure as possible, Sully reluctantly got into the passenger seat of Lowell's Land Rover, his uncle having promised to take Sully over to Dez and Eva's for the rest of the night.

Sully had hoped for a quiet ride, but wasn't remotely surprised when Lowell broke the silence during the drive to the Gladstone neighbourhood on the city's west side. Only, the break-in wasn't what Lowell had in mind as subject matter.

"You still got those pills I gave you?"

"No, they're back at the apartment."

Lowell reached into a pocket, producing a pill bottle he handed to his passenger. In the light from the passing streetlights, Sully recognized the label as the usual brand he was given.

"Figured you'd be running low by now, anyway. Here. Take them. You look like hell."

"I was sleeping fine until this happened."

"Right. But take one when you get to Dez and Eva's, anyway. You've always had a hard time nodding off."

That much was true, but Sully didn't acknowledge it, didn't say anything else about the matter. He hated taking pills. Most of the time, they kept dreams at bay, but sometimes they made it so he couldn't wake from nightmares. And there were times those nightmares were so real, he preferred the waking ones.

"You still don't like me very much, do you?"

Sully turned his head enough to realize Lowell was looking at him, stopped as they were at a red light. He refocused his gaze on the dark, quiet street ahead, wishing it was as easy to divert his thoughts. "I've got nothing against you."

"That's not altogether true, is it?"

Sully didn't say anything. There wasn't a right answer, nor was he anywhere close to thinking one up. Sully wasn't gifted in the art of gab at the best of times; chatting with Lowell typically hovered closer to the worst of times, as far as Sully was concerned.

True to form, Lowell picked up the one-sided conversation. "You know what I did today? I donated fifty thousand dollars to St. Luke's Childrens' Hospital. Fifty thousand dollars. It's enough to secure them the MRI machine they've been working toward purchasing. There's going to be a big story about it in the paper tomorrow. That's the kind of man I am, Sullivan."

Sully held his tongue. No right answer, he reminded himself.

"Still nothing to say? Even though I made sure you had a job after you finished high school? Come on, kid, you're smart and you've got a good head on your shoulders most of the time. But you've got no idea what you want to do with your life. I did my best to do right by you, didn't I? Where would you be right now if I hadn't?"

Sully shrugged, hoping that would be answer enough.

"What was that?"

Apparently not. "Thank you." The words emerged from Sully's lips through gritted teeth.

He heard the smile on Lowell's voice. To anyone else, it might have sounded innocently amused. "I'm sorry? I didn't quite catch that."

"I said, thank you."

The light turned green and the car pulled forward.

"You know your trouble, kid? You lived a rough life before Flynn and Mara took you in. You were treated badly, and you came to believe the whole world was out to get you. Problem is, that's not true. Some of us only ever want to help you, but you make it so damn hard sometimes. You can trust me or not, but the only one you're hurting is yourself. Now, I don't know what it is you think I did that was so bad, but—"

"You don't know? Really?"

"No, Sullivan. I don't."

And the sad truth was Lowell probably didn't know, probably wouldn't acknowledge it as fact even if Sully could present the distant past to him on a film screen. Because Sully had realized a long time ago the reason Lowell was so brutally capable of snowing the whole world. The man had spent his life practicing in the mirror. Whatever lies he told everyone else, perhaps he saved the biggest untruths for himself. And Sully didn't possess a shovel big enough to dig through all that bullshit.

"Never mind," Sully said. "It's not important. I'm tired. Wake me up when we get to Dez and Eva's."

This time, Lowell let the conversation drop, likely because he wanted to hear the answer to his question about as much as Sully wanted to say it out loud. Sully leaned his head against the window and shut his eyes most of the way, the sliver of sight allowing him to keep his eye on his surroundings outside the car. Lowell might have been lying about everything else, but he'd spoken some truth in there too.

Sully didn't like Lowell and he didn't trust him. He might never be able to say those words out loud to anyone who mattered, but *he* knew.

Even if no one else ever did.

3

IT WAS a rare day when Betty Schuster was late for work.

She might have been up half the night dealing with a break-in, but that wasn't enough to set her off her usual course.

When Sully arrived for work early that afternoon, Betty's car was already there. He found her in her office, trying to reorganize her scattered papers. It felt dark in there now with the window temporarily boarded up, the single sixty-watt lightbulb within a dusty fixture not up to the task.

She spared him a glance before returning to her task.

"Darker than a banker's heart in here," she said, squinting at one of numerous tax receipts she passed under the desk lamp's dim glow. He knew Betty needed reading glasses, but she refused to admit it, just like she refused to admit to any other weakness the rest of the world could see she was subject to. "Thanks for boarding up the window last night. I went to check if you were still here, but I guess you left after I did."

Sully smiled. "You know Dez. He wasn't going to let me stay last night."

"He knows you're a grown man, right?"

"He knows, but conveniently forgets. There's no point arguing with him. I tried after the last break-in and almost ended up cuffed in the backseat of his cruiser."

Betty snorted, which might have been a sign of amusement or an indication of derision. Often with her, the two went hand in hand.

She plodded away at her task a few more minutes while Sully lent what help he could, relying on younger eyes to look for dates on papers, until a glance at her watch had her changing tacks.

"Right," she said. "Business. Would you mind changing out a couple kegs for me while I get the till ready to go?"

In the bar, Sully busied himself with his task as he listened to Betty counting out the day's float, something she always did in an audible murmur.

There was plenty Sully appreciated about her: he enjoyed her black humour; the way she was able to settle most rowdies with little more than a glare and, failing that, her booming yell; and the stories she told about the characters she'd known over her many years of running the bar for its variety of owners.

Betty was a fixture at the Fox, like the dark oak panelling, tin ceiling and wide mirror behind the bar that provided patrons with a view of the offerings on display and, as the night wore on, a glimpse of their own drunken reflections. Betty was one of few bar workers Sully knew who had bemoaned the recent bylaw outlawing smoking in businesses, as she'd been commonly recognized for the lit cigarette she used to dangle from the corner of her mouth. She'd taken to tucking a cigarette behind her ear for future, and still-frequent, use. While she would have enjoyed taking her outdoor smoke breaks more often than she did, she'd say the bar wouldn't run itself in the meantime. And, with her, her job came first.

As much as Sully liked Betty, he appreciated her competence the most—in no small part because it kept Lowell from coming in on a regular basis to check on things. His presence here last night had been down to the break-in and nothing more, his visits usually reserved for special events or catastrophes.

Sully set down a keg of Guinness—nothing but the best for Lowell Braddock—making sure to connect it to the proper stout line. Betty had finished counting and was now working on a stain on the polished bar. She'd been scrubbing at it since he'd started working here and had not budged it an inch as far as Sully could tell.

"We're still good for Stella," he said. "But I'll probably have to change out the keg after a few."

Betty didn't respond in words, just nodded what Sully assumed was her acknowledgment. Sometimes it was hard to tell if Betty really heard him at all. The woman tended to live in her head and, once in a while, would get lost there, disappearing into her office for as long as an hour at a time and leaving the running of the bar to her assistant manager. Once she'd been in there a solid two hours before Sully finally got worried enough to check. She had done her best to hide it that night, but the redness in her eyes told him what she would not. Betty was what one of the regulars called a "tough broad." Crying was not one of those "human frailties" she willingly allowed in herself. She'd laughed it off, said she was allergic to the smell of Edgar Maberly, an elderly guy who came in every day for the cheapest scotch on the shelf and who likely hadn't taken a proper bath in close to three months. Then she went back to work as if nothing had happened, and Sully made sure to never bring it up.

But there were days like today when Betty got quiet, days Sully knew would eventually include a lengthy visit to the office by his boss under the guise of "paperwork."

It didn't mean he couldn't try.

"Everything okay?"

She responded as he'd expected, glancing up with a "Hmm?" as if just noticing he was there. He repeated his question, and she returned to scrubbing at that spot. "Goddamn stain. Stupid, goddamn stain."

Sully left her to it, half-thinking she'd put it there herself just to have a distraction when she was in one of her moods. Sully had enough distraction of his own for now, having found two other beers on tap were spitting out the last of their kegs' contents. He pulled out the first of the empty kegs and carried it to the back.

The alley door was propped open as usual, allowing fresh air in and, on those occasions when she had the chance, Betty out.

Given last night's shenanigans, Sully made an executive decision, setting the empty keg next to the others by the wall and approaching the door with the intention of pulling it shut.

He saw the barrel of the shotgun first. Sully barely had time to step back before a body followed, the form of a large man dressed in oversized dark jeans, a baggy overcoat, gloves and a Halloween mask with mesh eye sockets that revealed nothing. The ghoul's mouth was open in a wide, startled "O" shape.

Despite the mask's expression, the surprise was all on Sully, who tried to keep his eyes on the mask's eyeholes rather than the gun's barrel, levelled at his chest with just feet separating them.

"We haven't opened yet," Sully said, keeping his voice loud enough for Betty to hear in the bar. She was smart and steady, and he figured she'd get on the phone to 9-1-1. "We don't have any money here but the float. I'll get it for you, but I'm going to need you to put the gun down first."

There was no response, which didn't come as a shock. Sully raised his hands in a show of submission and was thinking through options when he heard Betty's shouted command.

"Drop the gun and get out! Now!"

The barrel shifted at the first word and Sully, aware the aim had moved to his colleague, rushed forward, grabbing hold of the shotgun and trying to force it upward where any blast would be felt by nothing more than the ceiling. But the man proved stronger than Sully had anticipated, and they were still fighting for the weapon when a deafening boom filled the room, loud enough to drown out any other sound. Wrenching away from Sully, the man spun and ran out the back door, any thoughts he might have had of cash having passing as quickly as the muzzle flash from the gun he'd dropped on the floor.

Sully followed close behind, sticking out his head in time to see the man headed north, in the direction of the river. The foolhardy part of his brain was thinking about following when he suddenly—inexplicably—saw Betty in front of him.

The way she was standing held Sully back. Her face was ashen except for the blood she'd coughed up onto her nose, cheeks and chin, eyes holding a combination of shock and horror as they drifted from Sully down to her chest. He looked too, but only for a second, long enough to see the bloody, torn front of her blue and white button-down.

And he knew. Knew without having to check any further.

He found her body where he knew it would be, lying on the barroom floor, shirt torn by the shotgun blast, blood spattering her front and pooled beneath her. Her right arm was splayed out to the side and a nickel-plated snub-nosed revolver lay about a foot from her limp hand.

Sully ignored the gun as he knelt next to her and called 9-1-1.

"There's been a shooting," he said. "The Black Fox on Second Avenue."

The operator talked him through the usual procedures for checking on a victim and starting CPR. He tried, but there was no point. He didn't need a paramedic or a doctor to tell him she was already dead. She was still standing there, after all, next to her body, the ghostly legs solidly visible to him even as he pumped at the broken chest over her heart. The sound of bone grating on bone turned his stomach but he continued anyway, if for no other reason than so she could see he was trying his best to save her. As he pushed, he noticed the pool of blood below her was widening, covering the floor and touching his knees. The thought came out of nowhere, uttered inside his brain in his brother's voice rather than his own: Betty, the bane of stains, is leaving a doozy of one herself.

Given the shooting had taken place at the back door, the operator asked him to unlock the front once police arrived. Four police officers trooped in, one of whom took over CPR as two others headed into the back for a look around. The fourth was asking Sully questions, presumably about what had happened and for the shooter's description, but Sully had already given all that to the operator. With the physical situation in hand, Sully's attention now went fully to the woman standing next to her body, mouth open and eyes no less panicked as she regarded her mirror image on the floor. He was seeing her as if looking through a tunnel, the officer's repeated use of his name muffled as if spoken through a wall.

Then came a sense of the familiar, and Sully released a fractured exhale as he heard his name being spoken again, this time by a voice he knew as well as his own. He finally pulled his eyes from Betty's ghost, finding Dez in front of him, dressed in his police uniform.

Dez grasped Sully's face gently, tilting it to look up to his own. "Look at me. Look at me, Sull. Are you okay?"

The other officer spoke for him. "He's in shock, but he wouldn't let me move him. I didn't want to force him."

Dez wouldn't have any similar hang-ups. "Let's get you sitting down somewhere. Come on."

Dez got one long, solid arm around Sully's shoulders and, in a combination of pulling and guiding, moved him from the bar area, trying to place himself as a visual barrier to the body. As if Sully hadn't already gotten an eyeful.

Sully's eyes drifted to his hands, finding them covered in blood. "Can I wash up?" His words sounded garbled, even to his own ears, but Dez understood without the need for further explanation.

"Sorry, kiddo," he said, and his tone suggested he meant it. "Ident's going to want to grab some swabs, test for gunpowder residue and all that. Just hang tight, okay? They won't be long."

They were headed toward the back of the pub where they usually sat during Sully's breaks or when there was a lull in business. Sully didn't make it that far before he lost the battle, slamming into the men's room and vomiting into the closest sink.

A large hand was on his back by the time he finished and spat, staying there while he rinsed the mess down the drain. Sully didn't move, just went on gripping the rim of the sink as he stared down, focused on nothing, pale brown hair flopping around his face.

"Sull?"

"It's my fault."

"What's your fault?"

"She'd still be alive if I hadn't been so stupid."

"Explain that to me." Dez's tone had moved from gentle to slightly dangerous, and Sully could sense his brother was waiting for the explanation only so he could beat Sully over the head with it.

Knowing he was fighting a losing battle, Sully forged on anyway. He knew the truth, even if Dez would never acknowledge it. "The guy shifted his aim from me to Betty. I was so close to him, I thought I could get the gun away or at least get it to discharge in another direction. But he was stronger than I expected, and he fired. Or maybe I fired. I don't know. It happened so fast, and I know my hands were around his. I could have fired the shot that hit her. I could have killed her."

The hand on his back moved to his arm, gripped and pulled until Dez had turned Sully to face him. Dez held him there, in both gaze and grasp. "Listen to me, Sully. You did nothing wrong, all right? Nothing. You were trying to save her and yourself. There's no way to know right now exactly what went down in those few seconds, but I'll tell you what I do know. If that guy hadn't burst in here with a loaded gun, none of this would have happened. You did what you could with a shitty situation. And, so help me, if you fight me on that point, I will bounce your skinny ass off every wall in this room, you hear me?"

Sully nodded slowly. There was no sense arguing when Dez took that tone, no way his brother would allow it. Instead, he blew out another shaky breath and heard Dez respond with one of his own.

"There wasn't a lot of info on the call," Dez said. "When I heard it, I thought it was you. I thought I was going to get in here and find you …."

He didn't finish the statement. And he didn't need to. Sully hadn't had a whole lot of people in his life who really gave a damn about him, but he sure as hell had this guy. Dez wasn't his brother by blood, but they were brothers all the same, and he knew he could count on Dez to have his back and to freak out about it on those rare occasions when he couldn't.

Dez's grip tightened, and he pulled Sully forward into a hug, his voice cracking around his words. "Damn glad you're all right, bro. I'll get you through this, okay?"

There was no sense trying to provide a verbal answer, Sully's face snugged between Dez's shoulder and one tree trunk of an arm, so he nodded instead.

As usual, where Dez was concerned, there was no need for words anyway.

4

By the time Dez and Sully left the bathroom, a paramedic crew had arrived to confirm what everyone already knew.

Betty Schuster was dead.

Dez explained that, as a witness to a homicide, Sully would have to go to the police station to provide a statement to one of the Major Crimes investigators. The brothers were barely back in the main bar when one of the other officers on scene, a particularly likeable guy named Constable Jeff Whitebear, said he'd been given orders to drive Sully over.

Dez dropped Sully into a chair and pulled Jeff to the side for a quiet conversation.

"I can take him over myself," Dez said. "I'd like to keep an eye on him. He's really shaken up."

Jeff smiled apologetically. "I get what you're saying, man, and I wish I could help you out. But you know the rules. Major Crimes isn't going to want him talking to anyone except them until they've got his statement. It's probably bad enough you were alone in the bathroom with him a minute ago."

"We weren't exactly having a long conversation," Dez said. "He was too busy puking."

"You know what I'm saying."

Dez knew. And he knew Jeff was right. He wouldn't be doing Sully any favours by giving the homicide investigators something else to question. Despite what he'd told Sully, he knew every detail was dissected in murder inquiries, and that would include Sully's handling of the situation. All Dez could do was be there to pick up the pieces.

With Jeff beside him, Dez returned to his brother. "Jeff's going to drive you to the police station, okay? They're going to want to take some pictures and swabs first. And they're probably going to seize your clothes as evidence, so I'll get a few things for you from upstairs and bring them over. After that, you'll have to give a statement, so just tell them exactly what happened and everything you know. All right?"

Sully hadn't looked at him, prompting Dez to try again. "You hear me, Sull?"

"Yeah. I hear you."

Dez stood and helped Sully up before passing him reluctantly to Jeff, who met Dez's eye with an encouraging smile before guiding Sully out the front door of the bar.

DEZ SUSPECTED he got to headquarters roughly five minutes after Sully and Jeff, but they were nowhere to be found by then. Dez expected an Ident officer was processing his brother already, checking for evidence on his body or clothing.

There was nothing Dez could do at this point, and he knew hovering wasn't going to help his brother. Sully was twenty-two and, while he'd always be three years younger than Dez, he was an adult. Not that Sully didn't come to him with problems anymore, but he'd been able to stand on his own two feet for a while now. And Dez knew his hanging around playing guard dog changed the dynamics of their adult relationship, held the possibility Sully would revert back to the shy, uncertain, scared kid he'd once been.

And so, after dropping off the bag containing Sully's change of clothes with one of the members on hand, Dez gave the interview area a wide berth.

Apparently his father, Deputy Chief Flynn Braddock, didn't subscribe to the same view. Dez was headed to see him when he ran into him on the stairs.

"I was just told they brought Sully in for questioning on his boss's murder," Flynn said. "Where is he?"

"I think Ident's processing him."

"How's he doing?"

"In shock. A bit of a space cadet right now, honestly."

"Was he hurt?"

"Not physically, no, but he's pretty messed up. He'll be okay, though. It's Sully. He's always been tougher than he looks."

"You were with him?"

"Afterwards, yeah. I got there a few minutes after the call came in."

"And you think he's got his head screwed on straight? For the interview, I mean."

"As straight as it's going to be in the circumstances. Don't worry, Dad. He's on the quiet side, but he's not going to let himself get railroaded or anything."

Flynn paused and looked to be taking an internal breather. "Right. Okay. Good."

Dez smiled. "You were going down to see him, weren't you?"

"Damn right."

"Maybe we could watch the interview from the monitoring room."

Flynn's obvious worry-created semi-panic had largely abated, and his answer proved it. "I don't think that's a good idea. Questions are going to be asked that will have the two of us fighting to hold ourselves back. Let's you and I go grab a coffee in the cafeteria, okay?"

"Cafeteria coffee's sludge, Dad."

"It's every respectable cop's duty to drink sludge, son. Come on."

SULLY READJUSTED a sock he'd rapidly slid his foot into after being relieved of the pieces of clothing that had either gunpowder residue or blood on them—which, as it turned out, was everything except his underwear.

He was grateful for the change of clothes Dez had brought, a welcome alternative to the cold plastic coveralls he would have been wearing otherwise. Unfortunately, Dez had forgotten extra shoes, leaving Sully sitting here in his socked feet.

His phone had also been taken, leaving him nothing to do but stare at the walls and think—not a good thing, given what he had to think about.

He was actually grateful when the door opened, heralding a start to his videotaped statement. Relief ended when he saw who it was.

Sergeant Forbes Raynor flashed a smile that was all teeth as he introduced himself, before taking a chair across from Sully.

"I know who you are," Sully said in response. The Black Fox was a regular drinking hole for some of Riverview's less-privileged denizens but, thanks to Dez and his popularity among his colleagues, it had also become a favoured spot for cops looking to wind down after hours. Forbes had turned up a few times, although not likely on Dez's invite.

Forbes loathed Dez, a guy who didn't have a truly unlikable bone in his body. Dez could be gruff and even outright intimidating when angry, but he was generally an affable goofball, always ready with a joke or a prank. Dez had more friends than Sully could count—always had—and most times when he brought a group of colleagues to the Fox, he was their boisterous centre.

The times when he'd shown up, Forbes had spent the evening

stewing on a bar stool, burning through Dez with largely unbroken glares until, once in a while, someone took pity on him and sat down to share a drink.

Forbes's jealousy was clear. Dez—unnaturally tall, athletic and good-looking—gave a lot of guys plenty to feel jealous about. Most took it in stride, were happy enough hanging out with him. Forbes wasn't the hang-out kind of man, and Sully recognized a fellow introvert when he saw one.

He also recognized someone who hated himself. Sully had spent years thinking of himself as a freak until, gradually, his time with the Braddocks straightened him out. He suspected Forbes hadn't had anyone to do him the same favour, although what his problem with himself was, Sully didn't know.

What he did know was that Forbes disliked him, as Dez's brother, out of principle.

This wasn't going to be an easy interview.

"I suppose you've seen me at the Black Fox on occasion," Forbes said.

Sully nodded.

"For future reference, answer in words, please. If we could get the preliminaries out of the way first, I need to double check your full name, date of birth, address and phone number."

Sully ran through the list as requested.

"You never took the Braddocks' last name," Forbes observed. "Why?"

"I was a foster, not adopted. It became a permanent placement, but it would have been tricky to change my name."

"Do you know anything about your birth parents?"

"I thought we were here to talk about what happened at the Fox."

"We are. Just curious."

"No. I don't know anything about them. That's no secret. Apparently, it was all over the news when I was left on that doorstep as a baby."

"You never wanted to find out?"

"What for? They abandoned me."

"Some people would still want to know."

"It's never really been an option, and I guess that's never bothered me much. At first, I was too young to do anything about it, even if I'd wanted to. After that, I ended up with the Braddocks, and that was way more than enough for me. They're my family."

"But not really, right? I mean, they're not blood."

"They're family in every way that counts. To some people, blood doesn't mean a thing."

"I don't know," Forbes said. "I'd be curious."

"No, you *are* curious," Sully said. "You're adopted, aren't you?"

He wasn't surprised that got Forbes back on track. "Why don't you take me through your version of what happened today."

Sully noted Forbes had requested his "version," rather than simply asking what had happened. He suspected that didn't bode well.

Sully provided the rundown, managing to make it through without losing it. He was far better at regulating his emotions than Dez was, far better at the poker face. Were this anyone else sitting in front of him, Sully might have allowed himself to let go a little, to reveal more of himself in that description. As it stood, the last person to whom he wanted to show vulnerability was Forbes Raynor.

Forbes's eyes were focused uncomfortably on Sully's face as he talked, and they remained there once he'd finished the narrative. Sully didn't have to be told the detective was searching for a lie.

Sully forced himself not to fill in the gap. Given he had family members who worked as police officers, he was aware spaces sometimes got dropped into interviews to see whether the person being questioned would fill them with something stupid. Sully was a lot of things, but stupid wasn't one.

Finally, Forbes picked back up. "Did you consider Betty a friend?"

"Yeah, I did."

"Pardon the observation, but you don't seem overly broken up for someone who just watched a friend die."

Sully bristled. "Excuse me?"

"Sorry." Clearly, Forbes wasn't sorry at all. "There was a break-in at the bar recently, I understand."

"Yeah. Last night, actually. I reported it."

"I know you did. And you reported the shooting today too. No one's been arrested in either of those. But, you know, what's really interesting to me is the fact no one but you saw either of the suspects. Your own brother didn't see the guy who supposedly broke into Betty's office last night."

"What do you mean, 'supposedly'? You think I made that up?"

"Did you?"

"No, of course I didn't. Why would I do something like that?"

"I don't know. Why don't you tell me?"

"There's nothing to tell."

Forbes sat forward, resting beefy forearms on equally beefy thighs. "Well, here's one thought. You were after something in Betty's office, but she's the only one with a key, so you had to break in. You couldn't just kick in the door because that would be a sign of an inside job, so you smashed the window out, instead. But you didn't find anything, did you?"

"What?"

"That left you with a problem, though. Whatever you were looking for was still out there. She had something on you, something you didn't want anyone to find out. So this morning, before the bar opened, and before anyone else was around, you confronted her about it. You had the gun on her, but she managed to get into the bar where she kept her pistol. She turned, you saw the gun, and you blew her away. Isn't that what happened?"

"No, it isn't what happened."

"Which part?"

"None of it. I didn't break into her office and I sure as hell didn't kill her. I described the suspects for you."

"Very conveniently, both men in masks and gloves. No

evidence left at either scene. Meanwhile, your shirt, face and hands are covered in blowback, and the shotgun with your prints on it is found at the scene. And there's no sign anywhere of your mysterious masked shooter." Forbes looked down, playing at studying a fingernail before staring back up at Sully. "Nothing to say?"

Sully had plenty to say, but his thoughts had stopped finding a coherent path to his mouth. He'd expected some uncomfortable questions, but he'd never anticipated being interrogated as a suspect.

"No?" Forbes said. "Maybe that's my answer."

Cold shock giving way to the necessity for speech, Sully at last found his tongue. "I didn't do it. I didn't break into Betty's office, and I didn't kill her. She was my friend and, no, she had nothing on me. There's nothing hiding in my past or present that I'm ashamed of, so there's nothing there to get."

"Maybe it's not that you did something to be ashamed of. Maybe she found something out about your past you wanted to know. There's a lot of shadow behind you, Sullivan. Maybe she found something out and wouldn't tell you. Or maybe she found something out you didn't want anyone else to know."

"Look. You can believe me or not. There's nothing I can do about that. But while you've got me in here, accusing me of something I didn't do, the real killer is out there somewhere."

"Maybe," Forbes said. "Maybe not."

"Are you arresting me for this?"

Forbes sat back. "No, you're free to go."

Sully took that as his cue to leave and headed for the door, but Forbes snagged his wrist.

"Sullivan? Don't go anywhere we can't find you. This isn't done."

5

WERE it not for his father, Dez would have been next in line for questioning over a serious crime.

Only, in his case, it would have been an assault on Forbes Raynor.

It had taken every ounce of self-control Dez possessed to keep the explosion in check until Flynn bustled his sons up to his office. Safely there, Dez paced the room as he vented, stopping only when Flynn held out a hand for quiet.

"Feeling better now?"

"No."

"Good." Flynn turned to Sully, slouched in the chair next to him on the visitor side of his desk. "It's possible Raynor was just testing you, seeing if you'd bite on something. It's normal for an interview like that, where we don't have a line on suspects."

"Sully's not a suspect," Dez said. "He's a witness. A victim, actually."

Flynn offered Dez a placating smile before returning his attention to his other son. "Sully?"

"He didn't really ask me anything about the guys I saw," Sully said. "He just wanted to know about me. Then he threw out that theory I told you about, that I might have been behind it."

"But he didn't arrest or charge you, so he knows it's nothing more than a theory," Flynn said. "You didn't do it, so there's not going to be enough proof to charge you. Simple as that."

"Except he pointed out my clothes are covered in gunpowder residue and my prints are on the gun."

"For which you have a solid explanation."

"Solid if they believe the truth," Sully said. "I don't think they do."

"First of all, Forbes Raynor doesn't count as 'they,' " Dez said. "Second, Dad's right. Your explanation makes sense, and it's going to be pretty hard to get around that if Raynor wants to lay a charge against you."

"Did Lowell ever get around to installing those security cameras you'd been asking him for?" Flynn asked.

Sully shook his head. "He keeps promising, but it hasn't happened yet."

"Don't worry," Flynn said. "Someone will check surveillance cameras on other area properties, see if anything picked up some guy running from the scene on either occasion. Chances are the suspect you caught breaking in is the same guy behind the shooting. Raynor might be looking in the wrong direction, suspect-wise, but his logic's not completely off.

"It makes sense someone might have gone to the Fox searching for something, and returned the next day when he didn't find it. Showing up with the gun like that, he might have intended to just use it to threaten Betty into revealing whatever he thought she had. Maybe he didn't anticipate you being there, or maybe the fact she emerged with a gun of her own set him off. Whatever it was, it's possible that changed the game plan for him."

"Or maybe it was because I tried to get the gun away," Sully said. "Maybe if I hadn't—"

Flynn cut Sully off before Dez could. "Don't you go there. You're not taking the blame for this, you got that? As far as I can tell, the whole thing was decided when Betty grabbed her gun, maybe even before. Hell, for all we know, the plan was to kill her all along."

"Why not me too?" Sully said. "I was a witness. But he didn't even try."

"Well, for one thing, he was masked so you couldn't ID him," Dez said. "And, as I understand it, it was a single-barrelled shotgun, right? He had just the one shot, and he'd used it. And even though I like to ride you about being scrawny, you're actually pretty solid. It would have been an idiot move for him to get into a physical battle with you. Running was the far better option for someone looking to avoid capture."

"You know Raynor's just going to say I walked away from the whole thing because I was the one doing the shooting."

"He can say whatever he wants," Flynn said. "It's what the evidence says that counts."

"Speaking of evidence," Sully said. "Anyone find a light blue thumb drive anywhere? Betty dug one out from somewhere in her office after the break-in, and she seemed relieved it hadn't been taken. She said it had family history and photos on it, but I had the feeling she wasn't telling me everything. Maybe there's something on it that someone wanted to get their hands on."

"Did you tell Raynor?" Dez asked.

"He didn't give me the chance, and once the accusations started, I forgot all about it."

Sully's reveal got Dez thinking, and his thoughts weren't emerging in a happy place. "If it was about a thumb drive, the shooter obviously left the Fox today without getting it."

"So it's possible he'll be back," Flynn concluded, eyes focused on Dez with meaning that didn't require words.

"We've got plenty of room for Sully," Dez said. "I don't imagine they'll let us in yet to get his stuff, but we can swing by somewhere after work and buy him a few things." He looked down at Sully before he could say anything to deride the plan. "And no arguments, Sull. Break-ins are bad enough. Murder's something else entirely. Until we get to the bottom of this, you're not going back there. Uncle Lowell can shut the place down for a while. His bank account won't suffer for it, believe me."

"So what am I supposed to do all day?"

Dez quirked up a corner of his mouth. "Staying out of trouble would be a good start."

DEZ AND SULLY waited while Flynn checked in with Ident on the thumb drive. Dez wasn't entirely surprised to learn no such drive had been found at the scene or on Betty's person.

"She must have done something with it last night," Sully said. "She knew the office was being searched, and it would likely be found if she left it there."

"So it's possible her house will be the next target," Flynn said. "Does she have any family there?"

"I think her son," Sully said. "But her husband's been out of the picture for years, so it was just the two of them."

"Do you know much about her son?" Flynn asked.

"Not really, no. Betty didn't talk much about family. Whenever I asked, she changed the subject."

"That's kind of weird, isn't it?" Dez said. "I mean, if he was living with her, they were probably close, right? And you and Betty got along well. Why wouldn't she talk about him?"

"Just the way she was, I guess. Betty didn't share a lot of personal info. She'd talk about being a kid, growing up and everything, and she'd tell me stories about her past working life, but she never really said much about her family."

"Do you know her son's name?" Flynn asked.

"She only mentioned it once, but I remember it was the last name of an author. She always stuck to romance novels and thrillers, but her husband loved the classics. She told me that when she explained why her son had the name he did."

"And you don't remember it? Was it Austen, maybe? Poe?"

"No, it was pretty unusual."

"King?" Dez suggested.

Sully smirked. "Like Stephen King?"

"Yeah. So?"

"I said classic."

"King's a classic."

Sully rolled his eyes. "Okay, old-school classic, then."

Flynn was still shooting out names of his own. "Brontë? Doyle? Twain? Thackeray?"

Sully turned fully to Flynn. "What was that last one?"

"Thackeray."

"That's it, I think. It sounds right, anyway."

Flynn tapped the name into his desktop computer, pinching at his lower lip as something popped up on the screen. "I think I get why Betty didn't talk about him much."

Dez and Sully circled the desk to see what Flynn had found. It was an arrest record, and the charge attached took things up yet another level.

"Possession of child porn," Dez observed. "So Betty's son was a pervert. No wonder she didn't want to discuss him."

Flynn eyed the screen for another few seconds before slapping his thighs and standing. "Well, pervert or not, we'd better ensure he's alert to the possibility of the house being targeted. I'll touch base with Raynor, make sure he's onto that."

Dez smirked at his father, easily reading between his lines. "You sure that's all you're going to discuss with Raynor? I mean, there's no chance Sully's name's going to come up during your chat, is there?"

Flynn smiled back, following up by grabbing Dez in a headlock and knuckle-rubbing his scalp. "You're a real know-it-all, you know that, kid?"

As Dez drove the police cruiser toward the freeway leading to his end of town, Sully was his usual brand of quiet in the passenger seat, staring out the window.

Dez knew that a lot went on in Sully's brain in these quiet moments, and it didn't always occur to him to share. Nor did it always dawn on him that sharing might be the key to staying sane.

"What are you thinking, Sull?"

An answer came after a few seconds' pause.

"Nothing."

"So you're just enjoying the scenery?"

Sully turned to him, expression suggesting he'd just realized he wasn't alone. "What?"

Dez chewed on the inside of his lower lip, studying Sully in between necessary glances at the road. His brother tended to do a good chunk of daily living inside his own head, but he wasn't often far from the surface. This was different, and Dez didn't like it.

"You doing okay?"

"Yeah, I guess."

The answer didn't do much to ease Dez's worries. Nor did the fact his brother quickly broke eye contact to return his gaze to the streets. "Listen, Sully, what you went through today, it's—"

"Dez, stop."

"What?"

"Stop!"

Dez pulled to the curb and made an unsuccessful grab for his brother as he bailed out of the cruiser. Pulling the keys, Dez rushed after Sully as he disappeared down an alley on the opposite side of the business they had pulled in next to.

As inexplicable as had been Sully's sudden flight from the car, it had nothing on the fact Dez could see his brother flattened against a brick wall, staring wide-eyed into the air in front of him.

And yet, there was no question what that meant. If he had no concern for Sully, Dez would have stayed where he was and waited until his brother showed signs the ghost had gone. As it stood, he couldn't do nothing, not when Sully looked like that—like he had when, as a seven-year-old kid, he'd spent hours shaking next to Dez in bed as he sought refuge from the things only he could see.

Dez was terrified of ghosts, but he was a big brother first, so he gained Sully's side in several strides and placed himself directly in front of him.

Dez felt the chill immediately, as if he'd stepped into a freezer, and it took every ounce of courage, self-control and love for his brother not to move. The cold seized him, biting into muscle and bone hard enough to cramp, and he felt a terror so strong it effectively rooted him to the spot. He sought strength, as he often did, in Sully, in watching the fear dwindle from in his younger brother's eyes, matching the lessening cold.

Sully reached out, grasping handfuls of Dez's uniform shirt as he dropped his forehead against his older brother's chest. "I'm sorry."

"What the hell was that, Sully?"

Sully's voice was slightly muffled against Dez's front. "The sort of thing you'd rather not know about."

Under normal circumstances, Dez would be happy to agree. They had left normal behind in that blood-soaked bar. "Tell me anyway."

Sully lifted his head and tugged back handfuls of hair as he leaned against the wall. "I saw him for the first time last night, just before the break-in. I hadn't seen him since. Not until now."

"I thought maybe you were going to tell me it was Betty."

"I saw her, too, after the shooting. She doesn't do this to me."

"Do what to you, exactly?"

Sully blew out a slow breath before answering. "This guy scares the hell out of me, and I don't know why. I haven't felt this way since I was a kid, and I hate it."

Dez dropped a hand solidly on his brother's shoulder. "Hey, we'll figure this out, okay? We always do, right?"

Sully managed a weak nod, albeit an unconvincing one. Dez pulled gently on his shoulder.

"Come on, let's get out of here."

"Not yet. There must be something he wanted me to see."

"I know what I want to see," Dez said. "The back of this alley." With Sully returning to his normal levels of calm, Dez felt his own anxieties bubbling back up. Dez sometimes joked the two of them were like a seesaw, only one allowed to hit the dirt at any given time. "Dude, tell me something. Did I just step into a ghost?"

Sully patted Dez on the chest as he pushed past him. "Yeah, you did."

Dez shuddered so violently it came out as a verbal sound.

"Thanks for that, by the way," Sully said as he scanned the ground around them.

"Jesus Christ, Sully ... Jesus Christ."

Coming up with nothing but a few discarded cigarette butts and a handful of candy wrappers and crumpled papers next to the business's rear exit, Sully moved further down the alley toward a dumpster. Dez's mind turned to the possibility of what that garbage bin might contain, given the recent presence of the ghost, driving Dez to overtake his brother and hold him back before he could pull up the lid. Sully had seen enough death for one day. As much as Dez hated being around dead bodies—mostly because he knew their former owners were sometimes nearby—he figured he was still psychologically sturdy enough to handle finding a corpse in a dumpster.

Holding his breath against the anticipated smell of dead flesh, Dez lifted the lid.

"What is it?" Sully asked.

Dez stared at what appeared, at first, to be a small body. Doing a double take, he realized it was just a bundle of clothes. "Just clothing, man. Nothing much."

"Can I see?"

Dez held onto the lid but stepped slightly to the side to allow space for Sully to peer in. "Mind if I move things around a bit?"

Dez used his free hand to pull his pen from his front pocket. "Go ahead, but use this. It beats handling garbage."

Sully leaned over far enough he could pick at the clothes with the end of the pen, shifting the dumpster's contents until they had a good view of a balled-up black overcoat, a pair of jeans and a rubber ghoul mask.

"Dez, how far are we from the Black Fox?"

"About three blocks, I think. Why?"

Sully straightened up and handed Dez back his pen. "Because this is the stuff the guy was wearing when he shot Betty."

6

Dez supposed he should have expected Raynor to be unimpressed with their find.

What he hadn't anticipated was an outright accusation of evidence-planting.

"It just seems very convenient, that's all," Raynor told Dez once the latter had pulled the Major Crimes investigator aside.

"What's that supposed to mean?"

"That means what it sounds like. Think about it. There must be close to two dozen dumpsters just like this one in a three- to four-block radius of the Black Fox. You're telling me you and Sullivan pulled over minutes after leaving the police station and just happened to head to this exact dumpster where, lo and behold, you find the suspect's clothing and mask?"

"Yeah, that's what I'm telling you."

"And I'm saying that sounds very convenient."

"I know it might seem that way," Dez said. "But it's what happened."

"And how do I know the two of you weren't just waiting for the opportune moment to plant this?"

"Excuse me?"

"Come on, Braddock. You know your brother is being eyed as a potential suspect here. So the two of you figure out a way to pad his story about this masked shooter by planting items that happen to match those he described to us."

"You're out of your mind."

"Am I? Hey, I get it. I really do. He's your kid brother. You take care of him. And, well, look at him. A pretty-boy like that, he wouldn't fare too well in prison, would he? He'd be bent over so often he'd start walking crooked."

Dez knew Raynor was baiting him, half-hoping to take a fist or two in the face just so he'd have cause to get Dez canned or, better yet, charged with assault. Dez knew it and yet, for a few seconds, he didn't care. He took a step toward Raynor, taking some satisfaction in the flash of fear he saw in the smaller man's eyes. Dez didn't say anything. He didn't have to.

"You're not thinking about assaulting me, now, are you?" Raynor asked, trying for cocky but getting to only half-mast with the smirk he appeared to be attempting.

"I'm thinking about it. And I'm enjoying every second of it."

He was interrupted by a hand on his arm and his brother's voice. "Dez? Everything all right?"

"Everything's good."

"I finished giving my statement to one of the constables. They said we can go."

"Uh-uh," Raynor said. "*I* say when you can go."

"Is there something else you need from me right now?"

"No," Raynor said. "You can go. Just don't leave town, as they say. This isn't finished."

Sully wasn't quite done yet. "Did you find that thumb drive yet?"

"The one the deputy chief mentioned to me? No, actually, we haven't. Which got me thinking maybe it doesn't exist at all. You're the only one who saw it, after all."

Dez was reaching the end of his rope and knew if he let go,

Raynor would be the form he'd crush in his descent. "You're a real asshole, you know that?"

Raynor shrugged and lifted an eyebrow. "Unlike some, I'm not here to win popularity contests, Braddock. Look, don't worry; we'll get your supposed evidence in for forensic analysis. But I swear to you, if it turns up with any of Sullivan's or your DNA on it, I'm dragging both your asses over the grill."

Only Sully's persistent tugging on his arm got Dez to follow him away from the standoff with Raynor and back in the direction of the car.

"Let it go. He's not worth it."

"He might be if it turns out he starts bending what he finds into an excuse to charge you."

"There's nothing to find, right? Like Dad said."

His shrugged and grumbled reply didn't make sense even to himself. He'd been around long enough to know the wrong people sometimes ended up charged. It didn't happen often, but it happened. And it sometimes also happened that investigators got tunnel vision, became so fixated on their working theory and preferred suspect that they lost sight of other possibilities—and even the truth.

No one liked to be proven wrong less than Forbes Raynor.

He wasn't about to share that with Sully, although he strongly suspected his brother already knew. He had, after all, come into their lives after being unfairly grilled as an un-chargeable child suspect over the arson-related murders of his then-foster family.

"What did you tell them about how we found the stuff?" Dez asked, instead. "I just said you seemed to have seen something and took off, so I followed. Figured I'd leave it to you to provide the explanation."

"I said I thought I saw someone I recognized in the alley. It's sort of true, I guess. I said I couldn't see him, so I started looking, and that's when I checked the dumpster."

"And did the constable seem to buy it?"

"As far as I could tell. I doubt Raynor's going to."

"Probably not."

"I couldn't tell them the truth, though, could I? I mean, Raynor would think that was more improbable than the explanation I gave."

"Yeah," Dez said. "You got that right. What I'm wondering is where that thumb drive got to. It doesn't sound like Raynor's about to go all-in looking for it."

"I was thinking the same thing. And maybe the reason it hasn't turned up is because the killer already found it."

"You think?"

"I've been thinking about it, man, and maybe he found it and decided he needed to get rid of Betty," Sully said. "I mean, she obviously knew what was on it and, if that's the case, she would have posed a danger, too, right? If there was some sort of evidence against someone on there, she would have lost her proof with the drive, but that wouldn't prevent her going forward with whatever she knew."

"Okay, yeah, but I'm thinking it's also possible the drive's still out there; that this guy hasn't found it, and he figured he'd better take Betty out to prevent her doing anything with it."

"You know, all this is dependent on my being right that there was more on that drive than Betty's family stuff," Sully said. "Maybe she was telling the truth."

"You're good at reading people, Sully. If you think she was lying to you, then she was lying to you."

Sully stuffed his hands deep into the pockets of his jeans as he walked. "I wish she'd let me help her. Maybe—I don't know …."

"Maybe what? Maybe you could have saved her? Or maybe, little brother, you would have joined her."

Sully shrugged but didn't say anything else, so Dez fell into silence too—although not for long.

"Where are your shoes?"

"Ident seized them earlier today, and I guess you forgot to bring some for me."

"Great," Dez said. "I guess we'd better stop off and buy you some. I don't think you're going to fit my skis."

SULLY HAD NEVER BEEN the kind of guy to go in for brand names or, for that matter, brand new, so Dez hit the army surplus store a few blocks away.

As his brother scanned the boots, Dez took in the posters littering a notice board just inside the front doors.

His eyes locked onto one featuring a warning reading "PEDOPHILE" across the top in big, bold letters. Beneath it was a pair of photos, both of Thackeray Schuster—one a mug shot and the other showing him in Riverview Park. The latter appeared to have been surreptitiously taken and revealed a couple children playing nearby. Beneath the warning were listed a number of personal details, such as birthdate, height, weight, physical description and even his home address.

Dez could see a store employee sitting behind the till, watching Sully like a hawk as if anticipating a theft. Dez didn't think his brother looked like a shoplifter, but then, this was the Riverview area. Shoplifters were a dime a dozen around here these days, and many didn't match the stereotype. Hell, he'd had to arrest an eighty-two-year-old granny last week for trying to make off with a stack of scratch-n-wins.

Dez plucked the poster from the tacks holding it in place and approached the employee with it. The man gave up the surveillance on Sully and stood to attention upon seeing the uniform—albeit with more anxiety in his expression than full respect. Dez sized him up during his approach: mid-to-late thirties, head shaved bald, well-tended facial hair, and a muscular build and lack of evident body fat that suggested he treated his body like a temple. He had a firearms magazine open in front of him, giving him something he could use to disguise his surveillance should he be spotted. His hands were out of sight, leaving Dez to question whether he had access to a weapon below the counter. And he had the cool, collected appearance of a man who had been there, done that and survived to tell the tale. He wore a long-sleeved T-shirt that couldn't help but fit tightly over his arms and pecs, and Dez suspected a range of tattoos sat beneath the material—one of them likely signifying the Armed Forces section in which he'd once served. The guy was shorter than Dez—most were—but he looked like he'd be a formidable opponent in a sparring match, nonetheless.

Dez plunked the poster atop the glass counter, beneath which sat a collection of knives, compasses and sunglasses. Always one to try the friendly approach first, Dez flashed a smile. "Are you the manager?"

"I am." The man's voice was deep with a slight scratch to it, suggesting he was either a smoker or had suffered some form of injury.

"What's your name?"

"Why do you want to know?"

"Nice to know who I'm talking to, is all."

The man didn't look fully satisfied by that response but answered anyway. "Terrence Waters."

"Retired Armed Forces?"

"Medical discharge." Terrence pulled up his left sleeve to reveal not just a tattoo marking him as army but, directly below it, the start of a prosthesis.

Dez had never been overly troubled about the idea of asking personal questions, even less so while in uniform. "How'd you lose the arm?"

"IED. Most of me's covered in one sort of scar or another but, quite frankly, I lucked out. They had to piece the guy next to me back together so they could send all of him home in a box."

"I'm sorry." Dez meant the words, and he supposed it showed as the guy granted him a nod and the hint of a smile. It disappeared as Dez pointed at the paper he'd placed on the counter. "I've got some concerns about this poster."

"So do I. Last thing we need is another pervert running the streets."

"That's not what I meant."

"Yeah. Figured. What's the problem, Constable?"

"Most glaringly, it contains a home address."

Terrence shrugged. "I don't really care. Wouldn't think you would either. You must get sick of dealing with assholes like him, guys who prey on little kids."

"I hate guys who prey on kids but, just to be clear, the man's been charged, convicted and sentenced. While I agree guys who get off on kiddie porn are repugnant, the law is the law. I'm required to uphold it. Like it or not, the guy's done his time. Listing his address like this and some of the details you have here, it invites vigilante justice."

"And that's supposed to bother me?"

"Whether it bothers you or not isn't an issue," Dez said. "I'm telling you, this is a problem. And I'm not sure if you heard, but there was a shooting this morning at the Black Fox. A woman was killed. This guy's mother as it happens."

"Sorry to hear that."

"You don't sound sorry."

"Apples fall pretty close to trees most of the time, don't they? Maybe she wasn't much of a human being, either."

Dez battled back the flash of rage that comment elicited, grateful Sully was too far across the store to have overheard. "You didn't know her. She was a good woman. A lot of the time, what you say about apples and trees is true, but sometimes there's nothing a parent can do when their kid starts going downhill. Thing is, this poster's got me wondering now if someone went after Betty Schuster because of her son. It would be pretty easy to track her since they've got her home address."

"So he was living with her, then?"

"He just got out of prison recently, as is mentioned in this poster, so, yeah."

"Then sorry, man. No offence to you, and I'm sorry for your

loss, but I really don't care. If she was supporting him, my sympathy for her is zero. The guy should have been left to fend for himself."

"You realize that only increases the chances of his reoffending?"

"He won't be reoffending," Terrence said, confidence rolling off the words.

"How do you know?"

"Because that poster's up all over the area, and it means people will be watching him. He won't get the chance to hurt another kid."

"Technically, he didn't directly hurt any kids himself, you know. It was a possession conviction, not producing."

"Two sides, same coin. It's because of dicks like him that the skinners keep feeding the beast. If there's no market, there's no reason to produce and sell."

Dez nodded, looking back down at the poster a moment before directing his attention back on Terrence. "You made these, didn't you?"

"So what if I did?"

"Take them down."

"Why?" Terrence asked. "Am I breaking a law?"

"You might have contributed to the death of an innocent woman."

"No way she died as a result of these," Terrence said. "People would go after him, not her."

Sully was approaching the till with a pair of boots, so Dez leaned toward Terrence to speak to him quietly. "If you've got that much spite for her, isn't it likely someone else felt the same?"

Dez swept the poster off the counter and folded it a few times, tucking it into his pocket next to his notebook as Sully reached the counter.

"Find something?" Dez asked.

Sully glanced between Dez and the manager. It only made sense a guy who dealt in beings made up solely of energy invisible to most everyone else would be able to sense mental and emotional strain among the living, as well.

"Yeah." The word was drawn out, the sound of questions waiting to be asked. But, for now, he simply fished some cash from his wallet and paid for the boots.

Dez waited until Sully headed out in front of him, then fixed Terrence with one last pointed look before following.

"WHAT WAS THAT ABOUT?" Sully asked, once back in the car.

Dez thought about keeping it to himself, but thought better of it, digging out the poster and handing it to Sully.

"This is Betty's son."

"Got it in one," Dez quipped. "Saw it hanging on the bulletin board at the front entrance. I didn't get a pat answer, but apparently the manager there, Terrence Waters, made it and posted them around town."

"This has their address on it," Sully said. "You don't think—"

Dez interrupted. "That someone saw this and took it upon themselves to start righting perceived wrongs? I think it's possible. I'm going to take this to Raynor just as soon as I drop you off. It's sure as hell worth investigating as a lead. Even he's got to admit that."

"Good luck with that. Listen, I was thinking, maybe I should go see Thackeray, pay my respects."

"First of all, the guy doesn't deserve any respects given what he went in for. And second, no."

"No? No, what?"

"No, you're not going near the guy. You need to stay the hell away from this investigation, all right? If you're seen to insert yourself in it, Raynor's going to start looking to others like he's not far off the mark suspecting you. I'm taking you home, and you're going to stay there."

Sully's mouth twitched like he was of a mind to argue, but he kept it to himself. Just as well, because Dez wasn't of a mind to listen. Instead, Sully changed the subject—although the topic wasn't much better than the previous one.

"Any chance you can help me figure out who that man is I've been seeing? I need to deal with him ASAP so I can get him out of my space."

"I'll do what I can. You wanna run that description by me, again?"

When Sully got to the ghost's clothing, Dez clued into something. "Were they pyjamas or the sort of garb they make patients wear?"

"It wasn't hospital stuff," Sully said. "Most hospitals in KR I've been to just have gowns for patients. Otherwise people have to bring their own clothes in."

"I wasn't thinking hospitals, exactly," Dez said. "I was thinking Lockwood."

"The psychiatric hospital? You think? That would explain so much, you know that? The fear rolling off this guy is intense. I can't imagine someone experiencing that in life and being able to function."

"Isn't it possible the fear is a result of whatever happened to him when he died?"

"Maybe, but I've seen some pretty awful things over the years, and I don't remember one who felt like this. There's something more to it. I think the fear is central to this somehow, like a clue I need to figure out. That would suggest it's about more than just his death. Can you drop me off at the university?"

"Why?"

"I thought I could go see Marc Echoles. He knows about this stuff, and I could use the advice if he's got some."

Dez didn't like the idea of Sully not being somewhere today where he was being looked after. But while Marc wasn't Eva, the professor had proved reliable enough over the past couple of years when these ghosts popped up. And, what was more, he was genuinely fond of Sully.

"Just promise me you'll head straight over to Eva afterward, all right?"

Sully was silent.

"All right, Sully?"

"I hear you."

Not until Sully was out of the car and headed onto the campus did Dez realize his brother hadn't promised him a damn thing.

7

Marc Echoles's office was located within the sociology department, halfway down a narrow hallway that always looked to be short a few bulbs.

Sully had never been able to keep the professor's schedule straight, recalling only that he taught two classes: History of the Occult and Social Deviance and Social Control.

Marc's office door was closed but he'd posted his schedule on it, and a glance at the clock on Sully's cellphone suggested the professor should be returning within the next twenty minutes or so.

There were chairs in the hall and Sully was about to drop into one when a familiar female voice called his name.

"Sully? Hey! I thought you'd dropped off the face of the earth."

He took a quick breath, steadying his nerves before turning to face Takara Watanabe. Sully had screwed up the courage to call her after meeting her two years ago, and they'd dated on and off since. Ara—as she insisted on being called—was happy most days to chatter his ear off, and Sully found he liked the sound of her voice. There was something bright and energetic about her, a clear morning sunrise to his haunted midnight, and he found a degree of comfort there.

But not always. As one could expect of any normal human being, Ara was not content to talk forever, and she at times asked more of him than he was prepared to provide. He trusted few with the gift—or curse—with which he'd been born, and he hadn't yet reached that point with her. Unlike with many, he didn't worry she would whisper his secret behind his back, nor did he think she—a practicing Wiccan—could handle his level of weird. Rather, there was something he liked about the idea of having someone in his life who didn't know that side of him, whose entire knowledge of who he was remained based on his character, his traits and the person he chose to be. Some days, it felt like there was little he could control, but he had at least retained the ability to decide what to reveal and how much should be left concealed behind his walls.

Not to say holding back was easy. Ara wasn't one to simply leave well enough alone, and her persistence—as well-intentioned as it was—had sent him retreating into his shell more than once. He hadn't seen her in a month. Their last date left him lying in bed beside her contemplating how best to extricate himself after fending off a tirade of questions he'd silenced with a kiss and everything that followed.

Nor was it easy to say no to her when she looked the way she did today: long, glossy black hair left to hang freely over her shoulders, just a hint of makeup on a flawless face, clothes that showed off both her quirky personal style and her petite build. And those almond-shaped, deep brown eyes that revealed her soul even as they threatened to dissect his.

"I've been busy with some stuff," he said. She graciously accepted the lame excuse, though it came with a gentle-but-knowing smile.

"I was a little hard-assed with the questions the last time," she said. "I'm sorry about that. It's in my nature. It's why I decided to switch to Journalism." She peered more closely at him, eyes back to that unnerving, soul-searching thing they did. "Something's off with you. Are you all right?"

Sully debated how much to tell her. He knew if he shared what had happened with the break-in and Betty, she'd insist on dragging him out somewhere for a coffee and a long chat—her chatting, him listening. The last thing he wanted, he decided, was for her to know he'd been pegged as a suspect in Betty's death. She wouldn't buy the idea of his involvement as truth, but he also knew she would insist on being there for him, which would end up creating more problems than it solved. Despite Dez's warnings, Sully fully expected he was embarking on another ghost chase—quite possibly two—and he didn't need or want a hanger-on, particularly one he wished to keep in the dark about that part of himself.

Even so, it felt wrong to lie to her, and so he did what he usually did. "It's not something I can talk about right now. I'm sorry."

"There's a lot you can't talk about—at least with me, isn't there? But you're here to see Marc, so you're obviously okay talking to him about it, right?"

"It's not like that."

"What's it like, then?"

"Ara ...."

"I've never demanded answers about why you clam up when things start getting real between us. I know you had a hard life before your family took you in, but you must know by now I'd never judge you. I get why there might be things your family knows about you that no one else does. But Marc? Sully, you're not even a student here."

"I never meant for him to know either, but he does. It wasn't my choice, but he's been helpful despite that. It isn't my intention to shut you out. You know everything about me except for this one thing. And I promise you, it's nothing you need to know."

She studied him another long few seconds in that unnerving way. "You're not some sort of pervert, are you?"

"Of course not."

"And you haven't killed or hurt anyone?"

"No."

"And is this about anything bad that happened to you that you don't think you can tell me?"

"No, it's nothing like that. I've told you all this before."

"I know, but I keep hoping you'll come through with a more detailed answer."

"I can't. Not yet, anyway. Okay?"

Ara looked to give it some brief thought before following up with a small smile. "I guess that's going to have to be good enough for now. But you do know you can trust me, right?"

"Of course I know that."

Ara stepped up and wrapped her arms around him in an embrace he'd done nothing to deserve. He responded and happily met the kiss she demanded by stepping back and pulling down on his shirtfront.

He allowed her to break the kiss first—about the only concession he seemed able to allow her.

"I've got to go," she said. "I've got a meeting with a prof I'm already late for. Call me later, okay?"

He nodded and watched as she rushed off, shiny hair bouncing behind her, book bag threatening to spill its contents along the hallway floor. In the end, the bag held its ground next to Ara, just as Sully had.

But, unlike Sully, the bag likely didn't feel guilty about it.

"Uh-oh."

Sully had just dropped into the chair across from Marc Echoles's desk. He turned his head at the voice and found yet another set of perceptive eyes fixed on him.

"Uh-oh, what?"

"Dark blue. You just ran into someone you had to lie to, didn't you? Someone important to you."

There were times when Marc's ability to see and read auras was a pain in Sully's ass. "Not lie to, exactly. Just avoid the truth."

"Same difference, isn't it? What happened?"

"Ara," Sully said. It was all he needed to say. They'd been down this road too many times in the past.

"I don't get why you don't tell her. I've met the young lady. She's not the judging sort."

"I just want one person in my life who sees me as a relatively normal person without some weird psychic thing."

"That weird psychic thing is part of who you are, like it or not. The things you've seen, the people you've helped, that's a big part of what's molded you into the man you've become. You were a young kid when you first started trying to find justice for homicide victims. That's a pretty great thing. Anyway, while I don't know your parents, I've gotten to know Desmond quite well. He doesn't think any differently about you because he knows, does he?"

"I don't know," Sully said. "Maybe he'd hover less if he didn't know about the things I saw."

"Desmond hovers because of the things *he's* seen. He lost a little brother in his childhood. You've become his chance to do things differently. Maybe you need to think about doing things differently yourself. In seeking to make yourself appear normal to Ara, you're creating just the sort of feeling you've been trying so hard to avoid. I know I've said this before, and I'm worried I'm a broken record on this point, but be honest with her. You might be surprised. Anyway, this isn't why you've come here today, is it?"

The change in conversation was a relief, albeit one that faded fast once he launched into this latest topic.

"My boss, Betty, was killed this morning. A gunman came in and he and I were fighting for the gun when it went off."

"Oh, Sullivan, no. I was wondering what those greys and blacks were about. Are you all right? Were you hurt?"

"I'm fine physically, but I'm not sure where I'm going to come out on this in any other way. I haven't had much time to try to process since I've been dealing with the police more or less since. The investigator in charge of the file is trying to pin it on me, saying I invented the gunman."

"Why would he do that?"

"I don't know, but he hates Dez. Could be he's trying to use me to get at my brother."

"That seems like a pretty drastic way to poke at a rival. I can't imagine a police officer would bend an investigation to try to meet a theory with no merit, simply to get at someone."

"It's not quite that simple." Sully explained about last night's break-in, the missing thumb drive and the morning's shooting, as well as what followed in terms of the ghosts he'd seen. "The problem is, there's no physical evidence so far on either of the incidents that connect them to anyone else. No prints were left, no DNA evidence, nothing concrete."

"But you found the clothes. Surely something will be found on them, whether blood or hair or even gunpowder residue."

"The shooter was standing too far back from Betty to get any blood on him, and there's no suggestion he was injured in any way that would leave his own blood on the clothes. Maybe hair or saliva will turn up on the mask, but that's my only hope. As of now, Raynor thinks Dez or I planted them, and he'll no doubt argue blowback can't be connected to any particular event. He'll say Dez could have fired his own gun while wearing the coat himself."

"Dez's gun could be tested for recent firing."

"That won't help. He had to re-qualify a few days ago for his firearms certification."

"Even so, I still think it sounds like this investigator would be reaching pretty far to continue to look at you for this. You'll keep me posted?"

"I will."

"So this ghost you've been seeing," Marc said. "What do you think is going on with him?"

"I was hoping you might have some answers. I can't figure out what he's after, much less why he led me to the alley where Dez and I found those clothes."

"Could be he's connected to the shooter in some way. Maybe he came to you to ...." Marc broke off, pressing his lips together and visually scanning his desk's surface.

Sully was never one to leave well enough alone, not when it came to finding the answers he needed to get rid of his ghosts. "Came to me to what?"

"Nothing. Never mind. Thinking aloud, that's all."

"No, you weren't. What were you going to say?"

Marc sighed and returned his gaze to Sully's face. There was regret in the upturn of his eyebrows, in the tiny, apologetic smile. "Maybe he came to you the night before to warn you."

The answer's full meaning settled over Sully like the feeling of standing in the pub's beer cooler for too long, leaving him chilled and numb. He slouched back against the chair, eyes drifting from Marc's face to a poster on the wall, an advertisement for a Beltane festival from years back. The poster featured a flame-lit phoenix and someone in a costume twirling fire. Sully had been in the office once on a particularly cold winter's day, frozen to the bone and shivering from the walk over from the nearest bus stop. While waiting for Marc, Sully had studied that poster and had gradually warmed as he imagined the feel of the fire. Today, he felt nothing, could do nothing but accept he was currently lost within a world too dark and cold for any warmth to find a way in.

"Sullivan, I'm sorry. But you need to understand it wasn't your fault."

"If he was there to warn me, I didn't see it. I didn't listen. And Betty's dead because of it."

"No. She's dead because of the man who shot her. Anyway, neither of us know anything for sure. You don't even know for certain whether the intruder from last night was the same man you saw this morning. Like I said, I was only thinking aloud. It's one theory, that's all."

"But a good one. It makes sense. Maybe he wanted me to stop the intruder. If I had, the police would have been able to arrest him last night. If it is the same man, he wouldn't have been able to hurt Betty this morning."

Marc held up a palm, a call to pause. "Let's not lose sight of one important detail. Most experienced psychic mediums would say that unless a person was able to do so in life, his or her ghost can't predict the future. It's possible those who cross over into the light can tap into some sort of grand life plan that might give them a few glimpses into others' futures. But earthbound ghosts are still very much tied into existence here, and don't have those abilities. He couldn't have foreseen the threat to Betty's life."

"Unless he'd been around the man who ended up killing her and realized his intentions," Sully corrected.

Marc shrugged but didn't respond, an indication he conceded the point but didn't want to say it out loud.

Sully sighed heavily, propping an elbow on the arm of the chair and dropping his face into his hand, squeezing the bridge of his nose to ward off the anticipated headache. Already, he could feel the tension building behind his eyes, around his temples, in the back of his neck. The day had been one long bout of it; the fact it had taken this long for his body to catch up was nothing short of a miracle. "All the stuff we know about, the weird abilities we have, and no one's sorted out how to go back in time. I wish I could."

"To do what, exactly?"

"I don't know. Something. Anything. Anything is better than nothing, which is exactly what I ended up doing last night."

"You didn't do nothing. You called the police and you tried to stop the man. You said he countered your swing and took you down, hard. Sounds like a professional job to me."

"If I'd called the police sooner, asked them to come there quietly rather than lights and siren ...."

"I'm pretty sure the police set their own protocol about lights and siren. And the outcome's the same, either way. Face it, son. You don't have a way around this. You couldn't have done anything differently here, no matter which way you try to dissect what went down."

There was no point arguing the subject any longer, Marc no more inclined to listen to Sully's self-blame than Dez. Instead, Sully pulled back to the other subject, the one he'd really come here to talk about.

"This ghost, the man I've been seeing. He scares the crap out of me."

"Which, to most people, is rather a normal response."

"And it was to me, too, when I was younger. But I don't react that way anymore. They shake me up sometimes, but they never terrify me. Not anymore, anyway. So why is this guy doing it? Is it just that I'm sucking in what he feels?"

"Yeah, I'd imagine that's exactly what it is. But I thought you had figured out how to block stuff like that."

"I thought I had too. I mean, it's not blocking, exactly. It's figuring out how to differentiate my own feelings from theirs so I can release the stuff that isn't mine. But this guy's not letting me do that. If I didn't know better, I'd think ...."

"What?"

"It's stupid maybe, but it kind of feels like he's trying to possess me. It's not just the feelings he's imposing on me. It's how close he gets and how intense it feels. I've had others come right up to me and touch me, but that was to pass along a thought, a vision, a memory or whatever. But not with this guy. It's like he's trying to figure out how to do something. I mean, if he was trying to get a message through to help me stop something, he could have done that like the others had, right? But he didn't."

"Maybe he doesn't know how to do that, either. But here's the thing. I teach the occult, so I've done a whole lot of research in this area. Between you and me, when it comes to ghosts, you're the expert. If you think he's trying to pull a step-in here, I'd say you'd better go with your gut. What worries me is you're not at your best at the moment. Your aura's weak and that means your defences are down. Do you ever meditate?"

"No. What would that do?"

"It grounds you, draws your energy together, calms and stills you. Given what you do, you should be building up to at least half an hour of meditation every morning. It will help to reinforce you so you're stronger and better protected going into these encounters."

"You're supposed to not think about anything when you do that, right?"

"Ideally, yes."

"I can't do that. My brain doesn't turn off."

"It takes practice, but you can get there. It's simply a matter of drawing yourself gently back every time you feel yourself straying. Give yourself something to focus on, whether it's your breathing or a mantra. That's what I do, anyway, and believe me, my brain is a pretty active little beehive of activity most of the time. It works."

"Okay," Sully said. "I'll try."

"Good. In the meantime, I want you to focus on something positive whenever you see this man. He can't overtake you if you're stronger than he is."

"No offence, but this isn't the best day to be trying to think up anything positive."

"Most people have something good in their lives. What about your family? That's a pretty big positive, right? Think about them when you need a boost or, better yet, stay physically close to them for a while. They'll get you through this, even if they don't realize they're doing it."

Sully thought about the incident in the alley earlier today. The ghost, directly in front of him, and was shifting uncomfortably closer when his image had suddenly morphed into Dez. Sully and the ghost seemed to become aware of Dez's intrusion into that uncomfortable connection at roughly the same time, the ghost disappearing and Sully's terror dissipating into relief. Since they'd met when Sully was a kid, Dez had been his rock, as had Flynn and Mara Braddock and, most recently, Dez's wife and daughter, Eva and Kayleigh. Sully had never known what family meant until he'd met the Braddocks; now it was the most important thing in his life.

"Thanks, Marc," he said. "I think that helps, actually."

"Good. So what's the plan? Obviously, you're going to want to do something about this guy."

"Yeah, and that involves figuring out what he wants."

"Should you be doing that, right now?" Marc asked. "I mean, if he's connected to the shooting somehow, won't you get in some serious trouble if you involve yourself more than you already are?"

"The ghosts usually don't give me much of a choice, and this guy's far from the exception," Sully said. "Besides, I'm already in serious trouble."

8

DEZ FOUND Forbes Raynor in the Major Crimes unit, sitting in what Dez could only imagine was his go-to position: feet up on the desk, leaning back in a chair while involved in a phone conversation that sounded far too relaxed to be wholly work-related.

Equally unsurprising was the fact Forbes was less than pleased to see him or to hear his opinion on the Betty Schuster murder.

"You know damn well I can't discuss that case with you."

"I'm not asking you to discuss it with me," Dez said. "I'm just here to inform you of some info that came to light today."

"Let me guess. This is info that will have your brother coming off all pure as the driven snow."

"Sully had nothing to do with Betty's death."

"That's for the investigation to determine," Forbes said. "As you very well know. But I'm up for hearing alternative theories, if there's a better one."

"What, you mean like the one where a guy came in and shot her? That theory?"

"Contrary to what you seem to think, Braddock, I'm not out to get Sullivan. Like I said earlier, we've simply got no physical evidence to back what he says."

"What about that clothing we found?"

"It's still with Ident, being tested. But, honestly, the only one who can put that clothing on the shooter is Sullivan. We need to do a little better than that, don't you think?"

The use of the word "we" had Dez bristling, the condescension clear in the older man's tone. Dez took a breath. It wasn't going to help Sully for his big brother to come in here and knock the block off the lead investigator on the file.

"Do you want to hear what I came here to tell you, or not?"

"I'm all ears."

All ass is more like it, Dez thought. But he bit back the comment in favour of launching into a narrative of the visit to the army surplus store and the poster he'd found there.

"Thackeray's home address is listed on the poster—his mother's home address," Dez said. "She took Thackeray back in after he was released from jail and he's been there since. We all know how kooky some vigilantes can get. A lot of people blame parenting for the reason people go sideways in life, and there could be some bad feeling against Betty."

"I realize that. Your father called me earlier after he looked Thackeray up, told me it was likely a good idea to warn the guy he might be a target."

"Did you?"

"I'll get to it."

"Don't you think it might be kind of important? I mean, if his mother's death was related, he'll no doubt be next."

"What sense does any of that make, really?" Forbes asked. "If the home address is the one listed, wouldn't anyone wanting at Thackeray go there to play vigilante? Why would anyone go to the Black Fox and target the mother?"

"I don't know, maybe no one was home? Come on, Forbes, everyone knows Betty runs the Fox. She's been a fixture there for at least two decades, probably closer to three. When people think of the Black Fox, she's an automatic second."

"Look, I'll talk to the son, all right? But I'm in the middle of something now. I'm waiting on that info from Ident you're so keen on, plus I've got patrol talking to neighbouring businesses, and one for sure is bringing in a surveillance tape as we speak. So, contrary to what you seem to think, I am looking into Sullivan's claims. All right?"

Dez took another breath, searching for that elusive feeling of calm. "Okay. Thanks. One other thing, though."

"There's always one other thing with you, isn't there?"

"The guy who runs the army surplus, Terrence Waters. He's an army vet. He'd know his way around firearms, plus he'd be good in a fight. Sully's no slouch when it comes to handling himself, and he said the shooter was pretty strong. Add that to the fact there might be some connection to the break-in and the possibility it's the same suspect, and it's got me thinking we're looking for a professional of some type."

"Let me ask you something," Forbes said. "Do you really think a professional is going to burst in the back door of a bar in broad daylight and fire off a round at a woman in full view of an employee?"

"Maybe, if he wants to pass it off as just some sloppy business robbery gone bad."

"No, Braddock. I'm thinking it's far more likely we're either looking at two separate suspects here, or it's the alternative you don't want to acknowledge."

"Sully didn't do it. How many times do I have to say it? He's not capable of killing."

Forbes curled his lips into the condescending grin again, the one Dez wanted to punch off his face. Unfortunately, Forbes followed it up with a piece of logic that Dez would never be able to wipe away as easily. "Braddock, you and I both know that given the right circumstances, everyone is capable of killing."

THE WARNING WAS STILL SITTING THERE, the earworm Dez had no doubt intended to plant when he'd told Sully to stay away from Thackeray Schuster.

But the more Sully thought about it, the more the reasons stacked up in favour of visiting the Schuster house until they'd finally cast a shadow long enough to eclipse the reasons not to.

And so, late that afternoon, Sully walked up the cracked sidewalk leading to Betty's small 1920s two-storey in the Riverview neighbourhood.

Judging from the state of the exterior of the house, Betty wasn't much for home renos. But she was a neat freak and an avid gardener; visitors could ignore the cracks in the sidewalk and the fact the house needed repainting as their vision drifted to the abundant flowerbeds that lined the house and coloured the small front yard. A veranda surrounding the front entrance boasted several healthy-looking potted plants and a porch swing, while window boxes held even more bright flowers.

Sully could imagine Betty out here every other morning watering her various plantings, enveloped for at least that short space of time within a world in which everything else could fall away. Mara Braddock loved gardening, too, and he remembered her saying she could tell when her flowers were smiling at her. If flowers could smile, Betty's were grinning a mile wide.

Sully's heart broke all over again.

Approaching the door proved easier than the idea of lifting his hand to knock. He wasn't here simply to try to piece together who had killed Betty and why. He'd been there when it had happened, had his hands on the gun when it was discharged. There was an apology he needed to make, words he wasn't sure he could find.

All he knew was that he had to try.

He stepped up to the solid glass pane, which made up much of the top half of the door and peered through, preparing to knock.

Betty stared back at him.

Sully took an involuntary step backward but caught himself

before the surprise-induced move could send him tumbling down the steps onto the pavement. He knew he shouldn't have been shocked by the fact she was here. He'd seen her, after all, in the moments immediately after her death.

She'd been there for a time at the Black Fox, staring down at her body, the disbelief written all over her face. From his experience, the people he saw sometimes found their way home if it was a place they found comfort. Sometimes they haunted the people who'd killed them but, more often than not, it was their loved ones to whom they gravitated, as if looking for some light in what had become a very dark reality.

Somehow, in his rush through this day, in dealing with the shooting and being pegged as a suspect and trying to cope with the terrifying vision of the man he kept seeing, Sully had lost sight of Betty, of the fact she was still here and needed help too.

It was one more thing to apologize for.

Her mouth was moving now, and he knew she was speaking but, as always, he didn't have the ability to hear what she said. Flynn had asked him once whether studying lipreading might help, but this situation proved once again it wouldn't. As usual, when Sully tried to focus on the ghost's lips, he found them moving in a blur, no way for him to make anything out. Whether it was because ghosts spoke at a speed too fast for living humans, or simply because this was another of the universe's annoying ways of telling him he was not to communicate with them in speech, he didn't know. None of this had ever made sense to him, and it likely never would.

"I can't hear you," Sully told Betty now. "I can see you, but that's it."

It occurred to Sully that apologizing to Thackeray was secondary, this opportunity perhaps his best chance of laying out what was tearing him up inside. "Betty, I'm sorry. I'm so sorry. I—"

"Who are you talking to?"

Sully spun to see a man coming around the side of the

veranda, a cigarette in his mouth. While the resemblance wasn't obvious at first glance, the way he held the cigarette between his lips so it bobbed as he spoke, was all Betty. Were this any other day, any other situation, Sully might have laughed at the thought of the two of them, mother and son, sitting on the veranda together, smokes bobbing simultaneously as they chatted about their day.

This was not that day, not that situation.

"No one," Sully said. "Sorry. I talk to myself sometimes."

The man pulled the smoke from his lips, held it between thumb and forefinger as if to throw it or use it as a weapon should need be. "Who are you and what are you doing here?"

"My name's Sullivan Gray. I worked with your mom at the Black Fox. You *are* Thackeray, right?"

Sully had expected the introduction to bring about an un-narrowing of suspicious eyes, perhaps a handshake. He got neither. "Oh, yeah?"

"Yeah .... Um, can we talk a minute?"

Thackeray studied him silently, gaze travelling up and down his body before settling back on his eyes. He was sizing Sully up, possibly looking for weapons, and it occurred to Sully this man had recently left prison. Considered a child sex offender, he would have been at the bottom of the pecking order, had possibly found himself being victimized more than once. While Sully's sympathies were minimal, the understanding was there.

He guessed he'd passed the test when Thackeray turned, showing his back as he disappeared around the corner of the veranda, making his way to what Sully guessed was a side door. While the invitation hadn't been spoken, he followed to where Thackeray dropped into one of two old kitchen chairs that had been placed—likely permanently, judging by the extent of the wear on their vinyl coverings—outside. The backyard was partly visible from here, enough to reveal further evidence of Betty's green thumb. Trees and shrubs formed a border this side, where the rickety fence was no longer up to the task, and an ivy-covered gated archway stood at the back of the property, leading to the alley. Like the front of the property, it was beautiful and peaceful.

That peace ended at the veranda railing as if by a wall. Thackeray was no longer behind bars, but Sully could sense them there all the same. He knew people, regulars at the Black Fox, who had been to prison. One parolee in particular he knew had done a fifteen-year stint for second-degree murder, and he was a living example that while most people eventually left prison, it never really left you.

Then again, Thackeray Schuster had at least one other thing that had to be eating him up today.

Sully eased himself onto the other chair, the one he guessed had been Betty's, alert for any signs should Thackeray not want him sitting there. He said nothing, so Sully launched into his reason for coming, staring down at his hands as he cupped one inside the other and rubbed at his fingers.

"I just wanted to tell you I'm sorry."

"Thanks."

Sully wasn't sure what he'd been expecting, but it was a little more than "thanks." Questions for sure, whether a simple ask about whether he'd been there, what had happened, had she suffered. Maybe Thackeray didn't want to know, or just didn't know how to ask. But, while there were no right answers in grief, Sully had come to understand it was wrong for loved ones not to have questions.

"I worked with Betty, and she's always been awesome."

"You didn't know her."

"I knew her pretty well. It's been almost four years since I started working at the Fox."

"I meant you don't know her like I do."

"What do you mean? What don't I know?"

Thackeray took a long drag on his smoke, then butted out the rest without finishing, grinding it down into a well-used ashtray. "Nothing. Doesn't matter. That all you came here for, to tell me you're sorry?"

"I guess. I don't know .... I guess I wanted to ask about something."

"What?"

"There was a break-in there last night. Did your mom mention that to you?"

"We weren't exactly chatty."

"So I don't imagine she said anything to you about a thumb drive, huh?"

"No, why?"

"She said it contained family photos and history, stuff like that. She was really worried whoever broke in had stolen it."

"It was stolen?" That had him turning his full attention on Sully.

"So you do know about it."

Thackeray narrowed his eyes, returned his gaze to the floorboards of the veranda in front of him—all the better to concoct a lie. "She was working on compiling our family history. She was big on that sort of thing, said she wanted to leave me something about my heritage. It's all I have left now, I guess."

"And there wasn't anything else she kept on there?"

Thackeray's eyes were on him again, shock replaced by controlled anger and suspicion. "Why are you so interested in it? It's none of your business."

"I was there when your mom was killed, and I was there when the place was broken into. I'm just trying to figure out what happened and why."

"Cops think you were involved, you know," Thackeray said. "When they came to notify me about Mom, they asked a lot of questions about my family, about me, but also about you. Seemed like they were trying to make out like you did it."

"Let me guess," Sully said. "The officer who spoke to you was named Forbes Raynor?"

"Yep. No friend of yours, I gather."

"I didn't have anything to do with this. I didn't hurt your mom."

"I know that. Cops get shit wrong all the time and, anyway, you probably wouldn't be here talking to me if you had. If you were really after something like that thumb drive, you'd have snuck in here in the middle of the night or waited till I went out. Not like this place is Fort Knox or anything."

"But you haven't seen it here? You're sure?"

"She told me she had something, but she never said where. I looked once or twice in the past, but I'm thinking she kept it at the office."

"Maybe we could look for it now. I mean, she must have taken it with her last night. No way she left it behind at work after all that happened, not if it was that important to her."

"I'll look for it again," Thackeray said. "I don't need the help."

What he'd no doubt meant to say was that he didn't want help, not from Sully, anyway. But there was something else on which Sully figured Thackeray could use the assistance.

"I stopped off at the army surplus earlier," Sully said. "The manager there has some posters he's put up of you. Sounds like there's more around town than just the shop."

"Yeah, I know. I've seen them."

"Your address is on them."

"Like I said, I've seen them."

"You don't seem as upset about it as I thought you might be."

"Look, I spent almost two years in prison for a crime I didn't commit, one that makes you a pariah in there. I'm on parole now, and my PO is just itching to throw my ass back in. I'm doing everything I can to keep from going back there, all right? It's hell. So, no, I'm not confronting some guy who's got it in for me."

"You didn't do it?" In Sully's experience—and he'd met more than his share of ex-cons at the Fox—few people ever willingly admitted to wrongdoing. He was skeptical of Thackeray's assertion, and it showed.

The tone of Thackeray's reply was that of a man who'd been down this road many times: exhaustion rather than indignation. "No. I didn't."

"But they would have found the stuff on your computer, right? That's usually pretty concrete."

"Yeah, I know. That's why they convicted me. I had a lawyer for a while, a Legal Aid guy who kept grumbling about his caseload. He kept at me to plead out, to take the deal the Crown was offering, but I told him I wasn't going to cop out to something I didn't do. So he withdrew on me, told the judge I was refusing to take his advice. I had no choice but to run the trial myself. You can see how well that went. Not only did I not get the sentence the Crown initially offered, the prosecutor asked for additional time since I'd pursued the matter in court. The judge had no problem with that given the size of the collection the cops found. The judge made some comment about it being the largest he'd ever seen."

"So if you didn't download it, how'd it get on your computer?"

"I have no idea, okay? If I did, I would have had my case made. And it wasn't just my computer. It was on some thumb drives that just turned up at my place, and someone had taken my digital camera and snapped a bunch of photos of kids at a nearby swimming pool. I was set up and, no, I don't know why. No one ever came at me for hush money or anything. One day, the cops just turned up with a warrant and seized all my electronics. Said they received information through an anonymous tip line that I was spying on kids. Surveillance didn't pan out—obviously because the tip was bogus—but they apparently found my IP address on one of those file-sharing sites used by perverts. I guess that got them their warrant, and everything else they needed was miraculously there. If I had to guess, I'd say one of the cops planted it because they were pissed they couldn't get me any other way."

Sully's brain had caught on one statement in particular. "You said police found some of the stuff on thumb drives. Do you think that has anything to do with what your mom was hiding?"

"Look, what's all this to you? It doesn't involve you."

"I know," Sully said. "It's just that the drive seemed important to her. I want to make sure it's safe. I guess I'm hoping to help her in some way, if I can."

Thackeray scoffed. "Yeah, well, don't bother. She doesn't need your help and, what's more, she doesn't deserve it. That thumb drive you're talking about? It contained information that could clear me."

"But that's a good thing, right?"

"She never did a damn thing but sit on it, like it would hatch a chick if she waited long enough. I knew she had something because she told me, but she never let me see it or make a copy. She wasn't there for me when I needed her. She never was. She was always more worried about my nutcase of a father than she was about me, and that's a fact."

Sully did what he could with the information Thackeray had provided. "Maybe if we found the thumb drive, we could at least clear your name. That would be worth something, right?"

"You don't get it, man. The amount of porn they found was beyond anything they'd seen before. My name was all over the news and reporters were at my trial. You think anyone will care if I'm exonerated now? Even if it's reported, you think anyone will listen or read it? Anyone will still be able to look up my name online and see the stories about my conviction. This is with me forever, no matter what I do."

Thackeray stopped, staring down at his knees and, with no other conversation forthcoming, Sully said the only thing he could think to say. "I'm sorry."

"Whatever."

Sully spotted movement, watched as Betty materialized behind Thackeray's right shoulder, blood still mottling her shirt front and seeping from her mouth as she stared down at her son. Suddenly, Sully knew the way to that thumb drive might be within reach, if only he could convince Thackeray to turn a blind eye for a minute or two.

"Hey, Thackeray? I'm sure you don't need me hanging around

here much longer, but I'm hoping I might be able to use your bathroom before I go."

But it seemed the veranda was as far as Sully was going to get today.

"There's a coffee shop down the street," Thackeray said. "I really think I want to be alone now."

9

SULLY SKIPPED the bus and opted to walk to the Black Fox, hoping to be able to get upstairs for some of his things.

Instead, he found himself standing in the parking lot with a view of the rear door, watching as the body removal service carted Betty away in a bag.

Death was always real to him—hell, it was stare-you-in-the-face real—but something about watching a friend's body being removed from a murder scene hit Sully as hard as last night's intruder had done in nearly this same spot.

Police tape still surrounded the area, cordoning off a section of the parking lot for good measure, and Sully expected he wasn't getting back in there any time tonight.

He walked for a while longer, lost track of time somewhere along the way, his mind playing through the events of last night and early this afternoon, thinking through the possibilities. It occurred to him, as the sky began to take on the first tinges of nightfall, that he hadn't heard from Dez in a while. His brother had taken a step or two back in the past couple of years, allowing Sully a little more room to move and breathe, but his solid and protective presence was always somewhere nearby. He would be off shift by now, and no doubt wondering why Sully hadn't made it to his house yet.

A check of his phone revealed the reason for the radio silence. It was drained, despite it being a relatively new phone which he'd fully charged before leaving Dez's and had barely used today. It happened a lot, this sort of thing. Ghosts liked to use him as a battery, but oftentimes they'd take advantage of whatever electronic devices were around too. It had taken a teenaged Sully a while to figure out why he couldn't seem to find a phone that held a charge. Now that he knew the answer, he could only hope manufacturers would come up with an app to prevent ghost drainage.

Sully took the bus out to the Gladstone neighbourhood, a suburb largely populated by young families and single, white-collar professionals. As expected, Dez was waiting at the end of the trail, arms folded and eyebrows lowered.

"Where have you been?"

"Sorry, lost track of time."

"I tried calling you, like, twelve times."

"My phone died," Sully said. "Usual issue."

Dez looked like he was about to launch into some form of lecture when his five-year-old daughter, Kayleigh, came flying down the stairs and into Sully's arms.

"Uncle Sully! We waited and waited for you and Daddy was mad, but we ate anyway. There's spaghetti in the fridge. And steak. Daddy barbecued."

"Steak sounds great," Sully said.

"There's none for you," Dez grumbled, but broke off in a smile that suggested he'd feed Sully regardless.

Unfortunately, the Kayleigh distraction proved only short-term with the emergence of a frazzled Eva. "Kayleigh. Bath and then bed. Now."

"But Uncle Sully just got here."

"Uncle Sully will still be here in the morning," Eva said. "Go."

Kayleigh rolled her eyes but gave Sully one last hug before running up the stairs almost as fast as she'd come down.

"Kayleigh! What did I tell you about running on the stairs?" Eva turned a quick smile on her brother-in-law. "Hi, Sully. Sorry. Talk to you in a bit."

With that, Sully was left alone with Dez and the explanation his brother would be expecting. Thankfully, Dez allowed it to come over a plate he and Eva had made up, letting Sully use chewing as an excuse to come up with better-worded answers.

Sully told his brother about the visit to Marc's office before realizing he'd have no choice but to mention his chat with Thackeray Schuster.

"You did what?"

It was Dez's quiet tone, the one that typically proved a prequel to a yell. Sully could see his brother one day becoming one of those paternal staff sergeants whom officers both loved and tried hard to avoid pissing off.

"I wanted to apologize and to ask him about the thumb drive."

"I thought I told you to stay away from there. Both he and you are being questioned on this. God, Sully, do you have any idea how badly Raynor wants your ass? You're making it easy for him."

"Do you want to hear what Thackeray had to say?"

"He'd better have had something to say, after all that."

"At first, he said he didn't know anything about a thumb drive, but he looked pretty startled when I mentioned someone might have tried to take it. Finally, he said his mom told him it contained some info that would possibly exonerate him, but that she never used it. He said he looked for it a couple times at the house but didn't find it. Obviously, that was because Betty was keeping it at the office."

"We're putting an awful lot on this thumb drive without even knowing for sure whether it's connected in any way to her death. And Thackeray's not exactly the most reliable source given his history. I mean, for all we really know, the drive contains exactly what Betty told you."

"Betty was there, Dez. At the house."

"Oh." Ordinarily, Sully would have found Dez's obvious and well-anticipated discomfort amusing, but he didn't expect he'd be in a laughing mood for quite some time.

"She put that drive somewhere, man, and the only way to know what's on it is to find it. I think it's more than possible she's still trying to protect it, so I'm going to need to talk to her. Thing is, Thackeray doesn't seem to be in any mood to let me in there."

"He just got out of prison. He's bound to be a little edgy."

"Fair enough, but that doesn't solve my problem."

"Sully, are you sure you want to go down this path? I mean, you've been through a hell of a lot today, and if the next-to-last place I want you is in the middle of an investigation, the very last place is somewhere you're going to mess yourself up. Have you even allowed yourself a moment to really process everything?"

"I did on the way over," Sully said. "I went for a long walk. That's why I was so late getting here."

"And? How are you holding up?"

Sully shrugged. "I don't know if I can answer that. When I saw Betty today ...."

"What?"

"She looked like she had after she was killed, all bloody and shot up. I tried to apologize, but ...."

"Apologize for what, Sull? It wasn't your fault. You need to get that through your skull."

"That's the problem. I *don't* know that. Not until I can figure out what happened and why. There are answers I need, and I'm not sure the police are going to find them. How can they when they don't even know what questions to ask or to who?"

"That's what investigations are for. To figure out what questions to ask and to who."

"And you're sure Forbes Raynor is the one to do it?"

Dez didn't have an answer, so Sully pressed on. "This isn't all about me, you know. It's not just about wanting to clear my name on this. I need to help Betty. Maybe that means helping Thackeray, I don't know. But I owe her at least that much."

Dez sighed, the sound of resignation. "Okay, what do you want to do?"

"I need to get inside her house."

"You said Thackeray wasn't letting you in."

"Even so."

Dez stared at Sully, a half-smile on his face suggesting he hoped his brother had been joking. "Sorry, it sounded to me like you were suggesting breaking and entering."

"Do I have a choice if he won't let me in?"

"Goddamnit, Sully, no. You are not breaking into someone's house. Forget it. Jesus Christ, kid, it's like you get off on making me crazy. I'm trying to keep you this side of the bars and you just keep looking for ways to put yourself in."

"I need to talk to her, Dez, and that's where she is. Maybe she's around the Fox, too, but I can't exactly get in there to check, now, can I?"

"They'll be releasing the scene soon enough. You can get in there then, see if she's around. In the meantime, you stay put here, lie low and try to get your head around all this, okay? Please, man."

"That's just it. I can't get my head around it until I've done something to help Betty. Until I know she's all right—and until I know for sure I wasn't responsible somehow—there's no way I'm going to be able to rest easy on this."

RESTING WASN'T COMING any easier for Dez that night.

He usually didn't have trouble falling asleep after getting off a shift, the twelve-hour stints—and the general business they typically entailed—resulting in an exhaustion only sleep would cure.

But not tonight. Tonight, his mind ran at top speed, stress and high blood pressure sending constant jolts into his brain that prevented its shutting down. He loved his family more than anything, but they were his Achilles heel too.

He had consciously worked at stepping back, particularly with Sully, having realized a couple years ago how much he was prone to hover—and how that was increasingly driving his brother batty. But it wasn't easy by any means; his natural instincts to protect those he loved battled the need to allow them space to live their lives.

When they were kids, Dez had caught himself a couple times calling his foster brother by the name Aiden. Sully hadn't made a thing of it, but Dez had, and he'd often repeated a mental reminder that Sully was not Aiden. As the years passed and he matured, he grasped the full meaning of the subconscious mix-up. It wasn't simply a matter of getting a second chance at having a little brother or the continued difficulty in accepting Aiden was gone. It wasn't even that Sully and Aiden were alike, because they really weren't.

It was, Dez had come to realize, connected to his own need to fix what had happened to Aiden, to go back and prevent it, to protect him, to be the big brother. Because he would never get that chance with Aiden, he'd visited those intentions instead on Sully. Transference, they called it. Sure, Dez loved Sully as much as any guy loved his kid brother, probably more than many come to that. But he'd learned to give him breathing room, which didn't come naturally. And he had to admit their relationship had improved because of it. In releasing his hold, Sully was more inclined to come to him as he always had in the past, more than he probably would have otherwise.

In the middle of the night, Dez heard Sully getting up and stumbling across the hall from the spare room to the main bathroom. He checked the bedside clock. 2:58 a.m.

During the couple of minutes that followed, Dez thought he could hear his brother talking to someone. Curiosity was not Dez's strong suit when it came to Sully's late-night conversations.

He knew full well he really didn't want to know who was on the receiving end of those chats. He chose the safer option, continuing to lie there, waiting for the eventual sound of his brother shuffling back to bed.

Instead, Dez heard smashing glass.

He wasn't alarmed, knowing Sully usually took a glass up to the bathroom before bed so he could brush his teeth. Dez guessed his brother had knocked the glass off the counter accidentally or, worst case scenario, he was dealing with a poltergeist that liked to throw things.

Whatever it was, Dez figured it merited a check, if only to make sure Sully wasn't in need of stitches.

"Everything okay?" Eva mumbled, half into the pillow, as Dez got up.

"Fine, Evie. Go back to sleep."

Eva's reply was incoherent as Dez slipped into his terrycloth robe and shuffled off down the hall.

The bathroom door was closed, a sliver of light showing from the crack where door met floor. Dez rapped quietly so as not to wake Kayleigh. Granted, she was a solid sleeper, but no sense taking chances. If this was a ghost thing, Dez wanted her kept as far from it as possible.

"Sully? You okay in there?"

When no answer came, Dez knocked again and spoke a bit louder. "Hey, Sull, you okay?"

Still no answer. Dez felt his heart thud against his ribcage.

He knocked one more time. "Okay, I'm coming in, man."

The door was unlocked, the knob turning easily in his hand. But, while Dez was able to inch the door open, he found some sort of force being applied against it, keeping Dez out and Sully in.

"Sully? Answer me, man. What's going on?"

Dez gave the door another little push, uncertain whether his brother was holding it shut, or if this was some otherworldly force. He'd seen that happen before, and he didn't like it at all.

He liked even less that fact Sully had yet to answer him.

Pushing a bit further, Dez was able to get the door opened just enough to catch a glimpse of the wall across from the sink, the one holding the towel rack.

What he saw was blood.

A lot of blood.

He called out Sully's name, louder now, pushed at the door with the strength of desperation, managing this time to move it. His brother, naked except for his underwear, fell across the floor in front of him, apparently knocked away from the door by the force of the shove. Dez entered the room fully, gasped at the blood soaking the walls, the floor, the sink, the broken mirror.

Soaking Sully.

Dez had been a cop long enough to know what blood spray looked like and what it meant, and it had Dez moving quickly, turning Sully—still prone on the floor—to look for the source. He found it at his brother's right wrist, a wide gash opened and spurting. Dez grabbed for a towel, and had just turned back toward his brother when he spotted movement from his right. Dez reacted on instinct, blocking the path of the large shard of blood-covered glass his brother was clutching in his left hand. Although Sully wasn't focused on Dez—he didn't appear focused on anything—the shard had been set on a course toward Dez's neck.

Grabbing Sully's uninjured wrist and pinning it to the floor, Dez wrested the makeshift blade from his brother's cut fingers just as Eva appeared behind him.

"Oh, my God."

"Eva, call 9-1-1 and make sure Kayleigh doesn't come in here."

He didn't need to look to know Eva had gone to do as asked, leaving Dez to deal with Sully. He kicked the door closed and created a tourniquet with the towel around Sully's right wrist. When he checked his brother's left hand, Sully struggled against him, and Dez shifted so he could draw his brother up against him and hold him there.

"Sully, stop. Just try to relax, okay? You're going to hurt yourself worse. Help's coming. Just hold on."

"Blue room." The voice had come from Sully, but it wasn't him —his voice, only far lower with a grating sound Dez had never heard in his brother's ordinarily soft tones. "Blue room."

The phrase was repeated over and over, louder and louder until Dez at last felt forced to press a hand over Sully's mouth, in part to prevent Kayleigh's hearing and in part to keep Dez from losing what was left of his sanity as he sat here, holding his bleeding brother on the bathroom floor.

Dez realized he was rocking back and forth, taking Sully with him, as tears pooled in his eyes and dripped down his cheeks. "Sully, shh. Please, listen to me, man. Come back. Sully, I need you to come back. Please. Please, Sull. I need you to be okay. I need you to be okay, buddy."

Muffled beneath Dez's hand, the terrifying chant had stopped somewhere along the way and Dez realized his brother was no longer struggling. Sully was trying to talk, the stifled sounds softer now; Dez removed his hand.

"Sully?"

"Dez? What the hell happened? How did I get down .... Oh, God. Oh, God. Dez?"

"It's okay, Sull. It's going to be okay."

The words, said to ease the fear evident in Sully's voice and in the way his body was shaking, felt empty to Dez as he lowered his tear-streaked face against the back of his brother's head.

He didn't let go until the ambulance came.

10

FLYNN'S LEGS were longer but Mara was faster, which probably explained how they managed to reach the ER soft room at the same time.

Dez knew he must look a wreck, hands, arms and face covered in Sully's blood, eyes and nose red and puffy from crying. He hadn't had a lot of answers for his parents when he'd called them from the ambulance, and his attention had been taken up trying to calm Sully before the EMT in back finally gave up the battle and sedated him.

But the expressions on Flynn and Mara Braddock's faces as they stared wide-eyed at Dez showed they'd be needing a little more info, and fast.

"He's going to be all right," Dez said, greeting his parents with a hug on shaky legs. "He's going to be fine."

"Define 'all right,' son," Flynn said. "Because it sounds to me like Sully tried to kill himself."

"It wasn't him, Dad. I don't know who it was, but it wasn't him."

Mara closed the door, sealing the three of them in the room for privacy. "Are you saying he was possessed?"

Dez hated thinking about it, but there was no other explanation. "It sure looked that way. First of all, he slashed up using his left hand, and Sully's right-handed. And then he was speaking in this weird voice, kept saying the same thing over and over: 'Blue room.' I kept talking to him and he eventually came around. It was like he had no idea how he'd gotten there, how he'd gotten hurt."

Dez didn't say anything about the attempt Sully—or whomever he'd been at the time—had made to stab him in the neck. That was one thing Dez intended to keep to himself. He sure as hell hoped to keep it from Sully if he could manage it. His brother would feel bad enough about the rest of this, and there was no telling how he'd react to the knowledge he'd tried to hurt someone he loved. Add the attempted attack on Dez to Sully's existing guilt over Betty, and Dez wasn't sure his brother had any place left inside him to put it.

"What's this all about, Dez?" Flynn asked. "It sure doesn't sound like Betty."

"I think it's this man who's been coming around Sully since right before the first break-in. Sully's really scared of him, and I haven't seen him this freaked over a ghost in a long time. There was this moment yesterday, right before we found those clothes in the dumpster, that the ghost came at Sully. He thought maybe he was trying to get inside him or something. Only I put myself in the way."

Mara smiled. "You did? Dez, you hate ghosts."

"I hate it more when they go after people I care about. Anyway, I didn't exactly know where the bastard was until I was standing right in the middle of him."

Dez cut the conversation short as his uncle Lowell came into the room.

"Sorry, I dropped your folks off and went to park the car," he said. "How's Sullivan?"

"He's going to be okay, I think. How'd you end up here?"

"I was at your parents' place this evening. I wanted to pick your dad's brain about everything that's been happening at the Black Fox. I was hoping maybe he was in on something."

"And you were wrong," Flynn said with a small smile.

"Yeah, I was. Anyway, Flynnie and I ended up having a couple drinks, so he figured I shouldn't be driving. We went to bed a few hours ago and woke up to this. What the hell, Dez?"

"I don't know, man. I can't figure it out."

"I know he must have been upset about Betty," Lowell said. "I mean, I think the two of them were pretty close. She used to tell me all the time what a good worker he is, how much she liked him."

"They were friends, yeah, but I don't think Sully tried to kill himself over it."

"So then, what?"

A knock on the door announced the arrival of the doctor, a man who appeared to recognize Lowell immediately, judging by the smile and the warm handshake.

"Mr. Braddock, somehow I didn't put two and two together," he said.

"Dr. Garva," Lowell said to his family by way of quick introduction. "Doctor, my brother Flynn and his wife and son, Mara and Desmond."

"I understand Sullivan was adopted?" the doctor asked. Dez noticed he was still addressing Lowell.

"Foster, technically," Lowell said, but Flynn cut in with his own firm handshake and an added comment. "Permanent placement, close as you'd get to adoption. How's my son?"

"Sullivan's going to be fine, physically," the doctor said. "He sliced into a vein, but it's sealed itself off and we've put in a few sutures. It may be that there's some muscle and nerve damage, but for now I just want the wrist immobilized, so time will tell with that. We cleaned and bandaged the cuts on his other hand, and he needed only a couple of stitches there. Frankly, it's his mental state I'm most concerned about. He seems fine right now, but I'm worried he says he's missing time. The last thing he remembers is walking into the bathroom, and the next he was being restrained by his brother. He's concerned, and so am I. It might not be such a bad idea to admit him to the hospital's psychiatric ward for observation and an assessment."

Dez met his mom's eye and shook his head just enough that she'd notice. A psych ward wasn't what Sully needed. Dez didn't want to think what would happen if that ghost got to his brother again with no one around who understood what was happening.

"I really think Sully needs to be around his family, right now," Mara said.

"No offence, ma'am, but he was around his family when this happened. And he can't explain why he did this, meaning there's no way to necessarily prevent a reoccurrence. Now, I'm told he's been under a lot of strain the past couple of days, so that might help to explain why he might be suffering some form of mental breakdown, but—"

"Sully's not suffering a mental breakdown," Dez said. "Yeah, he's in the middle of some bad stuff, but we can get him through that."

"My understanding is that 'bad stuff' entails the fatal shooting of a friend right in front of him," the doctor said. "That would be plenty to cause most people to suffer mental and emotional collapse."

Flynn lined up with Dez and Mara. "I understand what you're saying, doctor, but Dez and I are police officers, and Mara is a family counsellor. We're well placed to be able to take care of Sully. I promise you if there's any sign he's taking a turn we don't think we can manage, we'll bring him back in."

Dr. Garva smiled politely. "Of course, I can't force him to stay. If you insist on taking him with you, that's your prerogative. But if he runs into further problems, if you see any signs of more missing time or episodes of psychosis, I'd advise taking him to see Dr. Roman Gerhardt at Lockwood. He does some on-call work for us here, and he was actually planning to see Sullivan tonight if he was admitted. I can advise him you'll take Sullivan directly to Lockwood if there are any serious concerns."

Lockwood Psychiatric Hospital was known as the Lockwood Asylum at its inception in the Victorian age. Later, the facility was rebranded as an "institution" until improved understanding and sensitivity about mental illness had them changing it simply to "hospital." As far as Dez was concerned, it was the last place he wanted his brother, regardless of what it was calling itself these days.

"We'll bear that in mind, Doctor, thank you," Flynn said. "For now, I'd just really like to see my son."

Having been told they wanted no more than two in the room, Flynn and Mara went to sit with Sully until the discharge papers were signed. Dez went to the nearby bathroom to wash up, scrubbing until his brother's blood swirled little by little down the drain. He could have done it earlier, during the approximate hour wait for his parents to come in from the acreage, but he hadn't wanted to leave the soft room and risk missing the doctor.

That done, Dez returned to the room and his uncle, who had located a coffee machine. Dez gratefully accepted the styrofoam cup Lowell gave him.

"How you holding up, kid?"

Dez took a slow sip, finding the coffee too hot to manage just yet. He settled for holding it between his hands. Dez rarely got cold but the events of the night had set a chill inside him he couldn't shake.

"I don't know," Dez said. "I'll be fine, though."

"You sure? I mean, you and Sullivan are really tight, aren't you?"

"Yeah, we are."

"So it had to be pretty scary, what you walked into."

"I walk into that stuff all the time. It's the job."

"Not when it's your brother, though."

That was a fact, one that merited another sip of the hot coffee, temperature and scalded tongue be damned.

"Has he ever done anything like this before?" Lowell asked.

"If he had, you would have known about it."

"Look, Dez, I know this isn't what you want to hear—it's not what any of you want to hear—but maybe the doctor's right. Maybe Sullivan should spend some time being checked out. Just to be safe, you know?"

"Sully doesn't need checking out," Dez said. "He's one of the most stable people I know. He's dealt with a lot in his life and he still is, and he handles it. I don't know how, but he does. Between the two of us, I've always been the one more likely to fly off the handle."

"No offence, Dez, but what happened tonight is not a sign of a stable person. It's a sign of someone who needs some serious help. I know all three of you deal with mentally or emotionally unstable people all the time, given your work, but you know as well as I do that even the most experienced experts hand off personal matters to other professionals; being too close can blind you to the truth. He's got an awful lot going on in his life right now, and even the strongest people hit breaking points. Maybe he's hit his."

"He was fine before he went to bed."

"Maybe he seemed fine," Lowell said. "Maybe even to himself, he seemed fine. Sometimes things snap without a person knowing. He could have suffered something as simple as a PTSD-related flashback or nightmare, something that brought everything to bear all at once."

Dez had considered not saying anything to his uncle, but he knew his brother, knew without having spoken directly to him about it that Sully hadn't intended what he'd done. The left-handed slashing and the attempted stabbing of Dez were enough to prove that. It had been Sully in body only. Whoever had been inside him was responsible. Sully didn't belong in a mental hospital. If anything, he needed a bloody exorcist.

"Look, Uncle Lo, I know you don't go in for this stuff, but I don't think it was Sully. I think it was someone else, something else, at the helm."

"Something else, as in an evil spirit?"

It was there in spades, Lowell's skepticism. Since his childhood, Sully had helped the police behind the scenes solve some of their more challenging homicide and missing person cases, and no one was supposed to know. Which meant Lowell didn't know, giving him plenty of room to doubt. It was the one thing Dez hated about Lowell, his dismissal of Sully as attention-seeking or even crazy.

"Yeah, something like that," Dez said.

"Come on, Dez, you're a rational, intelligent person. You know there's no such thing as ghosts."

"Sure, I'm a rational, intelligent person, and I've rationalized Sully's telling the truth because he's shown me stuff I wouldn't have believed otherwise. Hell, if I could go back and not believe in this stuff, I would. I hate it. But it doesn't make it any less real."

Thankfully, Lowell was skilled at knowing when to back off. "I'm sorry. I know he's your brother and you want to do right by him. All I'm asking is that you keep your mind open to other possibilities, that maybe Sullivan needs the kind of help a professional can give him. Now, I've gotten to know Dr. Gerhardt over the years through the industry and he's a good man, and an unconventional one at that. He's not one to discount things. He has a keen interest in spirituality, so I'm thinking he would hear Sullivan out. Just consider it, all right? If Sullivan doesn't seem better or has any further spells, just take him to Dr. Gerhardt. If it's a mental illness, he'll know. If it isn't, he'll know that too."

Lowell seemed willing to accept only one answer, so Dez supplied it.

"I'll think about it."

IT HAD BEEN a few years since they'd been here, just the four of them gathered together around the breakfast bar in the kitchen of Flynn and Mara's country home.

Sully, still effected by the sedative he'd been given on top of the sleeping pill they found out he'd taken before bed, had slept throughout the ride home and was put to bed as soon as they got back. They bypassed Sully's old room, though, putting him in with Dez for the night. Dez recognized the intensified similarities with their old life here, Sully tucked next to him in bed as he sought refuge from a ghost Dez was helpless to stop. And yet, it had always felt like they'd found some sort of safety, some peace, together. Hoping for some peace, he had hoped for that overnight as he went to sleep with an arm draped across Sully's body, allowing him to remain alert to any movement.

At nearly noon, they got up and found their parents in the kitchen, coffee on. Flynn had called in sick for both him and Dez. They had more important things to do today.

"I know you might not want to discuss this, Sully, but you need to," Flynn said. "What happened last night?"

"I thought I told you something in the ER."

"You did," Mara said. "But you were still really groggy and you weren't making much sense."

Sully nodded and launched into what he could of an explanation. "I took a pill before bed to help me sleep. I figured I'd have nightmares, and I just wanted to get through the night without any. I woke up at some point, I don't know what time. My head felt off somehow, and I was really sick to my stomach, so I went to the bathroom thinking I was going to puke. When I got in there and looked in the mirror, this ghost was behind me, the man I started seeing at the time of that first break-in the other night. I remember thinking if I could just get some sort of response and figure out what he wanted, I could work on getting rid of him. But he just kept staring the way he always does."

"Why didn't you call me?" Dez asked. "I was up, I would have come."

"I couldn't," Sully said. "I could barely speak, let alone yell, and I was frozen solid. Last thing I remember he was coming toward me. He …."

Dez saw it in his face, the fear as he called up what had happened. He laid a stabilizing hand on the back of Sully's neck while Mara rubbed his back.

"Sully?" she said. "I know it's hard to talk about, but we really need to know."

He nodded again and continued. "Um, he … he stepped into me. I felt this chill, like walking into the beer cooler at the Fox. And I watched my face become his, like he was erasing me. The next thing I remember, I was on the floor, blood everywhere and Dez restraining me."

"You don't remember anything in the middle?" Dez asked. "Nothing at all?"

"Nothing," Sully said. "It's a blank."

That was a relief at least. Not only did it save Sully added emotional trauma, but it meant Dez could keep him in the dark about the apparent attempt on his life. There was one thing, though, that Dez needed to bring up.

"You …. I mean, *he* kept repeating this phrase over and over. 'Blue room.' That mean anything to you?"

Sully chewed his lip, but ended up shaking his head in the negative. "I don't know what it's supposed to mean. But I guess it's a clue, right?"

"I'm not sure I'm all that interested in clues right now, Sully," Flynn said. "You could have died last night. If it wasn't for Dez …." The unsaid words hung heavy in the air.

Sully's response was a pat to his brother's gut. "Thanks, man. I know that must have sucked for you."

"Understatement of the year."

"Are Kayleigh and Eva okay?"

"They're fine. Kayleigh, no surprise, slept right through it. And Eva sends her love. I'm going to go help her with cleanup in a bit."

"I'll help."

"No, you won't," Dez said. "I don't want you in there. It's handled, okay?"

"I'm sorry, D. I really am."

"It's not your fault. We just need to get to the bottom of this before the lunatic comes back, all right?"

"Lunatic," Sully said. "Remember we were thinking there might be a connection to Lockwood? Is there any way to check whether patients wear something like the clothing I saw on him?"

"Based on what Dez told me, I checked the Lockwood connection earlier this morning," Flynn said. "The clothes you saw match what patients wear, but there weren't any homicides or suspicious deaths that would explain your ghost."

"So maybe his death wasn't deemed suspicious," Sully said. "Maybe he was murdered and no one realized. It's a possibility, right? I mean, I'm still not seeing any obvious injuries on him or anything."

"How about his wrists?" Mara asked. "Did it look like they'd been cut? It might explain why this happened."

"I didn't notice," Sully said. "There's never been any blood on him anywhere that I can see, but I suppose it's possible he tried to kill himself in the past and that's what he made me feel last night."

"Or it's possible he was just trying to force you to kill yourself," Dez said. "Maybe this was an attempt on your life, a way to keep you from digging into something he doesn't want you involved in. You said he appeared to you the first time the night of that first break-in, right? What if he's acting kind of like an accomplice to the suspect?"

Flynn raised an eyebrow. "Seems far-fetched, even by our standards. A ghost accomplice?"

"Hey, since Sully came into our lives, a whole lot's become far-fetched," Dez said with a gentle elbow-nudge into his brother's ribs. "I'm just saying we shouldn't rule it out, that's all."

"Fair enough," Flynn said. "Sully, I hope you never see this guy again but, if you do, see if you can get a look at his wrists. If nothing else, it might be an identifying feature. I'm sure Lockwood is full of patients who've attempted suicide at some point, but methods differ. If we can track this guy, hopefully we can figure out what he's after."

Dez nodded at his father's assessment before adding his own. "So we can stop him before he tries to pull something like this again."

11

DEZ HEADED out immediately after coffee, planning to eat quickly at home before scrubbing the bathroom. He figured he'd have no stomach for much of anything by the time he finished.

He arrived to find Eva already hard at it.

"I thought you were going to wait for me," he said, forgoing plans for a sandwich as he moved toward the soapy water and bleach his wife was working with.

"I figured you had a long enough night."

Dez noted a bead of sweat rolling down Eva's forehead and the fact the bathroom already looked far better than it had. He took the rag she was using and gently ushered her toward the door. "I'll look after the rest. Would you mind making me a sandwich or something? I haven't eaten anything yet."

"Neither have I, and I don't think I could manage it now if I tried. How's Sully?"

"Better." Dez launched into his brother's recollection of last night, before adding, "He wanted to apologize for this. He didn't intend it."

Eva knew about Sully and, unlike Lowell, believed him. "That's really scary, Dez. You guys are working on figuring this out, obviously."

"Yeah, but so far, nada. By all appearances, the guy looks like a Lockwood patient, but there are no records of suspicious death investigations matching this guy. Sully makes the valid point it might not have been recognized as a suspicious death, so that could make things more difficult in terms of identification."

"Lockwood must keep a record of deaths at the institution."

"Sure, but I can't imagine they'd just hand them over without a warrant. They're big on privacy."

"We'll take it one step at a time, then. We'll figure this out, Snowman, okay? Don't worry." She wrapped her arms around him and warmth coursed back through his body.

Dez enveloped Eva in a return hug, loving the way the size of his arms all but concealed her upper body. It gave him the feeling of security, oddly enough, the sense that he could keep her safe and covered, even if just for a moment. He typically kept the feeling to himself; Eva was a tough, independent woman and a fellow police officer to boot. The last time he'd tried to play protector with her, she'd laughed it off and then taken him to the ground with a playful self-defence tactic. Nowadays, he reserved that kind of talk for their daughter.

"I didn't ask because I figured you had it cased, but Kayleigh's okay?" he asked. "I mean, she didn't see any of this, right?"

"I kept her out of the bathroom. She was pissed because we promised her uncle would still be here in the morning, but I just told her he didn't feel well and that you'd taken him to the hospital overnight. She seemed fine with the explanation and was okay when she left for school, but she's going to want to see him soon. You know our girl. She won't be satisfied until she can see for herself he's all right." Eva smiled before adding the statement that had become like a mantra around here. "Her father's daughter."

"Yeah, yeah," Dez said. "Now, get out of here. Go eat or something."

"Are you happy with grilled cheese? I can do those up pretty quick."

"Sure," Dez said. "Just skip the ketchup."

THE BATHROOM, it turned out, needed a coat of paint to hide some of the stains, and Dez put the first one on using leftover paint in the garage before leaving Eva to do the second later in the afternoon. There was something else he needed to deal with.

He was on his way across campus to Marc Echoles's office when he chanced upon the professor in the area called The Bowl, around which a number of the campus's original Victorian stone buildings were set.

Marc was in peak form in the aura-reading department. "What's wrong?"

Ordinarily, the aura-reading thing made Dez nervous, but today his anxieties were fully employed elsewhere. "You have a minute to talk?"

Marc ushered Dez toward one of several benches lining The Bowl, most already taken by students enjoying what was likely to be one of the last nice days before fall.

"It's Sully," Dez said. "We think he was possessed by something last night. He slashed his own wrist, would have gone further except I got there and stopped him."

"Is he all right?"

"Shaken up, and he needed a few stitches, but he'll be okay. My bigger worry is what happens next time. I can't be around him all the time, and neither can anyone else. We haven't made any headway on this ghost he's been seeing. He mentioned it to you, right?"

"The man in the hospital-type garb? He did. He said he's quite anxious about him and was worried about the possibility of possession."

"So he told you he thought the guy was trying to possess him?"

"I take it he didn't tell you prior to this."

"No, he did not." That gave Dez one more thing to stew over, but Marc cut in with a possible explanation that took some of the hot wind out of Dez's sails.

"He knows this stuff bothers you. I'm sure he thought it wouldn't help you to know. There isn't necessarily anything you can do about it and, as you say, you can't be around him all the time."

"Okay, point taken. At any rate, I didn't come here to sort through what happened in the past. I'm worried about figuring out what to do for the future."

"Ah," Marc said. "But the interesting thing about the world in which Sully's led you is you can't tackle the future without first knowing and understanding the past. Ghosts are, after all, a symbol of the past."

Marc did this sometimes, got philosophical. It drove Dez nuts. "I know I need to figure out this guy's past. First, I need to find out who he is. But that's *my* problem. In the meantime, Sully's got one of his own to deal with. I need to know if there's any way you know of to protect him from this guy getting inside him, anything we can do to prevent something similar."

"I suggested meditation and aura strengthening to Sully as a long-term thing, but I understand you're looking for something a little more immediate than that. I know a woman. Her name's Raiya Everton and she's a Wiccan high priestess."

"You didn't meet her in that Black Candle coven, did you?"

"I did, actually, but I can assure you she remained one of the good ones. She's since left the coven like I did, and practices mainly on her own. She's very wise and she knows more than I do about protection against evil. You might consider taking Sullivan to see her."

This wasn't what Dez had been hoping for, the suggestion he go and meet yet another person who walked in a world he dreaded, but if it would help Sully, he was game for just about anything. They'd both gotten to know and trust Marc over the past couple of years. If he believed this Raiya woman knew her way around possessions and evil spirits, Dez was willing to give it a shot.

"One more thing." Marc reached into his trouser pocket and pulled out a small wooden crucifix. "After Sullivan came to see me, I went home and did some digging through my wife's old things. Mariel was raised Catholic and, despite the fact she was also a practicing Wiccan, she held to some of her old beliefs. She had this crucifix made out of Palo Santo, a wood from the Amazon. It's used there by shamans to drive away evil spirits and other unwanted energies. While it's typically burned as part of those rituals, Mariel had some imbued with holy water and additionally blessed by Raiya back when we first met her. I think Mariel would be fine with my giving it to Sullivan for protection. She would have liked him very much."

Dez accepted the small cross, held at the end of a thin, black cord. Marc's offer was a selfless one, but Dez also found himself doubting. Mariel was, after all, dead; little good the amulet had done her in the end.

True to unnerving form, Marc read him without Dez's having to utter a word. "I know what you're thinking. But keep in mind that while amulets such as this can aid in protection against evil of a more ethereal nature, they hold little power against the evils of our physical world. It won't stop a bullet, prevent a car crash or—in my Mariel's case—cure cancer. I can't tell you how effective it will be, but I know my wife believed in it. And believing in something is the first step to making it so. Belief offers us a very powerful protection, Desmond, regardless of our choice of faith. Something to keep in mind."

"Thanks, Marc. I mean it. I'm really grateful to you for this. For everything."

"Anytime, my friend. Just look after your brother, all right? I truly think he has the power and the strength to help many lost souls, both living and dead. But he's still young and he's learning and, for now, that makes him vulnerable. Not just to this dark spirit, but to many others."

Raiya Everton lived in a small Victorian house in the North Bank area, just herself and three cats.

Dez hadn't provided a full explanation to his parents about where he was taking Sully. While they believed what Sully saw and experienced, Mara tended to get nervous about the idea of travelling too far down occult paths, particularly since none of them had any real knowledge of that world.

But Marc did, and Dez was giving that full weight right now. The alternatives, should they not explore every avenue before the ghost returned for Sully, were unthinkable.

Raiya wasn't what Dez had been expecting, a short, stocky woman with frizzy grey hair and no makeup on what had likely never been a particularly attractive face. And yet, there was something magnetic about her, about the confident and reassuring smile she showed as she answered the door.

"I've been waiting for you two."

Dez pulled up short, his hand on his brother's arm forcing Sully to do the same.

Raiya laughed, the sound soothing enough to relax Dez a bit. "Marc told me you were anxious, Desmond. Yes, he called. That's how I knew to expect you. Come on in, and let's see what we're dealing with here."

"Relax," Sully whispered as the two of them closed the rest of the short distance to the front door. "You're your own worst enemy when it comes to this stuff."

"Better the devil you know, Sull."

Dez was barely in the door before he found himself surrounded by a trio of cats, rubbing against his legs and standing on back feet against his shins as if wanting to climb him like a tree.

Raiya crossed her arms, pairing raised eyebrows with a surprised, open-mouthed smile. "They like you. I must say, they don't take kindly to many strangers. I'll take that as a very good sign. Come in. I've made tea."

Dez and Sully followed Raiya into a bright, plant-filled conservatory at the back of the house, which overlooked a wild garden full of trees, shrubs and tall flowers on their last legs as summer drew to a close. A set of white wicker furniture circled a sturdy-looking table onto which Raiya had placed a teapot and a few mugs, as well as other items that appeared to Dez's untrained eye like they might be Wiccan.

Raiya shook each of their hands before her eyes settled on Sully's upper chest where the crucifix dangled on its cord. "I haven't seen that amulet in many years. I'll cleanse it and re-bless it for you before you leave, but for now I'd like you to fill me in on what's been going on with this spirit."

Raiya listened attentively to the explanation the brothers provided before launching into her read of the situation.

"Marc tells me you're surrounded by bright light, Sullivan, which is a wonderful thing. It tells me you're a beacon to those who need help. But as with anything that attracts, you will never solely draw the good. There is a natural balance between the light and the dark; both must exist and both always will. But you're young and I get the impression you're not quite sure how to control the things you see and experience."

"I know a little," Sully said. "I've figured out how to block some of the feelings I get from them. And I've been seeing them long enough that I don't freak out about them anymore. Not until this guy, anyway."

"He's different."

Sully nodded. "Maybe it's just that he's more intense, or his emotions are. I'm not sure. I've seen people who've gone through some pretty awful deaths, and it always shows on their bodies. I don't see anything like that on him, and yet he throws off more fear than I've ever felt. It makes me wonder if he just lived in a constant state of it."

"That could well be," Raiya said. "Or it could be he's simply trying to make you feel that way. What concerns me is this connection he's been able to establish, which has allowed him to physically and mentally possess you for a short time. That takes the sort of power one rarely sees in a typical earthbound human spirit. Those of a Christian background would likely attribute it to demonic possession."

"He's not a demon. I'm not even sure I believe they exist."

"Oh, they exist, though perhaps not in the form Christians believe. There are spirits that were never human, ones that fall along the spectrum of light and dark. Some are benevolent—angels, in Christian faith. Some are not. But you believe this man you've been seeing was human in life, so let me propose an alternative. Perhaps he was, like yourself, capable of moving in the world most of us cannot see."

"You mean a psychic?"

"And a powerful one, I'd venture to say. Unfortunately, not all are capable of holding the power they're born with. Perhaps this man's gifts were too much for him and drove him insane. Now in that other world, there's something he needs to resolve, and he's found you."

"So why try to kill him?" Dez asked. "Why wouldn't he just try to possess Sully to do what he thinks he needs to?"

"I wish I had the answers for you, but I don't. As much as I've become a student of that world, I don't possess the gifts others do. I don't see the things your brother does. All I can tell you is what I believe to be true. Only you, I think, can find the answers you're looking for. What I can do is try to help Sullivan build and strengthen the protection around him and teach him to maintain it. It isn't foolproof. Nothing is. There will always be spirits that are stronger, and it could easily happen that he will attract them." She turned back to Sully. "But this will help, as long as you're diligent about maintaining it. There will be times you need to focus in order to keep them out. You'll know when. But if you're tuned into yourself, into your own strengths and weaknesses, you'll be better able to tune into them from a safe place."

For the next half hour, Raiya worked with Sully and, to Dez's chagrin, him as well. Dez came away knowing more about white light, protective circles and meditation than he'd ever imagined he'd be subjected to. Raiya then performed a cleansing ritual on both Mariel's amulet and Sully himself before preparing to send them on their way.

"Come back to me anytime," she said. "I will always be here to provide what help I can."

As he and Sully walked back to the SUV, Dez asked, "You buy all that?"

"Not everything. But I think what she said about this guy possibly having been psychic makes sense. It would explain why he's so strong—and maybe why he gives off so much fear. Could be seeing the things he did is why he ended up in Lockwood. God knows where I'd be right now if it wasn't for you guys."

Dez dropped into the driver's seat and waited until Sully joined him on the passenger side. "We didn't do anything, Sull. It was all you."

"All those nights when we were kids?" Sully said. "You put up with me even though you were almost as scared as I was. I felt like nothing bad would happen as long as you were around. That kept me sane, D. Don't think otherwise."

Dez couldn't hide the smile and responded by mussing up his brother's shaggy mop of hair. He'd turned to start the vehicle when Sully stopped him, changing the atmosphere in the vehicle almost as quickly.

"I think we need to go talk to Dr. Gerhardt."

"The psychiatrist? Why?"

"I need to find this patient."

"Sully, no. We're not going to Lockwood. In fact, we're not going anywhere near Lockwood. It's too dangerous for you right now."

"Things are already too dangerous."

"Listen to me. You've told me ghosts are strongest when they're in a place where they draw power. You said a lot of the time that means they're the most powerful where they died because of the intensity of the emotion connected with the location. If this guy you've been seeing is strong already, think how bad it might be if he died at Lockwood. I don't want you near there, Sully. No."

"And this doesn't have anything to do with the possibility this doctor might try to diagnose me as clinically insane and try to get me committed?"

"The thought doesn't help. You're not crazy, Sull, but to the unbelieving general public, opinions may vary. We both know that." Dez paused, giving it further thought. "Tell you what. I'll go talk to him, give him some story about being worried about you, wanting to explore options. That will get me in the door. Maybe I can go have a look around after."

"By yourself? No way."

"Relax, Sull. I'm built like a brick shithouse. It would take twelve orderlies to hold me."

"Which I'm sure they could find. I don't want you doing this. Not by yourself. If this guy was murdered there, someone's got a lot to hide, and they won't take kindly to someone digging around."

"So what do you suggest?"

"We go together. You keep the doctor busy with questions, and I'll have a look around. And if I get caught, hey, I'm crazy anyway, right?"

"And what if it isn't the staff who catch you? What if it's this ghost?"

"Then I'm just going to have to hope everything I've been given today is enough."

"Hope's not good enough for me," Dez said.

Sully gave him a reassuring smile. "Dez, I think the way things are shaping up here, hope might be all we really have."

12

THE AFTERNOON WAS NEARING its end when Dez steered his SUV off the main road and onto the lane leading to Lockwood Psychiatric Hospital.

A set of wrought iron gates marked the entrance to the property, having stood sentry there from the time the facility first opened. Dez imagined procedures had changed in that time, and he expected the treatment of the mentally ill had too. After all, Lockwood had become a place some people came of their own free will. While the hospital took medical committals, some deliberately came here when they felt overwhelmed by life. With the economic situation and everything that came with it, Dez had read that Lockwood had reached the point of having to turn people away.

It had also branched out from treating just the mentally ill. The first building they passed, which Dez thought had probably been a nurses' residence back in the day, was now a seniors' home, caring for those with dementia and other forms of mental illness and, again, some who just liked the place or the staff.

Lockwood had a decent enough reputation and had even achieved acclaim for the way staff here looked after their patients.

It didn't make Dez any more comfortable bringing Sully here.

Despite the desire to just turn the vehicle around and put the large stone building in his rearview mirror, Dez pulled into a spot in the parking lot.

"I still don't like this, Sull. I feel like we're opening a door we'll regret walking through. I mean, bringing you here is exactly what that doctor at the hospital wanted, and we both know he was wrong about you needing this place."

Sully, as usual, was the voice of reason. "Dez, I know you're not going to leave me here, all right? Come on, let's just go in. For all we know, Dr. Gerhardt's left for the day anyway."

He hadn't, of course. And he was more than happy to see them.

Approaching with a cane, Dr. Roman Gerhardt was only an inch or two shorter than Sully's six feet and was just as lean, save a small roll around his mid-section likely the result of aging. While his hairline showed signs of receding, his scalp still boasted a fair amount of now-grey hair, and he kept a neatly trimmed beard. He wasn't wearing the obvious garb of a doctor, clad rather in tan slacks and a pale blue polo shirt that revealed toned and sinewy arms. His handshake was firm, a small vice sealing itself around Dez's large fingers.

"Thank you for coming in," the doctor said, before turning to Sully for a similar handshake. "And this must be Sullivan."

"Must be," Dez said as Sully offered what amounted to a polite rather than warm smile. "Um, listen, this is kinda awkward. I don't really want to be here, but Sully wanted to see the place. He thought maybe it would help him decide some stuff."

"Of course," Dr. Gerhardt said. "That sounds like a superb idea. I can show the two of you around."

Dez took a step forward and spoke quietly. "Uh, actually, I really hoped I could talk to you in private for a few minutes. I've got some concerns about all this. Sully's aware. I was thinking maybe he could wait somewhere until we've had a chance to talk, and then you could take us around?"

Dr. Gerhardt smiled knowingly. "Of course. I understand. But it's getting near to supper time here and we don't typically allow visitors then. Tell you what, to save time, I'll have our head orderly Larson Hackman take Sullivan around, show him the hospital. That will give you and me time to speak. Then, if you're interested in seeing the place yourself—and I expect you will be—we can schedule a time tomorrow for you to return. How does that sound?"

Dez faked a grin. Sully wasn't going to get very far with an orderly on his arm. But to Dr. Gerhardt, all Dez said was, "Sounds good. Thanks."

As solid as Dez and only a couple inches shorter, Larson Hackman had the appearance of a man who had earned the spot of head orderly on sheer size alone. He smiled as he approached, hand extended in greeting, but Dez's police-trained eye picked up on something guarded and watchful in the man's expression. His grip was expectedly firm, but went one step further with a squeeze that seemed intended to challenge.

Dez met it with his own extra-solid grip, but tried not to make too much of it. It might be that Hackman was jaded by a tough job, one replete with emotional turmoil and more-than-occasional calls for physical intervention. Dez had dealt with his fair share of mentally unstable people during his career, and it always left him feeling drained, sad and helpless. To be surrounded by it day in and day out, that was a reality he wasn't sure he could bear.

"Mr. Hackman," Dr. Gerhardt said. "If you'd be so kind as to take Mr. Gray on a tour of our hospital, I'd greatly appreciate it. His brother would like to speak with me."

"Of course, Doctor." The orderly extended an arm toward the hall to the east. "This way, Mr. Gray."

Sully met Dez's eye, offering a flicker of a faked smile which Dez returned. Sully was on edge. Dez could only imagine. While Sully's ability to see the dead was restricted to those who had been victims of homicide, he'd told Dez once or twice he could still sense the spirits of others.

Like any other hospital, this place had to be crawling with

them. The difference was there might be some reasoning with those at a regular medical facility; here, there might easily be more just like the one with whom Sully was now struggling.

Dez felt a shiver coming on and gave up fighting it after the attempt edged toward futile. Gerhardt caught it and offered Dez a reassuring smile.

"Don't worry, Mr. Braddock. Your brother is in good hands here. Why don't we head to my office? We can speak there."

The doctor's office was on the main floor, behind a set of doors kept locked by key code. Gerhardt pulled a card from where it hung around his neck by a lanyard, beeping them into what proved to be the business offices.

They passed a reception desk staffed by a grinning young woman before making their way inside the doctor's large office. The room seemed dark to Dez, an appearance he put down to the wood panelling and what looked to be original light fixtures. Gerhardt slid behind his desk and flicked on a desk lamp, which helped some, but still didn't seem to suck all the shadow from the room.

Dez took one of the leather-backed chairs Gerhardt waved him toward and had barely gotten settled before the doctor opened with a comment.

"You and Sullivan seem close."

"We are."

"But I gather you're not blood brothers?"

"My family took him in when he was a kid," Dez said. "He was a foster placement and it became permanent. So as far as I'm concerned, he's my brother, blood or not."

"Of course. That would certainly explain your worry. Why don't you detail your concerns for me so I can address what I can?"

"The thing is, Doctor, Sully's not crazy."

"We don't use the word 'crazy' here, Desmond. May I call you Desmond?"

"Yeah. And sorry. I should have said mentally ill."

"Not to worry. Many people have a great deal to learn when it comes to mental illness. We all do, even me. We've made great progress in studying it over the years, and have arrived at a far more humane place in terms of treatment, but there are still a great many mysteries to be solved. People fear what they don't know, and—as you no doubt know as a police officer—it often causes them to lash out. That often makes the mentally ill a target for abuse of all kinds, including verbal. And so we're careful about the words we use here."

"Makes sense," Dez said. "My apologies again. Sometimes the drawbridge between my brain and my mouth gets a little stuck. At least that's what my mom used to tell me."

Gerhardt chuckled, one of those closed-mouthed ones that still managed to sound pleasant enough. Dez relaxed a little.

"How'd you know I was a police officer?"

"Dr. Garva told me a few things when he contacted me about Sullivan," the psychiatrist explained. "He mentioned you and your father are with the Kimotan Rapids Police Department, and had opted to look after Sullivan yourselves. No offence to either of you, nor your mother who I understand is a family counsellor. But there are times when it's helpful to have someone from the outside examine a situation or, in this case, a person. It's difficult to remain objective as a family member.

"Whether or not we have biases or pre-conceived notions about mental illness, I know of no one who wants to believe their loved one is affected. Many people live in a state of denial simply because they cannot or will not admit it to themselves. In the meantime, their loved one gets no better and sometimes even worsens.

"Many sufferers of mental illness, not understanding what's wrong or in no state to comprehend, begin to self-medicate. We have a great many patients here who were admitted only once they became too much for their families to manage, and many had chemical dependencies when they came to us. And sadly, many had already lost contact with family and were living on the streets. I'm sure you're aware of the problem. Like me, you must see it every day."

"Yeah, I do. Look, I'm not trying to devalue the work you do here. Not at all. It's just that I truly believe Sully doesn't need to be here. He isn't ill."

"Dr. Garva told me Sullivan described a blackout, and that he caused himself a serious injury as part of an apparent suicide attempt. I don't intend to sound critical of your assessment of your brother, but what other explanation can you offer for his actions and what he says he experienced?"

Dez's gaze dropped to his fingers, entwined around each other in his lap. He hadn't noticed until he looked, but they were clenched so tightly together they were showing white in places. He made a conscious effort to relax. He knew the truth about Sully, of course, but wasn't at liberty to share that here. Not with this man and not with anyone else.

Thankfully, Gerhardt didn't pursue an answer to his question, rather changing course slightly.

"Let me ask you something that might seem strange. Does Sullivan ever speak of hearing voices, or seeing people or images no one else can?"

Dez's head snapped up. The psychiatrist smiled, recognizing the unintended movement for what it was: confirmation.

"How long has this been going on?" the doctor asked.

Dez took a moment to consider how best to answer before deciding there was no best answer. "I really think Sully's the one you need to talk to about all that."

"You say last night was not the result of a mental illness, that your brother doesn't suffer from one. And yet last night happened. Did he report it as a spirit possession?"

Dez shifted in his chair. "Doc, you're kind of freaking me out here."

"I apologize. This often isn't easy for people to hear about, let alone discuss. While I would never presume to make a diagnosis without first spending a great deal of time interviewing a patient and observing him or her, I can speak of symptoms, and those I've just mentioned to you can be indicative of some form of schizophrenia. I would be concerned the sufferer is experiencing psychotic episodes, ones that are being acted upon in a violent way. Or …." Gerhardt paused while he sat forward, extending his wiry arms along the desk's surface and placing his fingertips together in prayer formation. His eyes fixed on Dez's in such a way that breaking the gaze was not an option. The man took a quick breath. "Or maybe Sullivan really is seeing the things he says he is."

Dez was stuck for a response, not wanting to confirm or deny. The doctor filled the gap.

"I've been told I'm unconventional. Some doctors within my profession think I should join my patients on the couch. Honestly, I started out believing we could experience the world only as it appeared to us through our five senses. I discounted those who reported having visions, prophesying the future, or seeing or hearing entities that were not there. I believed they were simply suffering from a form of illness I needed to treat.

"One day, a young woman came into my care who changed my mind. What she shared with me shook me to my core and shattered the foundations upon which I'd built my practice. She made me rethink many of my past diagnoses in a way that has caused a regret so intense I fear I will take it to my grave."

Gerhardt sat back, breaking eye contact to stare at his hands as he pulled them from the desktop. "I don't share this story unless I believe it needs told in order to help someone, but I lost my son many years ago. He was very young, only six. He was playing in the backyard of the house I shared with my late wife, and someone took him. We searched, the police searched and, thanks to many news reports at the time, the public searched, but we never found him. To this day, he remains missing.

"Fifteen years later, that young woman came under my care and told me my son was with me. She described him in great detail, which I initially put down to her having accessed news reports. I ignored the fact it made little sense a young lady who hadn't planned to come to Lockwood would have dug up dated articles about my tragedy. I believed she intended it as a means to get to me. But she continued, told me my son wouldn't leave her alone until she'd helped him. And as I began to hear her out, she told me things only known to my late wife and myself. And my wife, you must understand, was already dead by this point, so there was nowhere the patient could have accessed this information—save by the means she claimed to have come by it. From my son himself.

"She tried to help me find him. But she didn't want to be here, and she ran before she could tell me where to find the place he'd been buried or help me find the man responsible. To this day, I don't know what became of her. All I know is she convinced me there is more to this world of ours than we currently have the power to grasp, more than science has been able to explain."

Dez shifted in his seat. He knew there had to be more people like Sully out there, but hearing details of a specific case set him on edge. He grasped at the more solid information, the part he could easily process.

"I'm sorry for your loss."

"Thank you." The psychiatrist peered at Dez another few seconds before ending his study with a smile. "I can see you're uncomfortable. Forgive me. I tell you these things only so you can see I no longer go into any assessment with the immediate expectation of diagnosing a mental illness. Sometimes the things people claim to experience are simply the creation of a mind in need of the proper medication and treatment. But sometimes, Desmond, they're real. So, you see, I do not and will not enter into any assessment of your brother with the automatic assumption he is ill."

Dez rubbed his hands together. That chill had set back in, was threatening to work its way up his arms and into his chest. "Uh, sorry, but I'm not really sure what to say to all that."

"You don't need to say anything. It's just food for thought. Let me give you some more. Some people with this gift of sight find acceptance and peace within it. Others are tortured by it. It consumes them, causes mental illness where once there was none. I have seen once-stable individuals suddenly attempt suicide or even homicide upon reaching a point where they can no longer bear the things they experience, or even because something from beyond has taken control of them.

"I have been working on treatments for people like that. I believe the minds of these individuals are more open than most, and I have a keen interest in discovering where within the mind these gifts are accessed. In working toward that goal, I believe I have found a way to help them, to quiet their minds—at least until I can guide them to a stronger place. The ghosts probably still visit, but these patients are no longer aware of them. And, for some, that equates to the first sense of peace they have ever known."

"Do you have people like that here now?" Dez asked.

"For privacy reasons, I can't speak to specific cases," the doctor said. "But, yes, I do. And if you and your brother agree, I believe I can help him too."

THE WHOLE POINT in visiting Lockwood, at least as far as Sully was concerned, had been to try to find some clue as to the identity of the man he was seeing. But Larson Hackman was proving a very solid roadblock as he kept Sully firmly beside him during the tour.

Hackman was accommodating enough on the surface, guiding Sully through the parts of the building accessible to the public during visitor hours. But Sully had been a student of human behaviour most of his life—as a young child in foster care, it was a skill he'd been forced to learn early—and he honoured the unease he felt despite Hackman's attempts at niceties.

By the time they reached what the head orderly described as

the lounge area, Sully had become so wary of the large man at his side that he was all but oblivious to everything else around him. That changed the instant Sully made the effort to focus on the room around him.

There, sitting by the window in a wheelchair, empty, staring eyes locked onto the grounds outside, was the man from the bathroom mirror.

Sully had been seeing ghosts his entire life. If there was one thing he'd learned, it was that there was no predicting how or when they would reveal themselves. They had been living people at one time and, as such, they were as different as the personalities and the personal histories which had shaped them.

But there was something different about this man, something that made him far different from any of the ghosts Sully had seen in the past.

This one was very much alive.

13

Sully studied his brother's profile as they drove back into the city.

Dez's face was like stone, the look he wore when he was trying hard not to reveal some thought or emotion of which he wasn't overly proud. Usually Dez didn't stay quiet for long, but he was putting his usual short limits to shame on this particular ride.

After a solid five minutes with nothing to listen to but an annoying radio DJ spouting opinions about the city's sports teams, Sully decided he couldn't wait Dez out any longer. "You okay?"

"Huh?"

"I asked if you're okay."

Dez spared him a quick glance before returning eyes to the road. "Uh, yeah. Yeah, I'm fine."

"No, you're not. You haven't said anything since I told you about the man in the wheelchair."

"Yeah, I did."

"Dez, 'That's weird' doesn't count."

"What do you want me to say?"

"I don't know. Something. Anything."

Dez drove another couple of blocks, reverting to silence again. Sully had decided he was going to try to allow Dez whatever time he needed to process, when his brother suddenly veered into the parking lot of a flooring store. Sully was wondering whether his overnight bleed-out required the replacement of permanently stained tiles, when Dez pulled into a spot facing the street, far enough from the store's entrance for Sully to realize the stop was for his benefit, not his brother's.

Dez turned partway in his seat, draping a solid arm over the steering wheel. "I know you think talking helps me, Sully, but sometimes it doesn't. It really doesn't."

"Okay, I'm sorry. I shouldn't have pushed."

"It's just sometimes talking about it makes this shit feel more real to me. I mean, this latest crap. It's not enough you've got to deal with ghosts of dead people. Now you've got to contend with living ones too? I mean, how the hell does that work, anyway? How does some guy just randomly leave his body and get into yours so he can try to kill you? I hate this stuff, man. I mean, I really, really hate this stuff."

Sully fought the smile, forced it back before Dez could see. If everything else stopped making sense in his world—and there were plenty of days when it seemed likely to happen—he'd always have Dez.

"What's so funny?"

"Nothing," Sully said. "I wasn't laughing."

"You're doing that thing where you're trying really hard not to. Makes you look like you're constipated. So what's so funny? 'Cuz I could use the laugh right now."

"I'm sorry. Nothing's funny. I was just thinking how you're the most stable thing in my life. You don't change. And it's weird, but that keeps me solid."

Dez's scowl, while not disappearing altogether, faded by a good half. "So did you actually find out anything about this guy? You get a name or anything?"

"I made like I recognized him—which was actually true, I guess—and I asked Hackman about him. But he said their privacy rules mean they can't speak to any specifics about clients, including names. He did tell me the man I was asking about has been a resident there probably almost as long as I've been alive, so there was no way I could have known him outside Lockwood."

"Have you ever heard of anything like this? People leaving their bodies and possessing someone else's?"

"I've heard of out-of-body experiences, but this is going beyond anything I've ever known. Remember how Raiya suggested maybe the guy was psychic? Could be this is part of it."

"Okay, but there's the other thing. You only see the ghosts of people who've been killed by someone, right? This guy hasn't been."

"So maybe it's different than I thought," Sully said. "Maybe it's not just murdered people I see. Maybe it's people who are the victims of some sort of injustice. I mean, I know for a fact they've all had that in common. Or maybe ...."

"What?"

"It sounds stupid, but what if I'm seeing this guy because he's going to be murdered?"

"How the hell would that work? You don't see the future."

"No, but what if *he* does? Marc thought maybe the reason the ghost came to me at that first break-in was to act as a warning about what was going to happen to Betty. What if that's true? Maybe he foresaw it and tried to warn me."

"But it didn't work, so he's pissed now and trying to kill you? That sounds made up."

"Hey, I'm a little short on theories here. But the psychic thing, if it's true, it could change the playing field. That's all I'm saying. He might have the ability to do things others can't."

Dez nodded, but didn't say anything else, and Sully guessed that was as far as he was going to get with his brother on that topic. Even so, the way Dez was chewing at the inside of his lower lip was a clear indication he had something else on his mind.

"What?" Sully asked.

This time, Dez didn't delay. "Do you ever wish you could make it all stop? I mean, if someone had a solution for you, a way to end all this, make the ghosts go away, would you take it?"

"What are you talking about?"

"Dr. Gerhardt said he had some sort of treatment for people who see things the way you do. He told me he believes that stuff's real, and he gave me this example of some psychic chick who once tried to help him find his missing son. He buys that this sort of thing happens, and it sounds like he's dedicated a chunk of his career to studying it and looking for ways to help."

"Do you think I need help, Dez?"

Dez had been scanning the fingers of his right hand, but Sully's question had his eyes snapping onto his brother's. "I didn't say that."

"But you're thinking it."

"No, Sull. What I'm thinking is that the ghosts around you need help and, in trying to get it, they don't honour your space, boundaries or safety. You've handled a lot over the years. I've seen it, and I think it's awesome, the stuff you've been able to do. But it feels like the last few years, you've been getting in over your head more and more often. I don't like it. As much as all the ghost stuff freaks me out, the idea of something happening to you because of it, that scares me more. I just thought if there was a way to stop it, or at least to take a break from it sometimes, maybe that would be good for you."

Sully took a moment, searching for the right words before using them. He knew his brother might not like what he had to say. But it needed to be put out there, and Sully wondered whether he needed to say it to himself as much as to Dez. Because Dez's observation was true. There were times when not seeing the dead would be far, far easier.

"I know it's not ideal and, believe me, there are times when I feel overwhelmed and wish everything would stop. But I've been given this gift for a reason—even if sometimes it feels more like a curse. It's scary as hell sometimes. You know that. But there's no better feeling than knowing something you did helped save someone. You help people as a police officer all the time, and you risk your own safety to do it. I guess, in my own way, I do the same thing. And it's not just what I do. It's who I am. I've thought about it, believe me. I've thought about it a lot over the years. And I keep coming back to the same thing. If I lost the ghosts, I think I'd lose myself."

Dez didn't offer a verbal reply, eyes sliding slowly back to his fingers. This time, there was more to his silence than anxiety or fear. There was honour in it, evidence Dez hadn't just let Sully's words glance off his armour like an ineffective arrow. He was thinking about it and, as far as Sully was concerned, that was all he could ask of the brother who'd spent his life trying to protect Sully from the one bully he couldn't fight for him.

When at last Dez answered in words, it was through tones far quieter than he often used. "I'm never going to get used to your life ending up on the line because of you helping people whose lives are already over. But you need to know I respect what you do and, more than that, I respect *you*. If you need to keep doing this, I'll back you up. But I'm never going to like it, Sull. I can't change that any more than you can change."

Sully smiled, pleased when Dez returned it. "Thanks, bro."

"Let's head back home and eat and try to chill out a bit tonight, all right? If you can't give me a whole life's worth, I at least need a night without any ghost chasing."

IT HAD TAKEN some persuasion on Sully's part, but they made a stop at the Black Fox to allow Sully to get some of his things together.

The forensic examination done, police had finally released the scene, leaving the Fox an empty shell. Sully was used to being here alone, but this was different.

It was like the place had lost its soul.

The fire door between the employees-only area and the bar had been left propped open, and Sully's eyes immediately drifted to the spot where Betty had fallen. He didn't have long to dwell there, as Dez's insistent hands pushed him along from behind.

"Let's just go up and get your stuff so we can get the hell out of here. This place gives me the heebie-jeebies."

Sully gathered his toiletries in the bathroom while Dez bustled through the bedroom across the hall, stuffing random clothes into a duffel bag. Sully was just tossing in his shaver when he had the feeling of a presence behind him. The memory of last night compelled him to keep his head down, resisting a glance in the medicine cabinet mirror.

It was silly. He knew that. Spirit possession didn't rely on a person seeing it coming. And yet, Sully found himself hoping if he didn't see the man, if he could just keep his fear from spiking, he might be able to stay strong enough to prevent another possession.

But, as the seconds ticked by and the presence remained, Sully feared there would be no easy way around this—at least none that wouldn't involve wimping out and calling to Dez for help. If the man was behind him, then he was between Sully and the doorway, and his only means of escaping this room.

"Sully? You okay?"

The realization Dez had appeared in the door allowed Sully to turn and, as expected, he didn't just see his brother. But it wasn't the man from Lockwood standing there, staring at him. It was Betty.

Dez scanned the room, eyes wider than usual as if that might help him see what he couldn't. "There's someone here, isn't there? It's friggin' cold."

"It's okay, Dez. It's Betty."

"Jesus. You need a minute?"

"Yeah. Thanks."

"I'll be in your living room. Don't take long, okay? I'm hungry."

He slipped away, leaving the door open. Sully suspected Dez's rush was more about getting away from the ghost and less about the fact he was looking forward to barbecuing, but Sully didn't waste time ribbing his brother. He had something more important to do.

Sully turned full attention to Betty. On some level, he'd known to expect the rush of emotion that came with the contact. But there was something that surprised him nonetheless about the tears that clouded his vision as he searched for the words he'd wanted to say since the shooting.

In the end, there was no eloquent way to put it, no words in the English language for what he needed to express. After all, how did you tell someone you were sorry for the role you'd played in their death? So he was forced to settle for the inadequate.

"I'm sorry. I'm so sorry."

Betty shook her head side to side. Her mouth seemed to be moving once again but Sully, as usual, couldn't make it out.

"I can't hear you, Betty, and I can't read your lips. I can see you but that's all. I just need you to know how sorry I am about what happened. I've been going over and over that moment in my head, and I keep thinking there's something I could have done different. If I'd caught the guy from the break-in the night before, none of this ever would have happened. I just wish—"

He broke off as, in the blink of an eye, she'd gone from standing near the bathroom door to directly in front of him. Her hand reached up to his cheek and she shook her head slowly as her eyes regarded him with something he could only describe as sorrow. The message was clear.

She didn't blame him and she didn't want him to blame himself.

The unspoken absolution tore a choked sob from his throat and he had to swallow it before continuing. "But Betty, I didn't—"

She glared at him now. His chuckle was an automatic response to that face, the one she made whenever she felt someone wasn't listening to what she knew was very solid advice. She'd directed it at him more than once, and routinely wore that expression whenever Dez came around with his playful ribbing.

The realization he'd never see that scowl again once he found a way to help her struck him like a physical blow, wiped the smile away almost as fast as it had come. He didn't want to see the back of this woman, couldn't imagine working in a Black Fox where she wasn't. And yet he knew she needed a way to find peace. She might never allow Sully's guilt, but he felt it nonetheless, and if giving her peace was the one thing he could do to try to make up for everything, he would find it for her.

"Betty, I can help you, but only if you let me," he said. "The thumb drive you were worried about after that break-in. It's important, isn't it? I mean, there's more to it than just family stuff, right?"

Betty paused and Sully waited for it, the moment when she came to a conclusion: whether to trust him with this or not. Sully knew it all came down to this. Thackeray, he was convinced, didn't know where the drive was and wouldn't show him even if he did. And Betty, having gone to great lengths to protect the drive, might never be able to work herself up to trusting someone, particularly a person who was effectively an outsider to whatever secrets that device might hold.

Without Betty's cooperation, there might never be a way to figure this out.

As Sully was thinking up what to say to convince her, he got the reply he needed.

She nodded.

"I need to find out where it is."

Another pause. Another delay as she considered.

Sully waited her out, hoping for a similar response. But this time she shook her head.

"Please. I want to help you and I can, but I need to know about the drive. I mean, that is why you're still here, right? You're trying to keep it safe."

A nod.

"Safe for what? If it's not meant to be used, what's the point in having it? I need you to help me find it, Betty. Please."

He wasn't obeying her, was going so far as to argue with her. Ordinarily, that would have earned him one of her patented glares and a cuff on the arm, but this time, what he got was a warm smile.

It was the last thing he saw before she disappeared.

"Betty? Betty, please!"

Dez's voice drifted in from the other room. "Sully, you okay in there?"

Sully ran from the bathroom and covered the entire interior of the Black Fox as well as the back parking lot with a confused and anxious Dez hard on his heels.

At last, back inside the empty building, Sully dropped onto the stairs leading from the main floor to the apartments on the upper level.

Dez stood in front of him, wide eyes scoping the room before returning to his brother. "What the hell, man?"

"She won't tell me," Sully said.

"Tell you what?"

"About the thumb drive. She told me it's important, that it's why she's still here, that she's trying to keep it safe. But she won't let me help."

"What was all that a second ago? Were you looking for it?"

"Looking for her. She disappeared on me. And I'd imagine she's going to go to some pretty great lengths to avoid my seeing her again."

"Why wouldn't she show you?" Dez said. "I know she trusted … trusts you. If anyone could help her, it would be you. Why not give you what you need to do that?"

"I don't know. Maybe it's not about trusting me. Maybe she's just kept it secret for so long, she doesn't know how to do anything else."

"So, what? She's going to stay here forever, guarding the thing?"

"Some ghosts do that. There are stories about spirits that are hundreds of years old, ones where people have died and stayed to guard some family treasure or secret. When people's lives are consumed by holding onto something, they don't just let it go because the body dies. Nothing's that easy, man. People are the same, whether living or dead. So are their hangups."

"What do you want to do?"

"She's not coming back here, at least not while I'm around. I need to try to talk to her again, to convince her. I'm thinking my best bet is to look for her at her house. Anyway, I could search for the thumb drive while I'm there."

"I thought you'd given up on that because Thackeray wasn't keen on letting you in. You can't be serious about breaking and entering still."

"I need to get in."

"You can't, Sull."

"If—"

"No. Forget it."

"Dez—"

"No! You're already being investigated for a murder. How the hell do you think it's going to look if you get caught breaking into the victim's house? You know what Raynor will do with that? He'll say you were in there looking for something Betty might have had on you, or for something you were after when you supposedly killed her. How are you going to explain that?"

"I won't have to explain anything if I don't get caught. Can you do me a favour and check whether Thackeray is scheduled to go to the police station again at some point to give another statement? I was thinking they might want to talk to him about the possible connection to his charges and the poster you found."

Dez sighed, lifting a hand to squeeze the bridge of his nose between his knuckles. "Damn it, Sully."

Sully waited, recognizing Dez's most recent response for what it was—resignation. When Dez looked back up at him, he was no happier.

"Let's just go home for now, okay? We can discuss the rest tomorrow."

14

IF HE'D GOTTEN nothing else from the brief talk with Betty, Sully felt as if a small weight had dropped from his shoulders.

Whether or not he deserved it, the knowledge Betty didn't blame him for her death proved enough of a relief that Sully managed close to a full night's sleep without one of Lowell's pills.

Wanting the comforts of home and contending with requests from Kayleigh to see Sully, Dez had opted to return there instead of heading back to their parents' place for the night. But, as well as Sully had slept, he was left with a new measure of guilt as he looked at Dez's face the next morning.

"Didn't you sleep?" Sully asked.

Dez scrubbed a hand over his face and stopped to scratch at unshaven stubble as he watched the coffee perking. "Here and there. I was trying to listen for you, make sure nothing was happening that shouldn't have been."

"I'm sorry, man."

Dez turned, jabbed a finger against Sully's shoulder. "Don't. Not your fault."

Sully was pulling a few mugs from the cupboard when Dez cut in with the expected question. "No visitors last night?"

"Not that I know of. I mean, I had this feeling right before bed like I was being watched, but nothing materialized."

"I guess that's a good thing. Have you rethought your stupid plan for the day?"

Sully smiled. "If you mean heading over to Betty's house then, no, I haven't. I need to get in there."

Dez huffed out a breath but said nothing, which Sully took as a win. It wasn't that long ago his brother would have threatened physical confinement to keep Sully from doing something inherently stupid, so the lack of argument was a huge step forward.

"I don't like this."

"You don't have to. And honestly, I don't know what I'd think if you did."

Dez dropped Kayleigh off at school on his way to work the last of his day shifts this stretch, leaving Sully with Eva for the morning. Sully said nothing to his sister-in-law about the plan, wanting as few people involved as possible. The worst thing, if he got caught, would be to take anyone down with him.

It was after eleven-thirty when Dez called Sully's cellphone with news.

"Raynor's asked Thackeray to come in at one this afternoon to talk about the posters and a possible connection there. Apparently, he already talked to Terrence Waters about it, and Raynor keeps grumbling it's a waste of time, following this line of inquiry. Anyway, just letting you know."

"Thanks, Dez."

"I'm not sure how I'll manage it yet, but I'll try to figure out a way to meet you there."

"Why?"

"If you're playing cat burglar, you need someone outside, standing six in case Thackeray comes back earlier than expected. And I wouldn't count on Raynor to be interested enough to make it a long interview."

"Not that I don't appreciate it, but I don't want you anywhere near there. If things go sideways, you'll be considered an accomplice."

"I'm an accomplice anyway. I'm getting you the info you need to pull this off. That makes me a party to the offence, if not a co-conspirator. This is really stupid, Sully."

"Maybe, but I don't see that I have much of a choice."

"Okay, look. I'll stay away, but you still need someone there who can warn you and maybe stall Thackeray if he gets back before you're out. I'll see if I can reach Bulldog. Don't move until I do."

Sully smiled. Billy "Bulldog" Bird had gone from being a street source for Dez to a friend in a short space of time, and he and Sully had bonded a couple years ago during the search for Bulldog's missing niece. Somewhere in his mid-to-late forties, the guy had one of those hangdog faces that had helped earn him the nickname, and his appearance had been enough to cause a few people to seriously misjudge him. It belied the quick mind and ready instincts that made for a man who could talk his way around just about anything and, in the event that didn't work, he was a solidly built miniature tank of a man capable of holding up his end of a physical battle.

At one time, Sully had grumbled about Dez's desire to send Bulldog with him as backup. Now, with a little more age and experience to guide him, Sully was grateful for the possibility.

In anticipation of Bulldog's presence at the house, Sully headed to the nearest bus stop. After the usual transfer into Riverview, Sully opted to walk toward Betty's, happy to make the trip last as long as he could. Having grown up with a police officer as a foster father, Sully had been raised with a healthy and sometimes overly enthusiastic respect for the law. The idea of breaking it, whatever Dez might think, was nerve-wracking, causing him to regret the eggs and greasy bacon he'd eaten for breakfast.

There was a park near Betty's, close enough to afford a view of the house and large enough he could stand some distance away, ensuring he wouldn't be easily spotted by Thackeray. Sully saw a car still parked next to Betty's old beater and guessed it must belong to her son. A glance at the face of his cellphone told Sully there were still forty minutes before the interview time. If driving, it would take Thackeray only about ten minutes from here.

Unfortunately, that gave Sully more time than he wanted to think, so he was grateful when he heard the gruff voice behind him.

"You sure know how to find trouble, don't you, kid?"

Sully tilted his head up from where he sat cross-legged on the grass, squinting against the sun as he took in the stout form of Bulldog Bird. "Thanks for coming."

Bulldog grumbled a reply that was likely meant to signify a "you're welcome," before lowering himself and ultimately collapsing into a spot on the grass next to Sully. "Fucking hell."

"You okay?"

"Okay? I'm bloody old, that's what I am. Falling apart, piece at a time. Buggered up my knee."

Sully was happy for the change in topic, any excuse to think about something besides dead people and housebreaking. "How'd you manage that?"

"Got in a fight. Asshole hit a woman, so I got one in for her. After that, guy refused to back down so I played it through."

"I thought you always said you were a lover not a fighter."

"Hey, in my twenties, I was one hell of a fighter, Sully. I was the Rocky Goddamn Marciano of Blackwater First Nation. People saw me coming, they moved the hell outta my way."

Sully might have laughed but for the fact he fully believed it.

"So how's the other guy?"

"Unconscious, last I saw him. Won't be picking on women for a while, tell you that much." Bulldog grinned wickedly. "I made sure his dominant hand won't be good for much for at least six weeks. So, what's all this about today, then? Copper only gave me the Reader's Digest version."

Sully had never been sure whether Bulldog's nickname for

Dez had to do with his line of work or the colour of his hair. Sully had always intended to ask, but never found the right moment. This wasn't it, either.

Instead, he divided his time between filling Bulldog in and watching what he assumed was Thackeray's car. As soon as the guy pulled away, Sully would move in. Bulldog was one of few people who knew about the things Sully saw, and one of even fewer who believed it, thanks to the incident with Bulldog's niece —which also involved the ghost of his murdered sister, Breanna. Since then, Bulldog had been full of questions on virtually every occasion the two of them had run into each other.

Right now, though, his queries were focused on just one thing, and it wasn't of a spiritual nature.

"Just how the hell you planning on getting in there, anyway? Guy that paranoid, especially one who's been to prison, he's not leaving the place unlocked."

"If I've got to break a window, I'll do that."

"Yeah? And I'm supposed to be your six on this. How's that gonna look when the neighbours peer out their windows and see some Indigenous guy standing around? You think they're just going to shrug their shoulders and go back to watching their soaps? Racist bastards will have the cops here for me so fast it'll make your head spin."

Sully started to suspect his brother had an ulterior motive in sending Bulldog here. "Dez asked you to talk me out of this, didn't he?"

"You're a wise one, grasshopper."

"It's not going to work, Bulldog. I need to talk to Betty or just look for that drive."

"What makes you so sure either of them will be here?"

"I don't know about the drive, but I saw Betty here before."

"Okay. So why don't you just ask her to let you in, then?"

"Huh?"

"I've been with you before when ghosts held doors shut and

got them open, remember? My sister? Maybe Betty could do something like that too."

"I have a feeling she'd prefer it if I was nowhere near this place."

"Question for you: If no one wants you here, why are you here?"

It was a good question, good enough that Sully was still trying to come up with an answer when he saw Thackeray emerge from the house and slide behind the wheel of the car Sully had pegged as his. Sully and Bulldog lay back, obscuring their heads from view of the car passing this way. By the time they sat up again, Betty's son had driven past.

"Come on," Sully said, standing and helping Bulldog to his feet.

Bulldog wobbled a little but held his ground. "This is stupid. And you're stupid for thinking it isn't stupid."

"Look, I won't break any windows, okay? I see your point. If there's no obvious way in, I'll think of something else. Maybe one of the neighbours has a key."

"This is Riverview, not Gladstone or Jasmine Park. People don't share house keys around here. Neighbours are more likely to use them to go in and help themselves to electronics than to call the cops on someone burgling the place."

The pair made their way across the street, and Bulldog took a seat on a swing on the front veranda while Sully made a show of knocking. Unsurprisingly, no one answered and he took a moment to look around to see whether anyone was watching.

"Stop it," Bulldog said. "You look obvious. I'll be your eyes. That's the whole point of having a six."

"So I'm good?"

"For now. Hop to it, kid. We don't have all day."

Sully searched the areas beneath the mat, inside the outdoor light fixture and beneath several flowerpots, hoping Betty had been in the habit of hiding a spare key. But she wasn't the kind of woman to misplace house keys, and he knew she was too cautious to risk leaving them someplace where a potential intruder would find them.

Bulldog was just as doubtful. "You really think she'd just leave a key sitting around?"

"I don't know. I just thought—"

Sully broke off mid-sentence, his attention caught by a gathering presence just the other side of the glass. He expected Betty. What he got was Mirror Man.

"No."

"What?" Bulldog's question sounded as alarmed as Sully realized his one-word statement had been, and it merited a reply.

"Did Dez tell you about this man I've been seeing?"

"He said something about it, yeah. Said to watch your back, just in case. Why?"

"He's here. I have no idea why, but he's standing just inside the door."

"Fucking hell. What's he doing?"

"Staring," Sully said. "Just staring."

"Think he'll let you in?"

"If he does, I'm not sure it'll be for any good reason."

"Maybe we should leave. Copper said this guy almost killed you. Freaked him out pretty bad, from what I could tell."

It had freaked Sully out, too, if he was being honest. But saying it out loud wasn't going to help. What he hoped *would* help was what Marc and Raiya had taught him, and Sully fought every urge he had to watch the ghost inside the house as he closed his eyes and focused inward, breathing deep as he pictured a steady light surrounding and protecting him.

"What the hell are you doing?"

"Ssh," Sully said. "Grounding."

"This is the worst break and enter I've ever seen."

Hoping for the best, given he didn't have time for much more, Sully opened his eyes. The ghost was still there, still staring at him, but Sully felt like his own fear was lessened a little—still there, but pleading with him to run rather than screaming it in his ear. It wasn't ideal, but he could cope.

"I don't know who you are or what you want from me, but I'm trying to help," Sully told the man, a quiver sounding in his voice despite his best efforts. "If there's a way you could let me in, I'm hoping you can do that for me."

For a moment, there was nothing. No reply, not even a sign the catatonic-looking man had heard him. But then, as Sully continued to watch, the man lifted a hand. Held between finger and thumb was a key.

The man knelt slowly and Sully's eyes followed him down, noting as he pulled his sight back a bit he could see the reflection from outside in the door's glass. And Sully could see it as the man lifted one reflected corner of the outside doormat and place the key beneath. Sully looked down at his own feet. The mat hadn't lifted, of that much he was certain. And yet, he could see the man now settling the reflected mat's corner back into place before standing and slowly backing away from the door. Sully watched him go until, finally, he faded away into the shadows cast in the narrow hall between stairs and wall.

Sully looked back down at his feet, and then repeated the man's recent movements, kneeling and peeling back a corner of the mat. There, resting on the veranda's floorboards, exactly where his search had come up empty only moments ago, was the key.

Bulldog eyed Sully's find. "Get out. You just looked there."

"There wasn't anything there to find until just now. I think he put it there."

"How'd he manage that?"

"No idea. But there it is."

"Okay, great. You sure it fits the door?"

Sully tried it, heard the click.

"Wonderful," Bulldog said. "Now I'm definitely staying out here. You need something, call. But I'm not coming in no haunted house unless it's life or death."

Sully patted Bulldog on the shoulder and headed inside.

There was no sign of the man, and Sully was uncertain whether the lingering chill he felt had more to do with the ghost or the fact the house was so dark inside. Betty had gone to great efforts with her garden, and the exterior gave the home the appearance of a small oasis in Riverview's growing desert of unkempt complacency. Inside was another story. Not only was it shrouded in shadow—all the curtains drawn so the only light in the front hall came from the heavy glass door—it looked as if it was in dire need of an overhaul. A couple pieces of the stairs' bannister were missing. The hall carpet was old, worn and tearing in places. The hardwood in the sitting room clearly was in need of some TLC. Dust drifted through the air in the cracks of light created by small gaps in the drapes, and Sully spotted pieces of sock lint and dust bunnies as he moved through the lower floor. It didn't smell of cigarette smoke—Betty had seen to that much—but there wasn't much else about the house's interior to suggest she'd cared for the place. Maybe it was evidence of a woman whose garden was everything to her, who opted to spend every moment of every day there rather than indoors, where she felt closed in. But Sully suspected differently.

Betty was a woman who scrubbed at stains at the Fox, who bussed tables seconds after customers had left, who was on top of it immediately whenever there was a significant spill or a broken glass. The Black Fox was a shining beacon of neatness thanks to Betty. But this house revealed another side to Betty, a woman who didn't care, who'd given up trying for anything other than appearance. The exterior was bright, sunny, charming and welcoming; the inside made you feel cold and lost.

This house wasn't just a clue to who Betty was. This house *was* Betty. The only question that remained was why. It had gone unloved far longer than her son had been in prison, so the depression in this place had to come down to far more than that.

The answer came in a heart-stopping glimpse at a handful of dusty photos propped on the fireplace mantle in the front sitting room. Sitting between Betty and a child Thackeray, smiling into the camera with a relaxed expression, the man was nearly unrecognizable to Sully.

But he would know those eyes anywhere. He'd looked into them only seconds ago through the glass door.

The man who had possessed him and had tried to kill him—the man sitting right now in Lockwood Psychiatric Hospital—was Betty's husband.

15

THE AFTERNOON PROVED QUIET, the police department's usual clientele taking an uncharacteristic break from their shenanigans to enjoy the warm, sunny weather.

It meant a shift in which Dez had some time to visit his father.

He'd debated whether coming here was a good idea. He had no intention of telling Flynn what Sully was up to right now, and he always worried his father could read his mind. But Flynn also had a way of soothing Dez when his blood pressure was reaching roof-high levels and, with Sully getting himself into untold trouble, Dez figured he could use all the calm he could get.

Flynn was just getting out of a meeting with the chief and waved Dez in as soon as he was free.

"What was that about?" Dez asked.

Flynn took a seat at the table and motioned for Dez to join him. He looked exhausted and pale, and didn't immediately answer as he slumped back in the chair and massaged his forehead. The movement served to conceal his eyes from Dez, and it was a good thirty seconds before he looked back up at his son.

"Because the son of the deputy chief is being looked at as a suspect in a murder investigation, the chief has asked to be kept up to speed," Flynn said. "He was just updating me, as much as he could, on what's been found so far, and Raynor remains convinced Sully was more involved in this than he's saying."

"Raynor's got his head up his ass. What about those clothes we found? Did they test them?"

"They're running DNA on some samples they took, but it'll be weeks before we get those back."

"Couldn't we send them to Uncle Lowell's lab? He'd be able to get us something in days."

"I can't imagine Raynor will be satisfied with results that came from the lab owned by Sully's uncle. We're going to have to wait this out, I'm afraid. In the meantime, the coat tested positive for gunpowder residue, but Raynor says it doesn't prove anything in our favour. He says Sully could have been wearing the coat himself, or that he could have worn it while firing a gun after the fact and then concealed the clothing somewhere he could conveniently find it later."

"Concealed it when?" Dez asked. "The first officer showed up within two minutes of Sully reporting the shooting."

"I don't know everything about Raynor's working theory," Flynn said. "Obviously, I've been kept out of the loop on a number of details. But maybe he thinks Sully didn't make the call immediately. Or, more likely, he thinks the items were planted later."

"That makes no sense. Sully had no access to the Fox while the scene was being held. And I have no doubt the building was searched top to bottom for potential evidence. Surely someone would have spotted clothing that matched the description Sully provided."

"Then it could have been planted in preparation of a pre-meditated killing. I'm not saying it's a good working theory. But it is what it is, and we need to make do with it for now. Not our call."

"What motive could Raynor possibly think Sully would have to kill Betty?"

"You know motive isn't the starting point in a homicide investigation," Flynn said. "It's the evidence you follow. It's too easy to get caught up in perceived motive and start bending the investigation to fit your working theory."

"But that's exactly what Raynor's doing."

"Dez, maybe we need to consider something we haven't had the heart to ask ourselves."

"No, Dad."

"Dez—"

"No! Sully didn't do this."

"Listen to me, please. Something's going on with him, something not good. He's struggled in the past with the things he has to deal with, but he's hitting up against something now I've never seen. If it wasn't for the other night—"

"Dad—"

"He's missing time, Dez. And he tried to kill himself. He's never done anything like that before."

"Yeah, he tried to kill himself, not someone else." Dez stopped as suddenly as he'd started, mind flashing back to that moment in the bathroom, to that shard of glass aimed for his throat.

"What?"

"Nothing."

"Dez. What?"

Dez considered not saying anything, had intended to keep that moment safely buried. But this was his dad, Sully's dad. And the more Dez sat in the middle of this, the more uncertain he became about how best to help his brother. Their dad would know, and he'd do whatever was in Sully's best interests.

"There's something I didn't tell anyone about what happened in the bathroom the other night. Sully … or whoever was controlling him at the time, tried to stab me in the neck. I saw it coming, and I was able to stop him and get the piece of mirror away, but it was close."

"Sully doesn't know?"

"No, and I don't want him to. He'd be wrecked over it. But, Dad, he remembers the thing that happened to Betty. There was no blackout, no missing time. He told me exactly what happened."

"Memory's a strange thing, Dez. You know that. You can go to a crime scene, speak to five different people and get five different stories. Then you put them on the witness stand two years later and you've got five different stories all over again. I've read that memory records events in snapshots and fills in the gaps. Sometimes what gets filled in is close to accurate, and sometimes it's completely wrong. If Sully had a similar blackout at the time of Betty's murder, isn't it conceivable he filled it in with something? Maybe something far more bearable to him than what actually occurred?"

"You don't actually believe that, do you?"

"Dez, I don't believe Sully's capable of killing anyone. But given what you've just told me, I'm concerned the man he saw—the man who possessed him—is capable. If Sully was possessed at the time of the shooting, isn't it possible he was the one holding that gun?"

"No, it isn't. He remembers it, Dad, and I believe him."

"There's no evidence anyone else was in there that day. They've found no eyewitnesses who reported anyone in those clothes, and certainly no one carrying a long-barrelled firearm. Surveillance video in the area has been checked, but that's come up empty as well."

"There's not a lot of outdoor surveillance video," Dez said. "Most of the cameras in the area are intended to watch business interiors and till areas. And if the guy was smart—and he seems to be, given he's avoided detection this long—he would have carried the clothes with him, geared up before going in and then discarded everything right after the shooting. Sully didn't run after him. He stayed to try to save Betty, so there would have been no one following the shooter, giving him plenty of time to change or take off an outer layer."

"What about the gun?"

"Duffle bag. It wouldn't be seen as a big deal around there.

Couch-surfers are always shuttling their possessions from one place to another in various bags. No one would have thought anything of it. So the guy carries the gun and clothes to the back door of the Fox, changes, arms himself, shoots Betty, dumps the gun at the scene and takes off. He stops a short distance away, once he's certain he isn't being followed, and he takes off the clothes he was wearing and stuffs them into the bag. He finds a nearby dumpster and gets rid of it, not realizing his plan is essentially perfect because the case's lead investigator is going to be too blind to see reality."

"Dez."

"I'm not apologizing. Raynor's a Class-A asshole. I have no idea why he's got it in for Sully, but he does. I mean, I know the guy doesn't like me, but holy hell. This is going a bit far, even for him."

"It's not about you, Dez, and it's not about Sully. It's me."

"What are you talking about?"

"I've never gotten into this with you, because I didn't want you involved, but I think you need to know this isn't about anything between you and Raynor. I'd rather you understand so you don't go trying to take the guy's head off and get yourself arrested. You know Raynor's dad is Charles Raynor, the mayor, right?"

"Everyone knows that. Raynor doesn't let anyone forget."

"A few years ago, we received a complaint about some corruption that allegedly involved the mayor's office. Due to the nature and sensitivity of the matter, it was brought to the chief directly, and he briefed me on it to get my advice. Because Charles Raynor's position also makes him head of the police commission, we decided investigating the matter would have been a conflict for our department, so we passed it on to the feds to look into. But they wanted someone local to provide information on the man, so the chief suggested I do it. I didn't have to deal with the mayor directly nearly as much as the chief, but I still had inroads to certain people central to the investigation. I asked some questions and word soon got around to the mayor he was being looked at for possible charges. In the end, nothing came of it, but Charles Raynor's been looking for a way to get rid of me ever since. Problem for him is I've never given him anything to go after. I think the fact Sully's being targeted on this thing suggests Charles put a bug in his son's ear to ensure my son gets buried on this. If one of my boys goes down for a murder, the mayor would have every right to ask for my resignation. The optics would be bad, the father of a killer in the second-highest position on the police department."

Dez leaned forward, enabling him to keep his voice as low as possible. "Do you think there's any chance Betty's murder was ordered by the mayor so he could get the wheels spinning on this?"

"No. That's going far beyond what I believe the man's capable of. But I do think he's been keeping his eyes peeled for any possible opportunity to remove me. This situation probably felt like Christmas morning to him."

"And what about Forbes? I mean, the guy's a dick and I'm still convinced he got his current position solely due to who his father is, but I never took him for crooked."

"I'm not saying he is," Flynn said. "I'm sure Forbes is genuinely convinced he's doing the right thing. But, like I said, it's easy for inexperienced investigators' minds to get clouded into believing their working theory is the only rational solution. Once you buy into it, you start to twist things to fit. I once saw a good investigator blow his reputation and career because he was convinced a particular convicted sex offender was responsible for a pair of attempted kidnappings of young boys. Turned out he was wrong, but by then it was too late. His suspect, believing he was headed back to prison, committed suicide before we received DNA results that exonerated him. A man's life was over, the department was thrown into a media firestorm and that investigator lost his job. I would hope Forbes would keep that in mind as he's going about his investigation, but I can't involve myself to remind him of that. In the meantime, all we can do is wait and hope for the best."

"That's not all we can do. If Raynor's not looking for other solutions, then I'll do it for him."

"Dez, no. I don't want you getting involved in this, either. We're both too close to the situation, and the last thing I want is you getting suspended because you tried to interfere in an active investigation."

"I'm not looking to interfere. I'm looking to help. And I know what you said, but I know what Sully said was true, Dad. He didn't do this. Not consciously or unconsciously. It wasn't him."

"I'm not saying he did. Please understand that, Dez. I don't believe it, either. All I'm saying is we can't expect Forbes Raynor to keep an open mind if we're not willing to do the same. Something's going on with Sully and it's worrying me, especially given what you just told me about the attempt to stab you. Let me ask you something. The sleeping pill he took that night. He said Lowell gave it to him?"

"Yeah."

"How long has Lowell been giving him those things?"

"You didn't know?"

"No, I didn't."

Dez shrugged. "It's been a few years, anyway. Probably since shortly after Sully started working at the Black Fox. I'm guessing Sully said something to Betty about being tired, maybe word got back to Lowell, and he figured he'd help."

"Yeah, makes sense. I just wish someone had told me. Sleeping pills can be addictive."

"Sully doesn't use them often, just when things get bad. He told me he doesn't like feeling like stuff could be happening around him and he wouldn't be aware of it or in any state to handle it. Makes him feel too open to attack, I think."

"Okay," Flynn said. "That's good to know. Thanks." He checked his watch and looked back up at Dez with an apologetic grin. "I hate to cut this short, but I've got a meeting I need to get to."

"No problem. Thanks, Dad." Dez stood and headed to the door but Flynn stopped him before he could fully turn the doorknob.

"Dez? How are you doing, anyway? I haven't asked."

"Fine, Dad. Quiet day."

"I meant about Sully. What you had to deal with, I know that has to be doing a number on you."

"As long as Sully's okay, so am I."

"That's what worries me. You're a great big brother, kid, but sometimes you need to take a step back. I know what you went through with Aiden, and I know he's a big part of why you pour so much of yourself into being there for Sully. That's understandable. But you can't let your highs and lows ride solely on him."

"I don't," Dez said. "I mean, don't get me wrong. Sully's really important to me, but so are Eva and Kayleigh and you and mom. It isn't just Sully. It's all of you. I don't think I could cope if I lost anyone else."

"Yes, you could," Flynn said. "Because unless we all go in some sort of freak disaster, you're guaranteed to lose someone at some point. But this family will be here in whatever form to support each other should anything happen to any of us. That's what family's for, son. You need to remember that."

Dez smiled and nodded, hoping the response would be enough to convince his dad he would take the advice to heart. In all honesty, he was far from certain he'd survive any further changes to his family structure.

"Thanks, Dad." Dez's move to leave was once again interrupted before he got through the door.

"Dez? I meant what I said. I don't want you anywhere near this investigation, all right?"

Dez attempted a broader smile. "Got it, Dad. I'll see you later."

DEZ WAS happy enough to leave the investigating to Raynor—for about as long as it took him to get back down to his police cruiser.

He took it as a sign from the universe that he was barely back out driving the streets when he spotted Edgar Maberly, one of the Black Fox's now-displaced regulars.

Eddie was no fan of police, having been picked up several times this month alone for being drunk in a public place. Which was probably why Eddie picked up the pace when Dez's cruiser slowed next to him.

Thankfully, Eddie knew Dez was as likely to take him home as to the brief detox centre, as long as his condition was such that Eddie's wife was able to handle it. They were both in their early eighties now, but Mrs. Maberly was a tough nut, having grown sadly accustomed to her husband's alcoholism. Eddie wasn't a mean drunk, but Dez didn't imagine that made it easier for his wife, who had likely spent most of their married lives picking up pieces Eddie would just scatter all over again.

Dez stepped out of the car and jogged the couple of steps needed to catch up to the older man. "Eddie. Hey, Eddie."

"Oh, it's you. Big Red. I'm not drunk, so I'm not needing your cab services just yet."

Dez took the customary whiff of the air around Eddie and found he was inclined to believe him. There was a smell of alcohol, but it was faint rather than so pungent people were at risk of getting high just off the fumes.

"Where did you find to drink?" Dez asked.

"Some damn pub down the road. Place isn't friendly, though. Not like the Fox. I didn't like the way the waitress was looking at me, so I left. I've got standards, you know."

"You heard what happened at the Fox?"

"Yeah, I heard. Everyone's heard. Crying shame. Betty was one of the last good people out there. Did you catch the guy yet?"

"We're working on it," Dez said. "Problem is, the guy leading the investigation keeps looking at Sully."

"Sounds like the cops have their heads up their asses as usual

—present company excluded, of course," Eddie said. "I've been around a long time and I've met a lot of bad people. That kid doesn't have it in him."

"I know. I guess that's what I wanted to talk to you about. You've spent a lot of time around the Black Fox, and you knew Betty longer than anyone else I know of. Do you have any idea who might have done something like this?"

"I didn't know anyone with a bad opinion of Betty. Except, I guess, some of the people she booted out when they had one too many and got out of hand."

"Did she have to kick anyone out recently?"

"Hey, that's like a daily occurrence around there. Only thing is Sully gave her a hand as usual, so if someone had it in for her, they probably would have had it in for Sully too. And from what I hear, he was left alone."

"Unless the killer's plan all along was to set Sully up for it, get at him that way."

"No offence, Red, but most of the people of my general acquaintance aren't what I'd call skilled in the art of revenge. No one who hangs out at the Fox would know the first thing about framing someone for a murder, least not in a way the cops wouldn't see from a mile off."

"Fair enough. And you haven't heard anything else that might help us out?"

"Sully's really in trouble, huh?"

"Yeah, I think he's really in trouble."

"Then I'll keep my ear to the ground for anything that might help him."

"Thanks, Eddie. I'd really appreciate that."

"Keep in mind, though. If I've got my ear to the ground, it's likely I'm gonna need some help standing back up." Eddie broke into a wheezy laugh at his own joke, and Dez made like it was the funniest thing he'd heard all morning—which, given the state of the day, wasn't far from the truth.

Heading back to his cruiser, Dez checked his phone; a text

message from Sully showed on the screen: "Creepy guy at Lockwood is Betty's husband." Dez pulled up short and, once the shock had passed, returned to Eddie.

Eddie was grudgingly patient. "What now?"

"Eddie, did you ever meet Betty's husband?"

"Harry? Sure, I met him. Years ago."

"What's he like?"

"Disturbed. Very disturbed. Something wasn't right with him, you know? People said if he wasn't crazy already, he got there pretty quick because of the things he saw."

"What kind of things?"

"All sorts of things. Dead people sometimes. But mostly, he claimed he could see into the future. Harbinger Harry they used to call him. Finally lost what was left of his marbles and ended up in Lockwood."

"Did Betty still visit him there?"

"No idea, but she wasn't the type to just abandon people, so I'd imagine so. Hey, you think maybe he had one of his visions and said something to her about it? Maybe she tried to change whatever it was and pissed someone off. Or maybe Harry saw something he wasn't supposed to and told Betty, and she was killed to keep her quiet."

"You've been watching those detective shows on TV again, haven't you, Eddie?"

Eddie shrugged. "My wife never misses *Murder She Wrote*."

"Okay, but if your theory's true, wouldn't someone have tried to kill Harry too?"

"Seriously? What's the point? The guy's locked up in a nuthouse. It would be suicide to try to get in there and pick someone off in front of all those people. And really, who'd ever listen to him, anyways?"

It was a good point, one that merited further investigation. The question for Dez was how to go about it, given Raynor was unlikely to listen.

Receiving another assurance he'd get answers if Eddie heard one, Dez returned to the car and called his brother's cellphone.

"Where are you?"

"Still at Betty's," Sully said.

"Well, get the hell out of there."

"Did Thackeray leave the police station already?"

"I have no idea. I told you I probably wouldn't know when he did. Just get out. You've already found more than you were expecting."

"I haven't talked to Betty yet. I haven't seen her."

"Sully, I mean it. Get out of there. Now."

"Shit."

Sully's tone had been quiet, but it was the heavy kind of quiet, the kind that suggested something was wrong.

"What's going on?"

"I think Thackeray just got home."

16

SULLY HAD BEEN TIPPED off by a frantic pounding at the door, one that had him abruptly ending the conversation with Dez and dropping the phone into his pocket as he scanned his immediate surroundings for a way out.

His search had moved to the second floor and he'd made it partially back down the stairs when he realized there was no getting out that way. Through the glass of the front door, he could see Thackeray was indeed home and involved in conversation with Bulldog. There was no way to sneak past to get to the side door, either, not without Thackeray catching sight of him in his peripheral vision. Hoping instead for escape out an upper floor window, Sully retraced his steps, retreating into the room he'd just been searching.

Betty's bedroom overlooked the backyard with a large bay window, and Sully was banking on it that at least one of the panes would open enough to allow him to drop onto the veranda roof out back. He'd been paying attention during his search upstairs, and he knew he couldn't sneak around up here once Thackeray was inside. The floors didn't just creak with movement, the old hardwood full-out cracked under the weight of footfalls.

Unfortunately, it seemed he had picked wrong. The windows

in Betty's room weren't just locked, they were sealed shut. The locking mechanisms, when released, didn't help, and a closer inspection revealed nails had been driven into the wood frames from the outside. Why that was, he wasn't sure, but his suspicions ran in the direction of Betty's husband. If he'd begun to break down while still at home, it was possible Betty had been looking for ways to keep him inside to prevent his wandering the streets.

Of course, that left Sully just as confined.

He could hear the front door opening, the remnants of a tight conversation between Thackeray and Bulldog. He couldn't make out the words from here, but there was a higher tone to Bulldog's voice than normal, the sound of pleading that had Sully wondering if the guy had trotted out his lost dog story again.

For now, it didn't matter. Thackeray, unfazed by Bulldog's plight, was headed inside.

Eyes darting around for somewhere to hide, he settled on the small walk-in closet he'd poked through earlier. In the few seconds he figured he had before Thackeray heard someone upstairs, Sully dashed to the door and ducked into the cramped space, squeezing himself into one corner next to a laundry hamper and easing the door shut.

The space was pitch black, the sliver of light coming from beneath the door not nearly enough to illuminate anything, even once Sully's eyes adjusted.

He leaned back on the hamper, sitting on the edge and trying to decide how he was going to get out of this. At this point, unless Thackeray decided to go out again, Sully figured he was stuck here until nightfall and whenever Thackeray hit REM sleep. He'd just have to hope the man snored; there would be no other way to know when it was safe to make his escape.

Nothing was easy these days, and Sully found himself desperate for a quicker escape when the first sensations of cold crept into the closet. He knew the feeling coming with it, recognized it without needing to see. He closed his eyes, kept them squeezed shut for what felt like several minutes as he willed

Betty's husband to leave or, failing that, to build up the protection like Raiya had taught him. But it wasn't easy, the confined space and the knowledge the ghost was now standing directly in front of him creating that debilitating terror the man always brought with him.

Sully wondered if maybe this was why the ghost had let him inside. He hadn't been looking to help Sully unbury secrets. He'd been trying to get him alone, into a situation where, anxieties already heightened, he'd be most vulnerable to the ghost's will.

Unable to find the calm he needed within himself, Sully sought it elsewhere, keeping his eyes shut as he fumbled for his phone. He cracked one open enough to see the screen, caught sight of the ghostly glow directly in front of him, yellow pyjama pants and blue slippers.

Dez's was the last number under his recent calls, and Sully tapped his brother's name, pressing the phone to his ear and listening to the single ring before Dez picked up.

"Bulldog told me you're still inside. I'm coming to you. You somewhere safe?"

Sully kept his voice low, tried to keep the panic from showing through, but knew he'd failed when his voice caught on the first word. "Dez, I need you to talk me through something. I'm in an upstairs closet and he's here."

"You mean Thackeray?"

"No. The guy from Lockwood."

"Harry?"

"Who's Harry?"

"That's his name, Sull. I ran into Eddie Maberly on the street and he told me they called him Harbinger Harry; everyone figured he went nuts because of the stuff he could see."

Harry wasn't moving, which meant Sully wasn't either. But having Dez's voice in his ear provided just enough relief Sully could start picking through the terror as he searched for that so-far-elusive calm needed to build his defences against another possible possession.

"Sully? You still there?"

"Yeah."

"Keep talking to me, all right? I'm almost there."

"I still haven't found the thumb drive. But with all the stuff in this house, it's a needle in a haystack."

"You really think she would have taken it home? Maybe there's somewhere else."

"She kept it at her office, somewhere she could see it, make sure it was safe. I can't see her taking it somewhere she wouldn't be able to check on it. It's got to be here."

"Well, if it is, maybe we've just got to accept we're not going to find it."

"It's important, Dez. I know it is."

"Okay, listen, I'm at the end of the block. I'm going to ask to talk to Thackeray about his father. I'll get him to come outside which, given what you said about your earlier chat with him, shouldn't be that hard. Once that happens, you get yourself out, all right? No more searching, you hear me?"

"Believe me, right now all I want is to get out of here," Sully said. "Problem's going to be getting past Harry."

"Do what Raiya told you, man. Breathe and focus. You can do this."

"I'll try. Not guaranteeing anything, but I'll try."

Sully ended the call, not wanting to risk the possibility of Thackeray overhearing him. Losing Dez's voice left Sully alone in the dark with Harry, but buried within the fear the ghost created was an unexpected sense of calm born of the knowledge that his brother was nearby, ready to give him a hand—if only with the flesh and blood part.

But, for this moment and in this place, it was just the two of them, just him and this terrified-looking man standing within travelling distance of a breath should Harry have been capable of exhaling.

"Harry, I'm not sure if you can hear or understand me, but I need you to let me out of here, all right? I need to help Betty, but I can't unless you let me leave. Okay? Harry?"

Sully supposed he shouldn't have been surprised by the lack of response, by Harry's stubborn refusal to move from his spot in front of the door, leaving the younger man pinned back against the hamper.

That was bad enough, but bad only got worse when Harry shifted forward, closing the short space that separated the two of them.

There was no question what Harry intended and Sully allowed himself only the briefest moment of panic before deciding flight was the better option. Relying on science, on the fact the tightly packed molecules that made up flesh and blood beat the intangibility of spirit and energy, Sully pushed forward.

And hit a wall.

It was cold, like falling down on the icy surface of a frozen lake. And although he remained on his feet, falling was exactly what this felt like. Sully knew if it wasn't for Harry and whatever he was doing to defy the laws of physics, Sully would be lying collapsed on the floor of this closet.

Battling terror, he worked to drag a deep breath into his lungs, the intended first of many that would—he hoped—take him to that place where possession was rendered impossible.

But, as Harry's wide eyes reached his own, Sully knew getting to that place was the real impossibility.

THERE WAS no sign of Sully when Dez pulled up which, given the situation, was probably a good thing.

There was, however, a very obvious sign of Bulldog, waving his arms frantically from a bluff of trees in the park across the road.

Parking next to the house—no point hiding the obvious—Dez headed first to his friend.

"I don't have time for this, man," Dez said. "I need to get Thackeray outside so Sully can get out."

"So you're on top of this?"

"I talked to Sully, yeah. We can discuss what happened later."

"Okay. Just so you know, I told the guy my dog took off on me." Bulldog made a point of pulling out his beaten wallet and extracting a dogeared photograph of a black, long-haired mutt with soulful brown eyes and a lolling tongue.

"Where'd you get that? You don't have a dog."

"Found the photo lying in the street a couple years ago. The dog story's come in so handy in the past, I figured I could use the picture for a few extra points."

"You've taken lying to a whole new level."

"I prefer to call it 'occasionally necessary conversational creativity.' Anyway, I showed Schuster the photo, and I'm showing it to you too 'cuz I'm figuring he'll see us out here talking."

"Okay, got it, thanks. Head to the other side of the park and I'll pick you up there once I've got Sully."

With Bulldog on the move, Dez did the same, crossing the street back toward the Schusters' house where there was still no sign of his brother.

Dez made for the side door, deciding it gave Sully the best option to get out an upper floor window unnoticed, the quiet park across the road making the front a better choice for escape than on most properties. He was relieved when Thackeray came to the door almost immediately.

Dez hadn't had a chance to open his mouth before Thackeray proved Bulldog correct, that he'd been watching. "I didn't see the guy's dog, all right?"

"Good to know, but I didn't come here about that," Dez said. "I've got something I wanted to discuss with you that's a little more important than lost dogs. You have a minute?"

"I was just down at the station because I was told someone wanted to talk to me about the investigation. I sat there with my thumb up my ass for twenty minutes before someone finally came and told me no one had time to talk to me, and to call some jerk named Raynor later. If you're here to tell me to go back, you can forget it. I'm done with cops for today."

"I didn't come here to tell you to go back. And I'm not here to speak to you about the investigation into your mom's death. I wanted to ask about your dad, actually."

Thackeray's eyes snapped onto Dez's before narrowing perceptibly. "What about him?"

Dez, still conscious of allowing Sully the needed escape, motioned to two chairs on the veranda. "Mind if we sit?"

Thackeray looked no less suspicious, but agreed to the conversation anyway, and Dez guessed the fact the other man was shutting the door behind himself and lowering into one of the chairs had more to do with his own curiosity than a particular desire to cooperate.

Dez took the remaining chair. It resembled something he'd seen in his grandparents' old house, and he sat gingerly lest the object's obvious age rendered it too fragile for his solid weight.

"Your father is Harry Schuster, right?"

"What's this about?"

"I can't get into details just yet."

Thackeray crossed his arms. "Then neither can I."

Dez considered how best to move forward, decided some quid pro quo was likely necessary. "His name came up in an investigation recently. There's no file started at this point. I'm just making some inquiries. Someone reported he attacked them."

"That's impossible."

"Because he's at Lockwood?"

Thackeray had yet to uncross his arms. "Because he's physically incapable of doing anything other than drooling."

"The complainant said Harry seemed plenty capable of getting around. Does he have some sort of physical disability?"

"Sure, if a severe stroke counts. He had one years back, never recovered. He sits in a wheelchair all day and stares at the wall.

We used to put the TV on for him, mostly to make ourselves feel better. I doubt he had any clue what was on it. Once he got to be too much, Lockwood agreed to take him. They give him a nice window to look out. Not that it means much."

"You're sure he's not aware of anything?"

"My mom used to think he was more aware than we realized, that he was just trapped inside himself somewhere, but I think she just said that to keep herself sane. There was no sense both of them ending up in the loony bin."

"How long ago did he have the stroke?"

"Must be close to fifteen years now. I was a teenager."

"How old was he?"

"I can't remember, exactly. I'm not good with dates. But he would have been a little over forty, I think."

"Seems young for a stroke."

"Not for him," Thackeray said. "The way his brain worked—or didn't work, depending how you view things—I'm surprised he didn't have one sooner."

"What do you mean?"

Dez was reaching, he knew that. And apparently so did Thackeray.

"Look, I don't get what this has to do with whatever you're investigating. I told you he's incapable of attacking anyone. If you don't believe me, ask Dr. Gerhardt at Lockwood. I don't think he ever had good news for us about Dad's condition."

Dez gave it a moment, trying to figure out a next move. There was no good way to go about it, come right down to it, no way to find out what he needed without giving away more than he was comfortable revealing.

In the end, Sully solved it for him—although he created a whole new problem in the process.

Thackeray's attention was caught by the nearby sound of a vehicle door shutting, causing him to crane his neck toward the front of the house where he'd parked his car. Whatever he saw had him up and out of his chair with a shouted, "Hey!"

Dez followed, assuming someone was making off with the man's vehicle. His first thought was that he'd see Bulldog's stout form behind the wheel.

Who he saw instead was Sully.

Thackeray's eyes shifted wildly between Dez and his vehicle, now leaving its spot on the street and accelerating away. "He's stealing my car!"

The assessment was unnecessary and yet Dez realized he'd needed the verbal nudge to move past the shock at seeing his brother committing auto theft. It wasn't something Sully would do.

It *really* wasn't something Sully would do.

Dez ran for the cruiser and was behind the wheel and starting the vehicle before he realized Thackeray had gotten in beside him. There was no time to argue the fact, to order or wrestle the guy out of the car, and so Dez simply took off after Thackeray's beater.

The reason for the inexplicable theft was becoming increasingly and terrifyingly obvious to Dez, but he asked the question anyway.

"Hey, Thackeray? Did that used to be your dad's car, by chance?"

"Yeah, why?"

The affirmation, while expected on some level, nonetheless left Dez sitting in a cold chill. The last time Harry had possessed Sully, it had nearly killed him.

What it meant this time remained to be seen.

17

IT HAD BEEN years since Harold Schuster had last been behind the wheel, and it showed.

Thackeray's inherited car, a 1993 Toyota, swerved several times, narrowly missed two parked cars and blew through a stop sign before it started to show signs of corrected driving.

Dez wavered back and forth between thoughts of flipping on his lights and siren and simply following silently, wanting to attract as little attention to his brother—and to himself—as possible. Proper procedure was to call this in as a vehicle theft in progress, but that would mean alerting his colleagues to the fact his brother was behind the wheel of the car in question. Setting aside the fact no one besides Dez was likely to buy into the fact his brother was possessed by the wandering spirit of a man in a semi-comatose state, Sully was also a suspect in a serious crime. This was just the sort of thing Raynor would be looking for, an excuse to arrest and charge Sully properly, to hold him in custody so he could try to wrest a confession out of him on Betty's murder.

And it didn't help the optics of the situation, Sully breaking into the house of his dead boss and taking off in her son's car.

Dez figured he'd better try to get a handle on just how bad the damage was. "Do you know who's behind the wheel up there?"

Thackeray's eyes, when Dez looked to his right, were glued to the back of his Toyota. "Damn right I do. I saw him getting in. It's that guy from the Black Fox. The one who worked with my mom, Sullivan something or other. He was at my place two days ago. Now I'm wondering what he's got to do with all of this. Makes me think he was just there to scope it out."

Damn.

"Shouldn't you be trying to pull him over?" Thackeray asked. "You don't even have your lights and siren on."

"I'm trying not to spook him." It was a lousy attempt at an explanation and Dez knew it.

Unfortunately so did Thackeray. "That's bullshit. What the hell is going on here?"

Dez used a few silent seconds to consider his options and discovered he had none. None but the truth. "Listen, man, there's something I think I'm going to have to tell you. Sully's actually my brother and he's not really himself right now. This is going to sound weird but I think he's possessed."

Thackeray's response was about what Dez expected, the words proving enough to draw the man's eyes from his stolen car to zero in on the police officer beside him. "What the hell is this?"

"I know it sounds crazy."

"Crazy doesn't even begin to cover it."

That was probably true, and so Dez did what he could to fill in the rest, providing Thackeray with a brief history of what had happened and what they'd learned since the initial break-in and Betty's subsequent shooting.

By the end of it, Dez wasn't sure he was any further ahead in convincing the man, who sat firmly in silence as Dez continued to trail the Toyota at a distance.

Dez had never been what anyone would consider patient, and he quickly found his brain squirming with the lack of response. "You get all that?"

Another couple of seconds passed before Thackeray answered. "So you're trying to tell me my father's ghost or spirit or whatever is leaving his body and possessing your brother?"

"Yeah. Look, I wouldn't buy it either if I hadn't seen it with my own eyes."

"Maybe your brother's just crackers or something. Ever occur to you he's got some sort of dissociative disorder, one of those split personality things?"

"That wouldn't explain his seeing your father all those times."

"What you're telling me doesn't explain it either," Thackeray said. "He's still alive, so how can he be a ghost?"

"We're working on that. We talked to someone who wondered whether it might be because he was psychic though, and someone else told me Harry used to be able to see ghosts and predict the future. So I'm wondering whether that theory might hold up. I mean, what if he is like your mom said, completely aware and just trapped inside himself? Maybe he's figured out a way to leave his body."

"And possess random people?"

"Sully's not random," Dez said. "He's like your dad. He's got a gift."

"More like a curse." The words had been muttered, but loudly enough Dez had no trouble making them out.

"It's not easy for Sully, either," Dez said. "It took him years to get a grip on it, and he's still not all the way there. I mean, this wouldn't be happening now if he had."

Thackeray slumped in his seat, looking like a man who wanted to be anywhere else. "It probably would. They used to call him Harbinger Harry. He'd go into these trances like some bargain-bin Nostradamus and walk around the neighbourhood at all hours, muttering predictions. Spooked the hell out of people and made life at school a real bitch for me. He was exhausted all the time, self-medicated with sleeping pills and other garbage. But nothing helped. Mom used to say his gift, or whatever it was, burned through him. Doctors said all the pills caused the stroke.

Mom always believed it was more than that, that it had something to do with all the crap he saw."

Dez thought back to what Lowell had said about Sully, to that unsettling conversation about having him committed. "So no one ever talked about having your dad put in Lockwood? I mean, before the stroke?"

"Oh, lots of people talked about it. People at school, people in the park, people in the stores, people on the street. Everyone had an opinion on the matter and everyone felt the need to share. With me at least. My mom would have told them to take a flying fuck."

The accuracy of the comment regarding Betty's likely response drew an unexpected chuckle from Dez. "Yeah, I could see that. Betty obviously wasn't having it."

"She figured she could help him handle it. Turned out she was wrong. In the end, it took my father somehow managing to slash his wrists. It was Dr. Gerhardt and the guy supplying my father's meds who convinced my mom he should go into Lockwood."

Dez had already paid a visit to Gerhardt and was in no rush to see him again anytime soon. "Who was supplying the drugs?"

It took what felt like a long time for Thackeray to supply the name and, when he did, it had the sound of a man spitting out spoiled meat. "Lowell Braddock."

This time, it was Dez who fell into silence, shock at the revelation robbing him of thought and any immediate verbal response.

Thackeray, prison having fast-tracked his education in the subtle art of people-reading, was on it before Dez could recover. "You know him."

Dez thought about it, decided lying was off the table, too many truths having already been shared between cop and ex-con. "He's my uncle."

"Son of a bitch." And, just like that, the shaky trust Dez had built with Thackeray was gone, the man's voice resuming the edge it had possessed in those first moments on the veranda. "What the hell do the two of you want from me? What are you after here, huh?"

"We're trying to figure out what happened to your mom. The sergeant in charge of the investigation is wrongly assuming Sully had something to do with it, and he's going full bore trying to prove it."

"And he's wrong," Thackeray said. "Your brother didn't do it."

It was neither a question nor an observation of Dez's belief. It was a statement.

"You know," Dez said. "How?"

"I've met killers. I was on remand with a couple, spent time in prison with others. Sullivan's no killer." Thackeray paused a moment, as if thinking through what he wanted to say next. "Look, I know what it is to be wrongly accused. I didn't do what they accused me of either. You cops do that, get something in your heads and twist everything you find to fit it."

Conditioning over a frequent accusation had Dez meeting it with his usual defence. "No, we don't." Then, he considered Raynor. "Most of the time, anyway."

Up ahead, the Toyota navigated a turn which would lead to the freeway and, from there, toward New Town, KR's grandly designed and relatively new downtown core. Dez couldn't imagine the Harry Schuster he'd heard described spending much, if any, time in New Town. Someone like him would have been the sore thumb on an otherwise lily-white and well-manicured hand.

"Why would he be heading toward New Town?" Dez asked.

"How should I know? He's your brother."

"Right now, I think he's your father. Do you have any idea what he might want, what he might be after?"

"I never really knew my dad. He was already starting to lose it by the time I was old enough to really get to know him. We didn't exactly sit around and have long heart-to-hearts."

"And you don't visit him now?"

"What for? He wouldn't be aware of me being there, so why bother?"

"You're sure about that?"

"Not really your business, is it?" Thackeray said. "Mind your own."

Dez took a quick glance at the man beside him, eyes staring straight ahead at the back of the car. "You do appreciate, right now at least, your business and mine are pretty much intertwined."

Despite the truth of the comment, it wasn't enough to pull answers from Thackeray. And so the two of them remained quiet until they followed the Toyota into the northern edge of New Town, joining the slow sweep of traffic fighting to make headway at the start of end-of-day rush hour. New Town wasn't Dez's patch, but he'd spent enough time here to expect what they were getting, which was an increase in traffic snarls the further they crawled into the area's core. At this pace, it was just possible Dez could jump out, run to the Toyota, and drag his brother out. But every time he considered doing so, traffic opened up and sent them further forward.

Not until they approached a major intersection, one that sat at the very centre of New Town, connecting two major arteries, did the situation take a turn for the absolute worst.

Dez knew Sully or Harry, or whoever he was, had to know he was being followed by a police vehicle, and yet he'd avoided any real dangerous driving, limiting traffic infringements to a disinclination to signal. But now, he was up there blowing the start of a red light.

The two cars in front of Dez stopped as required and he flipped on his lights and blared his siren for a couple seconds to try to create the opening he needed to continue the semi-pursuit.

But the driver at the front of the line failed to notice immediately—long enough that New Town rush-hour drivers in the crossing lanes had already moved forward where they were now stuck in the middle of a crowded intersection, waiting on a light to change somewhere up ahead. That left Dez sitting here, watching helplessly as the Toyota maneuvered into a rare gap in traffic, managed a left-hand turn and disappeared from sight.

Dez slammed a hand against the steering wheel, the movement and the accompanying curse causing Thackeray, just visible in Dez's peripheral vision, to jump.

"What now?" Thackeray asked. "He's still got my car."

The answer hit Dez out of nowhere, had him whipping out of the traffic lane into a ten-minute loading zone outside one of the high-rise office towers. Pulling the keys, he issued a quick direction to Thackeray. "Wait here. I think I know where he's headed."

"Screw that. If my parole officer sees me sitting in a cop car, she'll want my ass in her office in five minutes."

"Suit yourself," Dez said. "But I can't wait for you. I think he's heading to my uncle's office."

For whatever reason, the theory proved sufficient to cause Thackeray to rethink any intention of joining in a foot pursuit, allowing Dez to sprint unhindered through the solid stretch of stalled home-goers as he crossed six lanes of traffic on each of the two major streets.

The high-rise housing LOBRA Pharmaceuticals's head office was visible, one of several towers glinting in the late afternoon sun. By the time he got close enough to see the main entrance, Dez had worked up a sweat.

While he ran, it had occurred to him there was another reason Harry had targeted Sully. Besides being more open to possession than a disciplined psychic or a non-gifted person, Sully was Lowell's foster nephew. If Harry wanted at Lowell, Sully could be the in he needed for easy access.

Dez's suspicions were confirmed as he spotted the Toyota parked a little crookedly outside the building's entrance. His heart, already thudding against his chest wall thanks to the physical exertion, picked up the pace as he saw no sign of Sully.

Dez yanked open one of the doors that made up a portion of

the building's glass-fronted north side and scanned the building's lobby for his brother.

He recognized one of the building's uniformed security team members hovering near the front desk. The man was staring in the direction of the elevators and, as he shifted his gaze back to the front entrance and the newest visitor, Dez noticed the bewildered expression of raised eyebrows and parted lips.

"You looking for your brother?"

"Where'd he go?"

Dez listened to the answer as he rushed past, headed for the elevators. "Mr. Braddock's office. He looked pretty wild."

Dez tapped the button repeatedly for the top floor, the display above the four separate doors counting down numbers at a maddening crawl. It was end of shift for many and it was clear employees were leaving the building for the day, tying up the lifts as they made to head down to the underground parkade.

"How long ago?" Dez shouted to the security guard.

"Only about a minute before you got here. Why? Should I be concerned?"

Dez kept the thought to himself: *God, I hope not*. Aloud, he said only, "Family thing. I'll handle it."

One of the elevators finally arrived, after heading first to the parking levels, and Dez was greeted by an empty car. Praying no one else had pressed the "up" button on any of the twenty-two floors separating lobby from executive offices, Dez watched the display as it counted toward his destination.

Luck was on his side, and he made it to the top floor without further disruptions, the elevator emitting a chirpy ding, which sounded out of place given the tension of the situation.

As anticipated, he arrived to an anxious-looking receptionist who, seeing him, pointed weakly in the direction of the hall leading to the offices.

Dez didn't bother to ask for details of his brother's arrival. Already he could hear signs of a struggle and it only intensified as he raced down the hall in the direction of his uncle's huge corner office.

Lowell was a big man, nearly as tall and muscular as his elder brother, Flynn. But even he was having a hard time warding off the attack from his small-by-comparison foster nephew as Sully strained to break Lowell's hold on his left wrist. Clenched in Sully's fingers was a long and dangerously pointed letter opener.

Dez didn't stop to yell a command, merely rushed forward as Lowell succeeded at last in using his free hand to shove Sully back a couple feet. It was all Dez needed to execute the tackle, taking his brother to the ground and relying on the solid weight of thick muscle to hold him there. Ordinarily, that would have been more than enough, many a lighthearted, brotherly wrestling match ending with a tap-out from Sully once they reached this point. But not today. Although Dez was sitting heavily on his brother's waist and hips and had Sully's wrists pinned to the floor, the younger man was still fighting. What was more, he was succeeding in lifting Dez a few inches into the air. It wasn't much and Dez didn't think there was any huge risk he would end up being bucked off, but Sully shouldn't have been able to budge him at all.

Focused as he was on his brother, Dez didn't dare look away to see what was keeping Lowell. "I could use some help here."

Lowell materialized at his side. "Think you can hold him still long enough for me to get at a vein?"

Dez risked looking away from Sully for a moment, enabling him to see the syringe in his uncle's hand. "What the hell is that?"

"It's a sedative. If you can't hold him, tell me, and I'll try for the hip instead. Vein would put him under quicker though."

Lowell knelt on Sully's right arm while Dez shifted his grip entirely to the left, placing the full weight of his upper body against Sully's shoulder and wrist as Lowell moved in with the syringe.

Sully had yet to speak, the sounds he was making restricted to grunts from the struggle. But now, with the needle moving in, words formed, the same two as the last time—"blue room"—

uttered repeatedly through a voice that sounded nothing like his own.

Dez fought to hold the arm steady as Lowell pierced the flesh near the crook of Sully's elbow, bringing on a fresh attempt at escape. But even Harry's frighteningly strong influence wasn't enough to shift two large men. Dez observed the liquid sedative slowly leave the syringe and disappear into Sully's arm.

"It's okay, Sull," Dez said as he watched the drug take effect, his brother's increasingly unfocused eyes losing the battle as they finally slid shut and remained that way.

Sully's voice changed in the moments before unconsciousness slid fully over him, becoming softer as he muttered just one word, the name a question. "Dez?"

"I've got you, buddy. You're okay."

Dez maintained both grip and pressure until he felt Sully go completely limp beneath him, body sinking bonelessly into the area rug.

Lowell slumped back against his desk, exhaling a slow but heavy breath through pursed lips. Dez felt for the pulse at Sully's neck, relieved to feel it slowing until it maintained a solid and healthy beat against his fingertips.

"How long does this stuff last?"

Lowell reached up and back, depositing the used syringe atop his desk. "Not that long, probably only an hour or two."

"Probably? You don't know?"

"I've never had to personally use it before."

"Are you in the habit of keeping injectable sedative in your office?"

Lowell's smile didn't move beyond a slight upturn of lips. "I've had my share of threats over the years. You never know when someone's going to burst in and come after you. I just never thought it would be my nephew. Thanks for getting here when you did. I don't think I could have held him off for long."

Dez didn't respond directly to his uncle's expression of gratitude, mind shifting instead to next moves. "If there's only an hour at the lower end, I'd like to get him back to Mom and Dad's pretty quick. Is there a less obvious way out of here so I don't have to be lugging him through the lobby with everyone around?"

"Dez." The way Lowell spoke his name was heavy with meaning, with concern not yet spoken and worry for what would happen once it was.

And Dez knew without having to ask that he didn't want to listen. He couldn't. "I need to get my cruiser and bring it around. Is there another way out of here?"

"Dez, you know we can't keep going like this. Sullivan's out of control. He just tried to kill me, for God's sake."

"It wasn't him, Uncle Lowell."

Lowell made no attempt to hide his incredulity as his eyes moved from Dez to Sully and back again. "Sure as hell looks like him."

"It's like what happened the other night when he slashed up. He was possessed. The guy who's doing it is making him do these things, stuff he wouldn't do otherwise. You know Sully. This isn't him."

"Dez, there's no such thing as ghosts, all right? Please, listen to me on this. I love Sullivan, too, and I'd like to believe him, but there's absolutely no scientific basis for anything you're saying."

"Okay, how about the fact he was using his left hand to try to stab you? Sully's right handed. Or there's this." Dez reached into the right, front pocket of Sully's jeans, extracting the Swiss Army knife he kept there for some of the odd jobs he was faced with at the Black Fox. "He always carries a knife on him, yet he went for a letter opener."

"Have you ever heard of dissociative identity disorder? It used to be called multiple personality disorder."

"I know what it is."

"It's often mistaken for possession, and there are documented cases of patients switching their dominant hand during an episode of fragmentation."

Dez loved his uncle, but there were times his patience faded with Lowell's opinions and constant need to be right. "Look, Uncle Lowell. You don't need to explain this to me, okay? I know about DID, and Sully doesn't have it. I know my brother. Now, are you going to help me here or not?"

Lowell's sigh was both frustrated and resigned. "I'll help you get him down to the parking garage on the executive office's private elevator, and you can bring your car down there to get him. But I can't look the other way on this much longer, Dez. By all rights, I should report this to the police. I can't promise no one else did."

Dez considered that and hoped the fact a uniformed officer had run in after Sully had been enough to keep people's fingers away from their phones' 9-1-1 buttons. If it hadn't been, there wasn't much he could do about the situation but convince Lowell not to lay charges.

"I swear to you, it wasn't Sully," he said. "We're working at getting to the bottom of this but, in the meantime, I'm asking you to trust me. I'm sorry this happened, but I'm begging you to just let me and Mom and Dad handle this for now. Okay?"

Lowell was silent long enough that Dez felt the creep of anxiety at the possibility his stubborn uncle would decide taking matters into his own hands was the only way to help Sully. In the end, though, Dez's pleas did not fall on deaf ears.

"I'll do what you're asking, Dez," he said, but then added the caveat Dez realized he himself had used. "For now. But I'm warning you, find a way to get Sully the help he needs, or I'm going to get it for him—with or without your consent."

18

When Sully opened his eyes, his surroundings, for a few moments, swam in front of him.

He blinked, clearing both his vision and his brain until memory returned like a jolt of electricity, a lightning strike through a storm-blackened sky. But it wasn't Harry Schuster's wide, terrified eyes and baggy, yellow hospital clothing illuminated in front of him.

He was instead greeted by the familiar, by his mother's concerned face moving in closer for assessment. The woman's expression did nothing to relieve the cold dread that dropped over Sully with the full return of consciousness.

His too-quick attempt to sit up was prevented by his mother's gentle but firm hand on his shoulder. "How are you feeling, Sully?"

"Mom? How did I get here?"

"Dez brought you over."

"When? What time is it?"

"He dropped you off about half an hour ago. It's getting close to six."

"But I went over to Betty's a little after three."

"Is that the last thing you remember?"

"Sort of, I guess. I mean, uh ...." He was uncertain how or even if he should be telling his mother—the wife of the deputy police chief—about the fact he'd committed a break and enter.

But there had never been any hiding from Mara—particularly when she'd managed to corner Dez first. "I know about you sneaking into Betty's, Sully. What I need to know is whether you remember anything about what happened after that."

"No, nothing. God, did I do something?"

"You could say that. But Dez says it wasn't you. He said it was Betty's husband."

"The last thing I remember was him coming at me in the closet where I was hiding. Is Dez okay? Bulldog?"

"They're both fine, although Dez was pretty shaken up."

"Where is he?"

"He had to go pick up Bulldog and drop off the cruiser. His shift ended while he was in the middle of dealing with this. Luckily for him—for all of us—it was a quiet shift. I don't know what he would have told dispatch if they'd tried to assign him a call."

"What happened after that? After Harry took over, I mean?"

"Dez told your dad and me you took off in Thackeray's car. Dez followed but lost you downtown. Luckily, he figured out you were headed for Lowell's office."

"Why would Harry want to go there?"

"Apparently, Lowell was involved in getting Harry committed to Lockwood," Mara said. "He'd been supplying Harry's meds back then, until Harry took a turn for the worse and attempted suicide. It was the last straw for Betty, and she decided Lowell and Dr. Gerhardt were making sense in recommending Harry go to stay at Lockwood. Dez thinks Harry has it in for Lowell because of it and used you to get to him. As his nephew, you have easy and immediate access to him."

"I didn't hurt him, did I?"

"No. Dez got there first. Lowell was holding you off, but only just. It took both of them to restrain you so Lowell could sedate you. Lowell agreed to keep what happened to himself, and Dez brought you back here."

Sully rubbed his palms against his eyelids, sealing out the image of Mara. He wished it was as easy to make the rest of this disappear. "I'm sorry. God, Mom, I'm sorry. I didn't mean for any of that to happen."

Her gentle hand settled on his shoulder, fingers kneading in and working to rub away tension. "I know, kiddo. I know."

Mara left the room with a promise of returning with a glass of water, allowing Sully a minute or two to pull himself together.

She wasn't gone long, and she pressed a glass of cold water into Sully's hand as she sat on the edge of the bed. "Drink this. Lowell thought you might be a bit dizzy or have a headache when you woke up. I don't want to give you anything right now since I'm not sure exactly what you were injected with. He's the chemist, not me."

Sully nodded and downed half the glass. Mara waited until the glass was safely on the nightstand before launching into another line of questioning.

"Dez tells me Lowell's been giving you sleeping pills for a while. Why didn't you tell us?"

"I didn't want you guys to worry. I have trouble sleeping sometimes with the stuff I see, and there are times when I get to the point where I can't take it anymore. The pills help. I don't abuse them. They're just for emergencies, when things are really bad."

"Here's the thing, Sully. Flynn told me that after Betty was killed, a search of your apartment turned up some pills. When no one was able to figure out what they were, they were handed off to a forensic drug expert. No conflict since she isn't associated with LOBRA. Flynn said she'd never seen anything like it before, that it appears to be a synthetic compound of some sort. I don't understand this chemistry stuff, but she said her initial tests showed some similarities between this drug and LSD. As such, she said she would be concerned someone using it might experience visual, auditory or other sensory hallucinations. Flynn said the lead investigator on Betty's shooting seemed quite interested in that information."

"Then someone must have planted that stuff. I haven't been hallucinating, Mom. I've never made up anything."

"I know you haven't made up the things you see, Sully. But things have been happening lately that don't make sense, even for you. You've never been possessed before. Until recently, we didn't even know it could really happen, not like this. You always said you believed ghosts could impact people's emotions, maybe even their thoughts, or that they could make people sick over time. But you thought the sort of possession where a person is completely taken over didn't really happen."

"That was before it happened to me," Sully said. "The longer I do this, the more I realize there's a lot I don't know."

"Sully, what if there's something else going on here? What if whatever you've been taking is responsible for what you've been experiencing lately? I'm not saying the man you saw wasn't real. Obviously, he was. I mean, you and Dez found him and identified him. But maybe you saw a picture of him somewhere and—"

"I didn't make him up, Mom. He's really been appearing to me. I've only taken a pill one time in the last few days."

"The night you tried to kill yourself at Dez's, when you said Harry possessed you."

"Yeah, but I've been seeing him plenty when I haven't taken anything. I didn't take one of my pills today, and all this happened anyway."

"Maybe the effects of the stuff are longer-lasting than anyone realized. If those pills are the ones you've been taking, LSD use often results in flashbacks. Maybe this is something similar."

"Mom, I know what this is and what it isn't, all right? Please. I need you to believe me."

"I do. I do believe you. But there are still questions here, and your dad and I are worried about you."

"Is he here?"

"He was," Mara said. "He left."

There was something in her expression, the way her lips drew in, a slight tension at the corners of her eyes. She was worried about something and, he suspected, she was equally worried about sharing it with him.

"Mom? What's going on?"

"Nothing, Sully. I need you to get some rest, okay?"

"Not until you tell me what's wrong."

"There's nothing wr—"

"I know you, all right? And I'm not stupid. Something happened, didn't it? Mom?"

She drew in a breath and let it out slowly, eyes fixed on him as if weighing how much, if anything, she should tell him. In the end, he must have passed her silent test.

"Your dad was very upset when he left," she said. "He wouldn't talk to me about it. He just said he needed to see Lowell, and would discuss it when he got back. He wanted to talk to you about something he found in your pocket."

Sully didn't typically carry anything but his wallet, keys and folding knife, so he was left at a loss as to what his mother was talking about. "What did he find?"

"I didn't see, not really. After Dez left, Dad was trying to get you comfortable and he emptied your pockets. He knows you carry that utility knife, and he wanted to make sure you didn't hurt yourself. Only he pulled something else out of your other pocket first. He didn't say anything about it, just went down to the office. A few minutes later, he stormed out, so I went to the office to see if he'd left any clues behind. All I could see was that the computer was on, set to the home screen. The only thing I can think is when he was going through your pockets, he found a thumb drive."

Sully wasn't going to manage any more rest, not with the possibility Flynn had found a thumb drive—*the* thumb drive.

Mara had been trying Flynn's phone repeatedly, but he hadn't picked up, nor had he responded to her voicemail pleas to call her back. Sully watched his mother pace as he dug through what he could on the desktop computer his father had recently used. He was no computer expert, but he wasn't wholly useless with them either, and he could find no trace of recent activity save the likelihood an external drive had been used.

Now there was nothing left to do but wait and worry.

"Mom, how upset was he when he left?" he asked.

Mara's face said it all as she gave up pacing and dropped heavily into the chair across the desk from Sully. She provided the verbal answer Sully probably didn't need. "Very. I can't remember the last time I saw him that angry. He could barely speak. I'm worried, Sully."

"Did you try phoning Lowell?"

"No answer there either, and your Aunt Kindra is having a very late day at work, so she isn't sure. She said she'd try Lowell and call me back once she spoke to him, but I haven't heard anything from her since, and now I can't reach *her*. I don't know what else to do. I was tempted to drive over, but I couldn't leave you."

"I'm awake now," Sully said. "Let's go."

They were in Mara's car, five minutes on the road, when it occurred to Sully they should notify Dez. Mara shot that down.

"I thought of that, but I decided I didn't want to call until I had some answers. You know how he can get. He handles stress fine on the job, but he's never been good at dealing with family problems."

Sully reluctantly agreed. If Flynn was agitated about something—a rare occurrence in Sully's memory—then Dez would quickly reach the same point if notified. Even so, it was likely Dez would want to check back in on Sully once he picked up his own vehicle, and it wouldn't be any better should Dez walk into an empty house and be left to worry about what that meant.

Sully was about to suggest they call Dez when Mara's phone rang.

"Oh, thank God," she said as she started to dig the phone out of her purse. Sully took over the search to allow Mara to continue driving and, when he at last found the smartphone, he didn't think she'd like what showed on the screen.

"It's Dez," he said.

Mara's sigh revealed distress rather than relief. "You'd better answer. Maybe he's heard from your dad."

Sully was already doing that, clicking the talk button as he lifted the phone to his ear. "Dez?"

"Sully, it's Dad! You need to hurry! It's Dad!"

Sully reacted immediately to his brother's panic, hand flying out and landing on Mara's shoulder. He felt the tension there and realized she'd heard Dez's voice even though the phone was not set to speaker mode.

"What happened?" Sully asked.

"Just hurry, okay? University Hospital. I'm heading there now. Hurry!"

"Dez, what happened?"

"Lowell called. He said Dad had a heart attack. It's not good. Jesus Christ, Sully. He said it's not good."

Something flashed in Sully's peripheral vision, and he knew without looking a third person was now with them in the car. And for the first time since he'd begun seeing him, Sully prayed it was Harry sitting in the backseat.

He stopped halfway to checking, unable to cope with a wholly new terror, one that dwarfed anything the vision of Harry had ever caused in him. Because he knew without the need to see. He'd spent much of his life protected and guided by Flynn Braddock, the man who had saved him, who had given him the family, the love and the hope Sully had never known and likely would otherwise have never found.

He would know his dad anywhere. And even if he couldn't bring himself to turn to see his face, he recognized the strong, lightly freckled hand that reached forward, settling over the fingers Sully still held against Mara's shoulder.

The hand remained there, fixed in Sully's wide-eyed stare for perhaps a minute. Then it was gone.

And Sully knew his dad was too.

19

Dez flew through traffic, four-way flashers blinking as he closed the distance to the hospital.

He didn't know what he'd find there, but he was experienced enough in life to fear the worst. There had been Lowell's tone for starters, deadened rather than panicked, the sound of shock or perhaps of the acceptance of a brutal truth. Then there was the fact Flynn and Lowell's father had died young of a sudden heart attack. They had blood pressure issues in this family, he knew that; he had his own to contend with. But Flynn had always managed to regulate his stress, was far more laid back than Dez. Sure, Flynn had moments periodically where he blew his stack, but those were few and far between, and he always needed some real incentive to get there.

He knew pessimism would be the safer approach, but Dez clung to hope, to the possibility it was just a colossal case of heart-burn that had led Lowell to request an ambulance. He passed that wishful theory on to Eva when he called to tell her, and she'd proven how well she knew him in opting to avoid pointing out the flaws in his suggestion. She didn't agree with him, either; he was aware of that. But she knew, as Dez did, hope was the only thing keeping him from blowing every maddening red light he came upon or screaming at slow-moving pedestrians crossing his path.

But hope could be an enemy sometimes, and it came at him with a sharpened blade the moment he found his uncle in the emergency room waiting area.

"Where's Dad?"

"Dez ..."

"Where is he?"

Lowell grasped his shoulder and attempted to guide him to a chair, but Dez wasn't moving, not for anything. He needed to see his dad and he needed to see him now.

"We need to talk."

"Not now. I need to see Dad."

"Dez, please. This is hard enough as it is. Please, son."

And it was there, the truth contained within Lowell's eyes, insisting on Dez's grasping it. It was exactly what he knew he couldn't do. "No."

"Dez—"

He didn't wait for the rest of Lowell's statement; he couldn't. He knew this ER well, had spent plenty of time here dealing with injuries to victims and suspects, as well as a few of his own. As he jogged through the department, scanning the faces inside the rooms for the one he was increasingly desperate to see, he struggled to ignore the sympathetic glances he was receiving from the nurses.

He found him in one of the trauma rooms, lying quietly upon the bed while a nurse gathered up items Dez recognized as his father's clothes. She looked up, her eyes enlarging and lips parting as a breath caught at the back of her throat. Behind him, he could hear rushed footfalls as Lowell, no doubt, caught up.

Dez stepped closer to his father, took his hand as he stared down into his face. He was still. So still.

Unnaturally still.

"Dez, I'm sorry."

"Why isn't anyone doing anything?" Dez asked. He broke his

gaze only long enough to fix the nurse in his glare, his agony finding an outlet in the words he shouted at her. "Why isn't anyone doing anything?"

"They tried, son," Lowell said as the nurse scurried off, closing the three men in the room. "They tried really hard. But there was nothing they could do. It happened so fast. I think he was gone within seconds, back at my place. He was a good man, a good brother. And he was a great husband and father to you guys. I'm so sorry. I'm so sorry, son."

Dez had been looking back down at his father's face, willing him to wake up, praying for a miracle, some sort of divine resurrection. But it wasn't coming, Flynn's body still, his hand limp, the chill of death beginning to creep in. And all Dez wanted to do now was to tear this room apart, to take it apart piece by piece until all that remained was him and his dad.

Instead, he turned on Lowell, his mind settling on one word, the last one his uncle had uttered. "I'm not your son."

"I know that. I didn't mean it like—"

But Dez wasn't listening, focus shifting again, this time to escape. He had to get away from here, from this place, his uncle, that body on the bed. He didn't know where he'd go, but anywhere was better than this.

He felt Lowell's hand on his arm, trying to hold him back, but it would have taken an entire army to stop him as he barrelled past and into the hall. One boot skidded on the waxed floor but he managed to catch himself before falling.

Then all he could think to do was run. It didn't matter he didn't know where he was going, what he was running to, not even what he was running from.

Nothing mattered.

Not anymore.

SULLY HAD HOPED to find Dez waiting for them at the hospital. Instead, they got Lowell.

Sully had a few inches on Mara, but she was doing her best to outpace him as they raced from the parking lot to the ER entrance. Sully had thought briefly about switching spots behind the wheel with Mara directly outside the entrance, which would have allowed her to go in more quickly while he looked for a parking spot. But he wanted to be there with her, didn't like the idea of her having to fall back on Lowell for support, even for a few minutes.

Because Sully knew what she faced going in there. He'd been working on getting his head around it himself since he'd seen that hand and felt Flynn's presence. For now, grief had taken a back seat to mounting anger. He didn't see ghosts unless they'd died at the hands of another person. If Flynn had died while in Lowell's company, then Lowell was responsible.

Lowell was waiting for them in the main waiting room, just inside the ER entrance. He got an arm around Mara and guided them down a hall to what Sully knew to be a soft room. Sully hated to think how many people had learned of loved ones' deaths in this little space; even more, he hated to think he was about to become one of them.

"Where's Flynn?" Mara asked. "I want to see him."

"Mara, there's something I need to tell you."

Mara must have read something in her brother-in-law's expression, because her face crumpled before Lowell had uttered the words, tears so far held in check at last giving way with the sob that tore from her throat.

"I'm so sorry, Mara. They tried but they couldn't save him."

"No."

"I'm so sorry. I'm so sorry, Mara."

Lowell tried to hug her, but she turned instead to Sully. Which was just as well, because Sully had been about to shove Lowell against a wall.

"What happened?" he asked. He could hear the accusation in his own voice and found he didn't care.

"We were arguing," Lowell said. "Things got a little heated and suddenly he just stopped and fell to the floor, hit his head pretty bad on the way down. The head injury looked bad, but I was more worried about why he collapsed in the first place. I remembered what happened with our dad, so I checked his heart immediately and it wasn't beating. I checked his carotid pulse as well, and same thing. I guess I've always been paranoid about going the way Dad did, so I keep epinephrine around, just in case. I injected some into Flynn, but I guess I was too late. It was so sudden, just seconds. I'm sorry there wasn't more I could do."

"What were you arguing about?"

"Sully, please," Mara said. "Not now." She pulled away from him to enable her to face Lowell. "Where's Dez?"

"He was here, but he left."

"He left?" Sully said.

"Ran off, to put it more accurately. I tried to run after him, but he was too fast and he took off in his SUV before I could catch up. I decided I needed to wait around here to talk to you."

Sully turned to Mara. "Mom, we need to find him."

"Eva's out looking," Lowell said. "She told me she'll call once she finds him. Listen, Mara, I think you should stay with Kindra and me for the time being. It'll be too hard going back home right now."

Mara nodded, but thankfully had a better solution to that immediate problem. "My sister's in town. I'll stay with her for now, but thank you for the offer."

She'd managed to get her emotions back under control, but lost it again as she made her next request. "I'd still like to see Flynn. Could you show me where he is?"

"Are you sure that's a good idea?"

One of the things Sully disliked about Lowell was the incessant need to control, not just his own business but that of others. Mara was a strong woman who knew her own mind, and the last thing she needed right now was to be treated like a fragile flower. "She wants to see him, Lowell. She doesn't need you to manage her, all right?"

Lowell looked for all the world like he'd been slapped, and Mara laid a gently restraining hand on Sully's chest. "Sully, it's okay. He's just trying to protect me."

"You don't need protecting." He didn't give voice to the thought that she definitely didn't need protecting by the man who was very likely responsible for their being here in the first place.

Lowell accepted Sully's assessment on that much, anyway, silently leading the way from the soft room and down a hall to one of several resuscitation rooms. He pointed to one with the door closed. "He's in there."

Mara nodded and took a deep breath as she stepped toward the door. Before she pushed it open, she snagged Sully's hand. "Do you want to come in?"

He shook his head, no. No way in hell. He had a hard enough time dealing with the walking dead; he didn't need the double dose. Mara nodded and squeezed his hand—or maybe he squeezed hers—before she pushed open the door. Sully spotted a flash of red hair and white freckled skin on the bed before he could look away.

Unfortunately for Lowell, he was where Sully's gaze settled.

Sully waited until Mara was fully inside the room, door shut behind her, before unleashing what he hadn't been able to in front of his mother.

"So what were you arguing about?"

Lowell blanched. Sully didn't fault him for that; he'd barely recognized the sound of his own voice, a low growl he didn't recall ever having made before.

"Sully, I don't think this is the time."

Sully took a step forward, causing Lowell to take one back until he was against the wall. "You don't get to decide the time, Lowell. I'm asking and I want an answer now. Where's the thumb drive?"

He saw the moment Lowell caught himself, mouth sealing into a line, brows crawling back down until they were in their natural position. It was the first indication of a lie to come. "What thumb drive?"

"You know damn well what thumb drive. Where is it?"

"I'm sorry, Sully. I don't know what you're talking about."

Sully had never been violent, had always been the sort of person to internalize rather than externalize torment, holding in and mentally evaluating rather than sharing his issues with others. But Lowell had just placed the last straw on the camel's back, and Sully felt it the moment something inside him broke.

He sprang forward, grabbing Lowell's shirt front and shoving him hard, back into the wall. Flynn appeared next to them, and Sully at last gave in, looking over at his father. Flynn, who knew Sully's limitations in his interactions with the dead, didn't try to speak, merely shook his head, no. And Sully could read it in his father's expression: "This isn't the way, Sully."

"Why didn't you take me with you?" Sully asked his father. "Why did you go by yourself?"

"Who are you talking to?" Lowell asked.

"You should have waited, Dad. I wish you'd waited for me."

Flynn reached out a hand as if to lay it along the side of Sully's head. There was nothing substantial to the touch, nothing but a sensation Sully could only describe as cold static. But the meaning behind it was there in Flynn's face, and Sully believed he could read his father's thoughts in his changing expressions, shifting from, "I'm sorry," to a more determined, "Find your brother."

The situation grew more complicated when Sully felt hands—these ones definitely physical—grasp his arms and pull him back, off of Lowell. This time, Sully was the one thrown back against the wall, putting him face to face with Sergeant Forbes Raynor.

"Are you all right, Mr. Braddock?" Forbes asked.

"Fine, thank you."

"Would you like to lay an assault charge?"

"No, of course not," Lowell said. "No harm done. Anyway, the boy's just suffered a loss."

"I heard," Forbes said. "I also heard him talking to air."

"As I said, he's just suffered a loss," Lowell said. "He's not rational right now."

"Interesting, isn't it?" Forbes said, before answering his own semi-question. "How, for some people under stress, violence is an automatic response." Forbes turned back to Sully, finally addressing him. "Now, I'm curious. Were you under any emotional strain before Betty was killed?"

"How dare you!"

Sully turned toward the voice as Forbes did, finding Mara standing there, face tear-streaked but set into a solid approximation of a mother bear prepared to defend a threatened cub. Forbes took a wise couple of steps away from Sully as Mara closed the gap, moving to stand at her son's side. "His father just died, and you choose this moment to level your ridiculous accusations at him? What's wrong with you?"

"Correct me if I'm wrong, but Deputy Chief Braddock isn't Sully's real father."

"He was every bit his real father, just as I am his mother," Mara said. "We raised him and we have always loved him as our own son. He has just as much right to grieve for his father as Dez does. Now I'd suggest you leave us the hell alone before I file a harassment complaint against you with the chief."

Sully suspected any complaints levelled against Forbes wouldn't hold much water, given his father's position as mayor and head of the police commission, but the threat seemed to be doing some good anyway.

"I'll give you some time tonight," Forbes said. "But I need to speak with Sullivan tomorrow."

He turned once again to face Sully. "I expect to see you at headquarters. Call me first thing to arrange a time." He glanced back at Mara, bowing his head as he spoke. "I am very sorry for your loss, ma'am."

Then he walked off, disappearing out the doorway at the end of the hall.

"Smarmy little bastard," Mara muttered.

Were this situation anything other than it was, the comment would have drawn a laugh from Sully; few people were less inclined to swear than Mara Braddock. That said, it was unlikely anyone in this ER was more entitled to it than she was at this moment.

She glared between Lowell and Sully, reserving her remaining fire for them. "I don't know what the hell was going on out here, but it ends now. Whatever happened this evening we will deal with later. Right now, this is all I can handle, and I'm not even sure I can do that. Sully, I need you to drive me over to Aunt Lyndsey's and then you need to help Eva find Dez. You can take my car and I'll have Lyndsey drive me around. If you or Eva find him before I do, you bring him to me so I can talk to him. Everything else can wait, you hear me?"

Sully nodded. No arguing with his mother when she looked at him like that. And no way he wanted to argue the point anyway. In his anger about Flynn's death, he'd lost momentary sight of his brother.

He wouldn't make that mistake twice.

20

It was close to eleven at night and the bars were in full swing.

Sully had talked to Eva and learned she was checking out a few pubs where she and Dez sometimes went for a drink on their date nights. She'd left Kayleigh with a neighbour who babysat for them and, like Sully, was operating under the assumption the little girl would be staying there tonight. None of them wanted her to have to see her father drunk, which was the state both Sully and Eva presumed Dez had put himself in by now.

He wouldn't be dealing with this well. Even a rudimentary knowledge of Dez would tell a person that much. For his part, Sully knew his own breakdown was waiting for him in the wings, standing there silently until the Dez-related drama was over. He was delaying the inevitable, using the drive and worry for his brother to keep him free for now of acceptance of the night's events, of all that would mean going forward.

Part of the problem—a huge part—was how to deal with his suspicions Lowell had caused his brother's death. Sully knew Mara, Dez and Eva would believe he could see Flynn; the biggest question was whether they'd be in any state right now to accept it. Sully and Lowell had next to no relationship, but Lowell was very much a part of everyone else's lives. They were devastated enough just coping with the death. They didn't need one more thing. Not yet.

At least not until Sully had something more solid than suspicion and a ghost.

It was too much to deal with now. It would be too much later as well, so he'd have to figure out a way to deal with it one piece at a time. The grief wouldn't wait long; soon, he would find somewhere private, somewhere no one would find him, to let it out.

But it would have to wait until Sully found Dez. He came first.

Sully had tried a few spots he and Dez had been for drinks when they'd wanted to avoid the Black Fox but, so far, he was coming up empty, no one having seen Dez for quite some time.

Sully thought through his brother's friends—most of whom were his work buddies—and wondered whether Dez might be with any of them. But he tossed the idea out the window pretty quickly. Dez was a social guy and, as a general rule, was not one to drink alone. He liked the company of friends, to be the centre of attention as he shared crazy stories from work or boasted about his daughter. But there would be nothing he'd be eager to share tonight, and he'd know he'd be lousy company.

Dez's buddies were people he enjoyed sharing the good times with, but Sully didn't think he'd take the bad to them. He had just a handful of people he trusted well enough for that. Sully was one, Eva obviously another. But Sully considered there was a third person Dez might not mind going to, a guy who wasn't likely to judge should Dez have a tearful breakdown in the midst of round seven.

Sully pulled over and dialled the number he had for Bulldog, hoping he'd been able to get his phone charged today. Bulldog didn't always have the money for bills, but Dez always ensured the guy's phone was topped up. He wasn't just his friend, after all; he was also his best contact on the street when it came to policing business.

Bulldog picked up just before the call went to voicemail.

"Hey, man," Sully said. "I'm looking for Dez. Have you seen him or heard from him?"

"As it happens, Sully, I can answer in the affirmative. I'm with him right now."

That would explain why Bulldog was keeping his voice low and why it had taken him a few rings to pick up. Bulldog sounded sober and Sully imagined he was keeping his head screwed on for Dez. Sully decided he owed the guy a steak dinner once things had settled a bit.

"Where are you?" he asked Bulldog.

"I was hoping you'd ask. I have no idea how I'm getting back to the city. No way in hell Copper's driving me anywhere, state he's in. I've never been here before, but I think I'm at your parents' place."

"On my way. I'll call Eva and Mom and see you in a few."

"Thanks. Oh, and Sully? We're not in the house. We're out back. Next to a river."

Sully felt a shiver run through him. Dez never went down there, not if he could help it. It held too many bad memories. Then again, it made sense in a way that was exactly where he'd go. He'd suffered his first major loss there, the spot they believed his five-year-old brother, Aiden, had fallen in and been swept away. Dez had never fully gotten past the death, had never stopped carrying the burden of guilt that first found footing inside him the day Aiden disappeared. Sully didn't believe for a moment Dez was there now to finally try to face up to the tragedy and his perceived role in it. More likely, he felt like he was sinking himself.

"Listen, I'm glad you called," Bulldog said. "My phone bill needs paid so I can take calls but not make them. Hurry, okay? I'm worried about him. He's kinda going off the rails here, and I can't get him to ease up on the drinking."

"I'll step on it, Bulldog. I'll be there as soon as I can."

Sully put his phone on speaker as he called both Eva and

Mara, allowing him to drive and talk at the same time. Everyone was headed out there now, Dez's makeshift intervention group.

Sully imagined at least one other member of that group was there already. Unfortunately, Flynn was no longer in a state to be able to help.

SULLY GOT THERE FIRST, which likely had something to do with his decimating the speed limit.

He kept up the pace on foot, jumping from Mara's car as soon as he'd skidded to a stop in the gravelled driveway and dashing around the house toward the waterway that ran on the far side of the expansive backyard.

The moon was nearly full, allowing Sully to make out the image of Dez sitting slouched on the reedy riverbank while, nearby, Bulldog stood silent vigil.

Dez's friend took a few more steps away from Dez as Sully approached, allowing the two to talk so as not to be overheard by the subject of their conversation.

"Glad you got here before the women," Bulldog said. "He's surpassed drunk and has moved firmly into the realm of asshole. I stopped trying to talk to him. Maybe you'll have more luck."

Sully wasn't so sure. Frankly, he couldn't remember Dez ever reaching the "realm of asshole" before. What that would mean for Sully's attempts to reach his brother remained to be seen, but he wasn't going down without trying.

Sully patted Bulldog on the arm and approached his brother's broad back. Dez sat with arms balanced atop drawn-up knees, one hand propping up his head while the other held a mostly empty forty-ounce bottle of dark rum.

Sully didn't bother to stand on ceremony, simply lowering into a spot next to Dez and roughly mirroring his posture.

"I said I don't want to talk anymore, Bulldog. Leave me the fuck alone."

"It's Sully, D."

Dez looked up and over. He'd been crying—heavily, if his swollen eyes and a nose that looked red even in the dark had anything to say about it. And he was certainly well past pissed at this point if the smell had anything to say about it. But it was the level of torment in his expression that toppled Sully, had him laying a hand against his brother's back.

"You know?" Dez asked.

Sully nodded. Neither of them was going to say it out loud. They didn't need to. Dez nodded his own reply and turned back to face the water. The moon was overhead, not at its peak yet, but far enough that it cast its sparkling glow on the water of the Kettle-Arm. It would have been beautiful were tonight's reality anything other than what it was, compounded by the drowning of a young boy at this location seventeen years ago. As it stood, there was little right now strong enough to pull either of them from the edge of this cliff. Sully could only pray he'd be able to give Dez something to hold onto.

"Eva and Mom are on their way," he said, hoping that would help, the reminder there were others left in this physical world who meant something.

"Fucking great," Dez muttered, the words slurred under the weight of alcohol. "That's fucking great, man. You call them?"

"Course I did. They're worried about you. We all are. We've been out looking for you for the past hour."

"I didn't need to be looked for. I just want to be left alone."

"So why drag Bulldog out here?"

Dez shrugged his response, and Sully dared to provide an answer to his own question. "You don't really want to be alone, Dez. You fear it. You always have."

"If I say I want to be alone, I mean it."

"You've got people who love you, and all we want is to see each other through this, okay? That's what family's for."

Dez turned on him and, this time, there was more than pain in his expression, lowered eyebrows and lips twisted into a snarl telling Sully he'd taken a bad step somewhere without knowing it. Whether it was intended or the result of intoxication, Dez's voice was a slurred bark. "Maybe I don't want to get through this! I'm sick of getting through losing the people I love! I'm done with it, okay? I can't do it anymore. I can't fucking do this anymore."

Sully tried to pull Dez into a hug but was shoved back, hard. "Leave me the fuck alone."

"I'm not going to leave you alone, Dez. I'm your brother. That means you're stuck with me when bad stuff happens. I know everything is really dark right now, but we'll get through this together, just like we've gotten through other stuff."

"Other stuff? What other stuff? There was nothing like this before with you and me. Nothing even close."

"There was for me," Sully said. "My whole life was black before I met you guys, before you took me in. All of you got me through, and you've been doing it ever since. You've always had my back, Dez, and I hope you know I've got yours. I'm not going to let you fall."

"It's too late for that." As if to prove it, Dez lifted the bottle and took a long pull.

"Dez—"

"I mean it, Sully, leave me alone. I don't want anyone around me right now."

That was too bad because Eva, Mara and Lyndsey had arrived, were standing with Bulldog now, a few feet away, as they allowed Sully a chance to try to get through to Dez.

"Listen, D, I know what you're going through right now. I—"

Dez turned back to face him, the moonlight exposing a humourless smile twisting his face and a sheen of tears pooling and spilling from his eyes. "You haven't got a fucking clue what I'm going through."

"I lost Dad too."

Dez turned away, staring back at the river, at the spot where they suspected Aiden had slipped into the current. "Yeah, well, he wasn't your real dad, was he?"

It was like being clubbed in the gut by a baseball bat, and it pushed a gush of air from Sully's lungs in the same way a physical assault would have. Dez had never, not once, reminded Sully of the fact he hadn't been born a Braddock, had always been prepared to go to battle with anyone who suggested any different.

Hearing those words from Dez hurt almost as much as learning Flynn had died.

There was nothing more he could say, so he stood and walked away. He knew the others had heard, felt it in Eva's sympathetic embrace before she went to fold Dez into one he was unable to fight.

"He didn't mean it," Mara said. "You know that. You're a part of this family, every bit as much as blood."

Sully nodded, the verbal answer he'd intended caught up behind the lump that had formed in his throat. Any attempt to speak right now would come out a choked sob, and that wasn't something he was willing to do. Dez needed people around him when he broke; for Sully, that would be added torture.

And Mara knew it, so she let him walk away. He knew she'd regret it the moment she saw him drive away in her car. But, right now, there was nothing else he felt he had the power to do.

He waited until he was out of the yard and on the gravel road leading to the highway, the house's exterior lights fading into the distance in the rearview mirror.

Only then did he allow the sob to tear from his throat.

HE DROVE THE CITY, aimlessly cruising streets and scanning faces that felt dark and empty.

He'd stopped crying awhile ago, enabling him to return what had been the fifth worried phone call from Mara. They were all going to stay at Dez and Eva's tonight to be together as a family, and she'd begged him to join them. And although she'd insisted Dez was sick over what he'd said—and while Dez himself had tried numerous times to call and text—Sully wasn't ready to be there with them. Not yet.

He wasn't sure what he was ready for. Not this. Not this pointless drive through a world where Flynn no longer existed in a physical sense, where he would no longer be available for a visit or on the other end of a phone call to provide help or guidance. And yet, Sully knew how lucky he was. He'd seen Flynn, held within his own visual memory the knowledge he was still here, that he wasn't completely gone because his body was dead. That was far more than Dez or Mara had.

And yet, it wasn't enough. Not when it came to Flynn.

Waves of grief had intermingled with anger bordering on rage, and a desire to return to Lowell, to confront him, accuse him, maybe even beat him into oblivion. He'd driven past the building in New Town that housed Lowell and Kindra's condo, had gone so far as to enter the lobby. But the doorman informed him the couple had gone to their country residence. Lowell had been very upset when they'd left, Sully was told.

If there was any justice on earth, Lowell would feel every inch of whatever it was he'd done to end his brother's life. Whether unintended or a yet-undiscovered murderous act, Lowell was responsible, and Sully would see justice done, one way or the other.

But he was never able to hold onto his anger long enough; continual glimpses of Flynn, popping in and out of the car as if trying to be everywhere at once, brought on fresh torrents of grief each time he disappeared.

The gas tank was riding the one-quarter mark when he finally pulled over on a dark street bordered by rows of brownstone apartment buildings from the turn of the last century. His brain was only half-working, caught somewhere between nightmare and reality—had him entertaining unrealistic thoughts that maybe he was asleep and none of this was real. Exhaustion had become the enemy and, as he looked up and fully clued in to where he was, he realized he'd been looking for a friend.

Ara Watanabe didn't turn him away, drew him into a warm hug as his attempt at explaining devolved into further tears. She didn't ask questions, simply guided him to the edge of her bed and held him while he struggled for some sort of control, until he was finally able to say the words. And with those words, spoken out loud like that, came the final nail, the irrefutable proof this was not a nightmare he would ever wake from.

Instead, she let him find some peace with her, Sully pulling back from the embrace far enough to deepen the needed connection, his lips against hers. She met him there, the two of them sinking back onto the bed. And, for a little while, thoughts of death strayed as Sully sought and found life here, in this temporary joining of bodies and souls.

She didn't let go after, warm fingers tracing a soothing path up and down the bare skin covering his spine as his forehead rested lightly against hers on a shared pillow.

Her voice was soft, the audible embodiment of that gentle hand. "I'm so sorry, Sully. I'm so sorry."

He wanted to return the words, to offer his own apology for coming here like this, seeking the emotional safety and pleasure she could give him after failing so utterly, over and over, at returning those gifts. He wanted to tell her she meant more to him than she knew, more than he'd allowed himself to acknowledge. He wanted to thank her and, right now, part of him wanted to beg her to allow him to stay here forever, in this space and time where, for a brief moment, every bad thing had fallen away.

In the end, she shushed him before he could start, rubbing his back until the impossible happened and a peaceful sleep settled over him.

When he awoke, sunlight was streaming through the window, and she was gone; a note on the pillow rested where her head had been. "Had to go to class. Coffee's on. Have some! I picked up your phone last night and talked to your mom so your family knew you were safe. All good. If you're still here when I get back, I'll make lunch. If not, remember I will be here if you need me."

She'd signed off with the initial of her first name and a series of Xs and Os, leaving Sully feeling both grateful and guilty. Ara deserved better than this, a guy who wasn't capable of sharing himself with her, who took without giving back, a guy who would be gone when she got home later this morning.

Because he would be. He had to be. There was a family death to contend with, a meeting with Forbes Raynor to attend, a killer to identify and a ghost who would, no doubt, return to torment him back into action all too soon.

But, for a few hours at least, he'd had a break from all of it and, right now, that was all he could ask.

He knew he shouldn't have been surprised to find Dez outside waiting for him, eyes reddened with a brutal combination of tears, lack of sleep and hangover as he unfolded himself from the driver's seat of his SUV and approached Sully with the most pathetic expression he'd ever worn.

Dez opened his mouth to speak but, like Sully with Ara last night, appeared to be struggling for the words. Finally, he gave up on the attempt, closing the distance between them and grabbing Sully in a hug he couldn't have escaped if he tried. In the midst of that, Dez finally managed to speak, his words, choked around emotion, sounding in Sully's ear.

"I'm sorry. I'm so sorry, Sull. I didn't mean it and it isn't true. Please tell me you know that."

"I know." There was nothing much else Sully needed to say. This was Dez, after all, and this was the two of them, two guys life had been kind enough to throw together when they'd both needed a brother.

A lot had changed within the past twelve hours, but some things blessedly had not and would never.

"I know, Dez."

21

Dez's fingers drummed the steering wheel as he took in the news Forbes Raynor had confronted Sully at the hospital last night, demanding he come in to talk to him today.

"Like hell," Dez said.

"I don't think I have a choice."

Dez drummed some more, reached up his other hand to rub at eyes that felt dry, hot and scratchy. Between grief over his dad and worry about Sully, he hadn't slept a wink last night and he felt every inch of it, his brain now twisting around Forbes's poorly timed accusations and demands. Dez knew his father would tell him to calm down, take a breath and let it go, and only then speak to Forbes and tell him unless he was planning on laying charges, Sully needed time to deal with personal matters before being dragged back into the investigation into Betty's death.

But Flynn wasn't here and all Dez could think to do was drive over to headquarters, find Forbes and create an open floor plan in the Major Crimes Unit by taking out a few walls with the man's body.

For now, they were still sitting outside Ara's, Sully having climbed in with him and allowing more time for Dez to try to wrangle his thoughts into words to ensure he and Sully were really okay. He'd gone completely off the rails last night, and he'd probably spend the rest of today apologizing to everyone. But Sully and Lowell had gotten the worst of it and, while Dez felt bad about what he'd said to Lowell, he fought nausea every time he recalled his words to his brother.

"I was only trying to get rid of you last night," Dez said. "That's why I said it, not because I meant it. Because I didn't."

Sully chuckled and Dez felt a swell of relief. It was an indication of normal, the sound his brother made whenever Dez cocked something up and felt the need to offer an apology Sully wasn't demanding. "I know that, D. We're good, okay? Promise."

Dez reached over, locking an arm around Sully's neck and pulling him in until their heads touched, Dez's forehead against his little brother's mop of brown hair. "I'm still an ass."

"I know that, too."

Dez released Sully and cuffed his brother lightly on the side of the head, drawing another laugh, this time from both of them. The levity didn't last long, as they both knew it couldn't.

"I know it's a stupid question," Sully said. "But are you okay?"

"Honestly? Not even close. I keep thinking it's a nightmare, you know? I used to have those all the time after Aiden, where I'd dream I was waking up in our house and it would be empty. And I knew they were all gone, my whole family. You were right last night, you know. I'm scared shitless about being alone."

"I think we all are, in a way."

"You like time by yourself," Dez said. "I can't handle it."

"I like being alone sometimes, but only because I know I don't have to be. I had to learn to deal with it before I met you guys. It's a hard habit to break, I guess."

"Childhood fucked us both up pretty royally, huh?"

Sully chuckled. "You got that right. At least I got something good out of the deal later on. Dad really saved my life when he took me home with him after the fire. You all did."

Dez smiled. "Back at ya."

"Listen, I know you don't like it, and I appreciate that, bro, but I need to deal with Raynor," Sully said. "He isn't going away, and I don't want to be sitting under the weight of this all day, waiting for him to come looking for me. I'd just rather get it over with."

"He doesn't have anything else on you, you know. If he did, he would have just arrested you and hauled you in. All he's after is getting you back in an interview room and seeing if he can crack you. He knows Dad's not around now to stop him, and he knows you're not going to be at your mental best. That gives him the upper hand in a big way. Don't let him have it, Sull. Trust me on this."

"So what am I supposed to do? It's not going away."

"I know that. You aren't going to do anything. *We* are, you and me. We'll get back into this thing, start asking around, doing some real digging."

"Dez, it's an open investigation. Dad told you not to get involved."

"Yeah, well, Dad's not here now, is he? There's you and there's me, and I'll be damned if Raynor puts you away for something you didn't do just to satisfy some stupid grudge. Look, I'm just going to say this because there's a lot of stuff I didn't get to tell Dad and I'm not making that mistake with anyone else. I love my job, but I love you more, okay? If it means getting you out of Raynor's crosshairs, I will gladly leave policing and spend the rest of my life working security at LOBRA's front desk. Got that?"

Sully sighed, the sound bordering on exasperation. "Love you too. And I appreciate that, but I'm not letting you risk your job for me. That's not going to make me feel any better about anything, all right?"

"Well, I'm not just going to do nothing. Hell, I can't do nothing. Sully, I can't just sit around right now, okay? I need to do something, keep my mind off things."

"So that's what this is about."

"That's not what it's about," Dez said. "Not most of it, anyway. It's about needing to protect what's left of my family."

Sully didn't argue that point, at least. "Okay. Given that, what I'm thinking is that the key to this thing is buried somewhere within another family."

"The Schusters."

"Yeah. Listen, I don't know how aware Harry is in a physical sense, but I'd really like to try to talk to him if possible."

"It might look kind of suspicious, us going back there again."

"Not if Harry's son is with us."

Dez studied Sully's face, didn't see any signs he was joking. "Sull, something kinda told me Thackeray wants nothing to do with the guy."

Sully shrugged. "Only one way to find out."

To Dez's surprise, Thackeray Schuster waved them in immediately, then closed the door solidly behind them.

The house's interior was bathed in shadow and, from what Dez could tell, all the curtains and blinds had been drawn.

It was a cloudy day, the forecast calling for light showers, so it wasn't the daylight that was bothering the man.

"What's going on?" Dez asked.

"Those damn posters," Thackeray said. "I've seen a couple guys hanging around outside today like they're hoping to bag themselves a skinner." As if to accentuate his point, he eased up to the sitting room window and edged a drape to the side to look.

"I didn't see anyone when we pulled up," Dez said.

Thackeray didn't acknowledge the statement. Instead he took two quick, measured steps toward Sully. Dez provided six-and-a-half muscled feet of disincentive as he shifted into Thackeray's personal space, causing the shorter man to take a step back. It didn't faze Thackeray in his accusations against Sully.

"You stole something yesterday. What did you take?"

Sully cast his brother a look and Dez shrugged. "I told him pretty much everything. I had to."

Sully nodded and returned his gaze to Thackeray. "I don't remember taking anything. I don't really remember much of anything from being in your house or what happened after. What I do know is that my dad apparently found a thumb drive in my pocket later on."

This was news to Dez. "What? Did you look at it? What was on it?"

"I didn't see it," Sully said. "Mom told me Dad took it into his office, and then left to see Lowell. From what we could tell, he took the thumb drive with him."

"So ask your dad what he did with it," Thackeray said. There was something beyond anger in his expression now, his eyebrows having risen and a notable widening of both eyes and enlarging of pupils speaking to fear.

"We can't," Dez said. "He ...." He stopped, blowing out a breath that whistled between teeth and lips. Sully came to his rescue, saying the words Dez couldn't.

"He died last night," Sully said. "It looks like he had a heart attack."

The appropriate thing would have been some expression of sympathy from Thackeray, but they'd moved well past appropriate—and Dez found he couldn't blame Thackeray. "Did it happen around Lowell? I mean, would Lowell have been able to get his hands on the drive?"

"He was with Lowell at the time, yeah," Sully said. "Thackeray, what was on it? You know, don't you?"

"Does Lowell have it?"

"I confronted him about the thumb drive at the hospital last night," Sully said. "I just threw the words out there to see how he'd react. The way he answered me, I think he's got it."

Thackeray's hands came up, raking through his hair and

getting caught up in the roots, tugging back hard enough to force a momentary facelift. "Son of a bitch. Goddammit. Why'd he fucking take it over with him? What the fuck was wrong with him?"

A bubble of irrational anger exploded inside Dez's chest at the insult to his father, and he started to move toward Thackeray without any real idea what he'd do once he'd closed the remaining short distance. Sully prevented anyone's finding out by throwing out an arm that miraculously proved enough of a barricade to stop him.

Thackeray apparently sensed the danger he'd stepped into. "I'm sorry about your dad, all right? But, fuck!"

"I know," Sully said. "And I'm sorry too. From what I can tell, Harry knew where your mom had hidden it and he's the one who made me pocket it. He obviously wanted to confront Lowell about something, but I don't know what. If it's about the thumb drive—"

"Give it up with the thumb drive, all right? It's family stuff, that's all. Just leave it alone."

"I think it's pretty obvious it was more than that."

"Look, I don't know, okay? That's it. I don't know!"

Dez had been working on taking some deep, calming breaths and found he was able to carry on his end of the conversation. There was no point pressing him further on the drive, but there was something else Thackeray might be able to help with. "When I got up to Lowell's office, Sully—or Harry, really—was trying to attack him with a letter opener. He kept saying the same two words: 'blue room.' Does that mean anything to you?"

Thackeray shook his head in the negative. "I don't think I've ever heard anything like that."

"So I guess that leaves us with the bigger question," Sully said. "Do you think we could ask your father?"

Thackeray's answering chuckle was devoid of humour. "You're kidding, right? You'd have better luck talking to a potato."

"I'd still like to try," Sully said. "I'm hoping I can at least get some sort of response, even if it's just eye movement. If he's got any sort of awareness—and, based on my experience the past couple of days, he does—I'm thinking there's a chance he could at least provide us with a clue."

"Far as I'm aware, you're free to visit without me."

"That's true," Dez said. "But if Sully and I keep showing up, visiting people we don't know, someone's bound to start wondering whether they shouldn't fix us up a room in there, too."

"You guys owe me big time for this."

It was the first thing Thackeray had said since they'd crossed the Kimotan for the north shore. Now, with Dez pulling to a stop in the parking lot outside Lockwood, Thackeray's nerves showed.

Dez put the gearshift into park before peering at Thackeray in the back seat through his rearview mirror. "You've really never been here in all this time?"

"Mom made me come here a couple times, but she eventually gave up trying. I think it was pretty clear neither me or my dad were getting anything much out of it."

Sully turned in the front passenger seat to face the reluctant passenger. "You going to be okay in there?"

"No, but if you think this is going to help get to the bottom of everything that's been going on, I'll give it a go. Someone's been screwing with me and my family for years, and I've got a pretty good idea who."

Dez knew whom Thackeray meant, but he wasn't ready to go there just yet. Lowell was his dad's brother and he'd always been there for them. Lowell and Kindra had rarely missed Dez's elementary school Christmas concerts or his high school football games, had always visited at Christmas with incredible gifts. And Lowell had supported Sully too, getting him set up at the Black Fox with a full-time job and a roof over his head. Lowell was family; Dez knew that reality carried with it a distinct possibility Lowell treated them differently than he might others. But he had a hard time believing that treatment would include what Thackeray was implying—helping to have Harry committed and, if Dez was reading this right, even playing a role in setting Thackeray up for child porn offences. Dez knew it was entirely possible Lowell was behind the first—he had, after all, spoken to Dez a couple times now about putting Sully into Lockwood—but there was no way Lowell was behind the other. It just didn't fit with the man Dez knew.

And he'd known Lowell all his life.

Dez glanced over at Sully to try to get a read on his thoughts, and found his younger brother watching him—or, if Dez was to be more accurate in the description, studying him. Dez raised an eyebrow, a silent question, and Sully responded with a put-on smile before turning away quickly enough to reveal a truth he might not have intended.

Sully shared Thackeray's suspicions.

Dez knew Sully and Lowell didn't enjoy the same close relationship Dez did with his uncle, and he'd always been aware of some tension there. But as much as Dez loved his brother, he bristled sometimes at how quick he was to doubt Lowell.

They let Thackeray pick his time and lead the way to the main entrance, giving Dez a chance to sneak in a quick word with Sully as they followed.

"You're buying into Thackeray's opinions about Lowell, aren't you?"

Sully's eyes were fixed on the ground as he walked, hands stuffed deep in his pockets so that his responding shrug was a minimal one. "I don't know, man. I guess I'm keeping an open mind."

"Look, I know the two of you haven't always seen eye to eye on things, but he's still our uncle. He wouldn't do the things Thackeray's implying."

Sully's only reply was another shrug. It was all they had time for with the steps leading to the door right in front of them, Thackeray waiting for them at the top.

"We'll talk about it later," Dez said.

Problem was, he wasn't sure it was a promise he wanted to keep.

22

THEY FOUND Harry Schuster where Sully had last seen him, sitting in his wheelchair, staring out the window overlooking the back gardens.

They'd gotten in with no issues, one of the older nurses working the front desk remembering Thackeray once he'd provided his name. Thankfully, this nurse didn't seem to be an avid reader of the city's newspaper or a watcher of any of the local news channels, and so showed no sign she knew the man in front of her as someone who'd recently left behind a prison term for a repugnant crime.

She had, however, heard about Betty, and the tears in her eyes appeared genuine as she offered her condolences to Thackeray and the two young men he introduced as friends. She'd pointed them in the direction of the sunroom without asking any questions, seemingly satisfied with Thackeray's explanation of wanting to see if he could rebuild a relationship with his surviving parent.

And so, moments later, here they were, back in this room and making their way across to the man whose spirit had been making Sully's recent life a waking nightmare.

Dez inched close to Sully, ensuring his comment remained between the two of them. "That's the man you've been seeing, huh? Jeez, no wonder he freaks you out. He's doing a number on me, and I'm looking at a living, breathing guy."

Sully glanced back to check on Thackeray, finding him dragging behind like a condemned man approaching the entrance to the gas chamber.

"Do you want to try to talk to your dad?" Sully asked.

Thackeray reached them, but kept a safe distance by using Dez as a solid wall. He looked only briefly at his father—who had yet to show any sign he'd so much as registered the arrival of visitors —before shaking his head quickly and moving off to stare out the window much as the older Schuster was.

Sully met his brother's eye, and Dez responded with a shrug. With little else to do now, Sully scanned the room to assure himself neither Dr. Gerhardt nor the orderly from the other day, Larson Hackman, were around. Satisfied on that count, he lowered himself to one knee next to the chair and peered up into the face, the alternate image of which had been haunting him.

"Mr. Schuster? I don't know if you can hear me, but my name's Sullivan Gray. I think you know who I am. I'm here with my brother and your son, Thackeray. Do you remember Thackeray?"

Sully gave it a moment, analyzing Harry's face for any indication of recognition, a flicker of eyelids, an involuntary twitch of a muscle around thin lips, a tensing of flesh in the deeply lined area between substantial brows.

There was nothing.

"I'm hoping you don't mind if I call you Harry," Sully said. "We've been spending some time together in fairly close quarters, so we've kind of gotten to know each other. You must know about Betty. Maybe you even tried to warn me. Is that true, Harry?"

Nothing.

"People say you can see the future. Are you trying to use me to prevent something from happening, maybe to Thackeray? Maybe to you? Is that why you used me to go after Lowell Braddock?"

No response.

Sully sighed. "I wish I knew if you could hear me."

"Oh, he can hear you all right."

Sully turned his head. Next to him stood a stout woman somewhere in her sixties, a pair of thick, round glasses enlarging her eyes and giving her the appearance of an owl. Her clothing—yellow pyjamas matching Harry's—marked her as a patient.

Sully stood, finding her close to a foot shorter than he was. Next to Dez, she looked like a garden gnome.

"My name's Phoebe but most around here just call me Snowy the Owl. You can, too, if you want. You know you were thinking it."

Sully met Dez's gaze, noted a set of upraised brows that no doubt mirrored Sully's own.

"I'm Sullivan," he said, returning his attention to Snowy with an outstretched hand.

Her small fingers wound around his gently, barely squeezing. "I know who you are, young man. He's talked about you, you know."

"Harry?"

"Yes, sir. He says things sometimes before they drug him up. The things he sees, they disturb him. Sometimes, he even wakes up screaming. Did recently, yelled his wife's name over and over. Two days later, someone killed her. Isn't that right, that she's dead now?"

Sully nodded. He sensed Dez beside him was finding new definitions of anxiety as this conversation unfolded, but there wasn't much they could do about it. If they couldn't get answers directly from Harry, it seemed Snowy the Owl was happy to act as stand-in.

"What did he say about me?"

"Nothing in so many words. He doesn't, you know. Never does. His brain doesn't work so well anymore, so his premonitions just come in bits and pieces. Never heard a last name, but I have heard him say the name Sullivan recently, quite a bit."

"Has he said anything else?"

"Not much, but there was another phrase I heard one night, something like 'red dead.' No idea what that meant."

If Sully was a betting man, he'd be prepared to lay down a few bucks on the likelihood it was a premonition of the death of Sully and Dez's red-headed father. It wasn't a subject he wanted to broach.

But there was something else he hoped she could tell him. "Have you ever heard him say anything about a blue room?"

Snowy's eyes had, to this point, been wide behind her glasses, giving the impression of a five-year-old child relaying a story to the class about how she'd spent her summer holidays. Now Sully watched as the light faded from the woman's expression, stealing years from her and making her seem far closer to her true age.

"We don't talk about that."

"Why not?"

"We just don't. They say bad things happen there."

Dez switched his weight from one foot to the other and back again. This time, Sully shared his brother's discomfort.

"I don't mean to upset you," Sully told Snowy. "But I really think it might be important."

"It is important," she said. "But some important things are best kept quiet. Like family secrets. You have some, surely. They're important, but saying them out loud .... Nothing good comes of that, now, does it?" She leaned closer, her voice near a whisper. "We aren't supposed to know about it, you know. That room. But Harry knows. Harry knows a lot. It's his greatest strength and his Achilles' heel, all in one. You don't want to know about that room, child. You don't ever want to know."

"What's going on here?"

Sully realized he'd been staring at Snowy, and the approaching voice had him blinking hard as he spotted Larson Hackman coming toward them.

"Who's that?" Dez hissed.

"Head orderly," Sully replied before Hackman could close the distance.

"Why are you bothering Mr. Schuster?"

Dez squared off against the large man, providing some substantial reason to pause. "We weren't bothering anyone. We were visiting. I wouldn't have thought that would be a problem."

"The two of you were here the other day," Hackman said, gaze flicking between the brothers, suspicion eking from the lowering of eyebrows and narrowing of eyes.

"I recognized Mr. Schuster," Sully said. "I worked with his wife, Betty." Sully motioned toward Thackeray. "We brought Harry's son with us. He wanted to see his father, but he didn't want to come alone."

Thackeray took that as his cue to rejoin the land of the living and, thankfully, he backed Sully's play. "I thought I did. Now, I'm not so sure. I thought maybe he'd know me."

"Harry barely knows who he is some days." Hackman's voice was kinder now, whether the result of Dez's imposing form or of speaking with Harry's son.

"That's not true," Snowy said. "He knows more than you think." She turned back to Sully. "And I wonder how much better he could show that if they didn't insist on drugging him."

Hackman addressed the accusation like one might explain to a child why dessert can't come before dinner. "We've had this discussion before, Phoebe. Harry's thoughts are very disturbing to him. They upset him badly and, what's more, they upset everyone else. You remember what happened the last time, when Dr. Gerhardt tried to lower his dosage?'

Sully was surprised when Thackeray provided the answer. "He tried to kill himself."

Hackman reached out a beefy arm, settling a solid hand on Snowy's shoulder. The weight of it shifted her body, had her reestablishing her balance as she turned narrowed eyes up onto his face. "We don't want to see that happen again, do we, Phoebe?"

"I'm not a grade schooler, Larson," she said. "Don't speak to me like one."

The smile didn't leave the orderly's face, but he did remove his hand from her shoulder after giving it a couple careful pats.

"What sort of drugs is he on?" Sully asked.

Hackman's eyes clamped back onto his face. "That's not really your business, is it?"

Thackeray took a step closer, edging in nearer to Hackman while managing to keep his distance from his father. "But it is mine."

Hackman, caught in a situation without a decent excuse to turn to for extraction, provided an answer. "I'm not aware of all the particulars, but he's on several drugs. One is an anti-psychotic and he's also on an anti-depressant and a mood regulator. And he often has trouble sleeping, so he receives medication for that at night. It's likely a combination of the drugs leaves him a little dopey, but it's better than the alternative. As I said, it's disturbing not just to him, but to everyone here, when he's in one of his states, and it has, on occasion, proved an actual threat to his life."

Thackeray's gaze fell onto his father's still form and, for the first time since they'd arrived, remained there longer than a couple seconds. "I'm aware."

"I know why you keep him medicated," Dez said. "But I think it would be helpful to both Thackeray and Harry if they had a chance to have a proper conversation. What are the chances he could visit sometime when his father's not like this?"

Dez might later tell him he was imagining it, but Sully thought he could see a smirk toying at the corners of Hackman's mouth, held in check by self-control and necessity. "Honestly? Probably never. I hate to say this, but Harry suffers from psychotic episodes frequently, and the risks are just too high. Phoebe can attest to that. I know it might sound trite, but I truly am sorry, Mr. Schuster. I deal with your father every day, and I just don't see that he'd be in any state to have a proper conversation, whether medicated or not."

Thackeray nodded, a tight up and down, before looking to Dez. "I think I'd like to go now."

"I'm sorry you were unable to get what you needed from the visit." The remark from Hackman had Sully looking up at him more sharply than he would have liked, afraid the automatic response might inadvertently prove the orderly right. Because there was something in the man's statement beyond a stated regret about the lack of communication between father and son; there was recognition of the existence of an ulterior motive.

Thankfully, Dez played it far cooler than Sully had managed, launching his response with a non-committal shrug. "Yeah, us too. Seems sad he doesn't understand his wife's gone. Sully and I had hoped we could explain it to him. Betty would have wanted him to know why she wasn't coming back to see him."

"We've done our best to explain," Hackman said. "But I don't think anyone really knows what registers with him and what doesn't."

Thackeray extended a hand to Hackman, shaking. "Thanks for looking after him for us. It's not that he and I were ever what you'd call close, but I wish there was a way I could know him better. More than that, I wish he didn't have to live like this."

As if sensing the visit was at an end, Hackman turned to lead the way to the exit, Thackeray falling in next to him. Dez looked down at Sully and gave his shoulders a shrug, but said nothing before making to follow the others.

Sully studied Harry's face one last time and, seeing nothing there but that same stony mask, turned to join his brother.

He was caught short by an iron grip around his wrist, coming so suddenly, he was unable to hold back an audible gasp. Harry's fingers clenched, vicelike, around his forearm.

The man's lips were moving as if to try and form words, and Sully leaned in as Dez regained his side, the larger man's body acting as a visually impenetrable wall between them and the orderly. At first, all Sully could hear was the in and out of breath, bent around a failed attempt at speech. But, as Sully put his ear right next to Harry's mouth, the indiscernible sounds of a mental hospital patient gradually came into audible focus.

"What's he saying?" Snowy asked.

"I'm trying to make it out."

"It's important you tell me."

Spoken through both inhale and exhale, Harry breathed out two words, repeated them three times. Then, as Hackman started back toward them, voice raised with demand as he asked what was going on, Harry fell silent.

"Quickly," Snowy said. "What did he say?"

Sully turned his attention from stilled lips and fingers unclenching from his wrist, meeting Snowy's wide eyes. "River boy."

Hackman regained their side just as Snowy shuffled off. "The two of you need to leave."

"One moment," Snowy called out over her shoulder. "I want to give them a present."

"Phoebe, not now."

The woman ignored Hackman, continuing off down the hall and leaving Sully and Dez with the orderly.

"I'm going to ask, again," Hackman said. "Were you doing something to upset him?"

Snowy had provided ample distraction to gift Sully with the time to invent a story. "I think I might have. I didn't mean to. I whispered to him that Betty had been killed. I wanted to see whether it registered."

Hackman stepped forward, lifting Harry's left arm from where it dangled next to the wheelchair and returned it to the armrest. "Something must have for him to have moved like that. I don't know why I should have to tell you this, but it is not your place to tell him things like that. Nor is it safe for him. It was left to Dr. Gerhardt to inform Harry about Betty's passing because only Dr. Gerhardt understands Harry's illness well enough to recognize potential impact and what to do about it when he becomes upset. Harry is susceptible to having another stroke. You telling him about that might well have killed him. Do you hear what I'm saying?"

Sully wasn't a liar by nature, but uttering false statements to Hackman felt as natural to him as the breath needed to speak. What was more, it felt necessary. "I'm really sorry. I wasn't thinking."

Snowy returned, a piece of drawing paper folded in her hands. "I'd like a word with Sullivan, if you don't mind, Larson."

"Not today, Pheobe. Sullivan and Desmond were just leaving."

Snowy turned so she was facing Hackman head on, determined eyes trained up on him and neck cranked back to make it possible. "Larson. It isn't everyday I get to visit with a handsome young man, and I want to give him a picture I drew. If you don't mind, I'd very much appreciate being treated like a human being. I don't see how that could be too much to ask."

Hackman drew himself up to full height and sniffed, but said nothing else before moving off a few steps to grant Snowy her request. The older woman angled herself away from Hackman for further privacy before unfolding the paper.

Sully's breath caught as a rudimentary drawing came into view: two orange-haired people standing next to a reed-bordered river, a dripping young boy's hand held by his father's.

Snowy's words didn't match the finger she was using to point to various elements in the picture, her motions clearly a disguise intended for Hackman as she provided her message to Sully. "Sometimes, I can see the things other people think. It comes and goes, but it comes far more often with Harry. He showed me this. He calls it 'River Boy.' I believe it means something to you."

Sully nodded and Snowy continued without the need for verbal confirmation. "You see things too. I think you've even seen Harry when he leaves this place. There are things you and I and Harry know about this world and the one beyond that others never will while they remain on this side of the veil. But there are people who wish to, people who will do anything in their power to gain that knowledge. That's the Blue Room. It's a place where they try to learn. You don't ever want to see it, child."

She refolded the picture and pressed it into Sully's hand.

"Leave this place, Sullivan. And don't you ever come back."

23

THE DRIVE back to Thackeray's house was long enough to get Dez's brain spinning, caught up in thoughts of dead family members and how they'd ended up on a drawing by a stranger in a psychiatric hospital.

"How you doing?"

At his brother's quiet question, Dez glanced over. Sully studied him from the passenger seat. Dez returned his eyes to the road, discovered he was back in Riverview, that he'd crossed the bridge without noticing.

"Fine."

"No, you're not. Neither am I."

Dez responded with a small upturn of lips before deciding Sully deserved better. "I don't get it. I've been turning it over in my head since you showed me that picture and I can't figure out what the message is supposed to be. I mean, I think it's pretty obvious it's Dad and Aiden, right?"

"Looks like."

"So, why? What's it about? And why is some random woman drawing them?"

"Apparently, because she draws what Harry shows her. Maybe she does the same thing with other people too. I don't know."

"But why is Harry seeing Dad and Aiden? I'd like to say it's a sign the two of them are together now and are at peace, but they don't look happy in that picture. They're not smiling. They should be, right?"

"I don't know, Dez. I don't know what Harry saw."

Dez was suddenly keenly aware Thackeray was still with them, a silent presence in the backseat since they'd left Lockwood. Dez would have preferred to save his next question for a private moment with his brother, but wasn't sure he'd get up the nerve to ask again. As it stood, it wasn't something he was convinced he really wanted answered.

"Sully, I've never asked you this. Not ever. Maybe part of me never wanted to know. But do you see them? Dad and Aiden?"

He tried to meet Sully's eye, but the need to watch the road got in the way. So was Sully's hair, falling forward across his face and acting as a curtain between them. It occurred to Dez once that Sully always kept his hair long enough that he could hide behind it when he felt the need. Dez tried to tell himself that wasn't what Sully was doing now, not with him.

Sully didn't answer right away, but Dez waited him out, convinced his brother had heard his question. The eventual reply came as softly as many of the utterances that had passed Sully's lips over the years.

"No, Dez. I don't see them. And I don't think you'd want me to."

Dez considered pulling over, forcing Sully to face him and repeat that statement, a move that would allow Dez to search for truth in his brother's words. Sully had never been able to lie to him convincingly, not when push came to shove. And Dez knew he could do some shoving now if he chose.

But his foot stayed on the gas, his eyes on the road ahead as they continued in silence toward Thackeray's. At some point—once the pain of losing his father was less fresh, once it had time to settle in and make itself comfortable—maybe then he'd be able to face the fact Sully had probably just lied to him. Right now, Dez had more than enough pain to contend with and he knew he was in no state to handle more. And if Sully was seeing their dad and Aiden, that meant more torment for all of them.

For Dez, there would be no peace were he to learn his loved ones couldn't find their own. He knew it, and Sully knew it. And Dez also knew there was a very real likelihood Sully was protecting him from that reality.

For now, Dez decided he was prepared to allow it.

The alternative was unfaceable.

THEY PARKED on the street outside the house, Betty's flowers waving a welcome in the late morning breeze.

The house's exterior was deceiving, as if it hadn't been told. Dez was reminded of the look on the face of a mother he'd visited with his sergeant a couple weeks ago, one of those notification-of-death visits that made most cops feel sick with dread beforehand and depressed as all hell afterward. Sergeant Granger had told him some parents seemed to know before he even got to the door. Not this lady. She'd been completely unprepared for the ultimate heartbreak, her expression open and welcoming as if expecting to find someone she knew and liked on the doorstep.

They'd left her a broken mess, with a kindly neighbour to take care of her until her surviving child could get there. Dez had been his own version of a broken mess later.

These flowers were that woman, and Dez didn't want to see this place a week from now.

Perhaps Thackeray didn't either, not yet having made a move to leave the SUV.

Dez had been inclined to wait him out for a bit, but it had gotten to the point of awkward, the question needing asked. "Everything okay?"

Thackeray, in the rearview mirror, was staring through the backseat window toward the house. "I think it's sinking in. My mom's really gone, and my dad's never going to be in any state to be anything more to me than someone I pity. Weird, when you realize part of you was wishing for something, almost behind your back."

"I'm sorry." Dez meant the words. He knew loss, had become intimately acquainted with the beast since childhood. There was nothing better to say than that, nothing that would magically change the situation. Dez was lucky by comparison; he had his wife and daughter, his mom and his brother. Thackeray had no one and, with a conviction like his clinging to him, probably never would.

The right thing to do would be to offer to come in and hang out for a while, but all Dez wanted was to spend time with Kayleigh. She made him laugh, and he needed that, even if it could only be for a few minutes.

Sully put a temporary end to that plan.

"Dez, there's someone in the house."

Dez ducked his head, trying to look through the passenger side window to see what his brother had spotted. "Where?"

"I saw someone in an upstairs window."

Dez repressed a shiver at the thought it might be one of Sully's "someones." "Was this person with body or without?"

"With. At least, I think so."

"Man or woman?"

"I'd say a man, but I didn't get a really good look."

Dez turned to Thackeray. "Were you expecting anyone?"

"I don't even really know anyone."

Dez scrubbed a hand through the stubble that had built on his lower face. The smart move would be to call 9-1-1, have some on-duty officers swing by and check it out, but that might well end in his being a laughing stock should it turn out the intruder was a Sully special. "Bloody hell. Look, I'll check it out. You two wait here."

He was annoyed but not surprised when he heard Sully's car

door open and close as Dez was making his way to the front door with the keys Thackeray had provided. "Sully—"

"You're not checking the house on your own."

There was no point arguing. "Stay behind me and don't wander off."

"The point is for me to be your backup. Hard to do that unless I'm at your back, isn't it?"

"No one likes a smart ass, Sull."

There was little question the intruder was aware of their presence. If Sully had seen him, no doubt the guy had seen them as well. He'd be looking for a way out rather than a hiding spot and, depending on the extent of his desire to avoid getting caught, it might be he'd be willing to go through rather than around them to get there. And there was always the possibility the guy had a weapon he'd be prepared to use. There was plenty enough gun crime in this city and it was getting easier for those who wanted one to get their hands on a firearm, giving Dez one more contingency to worry about.

No immediate sounds came upon their entering the house, nothing to tell them where an intruder might be lurking. Dez grasped a handful of his brother's hoodie and tugged him to the edge of the opening to the living room. "Stay behind the wall and keep watch on the stairs. I'm going to check the back door."

Dez found it secure, both locks in place, and there was no sign in the kitchen or living room of any broken windows.

Dez returned to Sully, whispering the lack of find to his brother.

"Maybe he left already," Sully suggested.

"Not through the door. The deadbolt's on. No way to lock it behind him unless he has a key."

Leaving Sully once more, Dez cleared the rest of the main floor, finding only an empty half-bath and a dining room Betty had partially converted to an office space.

Dez returned to the front hall, shaking his head at Sully as he moved to take the lead up the stairs. Sully fell in behind him as they made for the second floor, Dez shifting sideways and crossing foot over foot until he was high enough to glimpse the landing through the wooden bannister. There, he paused, forcing Sully to a halt beside him. Standing stock still, they each held their breath as they listened for any sounds that might tell of an intruder shifting in a closet or a window left open following an escape.

Sully seemed to have read his mind, tugging Dez down until he could whisper an observation directly into his ear. "The windows don't open, at least not in Betty's room. I think it's from when Harry was here, to keep him from getting out."

Dez nodded. If the windows in that room were sealed, it was possible others were too. Regardless, there was no sound to indicate a window was open, nor the sensation of breeze wafting through any of the open doors. Unless the guy had managed to get out a window and close it after his escape, that meant either the man was still here, or that it wasn't really a man at all—or at least not anymore.

Only one thing was certain: they weren't going to find anything standing here. Dez once again led the way and positioned Sully on the landing, away from the stairs. "Yell if you see anything."

Sully offered a half-smile. "No problem. You too."

One of the four doors up here was partially closed, and Dez could just make out the end of a floral bedspread—likely the most feminine item Betty owned—through the gap between door and jamb. Dez decided to try there first, mentally running through the list of hiding spots as he moved: behind the door, under the bed, inside the closet. There was no point trying to disguise his movement; his large, booted feet caused the hardwood to creak and crack with each step. And so, upon reaching the door, he threw rather than eased it open, sending it with a bang into the wall.

The movement garnered a response, although not the one he'd expected. The sound of his name on Sully's lips had him spinning in time to see his brother rushing a masked man who was making for the stairs.

Dez started toward them, but the intruder was quicker, delivering a blindingly fast roundhouse to Sully's jaw that sent him crashing back into Dez. The man didn't waste time, sliding down the heavy oak railing to the lower floor rather than bothering with stairs. Dez righted Sully and made to follow the man, his brother at his flank.

The intruder made it outside just before Dez burst through the front doorway. Thackeray stood beside the SUV's rear passenger side door, pointing dumbly toward the park. Thackeray's effort was needless, the suspect still in sight as Dez broke into a sprint, pumping long legs and arms in pursuit. One of his former partners called him Jack Rabbit and insisted on driving each shift to free Dez up should a foot chase be required. Dez was happy enough to go along with it, well aware his height and physical condition left him able to end pursuits quickly and still be in a state for a fight once he got there.

That was proving the case now, the distance quickly closing between him and the man. Just another few feet and Dez would be able to fall back on one of his high school football moves, a flying tackle that typically ended in bumps and bruises for the bad guy and, for Dez, reverential back slaps from his colleagues.

It didn't come to high school football moves today. This guy, it turned out, could qualify for the pros.

Up ahead was a playground, empty but for a few rusty pieces of equipment and a sandpit Dez would have checked for syringes before allowing a child near it. With just feet separating them, the man ran for the swing set and wrapped one hand and the opposite elbow around the steel bar that formed one of the support posts. The man swung himself around the post, slamming his booted foot into Dez's head. Starbursts flashed and the ground rushed up at him, leaving him flat on his back in the sand beneath the swing set. His heart skipped erratically, and the pain had him trying to determine whether it was worth staying conscious.

Darkness beckoned, but Sully gave him reason to stay present, arriving on the scene a moment later and taking his own run at the guy. Dez struggled to sitting in time to see his brother slammed to the ground hard enough to leave him gasping for air his rattled lungs couldn't process.

With just a couple of seconds to spare while the man repositioned himself for another attack on one of them, Dez fought through the off-centred world, dug deep, and managed the tackle he'd planned to execute earlier. The man went down, but he wasn't of a mind to stay there, getting his rock-solid left forearm up and braced against Dez's windpipe while readying his right for a blow. Dez shifted just enough that he was able to block the strike and relieve pressure on his throat, but that was about all the guy was prepared to allow.

Dez was used to sloppy street fights, the vast majority of suspects having no knowledge of proper defensive strategies. This guy was no street fighter and, if Dez hadn't already figured that out, the man's next move proved it as he hooked Dez's right leg, grabbed hold of his right arm and drove his hips up. With both leg and arm temporarily in his opponent's control, Dez was rolled sideways and ended with the other man straddling him. Dez was able to get his arms up as the suspect began throwing punches at his head, preventing two strikes but taking one to the side of the head that stunned him long enough to ensure a second found its mark.

He managed to get a leg up, intending to use it to nudge his assailant off balance, but Sully got there first, launching himself at the man's back and going for a choke hold. While the man grabbed at the arm Sully was using to restrict his air, Dez got in a pair of punches before following through with a knee to the guy's side. Busy with Sully, the man toppled, allowing Dez to regain the upper position while his brother tried to retain his own hold.

The guy wasn't done, directing a kick at Dez's thigh that pushed his leg from under him. Grunts of discomfort from Sully suggested he was being struck hard, and Dez found himself grateful for his brother's high pain threshold as he continued to hold on. Dez grabbed the arm the man was using to hit Sully—the left one—and twisted, angling to force their opponent onto his belly. There would be little he could do from that position, not with two of them on top of him.

But, once again, the suspect managed to thwart the attempt—although not in any way Dez could have foreseen.

The man's arm came off in his grasp.

As the arm pulled free of the man's jacket sleeve, Dez cursed between heaving breaths; it took a moment to see it for what it was: a dark-toned prosthesis.

The man's balaclava was well-fitted and had remained more or less in place throughout the fight. It no longer mattered. Dez knew who they were dealing with.

"Terrence Waters," he said. "Give it up, man."

The words signalled an end to the fight, and the army surplus store manager stopped struggling, allowing Sully to use one hand to pull the mask off. Dez hadn't really needed the confirmation, but there it was anyway: Terrence Waters glared up at them while drawing quick breaths through widened nostrils.

Terrence delivered one more hard elbow jab to Sully's ribs.

"Get the hell off me, kid."

Sully looked up at Dez, seeking approval, and Dez provided it through a nod. Sully rolled away and stood, Terrence refusing the hand Dez extended to help him up. Terrence rose to his feet and shrugged out of his jacket before seizing the prosthesis from Dez and starting the process of putting it back in place.

There was no point offering help, particularly given it was more likely to be seen as offensive rather than polite. It was clear Terrence was a proud man, and a tough one at that. He'd seen action, and the last thing he'd want was sympathy. He'd said as much at the store recently.

The struggle over, Dez recognized the taste of blood seeping from a cut inside his bottom lip, and he spit red, looking up to find Terrence smirking at him.

"Didn't hurt you too bad, did I, big guy?"

"Nothing I can't handle. Maybe you want to tell us what you were doing in the Schusters' house."

"You're taking some interest in that pervert. Why's that?"

"Asked you first."

Prosthesis back in place, Terrence shrugged. "Guess I figured I'd look to see if the man had any other dirty stuff kicking around. Skinners like him, they don't change. They keep going back to the familiar, looking to get their fix the same way as any heroin addict. There's no way to program that out of them, not once they get the taste for it. You know that as well as I do, being a cop, don't you?"

Dez did know that. He'd helped on more than one search and seizure with the Internet Child Exploitation team, and had been told on all but one occasion the guy they'd arrested was a repeat offender.

But, having spent some time with Thackeray and having heard his story, Dez was beginning to have some doubts about that particular ex-con. "Thackeray Schuster says he was set up."

"And you believe that? Of course, he's going to say that. No one wants to admit they whack off to kids."

"I don't know yet if I believe him. But he's raised some questions that need answering."

There was no point asking Sully's opinion. He stood off to the side, eyes focused on a spot just beyond Terrence's left shoulder. Someone was there, invisible to all eyes but Sully's.

Dez returned his focus to the problem he could fix. "You stay away from that house, you hear me? I'm willing to say you gave us the slip as long as you promise to stop harassing Thackeray. No more posters, no more stalking the house, sure as hell no more break-ins. I've got a lot of respect for you, given what you've obviously been through, so I don't want to have to arrest you."

"Don't do me any favours just because of my injury."

"It's not about your injury. My respect has to do with the fact you've served this country. I'm trying to return the favour, if you'd bother to take your head out of your ass long enough to listen."

Terrence's narrowed eyes held all the skepticism Dez would have expected from ex-military. While the world was full of cynics, few had earned the right as completely as those who'd served. People like Terrence Waters had witnessed some of the worst humanity had to offer, and it showed in his face—as well as in his body.

Dez took the chance, decided to ask the question. "Hope you don't mind me asking, but what happened to your arm?"

The eyes had yet to fully un-narrow, but Terrence answered anyway. "IED in Afghanistan. Hit our vehicle. I was blown out instead of up. In my case, all they had to look for was the arm. One of my friends, his arm was one of the only recognizable parts of him left. Some people call me lucky."

Sully's attention snapped back to Terrence. "Is that why you're doing this? Going after Thackeray Schuster?"

"What's that got to do with what happened back then?"

Sully shrugged. "It's about justice. Chances are no one was ever really held to account for what happened to your friend. Something like that, the memory, it doesn't go away. You've got a pretty solid reminder with your arm. And you've probably asked yourself why you survived, what that must mean about your purpose here."

Terrence's laugh held the darkness and threat of a gathering storm. "You think I give a damn about purpose, coming through what I did?"

"What are you doing here, if not because you give a damn?"

Dez guessed Sully had been on the money, given the two quick steps Terrence took to close the gap between him and the younger man. No doubt the veteran had been analyzed and re-analyzed during attempts at counselling once back home but, understandably, he wasn't about to listen to someone who had no clue about the horrors he'd seen. How did someone who'd been to hell and back accept help from a shrink in a white button-down shirt, patent-leather shoes and glasses carefully selected to fit his or her facial shape? It wasn't likely he was going to willingly take being read by a twenty-something bar employee in need of a haircut and a better wardrobe.

"You don't know me, and you sure shit don't know what I've been through. Keep your opinions to yourself."

Dez stepped closer, using his size in his favour even if his moves had proved less than perfect next to Terrence's. "Then you keep yours. In all honesty, I don't give a personal damn about Thackeray Schuster, but I do care about what goes on in the area I police. Stay the hell away from this, you hear me? That's your last warning."

Terrence's eyes were slits, his mouth a tight line, but he said nothing else before turning and storming across the park in the opposite direction from the Schusters' house.

"Who'd you see this time?" Dez asked. "His dead troop mate hanging around him?"

"Not just him. Betty was there too."

"Huh. Looking out for her son, maybe?"

"Maybe." The word from Sully's lips carried more doubt than its actual definition.

"Okay, what?"

"Hmm?"

"You want to let me in on whatever it is you're thinking?"

Dez rode out Sully's responding silence, pleased when more persuasion wasn't necessary before receiving an answer. "That break-in at the bar, where I caught the guy going through Betty's office?"

"You think that was Waters?"

"His moves were solid. I mean, I swung a bat at him, but he dodged it and disarmed me within what felt like the same second, and he had me on the ground the next. I've had to throw people out of the bar on occasion, so I'm not useless in a fight, but this guy, he felt like a pro."

"You think he went there looking for something on Thackeray?"

"I don't know. Maybe. But why go to that much trouble for something that didn't personally affect you? It doesn't make sense."

"Could be he's got a bigger stake in it than he's told us," Dez suggested. "You think he might be the one who killed Betty? Could be that's why you saw her around him. I mean, I don't get what motive he'd have to kill Thackeray's mother, not if his beef is with him. But it's a thought, right?"

Sully nodded, but his verbal response was less satisfying. "Maybe."

"You're big on 'maybes' today, huh?"

Sully's smile wouldn't pass any tests. "Right now, maybes are pretty much all I've got."

24

Just before noon, Sully's stomach provided a noisy reminder he'd been neglecting meals.

Unfortunately, it seemed Sergeant Forbes Raynor wasn't as troubled about food as he was the state of his investigation, his voice on the other end of the line as Sully answered his ringing cellphone.

"I thought you were going to come in this morning for a chat."

Sully was back in the passenger seat of Dez's SUV, his brother next to him behind the steering wheel. Still parked outside Thackeray's house, they'd been figuring out their next move when Forbes threw a spanner in the works. The quiet, the proximity and the natural volume of Forbes's voice had Sully holding his cell away from his ear. Dez snatched it away before Sully could stop him.

If Forbes Raynor's voice was thunderous, Dez's was the sound of an F-5 tornado.

"Do you have any fucking idea what we're going through right now? Our father just died, you asshole! Give Sully a couple days, or you'll be dealing with me instead. You hear me? ... Damn right, that's a threat. You wanna go there? 'Cuz I'm good for it."

"Dez." Sully restricted himself to just the one word, hoping it would prove enough. He had to repeat it a couple times, but his brother finally listened, handing back the phone while Forbes was mid-tirade. Sully waited until the man paused for a breath. "Sergeant? You're going to have to forgive my brother."

"I don't forgive threats, Gray."

"No, I mean you're going to *have* to. You know what we're going through. Any further pushing from you right now and I'll file an official complaint. Those don't go to the city, they go to the province. And, far as I know, your dad doesn't hold any clout there."

Even if Forbes reacted badly to Sully's promise, Dez's soft rumble of laughter made it all worthwhile. Unfortunately, Dez wasn't likely to find Sully's next statement so amusing.

"I'll come in to talk to you this afternoon, all right?"

Forbes's response sounded to be coming through gritted teeth. "What time?"

"I don't know yet. We're in the middle of something, right now. I'll call you. That's the best I can do."

"I'm warning you, Gray. If I don't see your ass in here soon, I'm going to find you and arrest you for obstructing an investigation, you hear me? Call me before four. Any later, you and I are going to have a problem."

As far as Sully was concerned, they already had a problem, but he found himself with a more immediate one the moment he ended the call and returned the cellphone to his pocket.

"Why the hell did you agree to meet him today?" Dez demanded. "We talked about this."

Sully suggested a mild correction. "Actually, you talked."

"And, as usual, you didn't listen."

"Like I said before, this isn't going away, Dez. I'm done with this hanging over me. Anyway, now that we know who it was who likely broke into the Fox the other night, I've got something I can give Raynor to follow. He can't charge me with anything until he clears that lead, right?"

"Damn it. I told Waters I was giving him a pass."

"You said you weren't going to arrest him. You didn't say anything about someone else doing it. Anyway, you hadn't thought about the possibility he was behind the break-in, not until I mentioned it after."

"Look, Sull, if it means taking the heat off you, I'll quite happily break whatever promises Waters thinks I gave him. I just don't want you talking to Raynor until you're in a state to handle it."

"That probably won't be for months. Look, you and me, we're probably kind of in the same boat right now, back and forth between shock and falling apart. There are moments where I think Dad's just a phone call away. Another couple of days, once reality's had a chance to really settle in, I don't want to think what state I'll be in. This is probably the best I'm going to be for a while."

"I don't like it, Sully."

"You don't have to. You just have to accept it. I'm a suspect in a murder investigation, and there's no way around it. I've got to find my way through it. Look, I didn't do it, and even if Forbes tries to twist every piece of evidence to fit, and even if he has the backing of his father, he's still got to have something for the prosecutor to make something of in court. If there's no way a jury's going to buy it down the road, no chance the prosecutor will either, right?"

Dez didn't respond, which Sully took as a win.

SULLY MANAGED to convince Dez to join him for lunch at a café down the road from the Black Fox, one where Sully took his breaks when he was short on groceries or sick of his own terrible attempts at cooking.

His appetite didn't match the sounds his stomach had been making, and he was fighting nausea by the time he'd forced down a burger and fries. Lunch done, Sully held onto his last request for his brother until they were back on the sidewalk. Once they were out of others' earshot, he told Dez he wanted to walk over to police headquarters. Alone.

He summed up with a statement he knew was sure to convince his brother of the merits of his plan. "It'll give me time to think and to calm down. I'll be less likely to say something stupid or step in whatever trap he's looking to spring."

"I still don't like this."

"You still don't have to."

To his credit, Dez did what he couldn't have a couple years ago.

Blowing out a heavy breath, he enveloped Sully in a hug and demanded a phone call once he'd finished with Forbes.

Then Dez walked away.

If Dez thought Sully was out of his mind for wanting to face questioning now, there was nonetheless method in the madness of the plan.

Of course, returning to face Terrence Waters so soon after the man had taken both of them on in the park was its own kind of crazy.

It might have been prudent to take Dez with him to have this conversation, as backup if nothing else. But the more Sully skirted around the edges of this foggy mire he was trying to slog through, the more the mists were lifting to reveal the person standing in the centre.

Dez was going through enough already and, although he was a stronger physical presence than Sully, he was more fragile emotionally. If this went the way Sully thought it might, Lowell Braddock was going to come out not only as having set Thackeray Schuster up for a fall, but possibly also as having been behind far more than that—including the death of his own brother.

But with no proof to present and nothing but suspicion to back him, now wasn't the time for Sully to drag Dez into this. If it turned out he was wrong about Lowell, any accusations he was about to make could serve to distance Sully from the rest of his family—including his brother.

That was an outcome he couldn't afford to risk.

And so he headed alone to the army surplus store, hoping Terrence Waters had made his way back there.

Sully wasn't surprised to find the man back behind the counter. Terrence, however, was plenty shocked to see him.

"What the hell you want now?"

Sully approached at the demand, closing the gap between the two of them so as to keep the conversation quiet. "Is there somewhere we can talk?"

"We can talk here."

"We won't be overheard?"

Terrence's sneer screamed sarcasm as he jutted his chin toward a so-far otherwise empty store. "Does it look like that's a problem? Damn glad I don't own this place. Loses more to shoplifters than to sales. So I'll ask again. What the hell you want?"

"I want to ask you about a break-in at the Black Fox four nights ago."

"There've been break-ins all over Riverview this past while. Someone tried to get in here not so long ago, too, but we keep it too secure."

"That's not what I was getting at. And I think you know that."

That Terrence did know was proven as he got off the stool and, casting one more dark look at Sully, waved his usable hand at him to follow. A private office was just the other side of the staff-only area, a room consisting of two desks—one stacked with papers and boasting a computer that had likely become obsolete several years ago, and the other holding a small bank of monitors showing front and rear doors, till area and a wide view of the store's interior. Terrence closed the door to ensure privacy, then positioned himself so he could keep an eye on the screens while listening to whatever Sully wanted to discuss, his imposing bulk and beefy crossed arms forming a dare only the truly idiotic would take.

Sully was that idiot today. "You're the one who broke into Betty Schuster's office, weren't you?"

"What the hell you talking about?"

"I think you know. I confronted the guy afterward in the alley, swung a bat at him. He moved around it like a pro and put me on the ground without really hurting me. That makes me think two things: the guy's trained in hand-to-hand combat and he either didn't want to hurt anyone or he was directed not to. Did someone pay you to do it?"

The sneer was back, less sarcastic now, more dangerous. "Those are some pretty serious accusations you're making there, kid. I'd be careful if I were you."

"All you have to do is deny it."

"I'm denying it."

Sully opted to play the trump card early. "Did Lowell Braddock pay you to break into his own bar?"

He looked for a tell, any tell, anything to indicate he'd hit the nail. He found it in a twitch of a muscle running along the left side of Terrence's jaw, a slight jump under the skin that came alongside a too-long break between question and response.

When Terrence spoke, it was a question rather than an answer. "Why would he want to break into his own bar?"

"My dad always told me answering a question with another question means someone's looking to buy themselves time. It can be a sign they're trying to come up with a good story. Why'd you do it? Did he pay you or did he blackmail you? Or did he just feed you a line that Betty had evidence somewhere her son was back at some bad stuff and that she was hiding it somewhere, trying to keep Thackeray out of jail?"

"You know, you're in a real dangerous situation, right now. No one knows you're here, do they? Real stupid move, laying accusations like that against a man like me. I could snap your neck right now and no one would even know."

"But you won't. You had a chance to kill me before and you didn't. Maybe you've had more than one. I think the person who broke in was looking for a thumb drive, and they didn't find it. So they were told to return the next day and just take care of the source of the info. If they couldn't find the drive, they could at least buy time to look if they took out the only other person who really knew what was on it. She was a threat, and there was a real risk she would reveal what she knew. You've killed before, probably, had to during your time in the service. You know how to put yourself into a frame of mind where you can stay calm doing it. Killing is messy and a lot of people leave evidence behind. It takes a cool head to ensure that doesn't happen."

Unfortunately, if Terrence possessed a cool head, he needed reminding. Sully couldn't get the door open before the other man was on him, good hand seizing a handful of his shirt and slamming him into the wall. Sully's back was still tender after the run-in at the park earlier; he grunted in pain as he met the wall and was held there in the solid grip.

"You ever kill a man, boy?"

Sully opened his eyes, found narrowed dark eyes piercing his. Sully had looked into the eyes of killers before, had once met a man who hadn't just killed, but had enjoyed it. There had been both steel in that gaze and the watchfulness of a snake looking for the best moment and location to strike. And there had been enough chill there to make anyone standing close enough shiver.

Terrence was not that man. These eyes, from this closer-than-comfortable view, were surrounded by a fine web of lines that spoke more to a life of strain than laughter. There was heat rather than cold. And there was something else, something it took Sully a moment longer to put a finger on. He'd seen it before, in the wide-eyed stare of a disembodied stroke patient housed at Lockwood Psychiatric Hospital.

Terrence Waters was haunted.

"I asked you a question. You ever kill a man?"

Sully shook his head.

"Let me describe it to you. Taking a life at a distance, that's one thing. You watch the body react to the impact of the shot. Maybe he keeps coming at you so you gotta spend another round. Maybe he drops right away. But that image stays, even if you can't see his face. Now, you kill a man close up, that's something else altogether. You see the moment he realizes he's hit. Sometimes he feels the pain right away, sometimes it's just shock at first. A head shot's quick and clean, ends things before they begin. Then you just gotta deal with the memory of the body lying there, head opened up, eyes—if he's still got 'em—staring up at you.

"Most times, managing a head shot's just not possible. There's pressure in the moment, people move. Maybe, if you're lucky, you get him in the heart. Even then, some people can run damn near a full football field before they drop. Takes the heart a while to clue in, enough time for the guy to give you something to remember late at night when you're trying to sleep. The visuals, that's bad enough. Standing that close, you see it the moment the light goes out from his eyes, the moment the chest stops moving, limbs stop twitching. But it's the sounds that can get you, the gasping, the gurgling, sometimes the screaming. You have a grown man in front of you, a tough, well-trained soldier, crying like a baby, begging not to die, that sticks with you. You take that with you, carry it so it comes out at the worst times. I can't go to funerals, I can't go to action movies, can't watch the news. I hear a man crying, I go back to Afghanistan.

"I heard how that woman died at the Fox, how some bastard went in and blasted her with a shotgun. I'm not cold enough to kill a woman, and I'm not strong enough to kill anyone, not anymore. Those days are behind me. You kill out of necessity in a war zone, and you take it with you all the same. Unless you're a fucking psychopath, your humanity's been torn out of you, or you're in the middle of a PTSD episode, most of us will do anything to never have to feel those things again. I didn't kill that woman. I'm not capable of it."

With those statements, and the level of pained truth behind

them, the fear left Sully. Sure, Waters might still be plenty capable of dishing out another beating, but Sully could cope with that. In fact, there were a variety of moves he could pull to get away from Terrence if he wanted. But there was no reason, because Terrence had been telling the truth. He hadn't killed Betty and he wasn't about to kill Sully.

And so Sully felt less anxiety about his next statement. "But you did pull off the break-in."

Terrence fixed him with one more heated glare before roughly releasing him. "What if I did? You just said nothing was taken. You gonna tell the cops it was me?"

Sully had been aiming in that direction, but that was when he'd suspected Terrence of pulling off both the break-in and the hit on Betty. Now he was back to square one on the shooting. "The lead investigator on the murder thinks I did it."

Terrence didn't bother to ask if he had. He just burst out laughing.

Sully took it as a compliment.

"Kid, that's the dumbest thing I've heard all year. You're about as capable of killing as I am of becoming a member of Cirque du Soleil."

"There are at least a couple people who would celebrate an early Christmas if they could lay a murder charge on me. The problem is, if they can't get me on it, there's always you to fall back on. Someone killed Betty, and if it wasn't me and it wasn't you, then that's got me wondering who it actually was."

"There've been a lot of robberies around here. People are saying that's what happened, robbery gone bad."

"I was there. The guy didn't say anything. Just came in, masked and armed, and fired almost as soon as Betty came into frame."

"Wasn't an accidental discharge? Some of the crappy guns around here have hair triggers. Feather landing on them would set them off."

Sully was forced to concede at least part of that point. "He and

I were struggling for the gun—or, at least, I was struggling. He felt pretty strong to me."

"So maybe the gun only went off because of that."

Which was exactly what Sully was dreading. "Maybe."

Sully's gaze had dropped to the floor, but he looked up at the sound of Terrance's voice. The man had his arms crossed, head tilted. "That's why you're so bent on figuring this out, huh? You think it might be your fault."

Sully didn't bother answering. Terrance probably didn't need an answer anyway, and he proved it a moment later by offering another observation.

"Let me tell you something. You might never know whose finger was on that trigger, or whether someone bumped it, or who shifted the barrel so it was aiming at her when it went off. I'm not going to tell you you'll stop thinking about it, because you won't. I was driving the TAV the day we hit that IED. I've replayed that moment in my head so many times, it's burned in there like a cattle-brand. It's never helped answer my questions. The road was full of ruts and bumps, so I didn't see anything out of the ordinary in the spot we hit. Maybe I should have, maybe I missed something. If I'd driven a little to the left or right, I might have passed right over. Then again, maybe that would have meant the next vehicle got it. I'll never figure it all out, and neither will you, no matter how many times you go through it.

"You can find the guy responsible, but maybe he's got the same questions you do. What are you going to do with your guilt, then? I'll tell you one thing. If that scumbag hadn't gone in there with a loaded shotgun, there wouldn't have been a struggle for the gun, and no one would have been shot. If no one had buried a fucking IED in the road, my buddy and I would have just carried on back to base. We didn't start this shit, kid, but you and me, we've got to figure out where to put it. I don't know, maybe we never do."

Sully had first seen him in the park, standing next to Terrence, a young man around the same age Sully was now. He was dressed in full tactical gear, although parts of it—along with parts of his body—were missing. One arm was gone and one leg, and there were pieces blown out of his torso and face, but he remained standing upright as only the dead can. Sometimes they appeared to Sully as if they were keenly aware of their injuries, dragging along the ground or bent around whatever wound had spelled their death. Sometimes agony marred their features as if they continued to feel whatever trauma had killed them.

Others, like this man, appeared oblivious—at least, to everything but the person standing next to him. There was not pain in his expression but a sympathy so profound it could only have been borne of the deepest friendship.

The ghost looked to Sully, and the meaning was clear. This might be an uncomfortable conversation but it was a necessary one.

"There was a young guy in the TAV with you that day, a good friend. His last name's embroidered on the left front pocket of his shirt. It's a bit torn, but it looks like Littlechief."

It took Terrence a moment to find his tongue. "What the hell are you talking about?"

"He was hurt bad in the explosion. He lost an arm and a leg and some pieces from his torso and lower face. He's got dark brown hair and is roughly your height."

"I asked you a question. What are you talking about?"

Sully drew in a deep breath, held it a moment and released it slowly, looking for calm in the movement. "I know how this is going to sound, but I see people after they die, usually as the result of something violent or criminal. He's standing next to you now."

Terrence took a step back, stumbling as his foot came down behind him so that he ended up hitting one of the desks hard enough it would probably leave a bruise. A lot of people didn't buy into the things Sully saw and so took some convincing, and he didn't want to have to try to persuade Terrence of the truth with a hand wrapped around his throat.

Sully talked fast.

"He's showing me a picture of the two of you with a couple other guys from the unit. He's pulling it out of that same front pocket, along with a photo of a young woman and a baby. They appear to be Indigenous like he is."

"That's his wife and little girl. He carried those two photos with him everywhere. How do you know that?"

Part of Littlechief's lower jaw was missing, and Sully was left to wonder whether he would have been able to understand the spirit even if he'd been capable of hearing him. Whatever the case, Littlechief didn't try to talk, instead raising a finger and tracing a shape in the air, twice over.

"It looks like he's making the shape of a 'B.' Does that means anything to you? He's doing it twice, and he's pointing back at the pocket where he's got the photos."

Tears had formed in Terrence's eyes, and he swiped them away. "He called those photos his babes and his bros. How the fuck are you doing this?"

"I told you how."

"That's bullshit. You can't know this. You can't actually be seeing him."

Littlechief exuded frustration as he looked from Sully to his old friend, and then refocused to the light fixture overhead. Within seconds, it began to flicker, gently at first, and then with enough violence Sully thought the lightbulb might blow completely. When at last the flickering stopped, Terrence's face had taken on a ghostly cast to rival that of Littlechief's.

"Why is that happening?"

"It's happened before, hasn't it?"

"Here, at home, sometimes when I'm out. Lightbulbs do that, the TV goes on and off by itself. Hell, I've even had to replace a microwave."

"Spirits are made up of energy and they can manipulate electricity as a way to interact. He's been trying to get your attention, and he's getting really frustrated."

Terrence had been breathing heavily, but now he stopped completely, round eyes fixed on Sully with what could only be described as dread. It took him a moment to form the words, as if he'd been debating whether he wanted to say them out loud. "He's pissed at me, isn't he? I've felt him sometimes, like he's around me. Like he's mad."

"He's not angry for the reason you think," Sully said, watching Littlechief for the confirmation he needed to forge ahead. The ghost provided it with an enthusiastic head nod, face turning between the two living people in what appeared to be an indication he wanted Sully to continue. "He's pissed at you because you're blaming yourself for something that's not your fault. He's sticking around because he's trying to help you, to have your back like he used to, like you used to do for him. But you're not hearing him, so he gets frustrated and starts screwing with your electricity. It probably happens mostly when you're having bad moments, doesn't it?"

Terrence's reply, coming amidst tears he'd given up on wiping away, was a whisper. "Jesus Christ. Chief? God, Chief, I'm so sorry, man. I'm so sorry."

Littlechief rolled his eyes and shook his head side to side.

"He doesn't want to hear it," Sully said. "He's rolling his eyes."

That drew a laugh from Terrence. "Jerk used to do that to me all the time. Knew it pissed me off. So, you're trying to tell me he forgives me?"

Littlechief shook his head again, leaving Sully to interpret. "I think he's trying to tell you there's nothing to forgive." Sully met Littlechief's eyes and received an approving head nod. "He's telling me I'm on the money. You've been blaming yourself, and it's been screwing you up for a long time. And he can't move on until he knows you're going to be okay."

Terrence's eyes swept the room as if trying to see his friend for himself, before finally settling back on Sully. "Chief knows me, so he knows I'm a skeptical S.O.B. I need one more sign from him, something just between the two of us. I landed next to him after the explosion, and there was a moment, before the next vehicle came up on us, where it was just Chief and me. He couldn't talk, but he did something right before he died, something he used to do to be a smart ass."

Sully waited while Littlechief played it through, revealing the answer with movement. "He's pinching your cheek."

Whatever walls Terrence had erected to cope with that tragic day's events crumbled to the ground, his throat releasing a sob that led to others. Sully waited him out, Littlechief standing at Terrence's side until, at last, he quieted and blew his nose into a fast food joint's napkin.

He didn't apologize for the breakdown, likely didn't want to acknowledge he'd even had one. Instead, his focus went back to Littlechief. "Is he okay? I mean, will he be okay if I am?"

"He can't really heal while he's stuck here, if that's what you're asking. He looks like he did after the explosion. I mean, he doesn't look like he's in physical pain like some people I see, but he won't be back in one piece until he can cross over."

Sully had been to the store a number of times in the past, and the smile breaking on Terrence's face was the first Sully had ever seen on the man. "Then he can go. I don't know how this is possible, but it feels like a weight's gone. I've been living in the dark all this time, and I didn't know I was keeping him there too. I thought there was no way to right my own wrongs, so I went out trying to right those of others. I don't know, man. I don't remember how to live outside of this box. But I'll figure it out, okay, Chief? You get out of here, stop fucking with my electricity. You're costing me money."

Sully passed along Littlechief's response. "He's laughing."

"Yeah, he would."

If there was a saving grace to seeing the dead, it was these moments, watching as death fell from the ghosts, as light filled and surrounded and healed them. Limbs appeared on Littlechief where they'd been missing, gaping wounds in his body filled and blood and gore faded from his now-crisp uniform. Littlechief's expression, at first one of surprise, gave way to serenity and strength, peace radiating from him and through him.

"I wish you could see him," Sully told Terrence. "You just healed him, man."

"So he's really okay?"

"Oh, yeah. He's more than okay."

Littlechief gave Terrence one last squeeze on the cheek before gracing Sully with a smile that sent a wave of warmth through him.

Then he was gone.

25

Sully did Terrence one more service, manning the till for a poorly timed customer while the store's manager got his emotions back under control in his office.

When Terrence re-emerged, he was a different man from the one who'd gone in there. This Terrence Waters looked a little sheepish, but it was tempered by a smile that only grew as he regarded Sully.

"Thanks for looking after that guy," he said. "He's not likely to be very understanding of me standing here blubbering like a baby. Sorry about losing my shit on you."

Sully returned the grin. "Forget it. If people don't lose their shit on me, I'm not really trying."

Terrence pulled up a stool, joining Sully behind the counter. "You helped me, now I wanna help you. Whatever you want to know, I'll tell you."

Sully was building up the nerve he'd need to face Forbes Raynor in an interview room. He'd come here looking for answers, expecting he might emerge with a suspect to pass along to the investigator. Now, the last thing Sully wanted was to hang Terrence Waters out to dry.

"Maybe I don't want to know."

Terrence wasn't having it. "If the cops are gunning for you on this, you need answers to give them, ones you don't have and likely won't find. After I was medically discharged, I came back here and found there weren't a whole lot of things I could do anymore. I was fucked with PTSD so bad I couldn't hold a job, and you add in the physical injuries .... Well, there just wasn't much I was trained in that I could still do. I tried to retrain, went to take a course in starting your own business, but I couldn't finish. My head just wasn't there. I damn near ended up on the street when money got tight. I got lucky, got a job here and worked my way to manager pretty quick. It's not great work, and the pay's crap, but it's something. Anyway, I've been trying to support Chief's wife and daughter with anything extra I have and, a couple weeks ago, I got a visit from a guy offering to pay me a decent amount of money to break into his business for him."

"Lowell Braddock."

"Yeah. Said there would be nothing illegal about it, since it was his place and I was doing it on his say-so. He'd actually come to me a few weeks before that with a bunch of posters he'd made up of that Schuster guy. Said he was out of prison and likely to reoffend, that I'd be doing everyone a favour by making sure the pervert stayed straight. Then, right before the break-in, Braddock came back and told me he believed his manager was using her office at the bar to conceal a thumb drive containing files that would incriminate her pervert kid, would prove he was back at the same shit. Braddock was worried if the drive was found in his business, he'd be implicated somehow, that people might think he was allowing it. He asked me to find the drive, but he warned me you lived in an upstairs apartment. He told me he passes you sleeping pills, but wasn't sure if you always took them. He said if you caught me at it, you weren't to be harmed—not like I needed that direction. Sorry, I took you down a little hard. Adrenaline was pumping and I was in a rush to get out of there before the cops showed."

"You didn't find anything."

"Nada. But then, I didn't really have a whole lot of time to look. Had to report back I hadn't had any luck. I'm glad I only talked to him on the phone. His tone suggested he'd have been looking for someone to bury his fists in."

The statement drew a smile from Sully. "I wouldn't have thought you'd be worried about going toe to toe with Lowell Braddock. Dez is bigger than Lowell and better in a fight, and you gave him a run for his money."

"I wasn't worried about getting hit," Terrence said. "I was worried about doing the hitting. Someone like Lowell Braddock doesn't take too kindly to having to explain a fat lip. He could make life real bad for me. It was one of the reasons I said yes when he came to me about the break-in, and the one you caught me at in the Schuster house. You don't say no to people like him. He's dangerous. Not in the way people like me are dangerous. But he's a man people don't refuse, and he's got the money, power and connections to see to it you regret it if you do anything but go along with him. He risked a lot, asking in the first place. Because it meant someone else knew what he was up to, which made me a threat right from the get-go. Signing on to help removed that threat, put me right in there with him. I'm not going to report anything because I'd be implicating myself and, for someone like me, a jail cell with nothing to do all day but think would be next door to hell."

"Did he approach you about killing Betty?"

"No, but I can guarantee he's got something up his sleeve to send me up the river for it if it starts coming back on him."

"You think he did it himself?"

"Break-ins are one thing. Him paying me to get into his own business, it's probably doubtful whether there's anything illegal in that. And the way crime's been going up around here, cops and folks in the courts have better things to do than chase some pharm bigwig over a break-in at one of his own businesses. As far as the Schusters' place, he had a key. Told me he owns the place, that Betty was just renting from him."

Sully hadn't heard that, Betty always having referred to the place as hers. It was possible, of course. Lowell owned a number of rental properties in the city.

"In any case," Terrence continued. "The risk's negligible to him, bringing someone else into that part of his plan. But involving someone else in a kill plot, that's something else. Some things you're better off doing yourself. Friends bury friends rather than do their time for them. Sure as hell won't get loyalty from strangers."

There was little Sully could say to that, his brain chattering on at him in a way that made physical speech next to impossible. He realized he'd been silent longer than intended when Terrence's voice cut into his thoughts.

"If you're thinking of a way to confront Lowell Braddock, let me give you a piece of advice. Don't. Just don't. I know this isn't what you want to hear, but I think you need to just leave this be. That woman's gone, and she's not coming back. You pursue this, you go after Braddock on this, you're going to come out the loser. People like him, they don't lose. It's not in their makeup, and I'll tell you another thing. Society's built to take the word of a rich man over a poor one, and a big business leader over a bartender or a manager of an army surplus store. Face it, kid, you're built to lose this one. Just let it lie."

"I wish it were that easy."

"Why isn't it?"

The answer to that one wasn't right here, staring Sully in the face as it so often did, but it was close, never far away, never forgotten. "What you said about the dead being gone and not coming back, that's true for most people. Not for me. They come to me for help, for justice, and they don't leave me alone until I get it for them. I could ignore one. Maybe I could ignore a dozen. But all that means is that I wake up one morning, and I've got twelve ghosts staring down at me instead of just one new one. I was given this ability for a reason, and I realized early on in life ignoring it isn't an option. And I've got my own conscience to wrestle with too. I couldn't just let someone suffer when it's in my power to help, and I sure couldn't leave a friend to fend for herself—especially one I might have had a hand in killing."

Terrence regarded Sully a long moment before offering a reply. "I've given you my advice, but I hear what you're saying. Conscience is a powerful enemy sometimes, and it's not one you can easily kill. I know that better than most. You and me, we've got our own ghosts to lay to rest, I guess. I can't come down on you for wanting to deal with yours when I've struggled under the weight of mine all this time. Listen, you helped me with mine. You need anything, you just tell me and you've got it."

Since he'd already ruled out the possibility of Dez's involvement, the idea of having a man like Terrence Waters at his back when facing Lowell was a welcome one. But Sully squelched it almost as soon as it formed. If Sully was right, Lowell was behind at least two deaths, both people he knew, at least one he claimed to love. Confronting Lowell would be a dangerous task, and Sully was entertaining no ideas that his foster uncle would spare him. And, if Terrence showed up, too, he'd be nothing more to Lowell but another walking and talking target. The last thing Sully needed was another ghost, another death on his conscience.

"Thanks, Terrence. I appreciate it. I really do. But I think I've got to deal with this one on my own."

"Let me give you one more piece of advice, then, all right? Don't turn your back on that man. He's missing something that makes a man human. He's damn good at hiding it, but it's there all the same. Whatever you do, don't get yourself into a situation where he has the upper hand."

Sully left Terrence with a warm handshake and assurances he'd do what he could to play this safe. He didn't make any promises, though, no way he could assure Terrence he'd ever find a situation where he had the upper hand.

This was Lowell Braddock, after all. There wasn't a scenario in existence between the two of them where Lowell wouldn't insist on coming out on top.

A COUPLE of hours before Forbes Raynor's imposed deadline, Sully was on the move again.

Sully needed to see someone else first, and another uncomfortable conversation needed to be had.

Thackeray Schuster was where he often seemed to be, sitting in one of the rickety chairs on the side porch, lit cigarette held at the corner of his mouth. His eyebrows lifted as he saw Sully approaching, and his cigarette bobbed in place as he asked the inevitable question.

"What are you doing back here?"

Sully closed the remainder of the distance, and slid into Betty's old chair. "We need to talk about Lowell Braddock."

Thackeray turned from Sully, eyes casting over the fence that separated his property from the neighbour's. It was in dire need of a paint job and a few new boards, but Sully guessed Thackeray wouldn't be in a hurry to do it. Thackeray had more important concerns and, if Sully guessed at this correctly, was haunted by his own sort of ghosts. Sully knew better than most, ghosts didn't often let you rest, let alone give you the time or inclination for home maintenance.

Thackeray had yet to respond, and Sully expected he didn't intend to.

"I know this isn't an easy topic for either of us, but it's necessary. That thumb drive, there was something on it concerning Lowell. I didn't bring it up earlier, because I don't want to involve Dez. If this is what I think it is, it's going to end with my brother having to pick sides, and I want to delay that as long as I can. Right now, it's just you and me."

He paused, waited. Again, there was no response.

"I know it was about Lowell, all right?" Sully said. "My dad found the drive in my pocket, and it looks like he viewed the contents. My mom doesn't know what was on it. She didn't see, but she said whatever it was, Dad was furious and took off to confront Lowell. That's the last time we saw him alive. Thackeray, I think Lowell did something to my dad to keep him from revealing what was on that drive. He told us Dad had a heart attack and that he gave him a shot of epinephrine. If I was to guess, I'd say he gave him enough to stop his heart. He talked about Dad hitting his head on the way down. I think it's more likely Lowell hit him and knocked him out. After that, it would have been easy to inject him. I don't know if there's any way to know the exact cause of a heart attack. And even if they tested and found a fatal dose of epinephrine caused it, Lowell would just argue he panicked and gave Dad too much. And it would be believable because why would he intend to kill his own brother, right?"

Sully took a breath, searching for calm as those images played in his mind; the likely reality of what had happened to his dad created a pain in his own heart. He battled emotion, sucked it back as he refocused on this conversation.

This non-conversation.

Thackeray allowed the silence to stretch, made no effort to fill it.

"Thackeray, I need you to talk to me. It may be nothing will ever come of this, but I need to know, okay? *I* need to know. He set you up for a reason, and I think it was about that drive."

"You don't understand."

"What don't I understand?"

"People like him, they get away with things. They find ways. He killed your dad, and I think he also killed my mom. He got my dad committed, he got me sent to prison. He's probably involved somehow in setting you up for Mom's shooting. He's capable of anything. Don't you get it? Pursuing this, it's not going to get you anywhere but dead."

"So why is he doing all this? I mean, for starters, why set you up?"

"To discredit me, no doubt. Who's going to buy anything a convicted pervert has to say? Thing is, he had access to the house, so he easily could have planted everything against me. He owns the place."

"But your parents had it before they met Lowell, didn't they?"

"Yeah, but when Dad started losing his marbles, and then with the stroke, he couldn't work anymore. Mom eventually had to remortgage, and she couldn't afford it on her own. Lowell took over the mortgage, agreed to rent it back to Mom at a decent rate. So, yeah, he figured he could come and go as he pleased around here. He came over quite a bit to talk to Mom, liked to have a hand in all his businesses, he said. But I think it was about more than that. I think he wanted to make sure he was still safe, that I would keep my mouth shut."

"About what?"

Thackeray fell back into silence, leaving Sully to fill in the blanks.

"Your father saw something, didn't he? Something Lowell did. And Lowell figured out a way to silence your father. Fact is, no one's going to listen to the word of a crazy man, are they? No one but you."

"Dad wouldn't stop talking about it. 'River boy, river boy.' He'd repeat it over and over until I sometimes wanted to just ship him off to Lockwood myself, just so I wouldn't have to listen to him anymore. But once in a while, he'd have these weird lucid moments, where the 'crazy' would go away, and you'd be able to have a proper conversation with him. I was at home with him by myself this one day, and he told me about a vision he'd had—not of the future, but something from the past. He said he'd seen Lowell killing a kid."

Sully had first seen the ghost of Aiden Braddock years ago, first standing behind Flynn in a police interview room, then next to the river running behind the family's home. He'd known then, even without a full understanding of his gift, something terrible had happened to the boy.

He rarely saw Aiden, but the fact he saw him at all meant his death was something more than a simple accident, more than a slip from the shore and the pull of a current. There was a human's murderous hand in it somewhere, and Sully had always felt his built-in finger of suspicion turning on his foster uncle.

But Lowell was a Braddock and, come right down to it, Sully was not. And while Sully had quickly learned to trust his family with his deepest secrets, there were truths he never dared speak for fear of running up against a wall that would separate him from the people who meant the most to him in the world.

Hearing those words spoken out loud by someone else, this darkest suspicion he'd kept to himself for years, set Sully's head spinning, sent blood rushing from his brain as quickly as the current that had carried Aiden's body from his home.

Sully's own voice sounded tinny, spoken from behind the thick pounding in his ears. "What else did your dad say?"

"He didn't know the kid's name, but he said the boy had red hair and freckles, was around five years old. He said Lowell drowned him in a river."

"Did … did you confront Lowell with it?"

"Are you kidding? No way. I was just a kid myself. But I did tell Mom. Back then, she wasn't putting much stock in the things Dad said, figured he was just off his nut. I was there when Mom told Lowell, though. She used to talk to him about Dad, about how she didn't know what to do about him. She always told him about the crazy stuff Dad said, and one day she brought up the 'river boy' thing. Only Lowell didn't laugh it off. He got really pale and quiet, and then he started talking about how we should put Dad into Lockwood. Said he was worried Dad might hurt me.

"He'd started his pharmaceutical company by then, and he had these pills he prescribed for Dad. Supposed to help settle his brain and help him rest, he said. He warned us stroke was a rare side effect. Dad's happened almost right away—so fast I've always wondered whether it was Lowell's intention in the first place. Even then, Mom insisted on keeping Dad at home. It took Dad a few years before he could talk again, and it turned out he was still having those visions. That's when Lowell started coming around again. He gave Mom a new drug and next thing we knew, Dad was slitting his wrists one night in the bathroom. After that, Mom finally gave in and committed him to Lockwood."

"So if your dad was out of the picture, why set you up? What was the risk to Lowell if you and your mom didn't believe Harry?"

Thackeray finally met Sully's eye. "I said Mom didn't believe him, I never said I didn't. I was almost done high school when Dad was committed, old enough to know how to research. I went to the library and found a newspaper story about a search for a five-year-old kid named Aiden Braddock who was found dead by the river. Lowell never talked about his personal life. It was all business with him, or my family's personal business. Never his. So he hadn't told us anything about losing his nephew.

"I showed Mom the articles I found, and I reminded her what Dad had said about the drowned kid. Mom brushed it off, said Dad could have seen it in the paper, too, and turned it into something else in his brain. I became fixated on it, though. It took years of stewing about it but, eventually, I decided to confront Lowell with it, and with what I believed he did to my dad. I arranged a meeting with him, and I recorded the conversation on a digital recorder. That's what was on the thumb drive."

"Did he admit to anything?"

"Of course not. But I thought I had something, even if it was just the way he initially froze and stuttered when I first brought up Aiden. I don't think I ever had any real idea what I was going to do with the recording, but I knew I wanted something to show Mom, to prove to her why she shouldn't trust Lowell. The week after that conversation, the cops showed up with a search warrant and turned up a pile of child porn in my room. Mom had held onto the thumb drive I'd made, kept it at the office, so it didn't end up getting taken along with everything else of mine. My mother didn't believe I'd been set up at first. She still swallowed the crap Lowell was feeding her, that I was disturbed like my father. We'd never been close. We fought a lot in my teen years, me accusing her of giving a bigger damn about dad than me.

"Anyway, Mom, it turned out, had some doubts after all, so she went to Lowell about what I'd told her about Dad's vision. He said I had obviously developed my father's mental illness and, if it got worse, he'd see to it I was committed to Lockwood with Dad. Without the income I'd been bringing in to help pay the rent, we'd lose our home pretty quick. Lowell offered to write off my share of the rent until I was released from prison, as long as Mom didn't go around spreading what he called false rumours about him.

"While I was locked up, there were three attempts on my life. Twice, I managed to alert the guards before the guys could stick a knife in. The third, I almost died. If money wasn't enough to shut my mom and me up, those incidents were. That's where Lowell really screwed up with Mom, I think. Those attempts ended up being what it took to convince Mom what I was saying was true."

"Did anyone in jail say they were acting on Lowell's behalf?"

"No, but they didn't have to. I knew. I was on a range with sex offenders. Nothing like that should have been happening. Skinners don't go after other skinners. There was something else behind it, and I can't think of a single other reason why I would have had a target on my back besides what I knew about Lowell."

"When did Lowell find out about the thumb drive?"

"Just recently, a few days before the break-in and Mom's murder. There'd been people watching the house, following me. Then Mom saw the posters about me, with our address. We both figured Lowell was behind all of it somehow, intimidating me into keeping quiet by lording some sort of threat over my head. The posters would have been the perfect cover, if he decided to try to kill me again. The police would have just put it down to some vigilante thing."

Sully hadn't seen her, focused as he was on Thackeray, although he guessed Betty had been here for much of the conversation. Now she moved into Sully's view, standing at her son's shoulder and placing a hand over it as she nodded at Thackeray's read of the situation.

"Your mom's here," Sully said. Then, to Betty, "Thackeray's right, isn't he? You confronted Lowell, told him there was a thumb drive with the recording of that conversation."

Betty nodded.

"Were you hoping to use it as leverage, to get Lowell to stop having Thackeray followed and threatened?"

Another nod.

The progression was obvious from there. Lowell had approached the manager of the nearby army surplus—the same guy he'd had plastering up posters and stalking Thackeray—and asked Terrence to find the thumb drive. It was likely he'd made his own efforts at the Schuster house first, using the key he'd have as the house's official owner. When both that and Terrence's search proved fruitless, Lowell had taken the last, bloody step, disguising himself and relying on the bar's non-operational surveillance cameras to kill Betty, silencing the one person he'd never be able to discredit. Betty wasn't perfect, never had been, but she had attained a level of respect for telling it like it was; people trusted her. If she talked, they would listen. And given the break-in, and the obvious reason for it, Betty likely would have been more inclined than ever to take the device to the one place Lowell couldn't get to it: the police.

Lowell had had to act quickly. With no time to hire someone, and no likelihood he would have entrusted a stranger with that level of dirty work, Lowell had shot Betty himself.

And when Harry somehow managed to slip the drive into Sully's pocket, it started a chain of events leading to Flynn's confrontation with his brother—and the murder of a man by one of the few people in his life he should have been able to trust completely.

Sully was not prone to anger, his emotions rarely shifting too far one way or the other. And so he barely recognized what he was feeling now, this sensation of bubbling rage turning his insides into a seething volcano nearing eruption. All thoughts pulled toward a confrontation with the uncle he now despised beyond anything else.

Flynn Braddock—the man who'd raised him, who'd allowed and even asked him to call him "Dad," who'd given him the love of a family Sully had once only dreamed of—had died because of his need as a father to settle a score over a wrong done to his child.

Now Flynn was dead, and Sully was the one with a score to settle.

"Where are you going?"

Sully didn't respond to Thackeray's question, nor did he stop when Betty positioned herself in his path, merely sidestepping her as he left the veranda.

He couldn't avoid her as she appeared in front of the gate separating yard from sidewalk, forcing Sully to a halt. She stood, glare fixed up on his face, arms crossed as she silently challenged him to disobey her obvious order to leave well enough alone.

"I can't, Betty," he said. "He's my dad."

His voice broke on the word, preventing any further explanation of his need to do this, to go toe-to-toe with the man who had killed Flynn, who had singlehandedly destroyed two families. Sully channelled his grief back into what he intended to be a more productive anger, something at the end of the road besides endless years without his dad. If he could deal with Lowell, it might be he could prevent his hurting anyone else.

Only one thing was left to say to Betty, the same words he'd repeated numerous times since he'd first looked down on her bloody, lead-riddled body lying on the bar floor.

"I'm sorry."

He ducked around her, hopping the fence and taking off in a run toward the nearest bus stop.

26

Sully had been about to board a bus for the New Town core when his plan to look for Lowell at his penthouse was derailed.

He considered it a sign that the text message showing on his cellphone screen was from Lowell himself: "Come to the bar. Need to discuss business."

Business definitely was far from all they needed to discuss, and Sully held onto his fury, allowing it to ferment while he jogged to the next stop for the bus ride that would take him to the Black Fox. Ordinarily, he might have run the entire distance, but he wanted to ensure he wasn't short of breath or exhausted—or in any other way ill-prepared for the anticipated verbal or physical battle—when he met Lowell.

En route, he turned off his cellphone, not wanting any distractions—or, more specifically, not wanting any from Dez. If he saw his brother's name and number pop up on his screen, there was a real risk it would throw him off this unfamiliar and dark path.

Of course, Dez wasn't the only one who'd be looking to influence him in that department. Sully was keenly aware of a presence next to him as he sat in the next-to-last seat on the bus, and he forced himself not to look. Flynn Braddock had always been a calming influence when Sully was anxious or Dez in a temper. The last thing Sully wanted now was calm.

There was no ignoring the hand that flashed in front of his face and settled on his chest, over his heart. Flynn had never been an easy man to ignore in life, and he was proving much the same in death.

Sully kept eyes facing front, his voice a whisper. "Please, Dad, don't. I need to do this. For you. For Aiden. For Betty. I need it for me. Please, don't try to stop me."

The stop nearest the Black Fox was right ahead, and Sully rang the bell, leaving Flynn behind as he went to stand at the rear door. Naturally, he found Flynn there, too, directly in front of him when the bus rolled to a stop and the doors opened, providing a barrier Sully would ordinarily be loath to break.

Not today, though. Today was different. Today, *he* was different.

He was able to avoid most of Flynn, no doubt raising a few eyebrows as he hugged the exit door rather than walking straight through. But Flynn was an imposing man, and it was impossible to avoid him altogether, Sully's shoulder passing through Flynn's left bicep. The chill was enough to cause a muscle cramp, but Sully merely rubbed at it as he continued forward, eating up the rest of the short distance to the bar.

He didn't bother with the front door, heading straight for the back alley. One of Lowell's cars, a Range Rover, was parked there already, and Sully headed for the rear entrance and the keypad that would get him inside. He'd expected another appearance by Flynn, was surprised when it didn't come. He didn't try to guess at what that meant, not wasting the time before keying in the entry code and stepping inside.

There, at the base of the stairs leading to the apartments, Sully saw his father. Only he wasn't alone. Facing him, staring with those wide, fearful, far-seeing eyes, was Harbinger Harry Schuster.

Sully had always wondered whether ghosts saw each other, or

if they passed each other without so much as realizing the other's presence. This—at least as far as these two went—answered his question, Flynn squaring off against Harry as if anticipating a physical battle. Harry's bushy brows lowered in response, for the first time revealing a face set more in determination than in horror.

Caught in a mixture of worry and fascination at what seemed to be an impending ghostly duel, Sully had momentarily forgotten Lowell. But, as usual, his uncle didn't allow himself to be ignored for long. His voice came not, as expected, from the bar, but from upstairs. Sully shifted over just enough to see Lowell leaning back against the frame of the second-storey landing's window, arms and legs crossed as if he'd been waiting.

"I thought we could talk in your apartment. Come on up."

Despite not sharing Harry's gift of foresight, Sully could hear the invitation's scream of danger. And yet, it was nothing more than the sight of the two spirits, suddenly meeting each other in the beginnings of a violent struggle, that kept Sully from rushing headlong up those stairs.

As in life, Flynn was sizeably larger and more skilled in physical confrontations than Harry, but the laws of physics were made to be broken in the spirit world. As the deceased cop attempted to catch Harry with well-honed holds or hand strikes, Harry disappeared from one spot only to reappear in another a moment later.

Flynn's purpose was obvious: having recognized the ghost of the man who had possessed Sully, he would do everything in his power from allowing the spirit anywhere near his son again. Sully didn't think one spirit could harm another—not in any lasting way, anyway—but there was plenty about this world he had yet to learn. And so he had to battle his anxiety over Flynn as he took advantage of the ghosts' distraction to ascend the stairs. Lowell was, after all, the reason he'd come here in the first place.

Lowell had moved, was standing next to the apartment door, and Sully fought against every instinct to lash out here and now, reason reminding him how close he was to the stairs. Lowell wasn't as big as Flynn, but he was still larger than Sully, and a physical fight wasn't likely to turn out well for the smaller man in any context. Starting anything from an even more precarious position was nothing short of stupid.

Pulling the keys from his pocket, Sully let the two of them inside, leaving the eerily silent battle behind downstairs with an unspoken prayer to keep Flynn safe.

Up here, he was waging his own battle, waiting until Lowell edged past him in the entry hall before lashing out with a fist, catching the taller man on the jaw.

Rarely in his life had Sully resorted to physical violence, and he'd forgotten how much it hurt to punch a man. It wasn't any more pleasant when Lowell, knocked on his ass as much due to surprise as the actual force of the blow, reacted with a push immediately upon rising to his feet, strong enough to shove Sully back into the wall.

"What the hell was that for?" Lowell demanded, his voice a shout in the otherwise-silence of the deserted building.

"I know what you did, you son of a bitch."

"What are you talking about?"

"You killed Dad. You fucking killed Dad!"

"Are you out of your mind?"

"Don't pretend you don't know what I'm talking about."

"I don't," Lowell said. But then the dawning of realization showed in his face, one eyebrow lifting as he regarded Sully. "You've been talking to Thackeray Schuster, haven't you?"

"What?"

"I went over today to offer my condolences, but I saw you there, sitting with him on the veranda. The man's apeshit crazy, Sullivan. Didn't Flynn or Dez tell you what he went to prison for?"

"He told me he didn't do it. He told me you set him up."

Lowell's laugh matched the scoffing tone of his reply. "He would say that. Easier than admitting to the world he gets off on kids. Think about it. His father's in the loony bin, Sullivan. Mental illness often runs in families, and a lot of people start suffering symptoms in their mid-twenties or thirties. That's what happened to Harry, and that's what's happening to Thackeray. Betty told me as much before she was killed, that she was concerned Thackeray was going the same way his father had."

"I've met with him a few times. I've never seen any sign of mental illness."

"No? Not even paranoia?"

"If he's paranoid, it's for good reason."

Lowell smirked. "Let me guess. He told you I set him up, sent his father to Lockwood, maybe even caused the old man's stroke. Hell, he probably told you I'm behind what happened to Betty, right?"

"That's not all he said."

"Yeah, the two of you also concocted this theory I'm responsible for Flynn's death."

"The day he died, Dad left our place in a rage, intending to confront you about something. Thing is, he'd found a thumb drive in my pocket, and he'd apparently looked at its contents. You know what was on it. You know because Betty told you."

"Betty didn't tell me anything. I don't know anything about any thumb drive."

"So why did Dad leave our place so pissed with you?"

"He found out about the sleeping pills I'd been giving you, all right? He was pissed off no one had told him. He said they're addictive and he didn't want you becoming dependent on them."

"You want me to believe that's the only reason he went to see you."

"It is. He was always protective of you. He knew you had issues, claimed to see things that weren't there. People like you tend to be more susceptible to addictions, he said."

Lowell was baiting him, trying to distract him from the central issue to all this, the one Sully had quickly realized Lowell was not ever going to raise. Even so, the words stung, required a response.

"He wouldn't have said that."

"He did say that, Sullivan. He knew how disturbed you are. We all know. Why do you think the police are so keen to see you charged with Betty's death?"

"How do you know about that?"

"Come on," Lowell said. "She was my employee. I was among the first people questioned about it. Let me ask *you* something. Did you do it?"

Sully stared at his uncle through narrowed eyes. "You know damn well I didn't."

"Right, forgot. I must know that because I did it myself, right? You're more ill than I thought if you believe that. And if you think anyone else will believe your little theory, you're beyond unhinged. I mean, what reason could I possibly have to kill my most reliable employee, let alone someone I considered a friend?"

"Because she figured you out," Sully said. "She'd realized, after several attempts had been made on Thackeray's life in prison, that her son was right about you. More than that, she figured out Thackeray was right about what you did seventeen years ago."

Lowell had to know what Sully was talking about. The pallor that settled over the flesh of his face caused the scattering of freckles there to stand out in contrast. He didn't ask what Sully meant, as if afraid to hear the response. The silence provided more of an answer than anything Lowell might say out loud in meeting the accusation.

"I don't know why, but I do know you killed Aiden Braddock. You were down with him at the creek behind the house, and you drowned him."

"You're out of your mind."

"Really? Here's the thing. I know you say you don't believe it, but I see ghosts. And I don't see them unless someone's done something to cause their death. Aiden hasn't appeared to me often, but I have seen him. And I wouldn't be seeing him unless there was more to his death than a simple accidental drowning. I've never asked, but I'd be willing to bet you were there the day he went missing. And I'd be just as willing to bet you know exactly what happened to him, and that Dad figured it out based on Thackeray's accusations on the thumb drive.

"You killed Aiden and then, when Dad accused you of it, you injected him with epinephrine—enough to cause a massive heart attack. You knew no one would ever accuse you of anything other than the explanation you provided. And you knew, if they did, you could just fall back on family history of heart failure and your own panic to explain how you 'accidentally' killed your brother. And, yeah, I know that wasn't an accident either because I've been seeing Dad too. He went to see you, Lowell, and now he's dead, and I'm seeing him. You might be able to explain away everything else, but not that."

Lowell's eyes had widened at Sully's accusations, and now they narrowed until he was fixing the younger man with a look that threatened to put Sully in the same state as Flynn and Aiden.

"You need help, Sullivan. And if no one else is going to get it for you, I will. You might not believe it, but it really is for your own good."

This was why Sully had opted to take the bus rather than run the distance to the Black Fox, leaving him stronger for the fight he now had on his hands. Lowell had size on his side but Sully had youth and, for a minute or so, the physical struggle between the two of them was more or less evenly balanced. No further punches were thrown, the fight consisting almost entirely of a close-quarters wrestling match through which Sully initially managed to stay on his feet.

The fight went to the ground within seconds. There wasn't much time for conscious thought, but fear was beginning to drive him now as much as the anger—fear about what would happen if he lost. Sully had wanted to confront the man, to drive a fist or two into his mid-section as he was currently doing. But it had been Lowell, after all, who had summoned him here. In his anger, Sully hadn't given that fact the consideration it deserved, so he'd put himself in a situation without first thinking through the possibilities, the end game Lowell had in mind.

Lowell was older, had lost some of the natural energy of youth. But he was by no means lacking in physical strength. As he did everything else in life, Lowell strove for excellence, for perfection, to come out on top. It happened so fast, Sully barely knew how he got there. But here he was, lying beneath Lowell's not-insignificant weight, the two of them panting from the exertions of the brawl while Lowell felt back in his pocket for what Sully knew, rather than suspected, was a syringe.

Movement to the right drew Sully's attention to the presence of two others, the combatants from downstairs hovering next to them. Flynn and Harry were no longer fighting, and Flynn's eyes had grown to near the size of the other ghost's as they watched for a moment the dwindling battle between the room's two solidly present occupants.

A look passed between the two spirits, eyes meeting as if one was looking to the other for an answer to an unasked question. The meaning became clear only when Harry moved to stand at Sully's feet, the chill of him causing Sully's body to seize as the ghost first sat and then lay down—not next to Sully, but *in* him.

Only, this time, Sully didn't feel the sensation of disappearing, of losing himself to Harry's utter physical and mental control. It was as if Harry had made room for him, was giving Sully a chance to be heard, seen and felt—empowering him as co-pilot rather than a slumbering passenger within his own body.

Sully felt his own youthful, controlled energy emboldened by Harry's frantic, pulse-like force, the two entwining until Sully could no longer sense where his spirit ended and the intruder's began. Beyond that, more disturbingly, were the joining of thoughts and feelings, Sully's anger turned to rage and his anxiety transformed into outright terror as he regarded Lowell through eyes that were currently only half his own. Sully had always distrusted and disliked Lowell; Harry, he could now perceive, loathed and feared him.

There was weakness in rage and terror, a terrible potential for loss of control when emotion rendered mind and body incapable of the rationality necessary for mounting a useful defence. But there was also unnatural strength and power to be found there, the kind that enabled a mother to move a vehicle that was pinning her child, or a horrifically wounded victim to outrun a pursuing assailant.

Sully felt every bit of that, this literal strength of two men he was now marshalling for the next, and likely final, phase of this battle with Lowell.

Sully stilled under the weight of the older man, a move Lowell appeared, through the lack of suspicion in his expression and movements, to accept as exhaustion. It had Lowell removing his hold from Sully's right arm and his weight from his upper torso, allowing Lowell to focus both hands on the task of readying a syringe full of what Sully imagined was the same sedative he'd used during the pair's last violent exchange.

Arms freed, and energy revving through him like high-octane fuel through a motorcycle's engine, Sully funnelled this strange combination of his and Harry's life force into one place inside himself, Lowell the target at the end of this particular range. He pushed against Lowell hard enough the syringe flew from his grip and rolled across the floor. Lowell reestablished his grip on Sully and, judging by the strained sound of his grunts and protests, it was all he could do to hold on. There was light at the end of this particular tunnel, a chance for escape, or even to finish this in such a way that Lowell would reconsider ever crossing Sully or anyone he cared about again.

Sully tensed his hips and arms, the energy of two people lifting and shoving, throwing Lowell partway across the room. Sully and Lowell climbed to their feet at the same time, Lowell's eyes having grown wide in the interim.

"I don't want to hurt you, Sullivan."

"You won't."

The two met again, Sully rushing him, shoving him back

against the wall hard enough to cause a sizeable crack in the drywall. Grabbing hold of the larger man's jacket, Sully pulled and spun, tossing Lowell across the room and sending him tumbling across the overturned coffee table. One of Lowell's thighs collided with a table leg, and he held the injured spot as he dragged himself backward, away from his advancing opponent.

An end to this was within sight if Sully wanted it. Harry desired it, no question, seeking to drag Sully's eyes over to the knife rack. But Sully was no killer, and he wasn't about to become one now. Not only did he not want it on his conscience, he didn't want to spend the rest of his life ducking Lowell Braddock's vengeful spirit.

The hall leading to the apartment door was close, no way Lowell could catch him if he ran. He could leave this place, disappear and stay that way until he could sort out what to do, come up with a plan that didn't require someone's death or the strength of a partial possession.

At this moment, he had both the upper hand and a choice to make.

Approaching footsteps echoed in the quiet room. Sully turned his head and knew his upper hand, his choice, had disappeared. This solid form of Larson Hackman blocked his only exit.

From his uncle's movement, Sully could tell Lowell had spotted the Lockwood head orderly at the same time, leaving Sully no opportunity to figure out what the man was doing here. "Hackman, help me. The syringe. Grab the syringe!"

For a few seconds, the appearance of the orderly proved more than Harry could psychologically manage, fear spiking to dizzying heights as he focused on the large man. Sully fought to pull Harry back, but the few seconds of distraction were costly, granting Lowell an opportunity to pull off a tackle his former high school and college football coaches would have praised. Sully landed on his side, skull thudding against the floor on the way. Head swimming, he could do little as Lowell turned him onto his belly, straddling his hips and holding him there.

After a few seconds, his spinning vision settled on his father, who was standing just a few feet away. If possible, Flynn appeared more terror-stricken as he stepped forward to rain ineffectual blows on his brother. And Sully had to struggle to redirect both his and Harry's attention, his own caught by the image of Flynn and Harry's by Hackman. The orderly ensured the substance within the retrieved syringe was ready for use. Lowell was the immediate barricade that needed to be cleared, the tether Sully and Harry needed to sever in order to free themselves of this threat.

But Harry's dread was not easily overcome, and Sully sensed this fear was not of something the man had envisioned, but rather a reality he himself had experienced. Hackman, Sully now knew, was something more than cocky, condescending and generally repugnant; he was dangerous.

There was little time to spare, Hackman approaching while Lowell continued to hold on. Harry seemed to understand it as he refocused himself, once again joining his energy to Sully's.

Flynn had taken a step back, was standing in the corner, watching the unfolding situation with an expression of the utmost dread. Sully recalled having told him the dead often used him like a battery, draining him of energy in order to replenish their own. Flynn would know Sully needed every bit of his right now and Sully's heart broke for the sense of helplessness once so unknown to his father.

Sully focused on ensuring he didn't feel the same helplessness, and he felt his Harry-strengthened torso lifting from the floor in defiance of both his uncle and gravity.

"Hackman, come on!"

Hackman knelt on the floor, setting the syringe down to give him two free hands to restrain Sully.

The words ran through Sully's brain like the nightmarish mantra Dez had described, "blue room" repeated over and over in an internal voice Sully did not recognize as his own. The words grew louder, matching the strength that funnelled itself into the fist Sully wrenched away from Lowell, into the delivery of the backhand he delivered to Hackman's jaw.

It should have hurt, but Sully felt little pain, distributed as it was between the two spirits currently residing inside his body. Hackman, on the other hand, appeared to feel all of it, the blow knocking him sideways and allowing Sully a few seconds to turn his attention to Lowell. A swift backward thrust of Sully's head met Lowell's nose, sending blood spurting and pushing the man off balance far enough that Sully was able to put him the rest of the way over with a heavy shove.

The weight gone from his torso, Sully squirmed free of Lowell's legs. The door to the apartment in his sights, he hurdled Hackman's form. Even Harry, adamant as he was about confronting Lowell, had decided flight probably carried a happier outcome than fight.

A hand closing around his ankle ended the run before it began, bringing Sully back down, the top of his head colliding hard with the wall. Once again, the pain was divided and tempered, but it wasn't easy to draw himself from the uncomfortable purgatory between waking and unconsciousness that also resulted.

It was into that momentary shock that Hackman and Lowell stepped, the weight of the two large men pushing him against the floor as Sully worked to shove himself up. Facedown beneath the two, there could be no further fight to freedom.

Harry knew it. Sully felt it the moment the spirit fled his body, leaving him alone with the two men, with the ghost of his fear-stricken father standing in the corner. With the dispersal of that power, energy and strength, Sully gave up as surely as Harry had just done, sinking into the floor, barely fighting as he felt someone work the boot and sock off his restrained left foot, as he felt the needle bite painfully into a spot between his toes.

All Sully could do was stare into Flynn's eyes as he waited for the inevitable, for that feeling of floating on a rapidly sinking raft in an open sea.

27

For all that Dez despised about Forbes Raynor, it was a phone call from the major crimes cop that ultimately alerted Dez that something was wrong.

But it was Flynn Braddock who saved them.

Having made one of the hardest decisions of his life—letting Sully go alone to an interview with a cop intent on charging him with murder—Dez returned home to Eva and Kayleigh.

Kayleigh was young, but she was bright, and she'd already grasped the heartbreaking fact her grandpa would no longer be a solid presence in her life.

So when Dez came through the door, fragile in a way he hadn't felt since Aiden's death seventeen years ago, Kayleigh was waiting with a hug and words that left Dez struggling to contain the swell of emotion.

"I'm sorry about your daddy, Daddy."

Dez, holding the little girl against his chest so he could feel her tiny heart beating near to his own, couldn't bring himself to set her down for a solid minute. And, to her great credit as a daughter and a human being, she didn't protest.

Eventually, she went upstairs to her room, leaving Dez with Eva on the living room sofa. Her arms encircled him immediately, allowing him the opportunity and the safe haven for the breakdown he'd held in check.

"How are you doing?" she asked, once he'd rid himself of another pound or two of tears and was sniffling back a few more that were threatening. One of her hands stroked his spine as the other covered his nearest hand, thumb running back and forth across lightly freckled skin.

Dez used his free hand to squeeze at the inner corners of his eyes, both wiping away moisture and discouraging any more. "I feel like my whole family's fallen apart, and there's nothing I can do to put it back together."

"Maybe it's not your job to do that, Snowman. Everyone has their own path in life. You can't walk it for them."

He didn't respond to what he knew to be a wise observation. He recognized the truth in it, but he also came equipped with a bit of his own. "No, but sometimes people need to be carried a bit."

"You ever stop and think maybe you need to let people carry you sometimes?"

Dez gifted her with a grin. "You gonna try carrying me, babe? How good's your chiropractor?"

"Shut up. Listen, before you ask, your mom and her sister headed out to your parents' place to get some more of her stuff. She's going to be alternating between our place and her sister's a while, until she's had some time to deal with things. I knew you wouldn't mind. How about Sully? Everything okay between you two?"

"Yeah, we're good. What isn't good is what he's doing right now. He's not going to be at his best in an interview situation, and Raynor knows it. If Raynor butts up against something Sully isn't answering the way he wants, all he's got to do is steer away for a minute and bring up Dad. That'll send Sully off-course pretty damn fast."

Eva's touch moved to the back of Dez's neck, where it squeezed gently, equally massaging and demanding his attention. "I know you don't like the man, but he's not completely inhuman.

Anyway, let's not forget, he'll have someone monitoring the interview who isn't going to have the same hang-ups. Could be that person will reign Raynor in if he goes too far off-course. Don't forget, if he pushes so hard a court views it as intimidation or a threat, anything Sully says will get tossed. And, Dez, let's not lose sight of the most important thing here: he can't get Sully to admit to something he didn't do."

Dez had a response ready when his phone interrupted him. He pulled it from his jacket pocket, and his heart thudded against his ribs when he saw Raynor's number come up. "I can't answer this."

He knew Eva's mind had gone to the same place when her words came with a tone intended more to sooth than to question. "You want me to?"

"Not really."

Both of them, he knew, were expecting this was what Raynor would define as a courtesy call. With no further suspects or evidence having been located, Sully's fingerprints on the gun and his clothes covered in blowback, with no physical injuries to back up his story about a struggle for the gun, Raynor had finally decided enough was enough and placed Sully under arrest. It might be there wasn't enough to lay charges just yet, but he could detain Sully at least overnight while he worked on breaking him down, piece by piece. With Flynn gone, the most significant barrier for Raynor had been removed, but a key incentive—impressing his own embittered father—remained firmly in place.

Dez didn't think he had the strength to deal with that right now.

Eva didn't have the same concerns, taking the phone and pressing the button to talk. "What do you want, Forbes? Now's not a good time. I'm sure you're aware of that .... Dez isn't up to talking right now. You've got me. What do you want?"

Eva listened for a moment, then held the phone away, her hand over the base to muffle their conversation. "Dez, didn't you say Sully was heading over to see Raynor?"

"Yeah, he was. Why?"

"He never showed up."

Dez pinched the bridge of his nose hard enough to hurt. "Damn it, Sull ... Tell Raynor we don't know where he is, but I'm heading out to look."

Eva passed along the message and, judging by the muffled sounds of speech coming from the earpiece, ended the call while Raynor was mid-tirade. She passed the phone back. "He's not happy."

Dez slipped the device back into his pocket, grabbing his vehicle keys at the same time. "That makes two of us."

THAT LEFT the question of where to look first. There were other questions, of course, and big ones—namely why Sully had seen fit to go off on his own—but those would have to be answered later, once Dez had found his brother.

His biggest concern right now had to do with the confrontation he'd learned had occurred at the hospital between Sully and Lowell after Flynn's death. If Sully had lied to him about his plans for the day, there had to be a reason, and Dez suspected it had something to do with his brother wanting to spare him any additional family drama. That Sully and Lowell weren't fond of each other was clear to anyone with the most base knowledge of either. With Sully having more or less blamed Lowell for Flynn's death, and having been interrupted at the hospital, that left the very real possibility he'd gone off to continue the confrontation.

The obvious first call was to Lowell, and Dez's concern rose a couple notches when no one picked up the phone.

Dez didn't wait for a callback, stepping on the gas and making for the thoroughfare that would take him into the city centre. If something bad was happening between the two right now, it had to be happening in the city rather than at Lowell and Kindra's country home. Mara's sister had come to pick up the car Sully had borrowed overnight, leaving him with no way to easily get out of town. That meant Dez's first stop would be Lowell and Kindra's downtown penthouse.

"Black Fox."

Dez's foot slammed down on the brakes, his body shooting forward and then back with the sudden movement. The voice—his dad's—had sounded directly in his ear, not a whisper or a yell, but a tone tinged with the controlled urgency more characteristic of Flynn's response to a situation demanding immediate action.

"Dad?" Dez's reply was hushed, and even he was uncertain whether it was from embarrassment in addressing what appeared, at a pivoting glance to be an empty vehicle, or if it was because he was scared he'd receive no answer. He knew the grief-stricken often reported seeing and hearing their deceased loved ones after their deaths. Part of the process, he'd been told, after he reported having seen Aiden in their house while searchers were still out looking for what would turn out to be the child's dead body.

Now, Dez wasn't so sure. He knew his Dad's voice. More than that, he knew that tone.

The vehicle's interior was silent, so still that Dez jumped at the blare of a horn from behind. He pulled to the curb, allowing the car to pass as he gave himself a needed minute to get a grip on himself. He needed to find Sully. There was no time to fall to grief.

"Now, son."

The words, same voice, same tone, sent Dez's head and shoulders swivelling; still, he saw nothing. After performing a quick shoulder check, he jammed his foot on the gas and peeled away, back toward the thoroughfare.

The utterance of the second command had erased any doubt. Dez entered the freeway, breaking the one-hundred-and-ten kilometre per hour speed limit as he raced toward the Riverview neighbourhood. Unlike his brother, Dez didn't know much about this spiritual stuff, but he did know his father.

And if his father was reaching out from beyond the grave to get Dez to the Black Fox, there was a reason.

HAVING PUNCHED in the back door's keypad code, Dez found no one in the Black Fox bar. Stepping over the dried pool of blood on the floor, he did a quick search, but found nothing in the shadowed stillness.

The answer, he suspected, lay upstairs, and it was to Sully's apartment he went next.

The door was locked from the inside, and no one responded to Dez's knock. He'd tried calling Sully's phone several times during the drive over, but received the message reporting the person he was calling could not be reached. Sully's phone was either turned off or dead.

His father's words held in his memory close enough he could almost physically hear them, Dez wasted no more time in the hall, kicking twice at the door near the lock until it gave under the weight of his leg.

The bedroom to the right was empty.

The bathroom wasn't.

Sully sat, fully clothed, in the tub, surrounded by reddened water. Next to him, on the rim of the tub, was an empty bottle of his sleeping pills. On the floor, a jagged-edged steak knife, blood still fresh on the blade.

The world went silent. Dez thought it likely he screamed Sully's name or a curse word, and repeatedly because his throat felt raw. He knew he dialled 9-1-1 because it showed on his phone's call history, and an EMS crew and a couple police officers showed up.

All Dez was fully aware of was the person in front of him, the pale and still form of Sully Gray, seated in a tub full of water dyed red by the blood from his opened wrists.

28

THE ER DOCTOR met the family in one of the department's soft rooms, providing a rundown of Sully's injuries.

The words ghosted around Dez, some sticking around to haunt him, others drifting past and disappearing into the ether. There was mention of self-inflicted wounds, overdose, blood loss, amnesia pertaining to the time leading to the attempted suicide.

They'd heard much of it before, the last time Dez had found his brother slicing through his wrists in a bathroom.

This time, Lowell Braddock—sitting with them—had taken matters into his own hands, summoning Dr. Roman Gerhardt to speak to Sully. Although he'd regained consciousness, he was still dopey from the overdose, and they hadn't let the family in to see him yet. Gerhardt was another story, and the hospital and Lowell viewed his presence as essential medical treatment.

Perhaps it was exhaustion over the number of tragedies they'd all had to endure. Perhaps it was fear about having to experience another. More than likely, it was both. Whatever the reason, Dez wasn't going to argue Gerhardt's presence in that room. Not anymore.

Some might see the suicide attempt as a decision resulting from loss of a loved one, compounded by the trauma of witnessing a friend's murder and being considered a suspect in that homicide.

Dez suspected otherwise. A man who spent his days staring out a window in Lockwood Psychiatric Hospital had answers he wasn't ever going to provide.

Dez's aunt Lyndsey had gone to stay with Kayleigh, allowing Eva to take Mara to the hospital. Had it not been for the presence of the two women, Dez thought he might have ended up in a position requiring a bed next to Sully's and a conversation of his own with Dr. Gerhardt.

As it stood, he had support in the form of Eva's soothing hand rubbing circles on his back, and each of his hands—since washed free of Sully's blood for the second time in a week—held by Eva and his mother.

It wasn't, it turned out, enough.

Gerhardt limped into the soft room, leaning into his cane as he sat in the chair nearest the door, fixing each of them in turn with a gaze Dez read as more scrutinizing than sympathetic. First he reported the good news: Sully would make a full physical recovery thanks to Dez's timely arrival in that bathroom. However, Gerhardt wasn't so ready to lift their spirits when it came to his psychological assessment of Sully.

"I've had a talk with Sullivan, and I'm very concerned about him. Although Lowell has informed me that Sullivan has spoken of seeing spirits, he hasn't said as much to me. In fact, he hasn't said much of anything to me. What is clear is that he's in a very vulnerable state. Within the past few days, he has made two suicide attempts. Given the trauma he's had to deal with lately, I'm concerned he's in the midst of a serious mental breakdown. I know this isn't the news any of you want to hear, but my recommendation is that you, as his family, speak to him about a voluntary stay at Lockwood Psychiatric Hospital. That way, I could assess him properly."

"No." Until all eyes turned to Dez, he hadn't realized he'd said the word out loud.

"Desmond, you came to me not long ago expressing your concerns for your brother. Now I see how right you were to worry. I know you have concerns about him staying at Lockwood but—"

"There's no 'but' here. He's not going."

"Even after what happened?" Lowell said. "Dez, if you care about Sullivan—"

Dez turned on Lowell, feeling the heat of the fire in his own eyes. "Don't you question how I feel about my brother. You've been trying to get him into that place ever since the last time we were here. Why?"

"Because I care about him, too, Dez. I know things haven't always been easy between him and me, but he's still my brother's son, and I want to do right by all of you. You need to see that."

Gerhardt stepped into the argument. "It's clear Sullivan is intent on ending his own life. If I'm not given a chance to help him, I'm not sure anyone can. You can look into my record if you need to. My staff and I have earned awards for helping people in this community. I can assure you, Sullivan will receive the best care imaginable. And don't forget what I told you. I can help him with more than just traditional mental health concerns. Maybe what your brother needs is simply some peace. I can give him that, keep him calm and safe so when he's ready to leave, he'll also be ready to cope with the stressors that are unique to him."

Mara spoke up for the first time since they'd been told about Sully's physical injuries. "Could we have a few minutes alone to discuss this, please?"

Gerhardt nodded his agreement with a smile, then leaned once again on his cane as he rose to his feet and left the room.

Mara turned to Lowell. "You too. This decision needs to be ours and Sully's."

"Mara, I don't think Sullivan can be trusted to make the correct decision right now. You know what—"

"Lowell, please. We need a few minutes."

It was her no-nonsense voice, one Dez had heard often while growing up. You didn't argue with Mara Braddock when she took that tone, and Lowell knew it, bowing his head in deference before following the doctor from the room and closing the door behind himself.

"We can't do that to him, Mom. No."

"Dez, listen to me. This can't go on, all right? It can't. You know that as well as I do."

"He's not suicidal, Mom. I know him. He isn't."

"I know that. But I also know he's susceptible to the things that come to him. If he was possessed this time, too, who's to say the same thing won't happen again tomorrow, or the day after, or a week from now? Are you going to quit your job to babysit him every moment of every day? Are you going to keep him hand-cuffed to you so he isn't allowed ten minutes alone to hurt himself again? Are you going to sacrifice your own mental and physical health for this, Dez? I can't. I just can't. We almost lost him again, today. I can't bury my son, not so soon after losing Flynn."

There was a solid sheen of tears in Mara's eyes, a few having spilled down her cheeks as she spoke. But her voice remained firm, her expression solid. She hadn't broken yet, but she was close.

They were all close. Dez could see the wide and jagged cracks in his own surface, created by the earthquake that had been Flynn's death. They needed only one more significant shock to open him up completely, to swallow him from the inside out.

He knew Mara was right. He knew it, and he hated it.

"I don't want to bring this up," Eva said. "But what about the investigation into Betty's shooting? I'm a bit concerned how this will look. Raynor might use this to discredit Sully's statement about the shooting. If it's learned Sully experienced blackouts prior to his suicide attempts, or during that confrontation with Lowell, Raynor could easily argue Sully was going through something similar when Betty was shot. That would give Raynor another piece of his puzzle, and it would cast doubt on Sully's description of the shooting and the man who did it."

It was a solid point, but Mara's was firmer.

"I hear what you're saying, Eva, but my biggest concern right now isn't about Sully's dealings with the police. It's with keeping him alive. Dez, what did Dr. Gerhardt mean about your previous conversation with him?"

Dez provided the explanation about his and Sully's undercover reconnaissance mission to Lockwood, and the discussion between him and Gerhardt initially intended only to give Sully time to look for clues about the man who'd been haunting him. Dez told them what Gerhardt said about his belief in otherworldly explanations for some things, and his attempts to find ways to help those people cope with their experiences, how he'd quieted people's minds so they didn't have to see if they didn't want to.

When he'd finished, Mara's reply was as he'd anticipated. "Maybe that's what Sully needs now."

"I asked him about it afterwards. He said if he lost the ghosts, it would be like losing himself."

"He's losing himself, anyway. These possessions, they're not just terrifying to him, but to all of us. Every time this man takes him over, Sully disappears and nearly doesn't return. We've all seen how badly the regular ones can impact him, the lengths he'll go to get them to cross over. I've always told myself that was his path in life, and he was learning to follow it. But this is different. This one has power over him in a way none of the others have. You've looked for solutions and they haven't worked. Maybe this is the only way. If there's a place inside his brain that allows him to see these people, maybe it needs to be sealed off for a little while, long enough he can heal from all of this. It could be like a vacation, in a way."

"Lockwood is no holiday destination, Mom."

"I wasn't meaning Lockwood. I was referring to Sully, to whatever it is inside him that connects him to that other world. We need to close the door, Dez. Just for a little while. I think you know that as well as I do."

The bitch of the thing was he did know that. But he also knew what he and Sully had been through together the past few days, recalled the words they'd exchanged before walking through Lockwood's front door for the first time.

"I feel like we're opening a door we're going to regret walking through. I mean, bringing you here is exactly what that doctor at the hospital wanted, and we both know he was wrong about you needing this place."

"Dez, I know you're not going to leave me here, all right?"

Now, that was exactly what Dez and the rest of Sully's family were about to do. It felt like betrayal of the worst kind, abandonment, like they'd given up on one of their own when he needed them the most.

Dez had always prided himself on being able to fight Sully's demons for him or alongside him. Suddenly, Dez came to the heart-sinking realization he couldn't chase Sully's shadows, because he'd gained too many of his own. The light within Dez, ordinarily bright enough for both of them, had faded to the dim glow of a flickering candle. One puff of air and he'd go completely dark. There wasn't enough left inside him to fight for everyone he loved. Not anymore.

His mother's voice cut in, a voice sounding from the topside of a deep, dark well.

"Dez? Sweetie, I know this is hard—"

"I understand why he needs to go," he said. "But I can't be a part of it."

Dez excused himself, muttering something about having to take a leak. He passed the bathroom. Walked past a waiting room. Heard the sliding glass doors to the ER entrance close behind him.

And kept going.

29

THERE WAS no such thing as time anymore, hours passing unnoticed through a fog, day and night marked only by light and dark.

A castaway in a life raft, Sully equated moments of clarity with ships passing within an endless sea. Before he had a chance to wave them down, the fog would settle back between them with the prick of a needle in his arm.

The first time he felt the full return of awareness, he awoke inside what looked like a treatment room, Dr. Gerhardt loading up a syringe at a counter along the righthand wall.

Sully was fully alert and, for a moment, revelled in that feeling. Relief faded fast as he became conscious of the fact his wrists and ankles were strapped to a bed. Testing the bonds, he found them strong, too tight to slip out of.

Then he noticed something else. The walls inside this room were covered in flaking paint the colour of a midday sky.

Harry's words and Snowy's warning came at him like a slap, pulling the whispered words from his lips. "Blue Room."

His eyes snapped onto Gerhardt's back, a desperate need to understand seizing hold of his insides and twisting. "What are you doing?"

"Ssh. Relax, Sullivan. You're all right."

"Why am I strapped down?"

"I need you fully conscious, and I don't want to risk you attempting self-harm."

On its surface, the psychiatrist's explanation gave the impression of doctorly concern.

Sully knew better.

Given the circumstances, there were two routes he could take: try to reason with the man or give in to utter panic. He opted for the former.

"I don't need the drugs anymore," Sully said. "I'm fine."

"You're fine because of the drugs. You have far too many demands on you, far too many emotional stressors in your life. I've only wanted to give you a rest." Gerhardt at last turned to face him. "You know that, don't you?"

"I don't need a rest. I need to leave here. I'm not mentally ill. I just need to be with my family."

Gerhardt smiled. To anyone else, the expression might have appeared kind. "Your family's here, Sullivan."

The doctor nodded with his chin, then went back to whatever it was he was doing. Sully followed the direction Gerhardt had indicated, angling his head until he could see just behind himself, to the right.

Lowell stared down at him.

Sully's heart drummed against his ribs as he teetered on the edge of panic. He heard the sound in his own voice, the way it turned a single word into a moan. "No."

"It's all right, son," Lowell said. "Dr. Gerhardt knows what he's doing."

"What are you doing here?"

Gerhardt answered for Lowell. "He's helping me with something I've been working on. His lab developed a drug that acts as a mind opener of sorts. I believe your ability to see the things you do originates somewhere within your brain. People with abilities like yours are able to tap into parts of the mind that remain closed to most of us once we pass childhood. Your ability is quite advanced, and very strong. That's why I've had to keep you sedated so heavily for the past couple of weeks. You needed a chance to rest."

Weeks? Had it been that long?

"Your uncle is a brilliant man," Gerhardt continued. "The drug he developed will, I believe, help us to control your ability, to channel it. It will open your mind and allow you to use your gift in ways you never could before."

"I don't want to use it in other ways," Sully said. Full reality hit him, called to mind the pills his uncle had prescribed in the days leading to the committal. "The pills you gave me. You passed them off as my usual sleep meds, but this is what they were, weren't they? A mind opener. Mom told me the police lab tested them and they came back as some sort of psychedelic."

"Psychotropic," Lowell corrected.

Gerhardt supplied a more detailed explanation. "He developed it for some of my other patients. But given what you'd told your family about your abilities, he thought it might be worth seeing if it would have a similar effect on you. I understand you experienced a full possession. That's highly unusual. Until you, quite frankly, I would have thought it impossible. What I've discovered about this drug is that it magnifies the existing abilities people like you already possess."

"Why? Why would you want to do that?"

Gerhardt replied without answering. "Lowell had his chemists develop an injectable and more concentrated form of the drug. The effect should be more immediate and give us an improved means of ensuring the appropriate dosage. It might take a couple tries to get it exactly right—that's why your uncle is here—but we'll manage, won't we?"

"You can't do this."

"I'm only trying to help you. If we can find the right combination of medications, we should be able to help you control your ability. Don't you want that? The chance to be able to turn it on or off at will?"

"Not if I feel the way I always do here. Not if I feel like I'm lost in a fog. I can deal with the things I see. I don't need your help."

"I think you do, Sullivan," Lowell said. "You're here because you tried to kill yourself."

Sully had no memory beyond that final fight with his uncle and Larson Hackman, not until he awoke in hospital with his arms badly slashed and a shellshocked Dez sitting next to him. Despite having no knowledge of how he'd ended up there, Sully suspected—more than suspected, really—it had everything to do with Lowell.

It hadn't been attempted suicide that had landed Sully in hospital with multiple stitches closing gashes in his arms; it was attempted murder.

He wished he could see his brother now. Dez would kick these guys' asses, would put them bodily through the wall and stick whatever Gerhardt was wielding into him. Gerhardt, and even Lowell, would be lucky if they escaped with their lives.

But Dez wasn't here, and there was nowhere that drug was going but into Sully's vein.

He had nowhere to go, no way to slip the restraints. But damned if he wasn't going to try.

He strained against the padded cuffs, the metal rings linking them to the bed frame clanking as he struggled. Lowell moved in, holding one of Sully's arms as a second person suddenly entered the frame. Hackman pressed his full weight down on Sully's shoulders, leaving him nowhere to go but back down the rabbit hole.

Gerhardt moved in, the needle pricking the flesh of Sully's inner arm as he released his terror and frustration in a howl.

Cool liquid entered his vein, flowed up his arm until the heat of his own body warmed it. The needle withdrawn, he was at first relieved to feel nothing.

But this was the Blue Room; relief had no place here.

Gerhardt had retreated back to the counter, where he remained for a couple of minutes, his back to the others. Whether he meant to allow the drug a chance to take hold, or to give Sully the opportunity to calm down really didn't matter. With these three men in control, no outcome would be a good one.

Lowell and Hackman had released Sully after the injection, granting him some space. It wasn't helping much, his brain running in overdrive with thoughts of what was to come.

He didn't have long to think.

Gerhardt turned, and Sully's heart caught in his throat at the tears in the other man's eyes. Emotion could make people dangerous, give them motivation they wouldn't possess were they more stable.

This emotion was the worst kind. In his hands was a stuffed rabbit, its fur matted and faded with age. The grimace twisting Gerhardt's lips and the deepening of lines across his brow told Sully a story before the doctor had said anything aloud.

"It was my son's. He had it with him the day he was taken." Gerhardt's gaze went from the rabbit to Sully. "I need you to find him."

"I can only see them if they're dead. If they've been murdered."

"I know. A patient of mine, a young woman, she told me he was gone. She left before she could tell me where to find him. I need to give him a good, Christian burial. But, more than that, I need closure. I need to know what happened, and to find the person responsible. You're going to help me, Sullivan. I need you to help me."

Gerhardt stepped forward and place the stuffed animal in Sully's restrained hand. "Focus on this object and tell me when you begin to see my son."

"It doesn't work that way."

"Just focus, Sullivan. Breathe deeply and focus."

Sully had never needed to focus to see the dead. He didn't need it this time, either.

Movement next to the bed, a gradual solidification of mist into human form, told him a spirit was materializing. The faint shape of arms, legs, torso and head sharpened as the swirling energy molded itself into the image of its former body—that of a young child, no older than five or six. Facial features began to reveal themselves as the ghost's hue changed from whites and greys to full colour: pale skin, the denim blue of jeans, the crisp yellow of a cotton T-shirt, green within the nearly formed eyes.

It was the strawberry blond tone to the hair that gave it away. This wasn't Gerhardt's son coming into view.

It was Aiden.

There was no doubt the dripping wet five-year-old standing next to him was the same little boy Sully had glimpsed several times in the past. The same little boy whose life had ended by the hand of the man standing oblivious to the presence on the opposite side of the bed.

The start of a word formed on Sully's lips, the desire to torment Lowell with this vision nearly as strong as the fear still coursing through him.

Tiny, cold, wet fingers touching his left hand forced Sully into silence as he was yanked from this room and into the consciousness of the five-year-old child.

He was next to a river, his hiding spot affording him a view of the house. Dez would come soon. He was angry with Aiden, but he'd look for him anyway. Dez always looked for him.

He knew he wasn't supposed to be at the river. Mommy and Daddy always said to stay away from it. It was dangerous, they said. But he wouldn't go in the water. He'd stay here, crouched in the reeds on the bank. Dez knew all his hiding spots inside the house already, and there weren't a lot of trees or bushes to sneak through. Eventually, Dez would come, and Aiden would jump out and scare him. Then his brother would giggle the way he always did, and they'd be best friends again.

Only it wasn't Dez coming this way. It was Uncle Lowell.

Uh-oh.

Uncle Lo was coming closer, coming right toward him, like he knew exactly where to find him. Aiden stayed crouched. He didn't like the frown on his uncle's face. Uncle Lo usually smiled. Today, he wasn't smiling.

Aiden knew there was no point hiding. Uncle Lo knew where he was. He would tell Mommy and Daddy Aiden was down here, and he would be grounded for a long time. No video games or TV, and Mommy would make him explain to her why it was so dangerous to come down here. And Daddy—he would be so disappointed in him.

Aiden looked up as hands parted the reeds. Uncle Lo was there, staring down at him, the same frown on his face. Daddy didn't yell much, but sometimes Uncle Lo did, and Aiden thought that would happen now.

Only he didn't yell. He stayed quiet, reaching a hand down for Aiden.

He took his uncle's hand. An apology was on his lips, as he expected to be taken back to the house and made to stay in his room until Mommy and Daddy got back.

Instead, Uncle Lowell stepped further down the bank, pulling Aiden along with him. He didn't stop until he was next to the water, standing on the big, flat rock Daddy and Dez liked to fish from. Uncle Lo knelt and pulled Aiden into a hug. His uncle's body started to shake and Aiden's heart beat fast as he realized Uncle Lo was crying.

This was even worse than Mommy's yelling or Daddy's disappointed eyes. Aiden had been so bad he'd made his uncle cry.

He said sorry again, but the crying didn't stop. It only got worse, and it seemed like it would never stop.

Uncle Lowell was still choking back sobs as he released Aiden. His uncle wasn't looking at him, and Aiden wondered if he'd been so bad Uncle Lo couldn't even stand the sight of him.

Then something happened. It happened fast. One second Aiden was standing on the rock, his uncle's big hands grasping his torso; the next he was going backwards, his body hitting the water.

Going under the water.

Uncle Lowell's hands were still on him, still holding him. Aiden's eyes had shut as he went into the cold water, but his mouth had been open in a surprised yell. Now he closed it, but water had already gone in.

He swallowed what water he could, but some of it felt like it went in his air pipe, the way it felt when he drank his juice too fast.

Only he couldn't cough. There was no air to cough. No air to breathe.

And Uncle Lo wasn't letting him up.

Aiden pushed his hands out of the water, grabbed at his uncle's bare arms. Pounded at them. He kicked out, trying to push away.

Uncle Lowell was too strong.

He would have to let him up. He had to.

But he wasn't. He wasn't letting him up.

Aiden's eyes opened.

It was a warm summer day, the sun high in the sky. He could see the rippling image of his uncle on the other side of the water.

And then he wasn't looking up at Uncle Lo. He was staring over at him.

Aiden was back on the big rock, standing next to his kneeling uncle. He didn't know how he'd gotten here, but here he was. He wasn't breathing, but he didn't feel like he had to. He still felt wet and cold, and he was afraid. He wanted to run from Uncle Lowell.

Then he saw his uncle was still holding something in the water. Something still, small, unmoving.

Something that looked a lot like him.

His uncle was still crying when he finally let the other Aiden go.

They stood there, side by side, watching as the other little boy floated away, the current carrying him down the river.

Past the reeds and the rocks. Past the big trees on the other side of the river, and the ones that had fallen partway into the water. Past the footbridge the neighbours had put up.

They watched as the other Aiden disappeared around the river's bend.

Then Uncle Lowell wiped away the rest of his tears and started slowly for the house.

Just as suddenly as he'd been pulled into Aiden's consciousness, Sully was ripped away. He found himself back in the Blue Room, gasping for air, three sets of eyes staring down at him.

One pair belonged to the man who'd just murdered him.

"Did you see my boy?" Gerhardt asked. "Did he show you what happened?"

Sully loathed Gerhardt, but every ounce of his hatred was currently focused on Lowell. Were he not strapped down, he would strangle the man, visit upon him the same feelings of helplessness and terror he'd brought a small boy—his own brother's boy—all those years ago.

Physical attack wasn't possible, so Sully poured every ounce of his hate into the words he growled at the man as he stared into his eyes. "He showed me. He showed me what you did. He knows. Aiden's here, Lowell, and he knows you killed him."

Lowell was usually good at playing it cool, but it seemed to be taking him a while to remember that. "I don't know what you're talking about."

"I saw you. You found him playing hide and seek in the reeds by the river that day. You took him down to Dad's fishing rock, you put him in the water, and you held him there until he stopped struggling. He was aware. He still is. He knows, Lowell. And we'll both see that you pay for it."

Lowell—the man who had spent his life doubting Sully's claims about his ability, who had called into question everything about the boy his brother had taken in as a foster—looked like he'd just seen a ghost. He sucked in a mouthful of air, then a second. A moment later, he ran for a garbage can next to the counter and vomited violently.

Gerhardt's train was still running on another track.

"I don't care about the Braddock boy." He gritted his teeth, issued his command through a clenched jaw. "Find. My. *Son*!"

But Sully didn't care right now about the Gerhardt boy. His own thoughts were with the child still standing to his left.

"He won't rest, Lowell. He'll never rest until you're brought to justice. He'll stay with you, and he'll see you never rest, either."

Lowell spat, wiped his mouth on the back of his hand. When he turned back to Sully, his face was twisted in torment, mouth pulled taut in a grimace and a moist sheen in his narrowed eyes.

"You don't know what you're talking about! You don't know anything! And I swear to God, Sullivan, I will end you before I give you the chance to spread your lies."

"Don't worry," Gerhardt said. "He won't be telling anyone. I've made certain to keep him heavily sedated when his family comes to visit. I'll ensure that continues. He won't be saying anything about our time here."

"You can't keep me here forever."

Hackman chose that moment to speak. "No? That's what Harry Schuster said."

Gerhardt shot the head orderly a glare that immediately silenced the man. A chill ran through Sully's body, the feeling nearly as cold as Aiden's gentle grip had been.

"What did you do to Harry?" When no one answered, Sully tried again, louder, as if they hadn't heard the first time. "What did you do to him?"

"We didn't do anything," Gerhardt said. "He just ... slipped away a little over a week ago. He's gone."

The tremble that had started a few seconds ago with Hackman's interrupted threat took hold as Sully grasped the truth Gerhardt would never voice. Whether because they'd determined he was no longer useful, or because he was too great a threat, they'd killed Harry.

And Sully knew, without a shadow of a doubt, he would eventually meet the same fate.

Lowell stepped to Gerhardt's side, his thoughts, as always, with himself. "You can't let him speak to Mara, Dez or Eva. You can't let him speak to anyone. Period. If anyone believes him, I will have to take steps. I don't think I can cope with any more. There's been too much death already."

Sully inhaled sharply as he recognized Lowell's statement for what it was. If the man was confronted with his crimes—even by Mara or Dez—he would see them dead before he'd face justice. With that, Sully felt one more shred of hope slip through his fingers.

Initially, he'd kept his concerns about Lowell to himself because they were nothing beyond suspicions; then he'd concealed the truth from his family because he dreaded exposing them to more pain.

The stakes had just changed.

Lowell had already killed two people he professed to love. There was no question he would kill more. As long as no one else knew, they'd stay safe. If it meant Sully ended up one day dying at Lowell's hands, he'd go happily as long as it meant his family was protected.

"I won't tell them," Sully said. "I won't give you reason to do to them what you did to Aiden or Dad. But don't think for even one second I won't find a way to bring you down. Alive or dead, Lowell, I will find you. And if I'm not the last face you see in this world, I will be the first you see in the next."

He took some pleasure in the fear that washed across Lowell's face, causing freckles to stand out starkly against the sudden pallor of his skin.

A moment later, Lowell stepped out of his view, and the sound of a door opening and banging shut and footsteps echoing within a corridor signalled his departure.

Any triumph Sully might have felt disappeared as his attention returned to the men remaining in this room.

"We have a couple more hours before shift change," Hackman said.

"Good," Gerhardt said. "There's no rush. Lowell provided us with plenty of doses, and we have all the time in the world." He redirected his gaze to Sully. "We have work to do."

THEIR VOICES WERE A DISTANT, dim light in Lockwood's dark, their chatter like a warm, refreshing rain at the top of a deep, dark, empty well.

Rarely did his brain work well enough to understand any of

the words spoken by Dez, Mara, Eva and Takara during their visits, but words didn't matter. The sound of their voices and the feel of their presence had brought a sense of familiar—a sense of home—to this godawful place. And while he was sedated too heavily to take part in the visits, he lived for those hours nonetheless.

He found temporary shelter there, aware that as long as his loved ones were beside him, Gerhardt, Hackman and Lowell were not. Nor was the fourth man, so often present in the Blue Room, the one who kept his features concealed beneath a rubber fright mask. That man—in his anonymity and silent observation of what had become brutal psychological torture—scared Sully most of all.

The terror never left him, not even in these moments when his loved ones were with him; there was no escaping the reality they would have to leave eventually and abandon him to the horrors Gerhardt would inflict.

The closest he got to a feeling of safety came during Dez's visits, the low, gruff rumble an incessant and comforting sound. Dez talked relentlessly, the fluctuating tones in his voice suggesting he was reciting a funny memory one moment and struggling not to cry the next.

Sully ached to answer, but there was no chance at forming a coherent thought, let alone uttering a word. So he sat there, clinging to the sound, and to the one making it.

Sometimes, his mind would slip back in time, to those nights of his childhood when he'd run to Dez for protection from the ghosts that haunted him. Those nights, he'd go to sleep with his cheek against his brother's chest, the rise-fall of his breath, the thumping of his heart and the vibration of speech each forming a reminder Sully was no longer alone. He'd discovered a never-before-known safety there, and he found it again during Dez's visits to Lockwood.

One day, it happened that the curtain parted just enough to allow Sully to make out more than muffled sound.

He could understand Dez's words.

Whether it was that they hadn't provided him the proper dosage that day, or that his tolerance level was changing didn't matter. All that mattered was what was being said—and what it would mean for him if he couldn't answer.

"... don't even know if you can hear me. I've been coming here every couple of days since you've been in here, Sull. But, Jesus, man, I don't think I can do it anymore." Dez's voice broke over the last word, and Sully's heart broke with it. "God, I miss you. I miss you so much, buddy. I wish there was something I could do to fix this for you. It used to be I could always fix things for you. Remember? You and me, man, we were a team. Nothing got at you without having to go through me first. But I let you down. I let you down, bad. And I don't know if I can face it anymore."

Sully felt movement, a pressure on his arm shifting to his hand. Something warm wrapped around his fingers, and it took him a moment to recognize the feel of his brother's hand.

"Remember when we visited Harry, and he grabbed you to pass along that message? He knew you were there, Sully. Well, I need a sign like that now. I need to know you're in there somewhere. Please, Sull, if you can hear me, squeeze my hand, okay? Please, kiddo, just squeeze my hand."

Sully tried. He summoned up every bit of strength and determination be had left inside him. But it was like he was trapped inside a vehicle for which someone else held the keys. As much as he willed his hand to move, to squeeze, to offer this one sign Dez so badly needed, he failed.

He knew he'd failed when he heard his brother's sigh, the sound shaky with heavy grief.

"I'm sorry, Sully. I'm so sorry."

He heard movement beside him, the sound of Dez standing. The hand remained in his for now while the other cupped his face. He felt Dez press his lips to the crown of his head before they shifted to his ear, whispering a few words.

Sully recognized them for what they were: a goodbye.

"I love you so much, bro. I always will."

The fingers wrapped around Sully's started to loosen.

It no longer came down to strength, determination or will; it was desperation. If Sully was floating at sea, Dez was his life raft. Without his big brother, he would sink. And if there was one thing that scared him more than the Blue Room, the men who confined him there and the repeated terrors he was forced to endure, it was losing Dez.

It happened without him having to put any conscious thought into movement, his fingers tightening around Dez's, squeezing so hard he might well dislocate his brother's pinkie.

A sob came from Sully's right. But it wasn't the sound of Dez's pain. It was relief.

Sully didn't ease his grip, even when he heard his brother sit back down.

"Okay, Sull, okay. I'll take that as a sign you want me to keep rambling. But ease up a bit, huh? You're crushing my fingers." Dez's voice was closer, quieter, when it next came. "I'm not going anywhere, all right? Promise."

Only then did Sully relax his grip. But Dez didn't let go.

Neither would Sully.

30

A LIGHT RAIN fell from an overcast October sky, lending an appropriate air to what would be another emotionally gruelling day.

Over at St. Joe's, the cemetery groundskeeper had dug a small hole in a plot next to Dez's grandparents' grave, large enough to fit Flynn's urn.

Flynn hadn't wanted a full funeral, but word was damn near half the city planned on attending the graveside service, once anticipated as a small family affair. For many people outside the Braddock clan, Flynn was family.

It had taken some convincing—and some strong words from Dez—but Dr. Gerhardt had reluctantly agreed to let Sully attend the service. Dez had demanded his brother be free of any drugs when he came for him, not wanting anyone to see Sully the way his family had to.

As much as Dez was looking forward to the possibility of an actual conversation with Sully, he wasn't sure what to expect. He'd never talked with his brother about the decision to commit him to Lockwood, had never learned whether Sully held it against them or had accepted it as a necessity. Rain soaked the shoulders of Dez's good blazer and washed away the product he'd used to style his hair this morning, but he didn't quicken his pace to the institution's front entrance. Truth was, if Sully's first words to him were to call him out as a traitor, Dez wasn't sure he ever wanted to get inside.

Mara had bought Sully a suit, had taken it out to Lockwood yesterday with the request her son be wearing it when Dez picked him up. Lockwood, Dez noted upon entering the lobby, had obeyed that request, as they had the one that Sully be drug free for the two days he'd been allowed out.

Dez's dread proved groundless when his brother grabbed him in a tight hug. But new worries sprouted as he felt the tremble racking Sully's body.

"Get me out of here, Dez. Please."

Dez had been happy to oblige, had kept Sully beside him for the day, providing himself with something to stew about besides the fact they were burying their father.

That evening, having changed into jeans and T-shirts for a family gathering out at their parents' acreage, Dez told the rest of the family he wanted to take Sully out to Winteredge National Park. Mara hated camping with a passion, so it had been an activity shared by Flynn and his sons, the three of them heading out for a week each summer to set up a tent, fish and hike in the Black Woods.

It was the perfect excuse now to get Sully somewhere the two of them could talk privately.

Flynn had had a favourite campsite, located so deep within the park the sounds of nature usually drowned out the noise from nearby human civilization. The rain-soaked ground left the driving paths hard to navigate, even with an SUV. Dez moved slowly, relying on fallen pine needles and, with any luck, his father's otherworldly guidance to get them to the spot.

Dez's breath caught as he came upon it, relatively unchanged since the last time they'd come. Few people asked for this spot, too far from a public restroom to make it comfortable for young families or partying youths, and unequipped with the power or water needed for those with campers. But the park had maintained it all the same, and Dez slid the SUV into the small approach so he and his brother could face the spot where, together, they'd shared so many happy memories.

The rain wasn't cooperating, making getting out of the vehicle a challenge, but Sully didn't look to be in a hurry to leave, anyway.

"It seems like so long ago."

Sully's words had come quietly, as they often did. But there was a quality to the hushed tone, something that felt more sad than reverent.

"I know."

"I miss Dad."

"Me too."

For a while, they sat, listening to the rain pattering against the roof of the SUV, watching as the campsite gradually obscured behind the blurry, wet curtain that flowed down the windshield.

But there was more needing said, things Dez needed Sully to hear, questions requiring answers. The day was dimming, quicker now they were this deep in the woods, and they hadn't brought sleeping bags or camping supplies for what was intended to be a short pilgrimage.

"Hey, Sull? I'm sorry. I know the last couple of months have sucked. I just need you to know I didn't want this for you. But I also didn't fight as hard as I should have, so I'm sorry."

Dez had been expecting a direct reply, whether absolution or condemnation. What he got was worse: abject terror.

"You can't let me go back there. Please, Dez. You have to get me out. If I go back, they'll kill me like Harry. You have to help me."

The plea had spilled out, and now a few tears joined in, more startling in their appearance than the words themselves. Among the various truths that described Dez's little family unit, one was that he tended to be the cryer among the group; Sully wasn't. Only the very worst of circumstances dragged tears from him and, even then, he tended toward stoic. That Dez was bearing witness to this wasn't just unusual; it was wrong.

Worse, it was terrifying.

"What do you mean they killed Harry? I thought it was another stroke."

"How do you know that? Did Thackeray tell you?"

"Thackeray? No. I haven't seen him. Uncle Lowell said he thinks he left town after his parents died."

"Jesus Christ."

"What's wrong?"

Sully took a series of quaky breaths, eyes wide as he looked to be processing something. Dez gave it a moment, but not long.

"Sully? What about Harry?"

"They found out he was getting out of his body. I don't know how. But if I knew, someone else probably did too. I haven't seen Snowy around there, either. They could have got to her as well."

Dez's first thought was, while Sully hadn't been insane before they'd put him in that place, Lockwood had driven him there. "I need you to slow down and walk me through this, all right? We've got time."

"Not enough. They're expecting me back there tomorrow."

"Well, you're here right now. Talk to me. What's going on?"

Sully took a deep breath, then a second, and Dez thought he could see the influence of centring techniques his brother had learned from Marc Echoles and Raiya Everton. Gradually, the barely controlled panic fell away, Sully's features settling into a familiar stillness, allowing Dez also to slip back into calm.

"I know what the Blue Room is."

Sully's words relieved Dez of any sense of tranquility he possessed. The rest of it—stories of confinement, injections, forced possessions and psychological torture—had Dez split between struggling not to vomit and wanting to kill someone. Sully had been taken to the room a number of times; he hadn't been able to say precisely how many. Sometimes, he'd be forced to endure the envisioned murder of one person; other times, he believed he'd experienced as many as two or three in the same session.

"Gerhardt and the others want me to use the spirits to learn things, but what they don't get is that spirits have a consciousness of their own," Sully said. "Ghosts don't care about anyone else's agenda, they just want me to help them. They show me things, Dez. They make me experience their deaths, and the drug makes me feel like every one is happening to me. One man was stabbed in the gut and took hours to die. He was in agony the entire time. I felt all of it, every minute. And this one woman, she was confined and tortured for three days and nights. I don't know how time works between these two worlds, but I was her throughout all of it. By the last day, I *wanted* to die, just to end it all. When I was pulled back into my own body, barely an hour had passed.

"Ghosts have shown me their deaths before from their perspectives, but there's usually some distance, or it's short-lived, and it's usually restricted to visuals. This was different. I could see, but I could also smell and feel. And it went on longer, sometimes what felt like forever. Under normal circumstances, I usually have a sense of myself. In Lockwood, I lost that. I couldn't pull back, couldn't separate myself. I wasn't just seeing them. I *was* them. I've never felt so much pain in my life. I've never been so scared."

Neither, for that matter, had Dez. Only his fear was something else, reserved solely at this moment for the person sitting next to him. Or, if he was honest with himself, for what would happen if he followed through on what he was thinking about doing right now. The last place he'd ever wanted to end up was sitting on the other side of the bars, serving a life sentence for murder, but that was where his thoughts were pulling him.

"Dez? Say something."

"What do you want me to say?"

"That you believe me. That you won't let them take me back there."

Dez turned; Sully stared at him, eyes round as if dreading what the response might be.

"Of course I believe you. And damn straight, you're not going back there. They'll need to go through me."

Sully's relief was pronounced through a heavy breath, in and out, his eyes sliding shut and pushing another tear past his lashes and down his cheek. Dez dropped a hand on his brother's shoulder, finding additional proof of trauma in the way Sully flinched at the touch. But Dez didn't let go, waiting until the tension eased.

"We need to figure something out, Sull. We could go to the police, launch a complaint."

"No one will believe me. Who's going to take the word of someone declared mentally ill over a psychiatrist who's earned all sorts of awards? Then there's the fact I was the suspect in a murder. I probably still am."

Dez didn't respond, which would be answer enough. The clothing they found in the dumpster that day had been checked for anything the lab could use to obtain a DNA sample. They'd found no hair inside the mask, and the sections around the mouth and nose—which could sometimes provide positive hits—came back inconclusive. All the testing had revealed for certain was the presence of gunpowder residue on the coat. The find didn't provide the proof Forbes Raynor had been after—showing Sully was guilty—but it didn't exonerate him either. All it proved, the investigator said, was that Sully hadn't been wearing those clothes when the shooting occurred; his own clothing, after all, had been covered in blowback.

Then there were the pills seized from Sully's apartment, the ones said to rest somewhere on the spectrum between psychotropic and psychedelic. Having spoken to Lowell, Forbes had determined Sully must have got them on the street; hallucinations were possible with high doses, further rendering Sully's story suspect.

In the end, the only benefit to Sully's committal at Lockwood had been the barrier it had created for Forbes.

If Gerhardt came out of this with one item in his favour, it was that he'd provided a report to the police that he didn't believe Sully capable of murder. At the time, Dez had been grateful to the psychiatrist for that assessment. Now, with Sully's claims, Dez saw it in a new light. Had Gerhardt suggested Sully could be responsible for Betty's shooting, he might have lost one of his prized psychics to an arrest warrant and, ultimately, to the correctional system.

Dez prided himself on his role as a support and a protector for his family. He was good at problem-solving, could usually see his way through to a solution, or at least the start of one. This time, the way out eluded him.

But with his brother's life at stake, failure was not an option.

"I'll sort this out, kiddo. Give me the night to come up with something."

"I think you already know what we need to do. There's only one way. I need to disappear. All you have to do is turn your back."

"Where are you going to go?"

"I don't know. Somewhere. Anywhere. Anywhere is better than going back."

"I'll talk to Bulldog. He'll have ideas about where you can lie low."

"I can't drag him into this, Dez. Not you, either, for that matter. No one can know about this."

"Hang on. When you were talking about disappearing, you didn't mean from us, right? We're your family. You need us. Hell, we need *you*."

"Not forever, okay? Just for a while—long enough to figure out a way to expose Gerhardt and the others."

"I don't get it. I mean, why? Why would these people do all this? I get it that Gerhardt wants to know what happened to his son, but you mentioned some guy in a Halloween mask. And they're giving you objects to draw you into more deaths than just the doctor's kid. For what purpose?"

"I've been thinking about it, and I keep coming back to one thing. There's money in secrets, and unsolved murder is the biggest secret anyone can hold onto. People will do anything to avoid having their crimes exposed. Even kill. Other people will do anything to make money, and what better way to do that than by blackmail? Whenever it's just Gerhardt in the Blue Room, everything is about his son. But when Mask Man is there, it's always about someone else. That's when they hand me trigger objects, and I get pulled into all those other deaths.

"I keep thinking if I can figure out who the guy in the mask is, I can find a way to end this. Not just for me, but for anyone else who gets pulled into that room."

"Are there others?"

"There was Harry. Snowy. I don't know about anyone else, but I'm sure there are. And if there's no one right now, there will be eventually."

"I don't know, man," Dez said. "The way you're describing this, it's big. Bigger than what you and I can handle on our own."

"I know."

Dez faced front, a brief slowing of the rain clearing the windscreen enough to bring the campsite back into focus. He didn't share his brother's psychic abilities, but he had his own ghosts in this place and his own way of seeing them. His memory conjured an image of his father, sitting on his favourite camping chair, feet up on the extendible canvas footrest while he listened to one of the few real arguments Dez and Sully had ever had.

Looking back, Dez couldn't remember what it had been about; all he recalled with any certainty was his father's response once he'd finally broken in with a firmly spoken, "Boys."

"The two of you are going to figure something out pretty quick in life. Maybe you'll get lucky and you'll find yourselves a buddy you call family, but chances are better there's no one out there who's going to be a better wing man than your own brother. You two go ahead and fight if you think you need to, but just remember when push comes to shove, you'd damn well better be at each other's backs, not at one another's throats. The older you get, the more you're going to appreciate the fact you two have each other. Look after one another and on your crappiest day, this world will feel a whole lot less lonely."

Dez had hit a point in his life where every one of his days battled it out for the supreme position of "crappiest." Now he had only to figure out how to put the rest of his father's advice into practice.

"I know you're asking me to turn my back on you, Sull. But I can't. You can't ask me to do that."

Sully didn't answer him, not right away. A lot went on within the younger man's silences, a world spinning within a skull that didn't allow outside bodies into its gravitational field. All you had was whatever Sully eventually chose to share.

This time, Dez found himself hoping his brother's response wasn't leaving anything sitting there, waiting between the lines to be read later on.

"Then I won't ask you to."

31

One of the park's hiking trails led to a cave system local spelunkers had once thrilled in exploring. A collapse a couple years back caused authorities to shut them to the public after a seventeen-year-old boy had been killed. With no safe way to excavate, they'd never been able to retrieve the body.

Sully knew it had taken everything for his brother to leave him there, the action contrary to all he stood for. Against Sully's wishes, Dez had returned with a duffel bag crammed with necessities and supplies, proving his stated inability to simply turn his back.

Whether Sully was repaying the kindness by holding back on his brother about Lowell remained to be seen. Dez would be furious if he found out Sully hadn't told him, but at least he'd be furious this side of a jail cell—or this side of a grave.

In steering their conversations away from Lowell, Sully sometimes asked about the Schusters.

"Did you find out where Thackeray went?" he asked Dez one day as the two sat deep in the woods, close to the spot Sully had been hiding.

Dez watched him a moment, then shook his head. "I don't know. He's gone. Neighbours didn't see or hear anything. They said his car was there one night, and was gone by the next morning. It never came back as far as anyone knows. Uncle Lowell said Thackeray didn't give him a month's notice or make last month's rent, so he thought that was kind of weird."

Sully imagined Lowell knew far more than he'd ever willingly let on. "Has anyone reported Thackeray missing?"

"Like who? He's got no one." Dez paused, the debate playing out across his face. "I actually filed a report a few days ago. I'm kind of worried he might have gone somewhere to kill himself. He was pretty unstable, and he's still got that criminal conviction hanging over his head. I don't know, man. I know he blames Uncle Lowell for a lot, but what if he actually did the things he was convicted of doing? I have a hard time believing Uncle Lowell would be behind something as bad as what Thackeray accused him of."

If life and death wasn't enough, Dez had just reminded Sully of the other reason Lowell's deepest secrets would need to stay buried for now. If Dez had a hard time accepting even that much about Lowell, he'd struggle with the full truth.

This time, Dez provided the subject change. "Do you see Harry anymore?"

Sully shook his head. "I haven't been able to see any of them since Lockwood. What if I can't anymore? What if all those drugs and all the stuff Gerhardt did to me made it so I can't see ghosts without some sort of chemical?"

"Would that be a bad thing?"

"Yeah, it would. I feel like I'm missing a part of myself I might never get back."

"It would also mean never being scared again like you were with Harry."

Harry. There had been a time Sully had feared him, had bowed beneath the weight of the terror that rolled off the man's disembodied spirit. That fear had created certain beliefs—ones Sully had since come to see as baseless and untrue.

Harry had tried to use Sully to prevent Betty's death and,

when he couldn't, had figured out how to possess him so he could kill the man responsible. In doing that, he could both avenge his wife and son—who had also suffered at Lowell's hands—and prevent future harms only he could see.

Sully still wasn't sure whether Harry had intended to kill him that night of the possession-induced suicide attempt at Dez and Eva's. With no way to see or communicate with Harry, Sully realized he might never know.

As things stood now, Sully had enough of his own problems, a constant toss-up between loneliness, uncertainty and an incessant worry for his family.

Despite Dez's lousy attempts at denial, Sully knew he had to be taking heat from Gerhardt, Raynor, Lowell and possibly even Mara and Eva. From Dez, Sully learned what the others had been told: that Sully had run from Dez, had gotten away while the two were in the park.

Search parties had been brought in, had scoured the area for signs of the Lockwood escapee. The bark of dogs had Sully shrinking further back into the cave where he'd been taken refuge, but the rain proved a godsend, masking his scent. The animals never came close enough to sense him.

The massive underground cave was nearly impossible to find unless you knew where to look. The brothers had found it years ago on one of their hikes with Flynn, what appeared at a glance as nothing more than a small crevice in the rocky ground. When Dez had agreed to aid in Sully's escape, it took the two a while to locate the entrance from memory. A tree had fallen across half of it, and moss, roots and dead leaves covered the rest so that only someone deliberately searching would spot it. The cave hadn't changed much, but they had. Sully was barely able to slither through; anyone bigger was unlikely to fit. Dez certainly wouldn't. So far, the cave had proved the perfect hiding spot, and

Sully had only to question how long he could continue to use it as such.

That first week, Dez visited Sully nearly as often as he had back at Lockwood. But Raynor had come sniffing around, had caught Dez in the area, and had demanded to know why he was there. His explanation, that he was still trying to find his missing brother, was believable enough that Raynor could do little to refute it.

But the confrontation shook Sully, the voices too close for comfort.

On the days Dez used the early mornings to visit, Sully occupied himself the rest of the day by exploring the tunnels branching off of the large cave. A single cramped passage led from it and connected to a series of nature-created openings. Some led nowhere, a couple ran on for some distance. One, he discovered, wove its way underground until, after several hours' exploration, it emptied into a larger cave that smelled of wildlife and was open to the outside world through a large fissure in the rock.

Given the possibility he might have to relocate his camp, Sully planned to tell Dez of the find.

A far-off rumble changed everything.

Sully's head snapped up, alert for any further noise before using his flashlight—courtesy of Dez—to find his way to his camp. Moving faster now than he'd come, he scraped his knees and hands as he scrabbled through the passage. Heart pounding, lungs aching from the exertion, he at last arrived back.

His makeshift camp, all of his supplies, were almost completely covered by a heap of rock and dirt.

From above came the muffled but frantic sound of Dez screaming his name.

Sully called back, heard the beginnings of a question from topside, confirmation Dez had received the message he was still alive. But a splash of dirt and a spray of stone against Sully's head, the scrape and rumble of rock on rock, had him scrambling away.

Sully ran, slipped through the passage. He barely made it into a small cavern just the other side when the whole thing collapsed behind him. The sound vibrated around him, the ground heaved, but the rock walls and ceiling held.

Dust swirled through the shattered air. Not until Sully stopped coughing did he realize he could no longer hear his brother.

His first thought was to find his way back toward the other entrance he'd found, the one a few hours from here. Once he was out, he could find a way to alert Dez he was okay. But, as he made his way through the cavern, a flashlight the only possession he had left, another possibility occurred to him.

Dez wouldn't be able to shift the debris to get to the cave—given the sheer amount of rock, it was doubtful anyone could—and the tunnel through which Sully had just escaped no longer existed. Even if someone managed to get into the now-collapsed cave where he'd been living, they'd never be able to search all of it. And, with no noticeable means for him to have escaped, the conclusions they'd draw were obvious.

Sully had just found the path to the ultimate safety, for him and for his family. If he were dead, he was of no further use to Gerhardt, Lowell or Raynor. Searches would be called off, warrants cancelled. He'd be in the clear to start over, free from being hunted.

Only the knowledge of his family's pain gave Sully pause, the awareness their grief—still so near to the surface after Flynn—would be reawakened and disinterred. But, he realized, emotional pain was the next-to-last thing he wished for them. The very last was a threat to their safety.

Sully had promised Lowell he'd guard his sins, to ensure the continued safety of the people he loved most. Lowell would have no reason to believe his dark secrets had been shared. And they hadn't. No one else alive within Sully's inner circle knew of it and, with Sully gone, no one would have reason to go looking. If Lowell considered himself safe, he'd have no cause to threaten the safety of others.

And there was that other fact, the one in which Sully allowed himself to take a small level of comfort as he began to envision this new future he was mentally carving out for himself. His family had gotten each other through Flynn's death; they'd get each other through Sully's. He knew it wouldn't be easy. But love healed. They'd be okay.

What he'd told Dez not so long ago had been true. Sully could cope with time on his own because he knew the people he loved most in the world were somewhere nearby, waiting to welcome him home.

For now, he'd have to search for peace in that. For now, there would be nowhere else to find it.

A flash of copper in his peripheral vision proved him wrong. There was one other place. Gerhardt's drugs had robbed him of the ability to see the dead, save in the ways the psychiatrist and his accomplices willed. As Sully had told Dez, he hadn't seen a spirit, save within the confines of the Blue Room, since he'd been taken to Lockwood. The image of Flynn walking next to him through the passages he was currently navigating formed a lump in Sully's throat—not only because this was his dad, but because it signalled a return to normal. It wasn't normal for most people, but this was his. And, more than that, this was *him*.

"Thanks for being here, Dad. Thanks for always being here."

As expected, there was no audible answer, Flynn knowing the parameters of Sully's gift too well to attempt one. He limited his reply to a smile and an intangible pat on the shoulder.

For the moment, it was enough.

With his father at his side and a rocky path laid out before him, Sully followed the glow of his flashlight into the darkness ahead.

UNTITLED

THANKS SO MUCH FOR READING. I hope you enjoyed it.

I hate to leave anyone hanging too much, so I've included the first chapter in the next Sullivan Gray novel, The Dule Tree—available now!

THE DULE TREE

1

HE HADN'T SEEN it coming, the blow to the back of the head that had sent him plummeting into darkness.

He awoke to pitch black and a deafening silence, the ringing in his ears doing what it could to fill the void.

His waking brain began to keep time with his heart, thoughts spinning faster and faster. He tried to skirt past the one that nagged at him, the one telling him the throbbing injury to the base of his skull had caused so much damage he had lost the ability to see or hear.

The panic caused him to squirm, the sound of his own movement reaching his ears and pulling an unexpected laugh from his throat. It was enough to further clear his brain, to get him reaching for his mobile phone within the chest pocket of his jacket. He closed his eyes and took a deep breath to steel his nerves as he moved to bring the handset to his face, hoping to make out the display once he'd lit it up with a click of the home button. His hand collided with something on the way up, something hard and yet encased in a fabric he could only guess was satin—its feel taking him back to the touch of his wife's negligee, the one she'd worn on those nights that promised great things.

Now he sought comfort where he could find it, praying to a God he no longer believed in as he manoeuvred the phone into a spot near his face, clicked the home button and slivered one eye open.

A second rush of relief hit as he took in the blessed sight of the display, a photo of the lake at sunset his daughter had programmed in the last time he'd seen her. The time read 10:24 p.m. Barely any time had passed since he'd started pursuing Raynor, since he'd first entered this ...

Cemetery.

The relief passed as quickly as it came, his mind turning to his current predicament, to whatever it was he'd managed to step into this time. He could practically hear Eva's voice in his head, her tone reflecting her position as both wife and cop: "Damn it, Dez, you've got a brain. Learn to use it."

It was too late to avoid whatever mess he was in, but he hoped he could use his brain to find a way out. Thumbing in the phone's password, he was rewarded with a second photo his daughter Kayleigh had put onto his home screen. Naturally, it was one of herself, the seven-year-old smiling impishly from behind the apps she'd also installed, most of them ones he'd never learned to use.

One was useful right now and he tapped the small square featuring a flashlight.

And immediately wished he hadn't.

The space around him lit up, the steady beam illuminating white satin and revealing the full horror of his situation within just three seconds, his heart back to pounding as he pushed against the surface above, finding it unmoving, himself sealed inside.

For some reason, it had taken until this moment to shift past the pain at the base of his skull, past the fear, to realize the discomfort the rest of him was in, curled up tight between two immovable objects, knees and shoulders pressed hard against the walls of his prison, head resting against something firm yet moveable. He knew what it was without looking, fought against the urge to turn his head. But he was unable to resist a look down toward his feet, bathed in the light from the flash and the pale satin. The full horror of the moment struck him like a fist as he saw not one pair of feet but two, the corpse's newly shined shoes resting against his own scuffed boots.

He resisted the urge to scream, a noise that sounded like a choked sob making its way from his throat instead. Kayleigh was still there on his phone's home screen, still smiling at him, dark ponytail defying gravity as she bounced on the trampoline he'd bought her for her last birthday. And he couldn't look anymore, couldn't face the possibility he wouldn't see her again.

Going into his contacts lists, he located Eva's number, hit the phone icon and waited.

Nothing.

He could see now there was no reception here, the tiny message at the top of the screen reading "No Service." He tried again anyway, waited until the phone stopped the call of its own accord.

Fighting the rising panic, he next tried to text Eva, not caring as his fingers fumbled over the on-screen keys, creating words no one would understand. She would know. If he could just get a message through to her, Eva would know.

He waited again, long enough to receive the message the delivery had failed.

With nothing left to do now but panic, he slipped deeply into it, hands pushing hard against the lid of the casket just inches from his face, his shoulder ramming against it as his hands made no impact. He shoved against it once, twice, three times, and reality trickled in with the sound and smell of soil sprinkling down the side of his tiny prison. The coffin wasn't locked or strapped shut.

It was buried.

He was underground, far enough down to render his mobile phone useless, trapped inside this small box, his only companion a dead man.

He knew what he should be doing with no air coming in. With likely no more than twenty minutes of oxygen—if he avoided further panicking—he had to do everything he could to conserve it, to allow Eva time to find him. He tried to ignore the reality she couldn't have any idea where he was, that even if she realized something was wrong she'd never get to him in time.

No one would, even if he managed to buy himself every second he could. No one else had been in the cemetery, no one but him and Raynor.

No one was coming for him.

He released the scream he'd been holding onto, the sound deafening in the enclosure, drowning out the satin-muffled sounds of his pounding hands.

He had no idea how long it went on like that, his terror robbing him of precious seconds of air, replacing oxygen with poison. He'd passed being light-headed, was edging back into what he knew would soon be unconsciousness. He welcomed it, relished the idea of it, arms too tired now to pound as he sank back into the space beside and above the emaciated body, his head finding as comfortable a spot as he could alongside the corpse's substantial nose. His breathing slowed as his eyelids began to flutter shut, the sounds of his pulse dull in his ears, muffled and yet persistent.

It must have been the lack of air playing with his brain that had him hearing what seemed to be two pulses now, his own and another coming not from below but, oddly, from above. The one beyond was a pace quicker, less even and yet no less constant, no less willing to give up on its life-sustaining rhythm.

It was going to have to give up. He certainly was.

His thoughts turned to his daughter, and he considered how Eva was going to have to break the news to her, the little girl he doted on, the little girl he didn't deserve. Would never deserve. There was no taking back the past, after all.

And yet, here he was, hearing the past in his head, the voice of his baby brother, forever five, echoing across time and space.

"Hold on, Dez. It isn't time. Please hold on. It isn't your time."

They were not the words of a five-year-old, and yet there was no mistaking the source. He heard Aiden's name on his lips, breathed it out like a prayer, the whisper of the word reverberating in his brain long after the sound had died in his ears.

"Dez, hold on. Sully's coming. Just hold on for Kayleigh. Sully's coming."

His brain caught on the name Sully, wondering what it meant that the little boy had uttered the name of Dez's foster brother, whose own grave had been added to this same cemetery two years ago. But the question fell away as he settled back into the feeling of the long-lost voice, Aiden's presence, so palpable to him now, so close he felt as if he could reach out and touch him.

He began to drift again, Aiden's voice not even enough to draw him back now. The darkness folded around him, enveloped him in warm nothingness as it slid over, under, around him, both lifting him and taking him down.

A sound like thunder broke through the soft arms, replaced by something substantial, firm, something that left no doubt it was part of the mortal world.

He initially fought to remain in that warm, dark place, where Aiden wasn't confined to videotape and memory. Hands—he knew that they were hands—tugged on his shoulders, urged him back into consciousness, pulled him back from the brink. They swept aside the fog inside his muddled brain as he made the yet-unwilling trek back into consciousness and into the horrors he knew he would find there.

But it wasn't a satin-lined prison and a deceased cellmate he saw greeting him; it was a lean, hooded figure crouched on top of the casket, hands holding Dez up to sitting. Above the hooded figure, just visible in the light of the moon that crested the edge of the grave, was the shape of a large dog peering down at him. The sound of panting mixed with the nighttime noise of crickets and a breeze rattling the branches of the cemetery trees.

He considered for a moment he might have gone farther down than he'd thought. "Is that a hellhound?" he asked, voice a croak.

"What?" The hushed voice from the hooded figure was not what he'd expected from Death, masculine but not deep, human rather than demonic.

More than that, it sounded familiar.

"This isn't hell?"

The reply came in the form of a quietly spoken, almost whispered, "That's a matter of perspective."

The hooded male helped Dez crawl out of the casket and it was somewhere between there and standing on solid ground that his senses fully returned, bringing with them a rush of emotion and nausea. He fell to his knees and vomited violently to the side of the grave, a hand against a pile of displaced dirt all that kept him from falling face-first into the mess.

He heard movement around him, the closing of the coffin lid, the shifting of fabric and earth as the hooded male pulled himself out of the grave, the pelting of stone and soil back onto the casket.

"Wait," Dez managed around a couple of heaving breaths. "My phone. I need my phone. I have to—"

A hand landed briefly on his shoulder, long enough to draw

his attention to the smartphone on the ground near him, just a couple feet from a large black dog. Ignoring the animal for now, Dez hit the home button and was rewarded with a glimpse of that lake. A few more clicks had him looking down at the smiling face of his little girl.

He couldn't resist the giddy laugh. "I'm not dead?"

"No."

Dez managed to make it to his feet, considered he should be helping his saviour re-bury the dead guy. He dropped his phone into his pocket and moved to help but was stopped by a hand on his arm. He straightened fully to standing, surprised to find he had a good five or six inches on the other male. He wasn't sure why, but he'd expected his rescuer would be gargantuan in proportion rather than six feet and lean bordering on skinny. The guy was wearing clothes he seemed to be swimming in, baggy cargo pants and a dark hooded sweatshirt tucked beneath an army jacket, both clearly a few sizes too big. The hood, which Dez had, in his initial daze, mistaken for a cloak or a robe, was still up, forming a halo for the strings of long hair that concealed the man's face in shadow.

"I've got this," the guy muttered, and Dez was again surprised by the familiar in that voice. "Get out of here."

"I can help."

"I don't need any."

Dez helped anyway, kicking dirt into the grave for the time it took to rebury the casket. They worked in silence, both huffing with exertion and exhaustion. Dez expected some sort of conversation at the end, was surprised when the other male simply whistled for his dog to come and started away from the grave, away from Dez.

Dez reached out, grabbing hold of the guy's arm, was instantly met by a light warning growl from the dog. Dez released the man, but did what he could to hold him with a question. "Did you get a look at the guy who put me down there, enough to provide a statement to police?"

"No."

Damn. "What's your name?"

"Does it matter?"

"You saved my life. Yeah, it matters."

There was again no reply, leaving Dez to fill the void.

"I'm Desmond Braddock .... I don't know you, do I?"

"Goodbye, Desmond." The male again turned to leave and Dez was unable to stop himself from grabbing ahold of him again. This time, he jerked him back a little too hard, causing the hood to fall away and the shaggy veil of pale brown hair to shift. The dog barked, but Dez's attention was locked onto the face of the young man rather than the potentially dangerous animal at his side.

"Oh, my God," Dez whispered as the light of the moon and scattering of cemetery lamps revealed hints of the other man's face, concealed behind the remaining curtain of hair and unkempt beard. It was the eyes—the slightly more visible right one, anyway—that revealed the truth, that and the finely shaped nose and cheekbones. It had been two years since he'd set eyes on him, but a decade and a half had made him an expert on Sullivan "Sully" Gray.

Sully put up what fight he could but was deftly taken to the ground by Dez, whose mental exhaustion had cleared with the return of both precious oxygen and his brother. There was another low growl from the dog but it didn't attack like Dez had anticipated, despite the fact its master was struggling futilely next to the resealed grave, pinned beneath the weight of the larger male. After a minute or so of useless fighting, Sully went more or less limp in his brother's grasp.

Dez used the defeat to sweep the remaining hair from the younger man's face, wanting to believe but needing the absolute certainty before allowing himself to give in fully to the joy and confusion of the inexplicable reunion.

"Sully?"

"Yeah, Dez, it's me. Let me up."

The sound of the voice, spoken now at normal volume and

tone, was the final proof, had Dez jumping up and staggering backwards as if attempting to escape another corpse.

"I was there when that cave collapsed. They told us no one could have gotten out. We held a funeral for you, damn near spitting distance from here."

Sully rose to his feet, eyes pinned to Dez's as he kept his own expression guarded. "I know. I was there."

"Where?"

Sully angled his chin toward the treed edge of the cemetery, visible just beyond the far row of lamps that lit the bordering driving paths. "In the trees."

"Watching?"

Sully nodded. "Hardest thing I ever had to do."

"Hardest thing *you've* ever ...." Dez let the parroted statement go midway, the rage rising unexpectedly and channeling itself into his fists. He barely saw it coming himself as he unleashed his fury in one solid punch, laying his brother out on the ground.

Sully lay there a moment before balancing himself on one elbow, cupping his jaw in his free hand and testing it cautiously before quirking up one side of his mouth in a smile. "Still pulling your punches for me, bro."

The raised eyebrow and warm smile were pure Sully, had Dez extending a hand and hauling his brother up in one fluid movement. He didn't let go until the smaller man was encased in a hug tight enough to restrict breathing. Dez ignored the fact he could feel Sully's ribs even through the jacket, and the smell that suggested the guy hadn't managed a shower in at least two weeks. Right now, all that mattered was his brother—a man who had shared everything with him but blood—was back.

At long last, he held Sully at arm's length, casting an appraising eye over him. "You look like hell, kiddo."

Sully chuckled, the sound ending in a lingering grin. "Damn good to see you, Dez."

He pulled away and turned, and Dez realized Sully didn't mean to stay. "Where are you going?"

"Away."

"You're going to have to do better than that."

Sully turned partway, enough to meet his brother's eye. "I can't."

"Listen, man, judging by the look, feel and smell of you, I'm going to take an educated guess and say you don't have anywhere to go. You can come home with me, all right? Maybe then you can fill me in on what the hell you've been doing the past two years."

"Dez, I can't. It's not safe."

"Hey. It's me. You always said there was no one you trusted more to have your back."

"I didn't mean it's not safe for me. I meant it's not safe for you."

Dez took a step forward, worried this was going to come down to another battle. He wasn't prepared to let Sully go. Not now, not until he had some answers, not until he knew his brother was safe. "Let me decide what's best for me. You look exhausted, you're clearly not eating properly and you're as weak as a kitten. You barely gave me a fight a minute ago. Never mind the fact you need a shower and a change of clothes like right now."

"Dez—"

"Don't. Don't even say it. I'm not taking no for an answer. If you wanna go toe to toe with me on this, I'm good to go, man. But I promise you, you'll be leaving this cemetery unconscious and over my shoulder. I'd rather we walk out together."

Sully was quiet a moment and Dez could see his brother studying him, looking for signs of a bluff. But the larger man was far from bluffing and it took Sully only a few moments to get that.

Thankfully, for both of them, he chose option two.

AFTERWORD

Thanks so much for reading! I am continuing to work on the next Sullivan Gray books, and would be pleased to keep you updated on future projects and release dates if you would like to join my mailing list. As an adding bonus, a growing anthology of short stories, entitled *Haunted: The Ghosts of Sullivan Gray,* is available as a gift to subscribers. Visit my website at hpbayne.com to sign up.

The books in *The Sullivan Gray Series* can be read as stand-alones to some extent, each with a plot that wraps itself up by book's end. But there is a deeper plot that threads throughout the series so, for that reason, I always suggest the books are best read in the following order:

Black Candle

Harbinger

The Dule Tree

Crawl

Hollow Road

Second Son

Spirit Caller

As always, a huge thank you to my eagle-eyed editor Hannah Sullivan. She not only catches the various typos that escape me, but asks the tough questions that have allowed me to make The Sullivan Gray Series the best it can be.

Thanks also to the brilliantly creative Fiona Jayde for designing another stellar cover. How she manages to turn a handful of photos into a work of art is beyond me.

Another thanks to numerous members of the writing community I've had the privilege to get to know, both in person and through social media. Your support and willingness to share your knowledge has helped make this journey far less terrifying!

I also want to thank the lovely folks on my advance reader team for perusing the manuscript and giving me that crucial early feedback. Your thoughtful comments and last-minute typo-snagging are utterly invaluable to me. I'm so grateful you've come on board.

And, of course, a massive, Dez-sized thank you to everyone who picked up *Black Candle* and bought this book. You are, each of you, enabling me to live out my lifelong dream of becoming a published author, and there are no words strong enough to express my gratitude for all of your incredible support.

ABOUT THE AUTHOR

Fascinated by ghost stories and crime fiction, H.P. has been writing both for well over two decades, drawing on more than fifteen years in a career in a criminal justice setting. Raised on a farm on the Canadian Prairies, H.P. enjoys reading, portrait drawing, travel and spending time with family and friends.

For more information, visit H.P.'s website at hpbayne.com.

Made in the USA
Monee, IL
01 July 2021